Praise for

"*Indigo Field* brims with multigenerational drama, earthy spirituality, and deeply imagined characters you are unlikely to forget. In tightly compressed, poetic language, Hudson weaves a mesmerizing story of loss, injustice, and revenge conspiring to darken the human heart—and the redemptive and unexpected ways the light comes in."

—Sue Monk Kidd, *New York Times* bestselling author of *The Invention of Wings*, *The Book of Longings*, and *The Secret Life of Bees*

"In her fascinating debut novel *Indigo Field*, Marjorie Hudson digs beneath the surface of the contemporary Southern world and raises up stories long repressed—stories of Indigenous and Black heritage. Miss Reba and her present-day antagonist, a retired white man from across the highway, are each on a journey of transformation in Hudson's shimmering world of a wild pasture filled with rising spirits."

—Lalita Tademy, *New York Times* bestselling author of *Cane River*, an Oprah selection, *Red River*, and *Citizens Creek*

"Get ready to be swept off your feet by Marjorie Hudson's glorious big-hearted novel *Indigo Field*. Her characters are as diverse, complicated, and compelling as any you are likely to find between the covers of a book, and she weaves their stories together with stunning mastery. I love this book, and every time I read it, I am filled with admiration and wonder."

—Helen Fremont, national bestselling author of *After Long Silence* and *The Escape Artist*

"*Indigo Field* is a rich tapestry of history and nature, and the many vivid characters who have lived in that place. From life in a contemporary retirement village to long forgotten graves and secrets of prior generations, Marjorie Hudson takes us on a compelling and surprising journey as these unlikely characters come together in moments of shelter and grace."

—Jill McCorkle, *New York Times* bestselling author of *Hieroglyphics*, *Life After Life*, and *Going Away Shoes*

"*Indigo Field* gives us genius in the ancient sense of that word—the spirit animating a place. Marjorie Hudson is a spiritual geographer, charting the landscape of a changing Carolina community and its intertwined lives, past and present, Black and white, rich and poor. The ancient pines on Gooley Ridge overlook Indian burials and bank foreclosures, bird and people migrations, secret murders and delayed vengeance, sweet love scenes and brutal assaults. Like Pat Conroy before her, Hudson writes up a mighty storm in this moving and satisfying novel."

—Dale Neal, Novello Literary Award Winner, author of *Appalachian Book of the Dead*

"Marjorie Hudson's stunning debut novel, *Indigo Field*, conjures a world anchored in the people and soil of the 'land between two rivers' in North Carolina. Like the deep roots of the ancient Gooley Pines know the depths of this soil, only one elder knows the depths and connections of history, love, and tragedy concealed in this blood-soaked abandoned field. Revealed here in lush, evocative prose and unforgettable characters, Hudson's tale intertwines old dispossessions with new losses, upscale retirees with longtime farmers, Black with white, foolish ignorance with startling revelation. As storytelling peels back each layer of history and memory, and present-time lives are called to acts of vengeance or courage, a wise woman reminds, 'There are moments in life in when everything you do makes a difference.' This is a book of Old Testament wrath and New Testament forgiveness—a magnificent, magical debut."

—Valerie Nieman, winner of the Sir Walter Raleigh Award for Fiction, author of *In the Lonely Backwater* and *To the Bones*

"*Indigo Field* showcases one of the rising novelists of the American South. Marjorie Hudson is a master storyteller like Bobbie Ann Mason; her characters come alive and engage the reader. Hudson vividly creates a sense of place with exposition as rich as any of Eudora Welty's fiction. This novel belongs in classrooms as well as libraries, weaving history, empathy, and spirituality."

—Lenard D. Moore, Recipient of the North Carolina Award for Literature, author of *Long Rain* and *The Geography of Jazz*

"*Indigo Field* is an expansive, engrossing saga of lives whose paths cross lines of race, class, and culture. As with the best Southern literature, it stirs up the past to illuminate the present, fills our senses with a richness of place, and makes memory a testament to our existence. Likewise, no story about the South is complete without the forces of nature and avengement in play, as dramatically here. I'll well remember these vivid characters who prevail with a moving faith in this unforgettable novel."

—Steven Schwartz, Sherwood Anderson Award-winning author of *The Tenderest of Strings*, *Little Raw Souls*, and *Lives of the Fathers*

"In so many ways, Marjorie Hudson's *Indigo Field* is a transcendent book, a rich and beautiful tapestry, woven with dazzling craft and an artist's touch. Deep, resonant characters and a powerfully human story lay the truth before us: more than all our differences, we are part of one whole that is both past and present, young and old, living and dead, spirit and fundament, man-made and born in nature. This novel will take you deep and send you soaring. It may be the most definitive novel ever written about North Carolina. But it is more than that; it's a story for all time."

—Walter Bennett, author of *Leaving Tuscaloosa*, winner of the Alabama Author's Award, and *The Last Kiss*

"Marjorie Hudson's *Indigo Field* is a beautifully crafted novel set in a North Carolina that has not been fully explored in literature before, one where Black, white and Indigenous narratives weave together to reveal festering secrets and powerful commonalities. Here is a sweeping story of forgiveness, love, family, loss, and friendship that begins with richly imagined characters. This haunting novel about memory, community, and justice marks the stunning debut of a provocative new voice in contemporary Southern fiction."

—Michele Tracy Berger, author of *Reenu-You*, and winner of the Carl Brandon Kindred Award

"Inhabited by unforgettable characters and haunted by unspeakable crimes, Marjorie Hudson's loamy Ambler County, North Carolina, is every bit as richly drawn as Faulkner's Yoknapatawpha. Cast against a rural landscape of rare beauty and heart-stopping terror, *Indigo Field* is a mesmerizing story of buried secrets and heart-wrenching struggles: a story of racial boundaries and those who cross them with hope and love and yearning. It's deeply researched and beautifully told—among the best of contemporary Southern fiction."

—Minrose Gwin, author of *The Queen of Palmyra*, *Promise*, and *The Accidentals*, winner of the Mississippi Institute for Arts and Letters Award in Fiction

"In her long-awaited debut novel *Indigo Field*, Marjorie Hudson's 'land that nobody seems to own' holds secrets and stories and trees whose towering crowns shower fertilizing, enlightening, enlivening pollen into the open mouth, into the eyes. O taste and see! Here, the histories of three peoples are braided together in a tale that promises its characters and us that the revelations belonging to story can enlarge our world and our time, bind us together, and bring on a spirited whirlwind of more life."

—Marly Youmans, author of *A Death at the White Camellia Orphanage*, winner of The Ferrol Sams Award for Fiction, and *The Wolf Pit*, winner of the Michael Shaara Award for Excellence in Civil War Fiction

"What a gorgeous book! *Indigo Field* is a powerful and perceptive novel with small town rural characters dealing with their greatest losses and trying their best to survive. You will be swept up in the arc of the story, in the astonishing imagery, but most of all you'll love these characters and the many migrations they take on the way to finding home. Unforgettable."

—Stephanie Powell Watts, author of *We Are Only Taking What We Need*, winner of the Ernest J. Gaines Award and an Oprah Summer Read Selection, and *No One is Coming to Save Us*, Winner of the NAACP Image Award for Outstanding Literary Work

INDIGO FIELD

Marjorie Hudson

Regal House Publishing

Published by
Regal House Publishing, LLC
Raleigh, NC 27605
All rights reserved

ISBN -13 (paperback): 9781646033256
ISBN -13 (epub): 9781646033263
Library of Congress Control Number: 2022935700

Interior by Lafayette & Greene
Cover design © by C. B. Royal
Cover image © by Markus Semmler/Shutterstock
Author photo by Annette Roberson

Regal House Publishing, LLC
https://regalhousepublishing.com

An early version of Part I: Abandoned Field was first published as "Accidental Birds of the Carolinas" in The Literarian at the Center for Fiction, Spring 2011, and was also the title story in the collection *Accidental Birds of the Carolinas*, by Marjorie Hudson. Winston-Salem, NC: Press 53, 2011.

The Rumi excerpt on the epigraph page is from "Where Everything Is Music," from *The Essential Rumi*, translations by Coleman Barks with John Moyne, Castle Books, HarperCollins San Francisco, 1997. Used by permission. All rights reserved.

One of the scripture quotations is from the ESV® Bible (The Holy Bible, English Standard Version®), copyright ©2001 by Crossway Bibles, a publishing ministry of Good News Publishers. Used by permission. All rights reserved.
The remaining scripture quotations are from the King James Version of the Bible.

Printed in the United States of America

So the candle flickers and goes out.
We have a piece of flint, and a spark.
. . . .
Stop the words now.
Open the window in the center of your chest,
And let the spirits fly in and out.

—Rumi

They that sow the wind, shall reap the whirlwind.

—The Book of Hosea

PART I

Abandoned Field

1

Tucked between the Cedar River and the monstrous pines of the Gooley Ridge lies an ancient field, tangled and wild, knee-high with last year's scrub, strewn with rocks the size of crouching men and sleeping deer. Its soil is deep and loamy. It has been planted but never plowed.

It is spring, and up on the Ridge, a breeze lifts the broad crowns of the Gooley pines, releasing yellow clouds of pollen that float across the highway and come to rest on every flat surface of Stonehaven Downs Retirement Village, including the hood of Col. Randolph Jefferson Lee's new Honda Accord.

West of the Ridge, across Spill Creek, the breeze raises wild bees from the hollow heart of Miss Reba's sycamore. The bees rise up from that dark cove of sweetness, hover over three strange cedar statues in the yard, then head across the creek and through the woods. They pause over Jolene Blake's tidy fields, then glimmer up the Gooley Ridge and gather among the old pines, humming. The pine boughs flicker with the wings of small birds in mating plumage—goldfinches and cardinals, bluebirds and jays, and a lonely painted bunting blown here from the coast in a wild storm.

The Gooley pines have lived through drought and flood. They know the glaze of ice and the glimmer of sun on their cracked, cupped bark, each scale like a small ear alert for sound. The giant trunks sense the movements of vast oceans. They taste the breeze and know a storm will rise along the coast of Africa. They listen to the stories of the Field. The human stories they hold happened a hundred years ago, or just yesterday, or maybe ten years hence, it makes no difference to the Gooleys, for time is eternal and flowing, caught in circles within circles, uncounted.

❧

Col. Randolph Jefferson Lee, retired army, prepares for his daily run, which he's lied about for months, telling Anne he will stay in the neighborhood, he will call her on the cell if he gets in trouble, and he will keep it down to a stroll, a slow walk, no running.

Rand glances guiltily at Anne sitting at the kitchen table, her fluffy, just-washed white-blond hair, her head tilted in that funny way of hers, peering through her fancy multicolor reading glasses at the paper. The lovebirds chatter in their cage next to the window. Anne's deep into her morning routine. Looking out the window now with pursed lips, something on her mind. He wonders sometimes if she thinks about Malaysia, their last posting, and all that happened there. But now she turns to the lovebirds in their cage, lifts the latch, and that mischievous grin, that morning joy is back.

God, she's a beauty. How did he ever catch a woman like her? By pretending to be a man who belonged in a place like this.

He slurps coffee, steals another look. Is she snubbing him, after their dustup last night? She asked him to come with her today to some crazy Spring Gala where all the ladies are supposed to wear sundresses and the men are supposed to wear straw hats. Croquet is involved, she said, or cricket, she wasn't sure which, and vodka-spiked lemonade, and it is all supposed to celebrate the first day of the Stonehaven farmers' market. "What does farming have to do with croquet?" he'd asked her. "It's the dumbest thing I ever heard."

"Don't be such a spoilsport," she said. "I think it'll be fun."

The social program here seems modeled after a summer camp for Southern debutantes. Tea and crumpets. Balls and juleps. My God, last April—when they were still new here, before he'd figured out their game—they'd bused the newcomers down to some coastal plantation for a party with hoop skirts and a Rhett Butler look-alike. Rand stood, cringing, in a corner, getting drunk as fast as possible.

Anne ate it up. Laughing, asking to see the elaborate pantaloons under those skirts, even dancing with the Rhett character, who was paunchy and fortyish up close and, from what Rand could tell, knew only one dance step. The man led Anne in an endless backward circle till they were both dizzy and had to sit down.

Rand avoided dancing. But he remembers a ridiculous twinge of jealousy about that Rhett character spending so much time holding his wife. Anne seemed to be enjoying that a bit much.

To be fair, she had agreed later that having the Black serving staff sing "Dixie" for them had been in terrible taste. "Maybe they were being ironic," she said, with her wry grin. "God, I hope so." Since then, Rand has picked and chosen his social events carefully. These days Anne goes to most of them alone or with her new friends Bess and George.

Rand finishes his ration of half a cup of black coffee, turns to the kitchen window, where he can just see the crowns of the Gooley pines across the highway, lit by the early slanting light. Strange gurgling sounds emerge from his gut. He ignores them, glugs bottled water at the counter, stretches his calves, aware that his once taut body is not taking punishment well these days, not well at all.

Anne comes up behind him, rests her fingertips on his biceps and peers out the window over his shoulder, her small breasts brushing against his back. *All is forgiven.* Her hair tickles his neck. It smells faintly sugary, like strawberries, with a sharper scent underneath, some lemony new perfume. He feels a stirring in his groin, which quickly fades. Old soldiers never die, they just get soft.

"Look at that light!" she exclaims. "It's positively—" she searches for the right word—"Roman," she decides. "That lovely slant and glimmer. Well, I guess Michelangelo could have painted those trees, they're old enough. What a painting he would have made!"

He agrees. But what he says is: "I don't think he made it here in his travels, dear, and if he had, the ones you see now would have been knee-high." He hears the sharp tone in his voice, a crabbiness that has seeped into his daily intercourse with Anne more and more, but he can't help it. The more she bubbles about this place, this county, its inhabitants, the more it annoys him.

He feels Anne's fingertips withdraw and smells her faint coffee breath as she turns away. A chill descends between them like a thin glass panel. "I'm just remembering Rome," she says, a little sadly.

"Ah, Roma," he says, softening. They had both been entranced by Rome. He's the one who'd made sure they flew via Rome and paused a few days there whenever they had home leave in their early days. That was a long time ago. Since then they'd raised kids, moved stateside, sold the house on Long Island, and just a year ago retired South, to this place that Anne loves and he—after giving it chance after chance—truly despises. He agreed to come only because, after all their foreign postings, it was time she got to decide where they would live. It is a pretty world, but he sees through it. Yankee duffers perfecting their golf game, as if a low score will ward off death. Wives planting petunias as if their lives depended on it. Only the running is keeping him sane. That, and coming up with new ways to avoid Anne's nutty social plans.

Now she's opened the birdcage, has one of the lovebirds in her hand, stroking it, humming a little song, peering at it over her glasses while it pecks seed from her palm. Anne keeps lovebirds in the breakfast nook and a pair of cockatiels in the den, presents to him for some anniversary or another over the years. They've had them for ages. She's fond of them, she feeds them and cares for them, but she claims they're really for him. "Let's face it," she always says, "you're a bird fanatic."

"True," he always says. "*Wild* birds." Not these caged muttering creatures. He can barely look at them. It seems to him, what they want is *out*.

He lets the cockatiels out sometimes when she's not around. Lets them walk up his outstretched arms and peck his hair. Lets them fly around the room. Like a damn kid, being bad. He always wipes off the furniture, as needed, before she gets back, and she's never said a word about it, although by glances and lifted eyebrows he knows she knows.

Their first days here, she tried to convert him into one of those doddering birders who travel in a pack, doing their Christmas counts and Audubon surveys. He tried that once or twice and hated it. Now he's the one who heads out alone and spies on birds, part of his "walking therapy," and she tromps out with a cast of thousands, scaring them all off.

"You make everything into a party," he said to her, complaining.

"And you pick the solitary sports," she'd said. "Running, for instance."

That was not true, of course. He ran with Kip Larsen for most of last year and enjoyed the company thoroughly.

She was always a people person, but now she's such a social butterfly, he finds it unsettling, and a little lonely, as if he's suddenly bunking with an unpredictable younger woman.

She catches him looking. "Going for your walk, dear?" she says.

"Right."

"I'm off to tennis."

So. She is skipping the Spring Gala after all. Good. The Cutest Farmers' Market in the World can start without them.

"Okay." Rand pulls his ball cap over his bristly military cut.

"Be safe," she calls after him. "And listen to the birds!"

"I will," he says.

Anne's lips curl in the slightest of wry grins from behind her coffee mug. *Forgiven again.*

He leans in to kiss her goodbye, an old habit that still suffices to warm him. "Lipstick," she says. She turns her head slightly. He gives her a peck on the cheek. That cheek his whole life has been soft, powdered, and gardenia scented, like a kept woman's, behind the compound walls of overseas military housing. Now it is lean and brown and salty, like a tomboy's, playing all that tennis through the mild winter.

Rand opens the door, steps outside, and lets the fine April day enter his lungs. It is, after all, the one beautiful time of year around here. He might see that pileated woodpecker, find its roost. He looks up, sees the pines glowing on the hill across the highway like a promise, and sets off walking down the asphalt path, watching his feet, one of which drags a little when he tries to go faster.

By the time Rand turns down Sir Walter Raleigh Way, his Achilles tendon is tight as a drum, and his left knee starts to catch and make that clicking sound. He speeds it up, starts "run walking," pumping his arms, letting his hips slide side to side in that peculiar-looking way. It gets the heart rate up. But none of Anne's spies will mistake it for running. He slips his hand surreptitiously into his pocket, turns off his phone. There are many spots in this new neighborhood where coverage fades out. That's what he tells Anne anyway. He hates the feel of something alive and demanding on his person, tracking his every move. He doesn't like the hard bounce of it in his pocket, either, and he's thought about "losing" it in a pile of pine straw in the woods, but she would just get him another.

Besides, it's part of the plan.

Their first year here he simply pretended it wasn't happening again, all the signs floating below consciousness like some watery checklist for drowning: shortness of breath, the lead weight in his legs when he tried to run, worse every morning instead of better. Finally, the sweating collapse six months ago on the pale-blue living-room carpet, shooting pains traveling into his jaw, nothing to do but stare up at the carved roses in the underside of the dining room table, at his gun collection display cabinet on the wall—his only contribution to Anne's new décor. Below it, Decker's chestnut table that Anne insisted be displayed in a prominent location. He lay there, clenching his jaw and trying to breathe.

Anne was lunching with her new friend Bess. He'd managed to call 911 himself, crush some aspirin between his molars, and hang on. The EMTs arrived in due time and took him to the hospital, where they reamed out his arteries, put him on cholesterol drugs.

"This isn't ordinary heart trouble," the Quarryville doctors told him. "You have a hole in your heart. Strange it was never diagnosed." That's what had made it hard to run up a hill since he was a young boy. He had few symptoms, and he's already lived longer than was reasonable. He could go at any time. He let Anne think it was one of those other heart conditions. No need to scare her.

So, he runs. He'll either get better or he'll die trying. Meanwhile, he is getting his papers in order, checking off the tasks—will signed and notarized, stock portfolio rebalanced, pension papers in files, life insurance on auto-pay. After he's gone she'll finally know. He did it all for her. And he won't have to watch anymore as Anne falls in love—blatantly, besottedly in love—with Stonehaven Downs.

She is in love with the Commons—gated and picketed to keep in some rare and exceptionally cute form of sheep, cropping away, as tourists snap photos. She is in love with the expensive little shops in the village square, the ladies-for-lunch café, the cappuccino wagon—the first, no doubt, in this dusty, hazy, forgotten scrap of the rural South, and one that attracts more flies than clientele on August afternoons. She's in love with the little town of Quarryville, the tiny Episcopal church, the quirky health food store, the farm supply place with its baby chicks. And all those places she volunteers—he's lost track, there are so many.

"Rand, you should come exploring with me someday," she used to say.

"Got to work on some paperwork," he always said.

On their brief visit to the new house last Christmas, the kids, Carrie and Jeff, who never used to agree on anything, looked around, looked at each other, and gave their approval to the move. Carrie, squinting through her fashionable LA catwoman glasses at the new décor, the sheep, the neighbors, saw the sense of the move. Jeff, sitting unshaven at the kitchen table in a ripped sweatshirt from the University of New Mexico Archaeology Department, dicing celery for the stuffing, saw that his mother was happy. Still, neither one of them could figure out why anyone would want to live in the South.

"It's weird here," Carrie said, twirling her wispy hair around a pencil. "I mean, at the gas station these guys were picking the filters off their Winstons and smoking up the room, I mean, isn't that against the law here, like it is everyplace else? Talking about NASCAR and chewing on Slim Jims. It's like that old show on Nickelodeon, where the sheriff goes fishing with Opie?"

"Andy Griffith," Jeff said. He lined his celery up and eased the blade through the ribs in straight lines. Then made careful cuts crosswise.

"Yeah. It's like that. A time warp, 1950s Southern Cracker Land."

"The South will rise again," Jeff says, his lip curled in a half-grin, half-challenge. "Isn't that what they say?"

"This isn't the South," Rand told them. "I'm *from* the South. This is Stonehaven Downs, a world unto itself."

Anne gave him a look. "We love it here," she said, turning to smile brightly at the kids. "It's perfect."

Rand turns down Queen of Scots Way. Now he remembers. No wonder Anne was so happy this morning, humming her little tune. He finally gave in last night and promised her a dinner party for twelve. She will at long last get to use her mother's ancient dining room table with matching chairs in English oak and chintz. The story goes that table was Tudor, stolen from a pirate ship and dragged to the New World by some colonizing ancestor. No doubt there will be ornate silver settings with her family crest and individual crystal salt bowls with tiny individual salt spoons. She's been wanting to use those ever since she got here.

"Help me add a leaf tomorrow?" she said.

"It's not for weeks," he said. "Why do it now?"

"I want to practice place settings."

"Oh for Chrissake." His usefulness to society these days seemed to be limited to changing light bulbs, putting out the trash, and moving furniture.

"Rand. You're going to enjoy this if it kills me. It's going to be a Strawberry Dinner—standing rib roast, strawberry shortcake. All your favorites. Bess said the farmers' market will have them then, first of the season."

"I'll enjoy the meat," he grumped. "But please, by all that's holy, don't put strawberries in the wine."

"Oh, why not. You don't drink wine anyway."

He has not yet figured out a way to get out of it. Dinner with six self-satisfied retired Connecticut couples, all strangers, is his idea of hell. The inane chatter, the sloppy drinking, the inevitable social climbing and one-upmanship. Civilians are just as bad as mid-rank military. They like to brag, while pretending not to. Here they brag about their kids and grandkids, their furniture and collections, their former lives, their travels. She can do that kind of thing without him soon enough.

Rand crosses Lady Jane Grey Way, breath coming ragged now. He passes a gaggle of garden ladies, all done up in grass hats and latex-dipped gloves, planting petunias, out early before the heat of the day. They wave. He nods, knowing they'll report any sign of weakness to Anne. He knows he looks more fit than their husbands, which makes him suck in his gut, which throws off his stride and, before he can catch himself, he trips on a chunk of asphalt—the new roads in this place are already dissolving—twists his knee, stumbles, bounces off the heel of one hand, and recovers.

The ladies call out, "Oh, Colonel, are you okay, Colonel?" They are coming this way. Crap. A new, hot nerve shoots pain from knee to ankle. He waves the ladies away, keeps going, waits till they are out of view to stop and pick the asphalt out of his palm.

"Have a good run, Colonel!" Another one of Anne's friends, picking up her paper from the driveway. He waves half-heartedly. This is one of Anne's spies.

After the heart attack, all her new cronies took Anne aside and instructed her on how to manage a bearish retired husband with heart trouble. It was just after Kip Larsen went to the hospital, and the Stonehaven ladies were on high alert.

One day when he breezed into the kitchen, having experimented with a new route home, he found her on the phone, looking worried, then guilty. She hung up quickly, saying, "*There* you are!" That happened often enough that it became clear she had some lady spies along his route, calling in reports of his progress. She gave him the phone with GPS tracking and made him promise to use it. Now, after six months, she's finally lost that vigilant look of wives who watch their husbands for signs of artery blockage. She's taken on a few more tennis lessons and let him go his way.

For his part, when he got home from the doctor he was terrified for the first time in his life—not about death, old friend, but that Anne might find him when the next one came. He who had faced off with four-star generals and Asian dictators couldn't stand the idea of her finding him helpless on the floor. And what would happen after.

She would call 911, they would bring him back, and him having no heart left to speak of, they'd hook him up to wires and tubes. She has read the DNR order he placed before her, but he knows she won't use it. Her heart is too soft. Hard cheek, muscled lean arms, brown legs, snapping blue eyes, she will cave the instant she sees him face down in the pale blue pile.

It happened this way to Kip, who lived an underwater life of breathing machines and slow drip feeding for months, his face floating and bloated in the blue light of his nursing-home room, the whoosh of oxygen into his lungs sounding just like Darth Vader's labored breathing. Kip, the most cheerful soldier/sailor Rand had ever known. Thank God he finally died.

Kip's wife, Adelle, lost the house. She is lucky some other Stonehaven widow with more resources has taken her in. He sees her from time to time, hunted and pale, fingering the budget-bin steaks at the grocery store. No, not that way for Anne.

He began to make a plan to be far away from rescue when he drops. The GPS on the phone will allow her to find him before the ants find his eyes.

Rand takes a furtive look around. No gardeners out in their yards, none of Anne's spies. He ducks down a dirt path between houses that leads to the highway. He crosses, heads down a side road, and looks up. The crowns of the Gooley pines blaze with light. He has timed it perfectly. If a heart attack does take him, it will take him up there, in the sharp-scented woods, birds calling overhead, cheek resting on clean pine needles. If it happens there, it will be quick. Running can be a trigger. Running uphill—well, that could finish things quite nicely, that and the sausage biscuits he's been sneaking afterward at the Sunrise Gas N Grill down the road, a pile of old tires out front, blinking lighthouse in the yard, off-brand gas, a place no self-respecting Stonehaven man ever goes—except him and Kip, he remembers with a guilty twinge. They used to sneak biscuits there.

He finds the pine needle path that leads up to the enormous trees, sucks in breath for the uphill sprint. *One Mississippi, two Mississippi, go.*

Rand is gasping for breath, forehead pressed against the bark of a behemoth pine, pulse pounding in his ears, when he hears the sirens winding down Route 177 from Quarryville, faintly at first, then whooping faster and closer as it rounds the bend and crosses the Cedar River. For an instant he thinks it's coming for him. He's imagined it so many times. He listens with dread, till he hears it turn in at Stonehaven, mute its sirens, and go about its business. It is not coming up the hill to the Gooley pines. He is not having a heart attack. He is not dead.

Once his pulse has settled, Rand walks along the ridgetop to spy on the old white frame farmhouse below, roof painted blue. Next to it, a smart new barn with a bright tin roof. When he discovered this place last winter, it seemed abandoned, last year's crops stubbled and burnt gray with frost, but there were signs of life. A thin stream of smoke trailed from the chimney, and sheets bellied on the clothesline like big square ghosts. He stood here, catching his breath, making up a story that perhaps an old widow lady lived here, and someday she would die or her children would decide to take her in, and then he would buy the place for a song, convince Anne to move there with him and fix it up. Abandon Stonehaven Downs and its excruciating social obligations.

Rand bends to tie his shoe, hears voices. A woman in bib overalls and a red kerchief is pushing a wheeled planter along the plowed furrows below, and a big kid tamps the earth behind her with the flat of a hoe. The boy dawdles. The woman calls out: "Bobo! Keep up now."

Keep up now. His mother used to say that. Back at the home place in West Virginia, in the narrow garden patch, tucked between the ridge and the crick, Ma called to him to keep up while she set seed potatoes, four to a hill. Him just a young boy, staring at clouds and bird migrations across a narrow slot of sky.

Rand lifts his bottle, sucks down water, coughs. The boy looks up, glances his way, searching. "Papa!" he calls out.

Christ on toast. Rand ducks behind a tree. He looks around. Is the kid's father up here? Nobody.

He waits a minute, peeks out. They've gone back to their planting. He watches awhile longer, but then it starts to drizzle, and then it starts to pour, and the woman and her boy go running to the house. He turns back the way he came, sliding down the pine straw path, rain pouring off the brim of his army cap, bouncing off his shoulders.

Rand jogs through the rain to the Sunrise Gas N Grill for his morning sausage biscuit and his cheat cup of coffee. At his table, he toasts an invisible Kip, swallows the bitter brew, wipes his forehead and eyes with thin paper napkins, but no matter how hard he rubs, the world is still a blur outside the plate glass window. Across the highway, an ambulance comes out of the stone entrance and turns slowly toward the hospital, windshield wipers going. No siren, no big hurry. *Another man bites the dust,* Rand thinks. *Not me. Not yet.* He has to admit that he is greatly relieved.

When Rand gets home, the spring shower is long over, the asphalt already dry, but their neighbor George is sitting on the kitchen stoop, head resting on crossed arms, arms around his knees. Napping? Drunk on gin and tonic more likely, even at this hour. George is a retired attorney from Connecticut. He drinks gin and scotch interchangeably, it seems, without seeming to care which, but it's always the good stuff, none of that army issue in plastic gallon jugs. His wife, Bess, is Anne's best friend, her most loyal tennis partner and lunch companion. Maybe George is going to invite him to lunch again, or for a round of bad golf. He thought George had finally given up on him. He had *hoped.*

Rand approaches, wheezing a bit, hoping his flushed face doesn't give away that he hasn't been just walking.

George looks up. It is the strangest thing. His face is red and splotched. His eyes are bloodshot. His shoulders shake. There's no mistaking it. He isn't drunk. He's crying.

That siren. That slow-moving ambulance.

"What happened, man?" Rand calls out, breaking into a jog. "Is it Bess?"

George shakes his head, miserable. Rand watches him try to stand. Watches George's hand reach out, a trembling, old man's hand. George's fingers grip his arm. His chest goes numb. There is only one other person it could be.

After the first jolt, like an electric shock to the heart, Rand pushes George away, charges into the house, and shouts her name, expecting to find Anne on the floor. But she's not there. He charges back into the kitchen and demands to know where she is. George swallows his drink, sets his glass carefully on the counter. "It was on the tennis court, old man. She just went down. She's at the hospital now. Bess is there. Buddy, there was nothing they could do."

Rand grabs his phone. "What hospital?" His voice is hoarse.

"Quarryville. I've got the number. I'll drive you. But first—" he hands Rand a juice glass filled to the brim with scotch. Rand drinks it down. He stares at George with loathing. Then he dials the number. A voice-mail system answers, "Thank you for calling Quarryville Hospital. If this is an emergency, please hang up and dial 911. Press one for visitor services, two for the rehabilitation unit..." Rand wants to throw the phone across the room.

He gets in George's Jag, redialing in the vain hope of reaching a real person, until they cross the bridge, where the signal dies out. He shouts,

"Can't you get any speed out of this thing?" but George is already speeding and weaving all over the road.

There has to be something they can do. There is always something they can do.

There was nothing they could do. When they couldn't find him, and she didn't respond to a tennis court geezer's rickety CPR, Bess called 911, but Anne was already dead. At the hospital, they took her straight to the morgue.

Someone takes him to her. Someone lifts the cover on her body.

Anne is not Anne. Here is a stranger with waxy skin, sagging mouth, a crust of spittle. He reaches out to wipe it away. His beautiful Anne. Her blue eyes sealed under pale freckled lids. A whiff of lemon under the hospital disinfectant and the room's pickle stench of formaldehyde.

Death squeezes Rand's heart till he cannot breathe, then settles around his shoulders like a numbing shroud.

Someone puts a hand on his arm, guides him away.

Someone fills out forms, hands him a pen.

Someone sits him down with a Styrofoam cup of coffee, he waves it off.

Someone drives him home.

Bess makes him a cup of tea with lemon. He hates lemon, but he drinks it dutifully like a refugee in a camp. He knows he's in shock. Sustenance shall not be refused. Your duty is to survive.

Someone makes phone calls in the background. The thought of Anne in the hospital, cold, fills him with dread, then rage. Bess's hand floats into his line of vision, takes his teacup, fills it again. He turns to her, croaks, "I'll sue the bastards. I want to call my lawyer." Bess fends him off, tells him they need to keep the lines clear, waiting for callbacks from the kids. The kids. Christ, the kids. Rand completely loses his courage at the thought of telling them. Someone else will tell them.

Someone finds him asleep in the recliner in the den and pulls off his shoes, covers him with a blanket. He wakes in the dark with a jerk. What is he doing here? Another spat with Anne? He makes it halfway down the hall to the bedroom before he remembers. No Anne there. No Anne anywhere. He turns and walks to the kitchen and pours himself a bourbon. Wishes he had a cigarette. Thinks there might be one in a drawer somewhere, though it's been twelve years since he quit. The kitchen phone starts to ring. He yanks the cord out of the wall.

In the morning, Bess finds him asleep at the kitchen table, his head resting on one arm, all the drawers in the kitchen pulled out and their contents scattered. She rests her hand on his shoulder. He raises his head, befuddled.

"What are you doing here?" he says.

"Oh, Rand," Bess says, her face collapsing in a puddle of tears. She turns and makes coffee and pours him some, then plugs the phone back in.

Neighbors come, Bess takes their casseroles and condolences at the door. He hears her whisper, "Massive stroke. On the tennis court. Poor thing. So unexpected." He has a dim sense of George hovering in corners, exuding a ginny smell.

That night he wakes up in his recliner, cockatiels muttering over his head: *Go to bed.* He hasn't fed them. He wonders if Bess did.

By noon the next day, Carrie and Jeff have been notified, picked up at airports, and brought to the front door. Somehow he endures their stricken faces, Carrie's desperate hug, Jeff's awkward clutch-and-pat. Carrie makes sure all Anne's relations are notified. She gets his dress uniform quick-cleaned for the funeral, sets out a dark suit for the wake. All is arranged. The women do it all.

The wake is brutal. They have dressed her in a blue flounced party dress, tan shoulders exposed, hair frosted and sprayed, gardenia on her breast, eyes closed with a dusting of blue shadow, as if she were taking a short nap before heading out—alone—to a fancy ball. Bess must have handled it. Damn her. What was she thinking?

And the flowers. Someone has sent lilies, reeking of death, and an arrangement of roses shaped like an enormous halter, as if Anne had just won a horse race, but the worst are the spring flowers. People somehow knew which ones were her all-time favorites: white daisies and blue larkspur. They are everywhere.

He overhears a complete stranger whispering to another: "There was a field behind her childhood home—on Long Island—and when she was a girl, she told me she used to run through the flowers, larkspur and daisies, lying down on them, smelling them, deciding they were proof there was a God."

He never knew that. All those people, whispering their stories about Anne, people who have known her for six months or a year at most, acting as if they knew her more intimately than he did, looking at him with an unsavory combination of sympathy and curiosity. His own children, Jeff and Carrie, standing beside him, glance at him from time to time with the same furtive expression: *How is he making out? Is he falling apart? And if not, why the hell not?*

There are people he barely remembers from their ten years in Huntington and from scattered months of home leave there. People Anne has known since childhood. People have also come from all over Ambler County, Quarryville, Green Hope, Poolesville. The sheriff is out front, guiding traffic, because people have parked all down the block. All Rand's paperwork, all his plans for his own orderly death, have not prepared him. He stands there, stunned, listening to people tell each other how sorry they are, watching people cry for the loss of beautiful Anne, watching them embrace her sister Celia, her new best friend Bess, then finally approach him with hesitant eyes, reach out for his hand, muttering, "I'm so sorry for your loss."

He hadn't known his wife's friends. He hadn't known his wife. Not very well at all lately. It eats the liver out of him.

The next day, all Rand has to do is dress for the funeral. His collar is giving him trouble—neck got thicker with age—and Carrie helps with the closure.

Jeff's face seems different this morning, shiny and pink, and it takes Rand a minute to figure out that his son has shaved off his mustache and his scruffy stubble. His suit is borrowed, too short in the sleeves. The boy looks young, vulnerable as a rookie recruit.

At the little historic church—apparently this is where Anne has been going on Sunday mornings—Rand tries to listen to the sermon but spends most of his energy trying to stand up straight. His body seems to keep wanting to sag to one side. Carrie stands beside him, gripping his arm. Then it is over.

When they get home, there is a moment when Carrie and Jeff have gone off somewhere and Rand is standing alone on the kitchen stoop, trying to see the world clearly, trying to see the world as Anne saw it. And failing miserably. At that moment he hears a crack, and an enormous tree limb falls out of the sky, bounces off the gutter, and lands on the pair of Adirondack chairs near the bird feeder. Birds hurtle in all directions—cardinals, juncos, goldfinches, jays—bursts of red, gray, yellow, and blue. She used to sit out there, watching "the common birds" at the end of the day. He'd tried joining her a few times, but the damn mosquitoes took after him.

God, he misses her. But it is more than that. Something twists in his heart, thinking of her voice, calling to birds. Her strong hand, filling the feeder. Her blue eyes, searing, accusing. Rand retreats inside, pours himself a bourbon over a single cube of ice. Gulps it down. Pours another. He lifts his glass to Anne's portrait over the mantel, a blue off-the-shoulder gown, skin glowing as if it were alive. He barely looked at it before, Anne's presence was so much more vivid. But now. Now it looks at him straight in the eye, and that blue gaze follows him around the room until he has to look away.

He remembers that he has not held back on his complaints about their new life. He hears his own voice needling, dismissing, complaining. He thought he was preparing her to live without him. Instead, he sees now that she was already living without him. Working four days a week at one thing or another—shelter, food bank, school—making morning coffee, sending him on his walk, rushing off, not returning till late afternoon, and then just long enough to make a plate for him, place it in the oven to warm, and go off to some party alone. Friday was tennis. He never saw her on Fridays. She'd tried, for a year, to lure him into the social whirl. She must have decided at some point: He could have the house, as his preserve, old growly bear. She, the bird, would fly through the open window.

2

In the morning Carrie is camped out upstairs in the guest room with her camcorder, her mother's letters and journals and photo albums, and her iPhone to keep her connected to her paralegal job in LA, from which she has taken a ten-day leave. Jeff is conspicuously absent, staying on Bess's couch rather than his father's. "Less mess for you, Dad," Jeff had said, cautiously, testing the waters. His father agreed. Jeff had clearly been relieved. Rand and Jeff have not gotten along well in recent years.

Let's face it, Jeff is kind of a bum—"shovel bumming" around archaeology digs, summer jobs, never anything that lasts, his only possessions a rucksack full of rocks and tools. A slew of short-term girlfriends, none of them good enough to bring home, apparently. The boy used to call Anne late at night, getting her up at all hours. Rand would find her sitting in her oversize flannel bathrobe in the kitchen with reheated coffee, talking out his latest failure, bad breakup, lost job. Who's the boy going to complain to now? Not him.

Rand gazes at the long oak table—someone must have added the leaf—now covered in piles of food brought by neighbors, remembers how it lay shining and expectant all these months, with a fresh flower arrangement in the center. Now funeral flowers cover every surface, including some of the chairs, and Anne's dream of a Strawberry Dinner tastes like dust on his tongue. She had been so happy that morning, and now he realizes she must have been hatching her plan—gathering recipes, guest lists, visions of table settings fizzing in her brain until that moment on the tennis court when it all exploded.

Casseroles, pies, brownies, baked chickens, deli chickens, green beans, baked beans, pound cake, even a baked ham. Some of it still warm, like the whole wheat cinnamon rolls Bess somehow found time to throw together. It is an enormous picnic—a mountain of food, really—for so few ants. He has lost his appetite. Carrie, thin as a rail, eats only desserts and Diet Coke and wheatgrass shakes. Jeff can really pack it in, but there is no way in hell he can eat a whole ham before he leaves Monday.

Rand rummages in a drawer for the Stonehaven Downs Community Resource Directory and starts flipping through. Ambler County Food Bank. That's one of Anne's things, isn't it? They take food, don't they?

"Hello," he says, surprised someone is there to answer the phone. "I have some food… Well, some of it's frozen. I don't really know what it is. It's from…a party. Casseroles and things. You can't? Oh. Oh, I see." He hangs up the phone. They think he's out to poison them. Nothing homemade. No pies or casseroles. No chicken curry. It is amazing that he cannot give away all this food.

Rand picks up two pies, a pound cake, and the baked ham and finds places for them in the refrigerator. Then he pulls a yard waste bag from the box, snaps it open, and begins to scrape the food from Anne's table into the garbage.

"Dad, what are you doing?" Carrie walks in, rubs her eyes, and stares at the casserole dish in his hand.

"Just cleaning up," he says.

"But, Dad—" Carrie looks at him quizzically. "It's perfectly good food. It's for us to eat. You know, so we won't have to cook for a while."

"I saved some of it. All this will go bad. It may already have gone bad, I have no idea how long it's been sitting here."

"Dad," Carrie says, her expression just like her mother's when Anne was about to decide to take charge. "I was just going to freeze it for you. There's plenty of room in the box freezer." She peers into the trash bag. "Don't like curried chicken anymore?" she says.

"I like your mother's curried chicken," Rand says. "The rest can go to the dogs."

"Oh, Dad." Carrie has tears in her eyes. "I miss her too."

He misses Anne. God, he misses her like an arm or a leg—no, you could lose one of those and get by. He misses her like a set of lungs. He misses her like fresh air. He has been drowning in this cheesy Southern thickened air, this false camaraderie, this pretty Disneyland For The Old, and she has been his only source of oxygen for months.

The phone rings. He hands Carrie the trash bag and picks up the phone. "Yes?" he answers. "Okay. Yes, it was. Yes, thank you. Goodbye." He looks at Carrie. Carrie is sorting casseroles by size and shape. "I don't even know who that was," he says. "She was *crying*."

Carrie stops sorting. "Dad?" she says. "Will you make a deal?" This is their old signal for serious talk. When she wanted to go to Berkeley and he wanted her closer at Swarthmore, she came to make a deal. When she wanted a strapless outfit for the prom and Anne wanted her shoulders covered, Carrie made a deal. When Jeff was winning at Monopoly but she had Boardwalk, she could always make a deal. Carrie the dealmaker. She usually made a *good* deal, where everybody felt like they got something of what they wanted. She would make a terrible lawyer. She thought about others too much.

"What's the deal," he says.

"The deal is, I'll answer the phone while I'm here. You don't even have to think about it. I'll keep it on speaker so you can pick up if you want. And if I'm not here, you agree to screen calls with the answering machine and only talk to people you want to talk to."

"Okay," he says. "You win."

Two hours later, the casseroles are sorted into What We Will Eat This Week and What We Will Eat Next Week and What We Will Never Eat in a Million Years But Jeff Might. Carrie is sitting at the kitchen table sneaking a coffee loaded with cream and sugar toxins, not on her vegan diet, when the phone rings. "Hello, Lee residence, Carrie speaking," she says.

"Talk tah Miss Ahn?" a childish voice says.

"Who is speaking, please?" Could this be a friend's grandchild, some special protégé?

"Miss Ahn, Miss Ahn!" the voice rises to a squeak.

"I'm sorry, I need to know your name," Carrie says.

"I am Bobo," the voice says. "Sorry you ah dead."

3

By Thursday, Jeff has long since run off to crash on some friend's couch somewhere in Chapel Hill, and finally, after a week of paperwork and commentary on her father's dietary practices, Carrie is packing to go. Rand wakes with plans to fit in a run before she leaves, but on his way to the closet for his shoes, he picks up the cologne spritzer on her dresser and reads the label: "Happy." He staggers to the closet and leans in, touching Anne's summer dresses, her linen suit jackets, clutching them to his breast and breathing in the faintly lemony scent, which he'd never known the name of till now. There's a whiff of stale cigarettes, as if Anne had a secret life as a smoker. All the parties she went to without him. Someone in Stonehaven must still have the habit.

Now his body slumps to one side and he slides to the floor, dragging a pile of clothes with him. When Carrie pokes her head in the bedroom door, she finds him huddled on the closet floor, his face buried in a tumble of cloth. "Dad? Dad! What's wrong!"

Rand pushes the clothes away, scrambles up. "Where the hell are my Nikes? Got to clean out this damn closet."

"Dad," Carrie informs him, "nobody cleans out a closet this soon. Anyway, I might want some of her things."

He looks doubtfully at his daughter, who has never seemed to know conventional wisdom about anything, much less closet cleaning and death. And she has never shared her mother's taste for tennis togs, silk dresses, and double-knits. Carrie's always been strictly a thrift store fashionista—her taste running to plastic purses, zigzag patterns, and polyester micro-mini dresses. For a moment he imagines Carrie in one of Anne's outfits. There's…a resemblance. Delicate nostrils, tilted eyes, and faint brocade of freckles. He can't breathe, looking at her. He needs to get out, run up a hill, inhale the hot incense of the Gooley pine grove.

Rand scoops his Nikes out of the closet, tells Carrie, "Time to get back to the routine. Doctor's orders, you know." Carrie opens her mouth as if to protest, then closes it and lets him go his way.

Rand heads down the road, not stopping for stretches, for fear that a passing car will stop, a neighbor look out at him, someone he's never met, and express sympathy, tell a story about Anne that he's never heard, some intimate moment of her life, make him feel even more a stranger in his own marriage. He looks both ways, crosses the highway, spies a big black beater of a car parked next to the field. That's new. Maybe some kids fishing by the river. He heads to the base of the trail that leads up into the Gooley pines. He does his stretches, massages the knot in his calf. *One Mississippi, two Mississippi. Go.*

At the top, back against a giant pine, he looks up, mouth open, gasping like a landed fish. The crowns of the Gooleys catch a breeze; their needles shimmer down at him, greenly. He remembers the day he stood here, watching an ambulance carry his wife away, so relieved it wasn't him. He slides down the trunk, holds his head in his hands, shaking it from side to side. *No no no no. Oh Anne, oh damn, oh hell. How am I supposed to do this without you?*

He hears a sound like laughter. Or crying. He crawls to the edge of the cliff and peers at the ragged field below. A dark figure there, kneeling among the rocks and weeds as if she owns the place. *This is my field,* he wants to say. *Nobody comes here.* Except those goats last winter. So maybe it belongs to someone. This person. Who now rises and stares up at the giant pines. Who now seems to be talking to them. Calling out a name. *Anne?* A trick of the bowl of land, the word now comes as clear as the bird chatter above his head: *Danielle.* He looks around for the person she is calling. But there is no one.

Rand turns back to find the forest path. He begins to run. He runs steadily, slowly, along the ridgetop into the shadows of the great trees, their scent like joss sticks, pungent and bracing. If someone catches him here, he will be sweating, working out, too busy to talk, not mooning about the past with his hands over his eyes. If someone finds him here, he will somehow still be moving.

That evening, after he's dropped Carrie at the airport—"Dad, I'll call you every day. The deal is, you pick up"—the house seems hollow, the air conditioner droning outside like a giant cicada. He turns on *The Weather Channel.* The map shows three hurricanes lined up like bowling balls, heading across the Atlantic toward Florida. Thank God they didn't retire there. "Unprecedented number of storms this early in the season...." A knock comes at the front door. What the hell? People never knock at the front door. More nosy neighbors no doubt. He opens it a crack.

A couple stands there in the dark, all dressed up. The man holds a bottle of wine. "You must be the colonel!" the man says, shifting the wine so he can shake hands. "Anne's said so much about you."

Rand leaves the man's hand hanging in the air. Is this that awful bereavement committee, come to check on him? "Who are you?" he says. "What are you doing here?"

The woman looks shocked, then uncertain. "Oh dear," she says, "have we got the wrong night?" She looks accusingly at her husband. Then back at Rand. "We're here for the Strawberry Dinner? We just blew into town from three weeks in Costa Rica, we're a bit frazzled. She said Thursday."

"We didn't get the wrong *night*," the man hisses to his wife. "I'm Fred Ackerman," he says, looking around Rand to the darkened house and looking increasingly concerned. "This is Judy. We're friends of Anne's. Met on the tennis court. Isn't this the Lee residence?"

Judy grabs her husband's arm, turns to Rand. "We didn't see a house number. We just guessed. She told us the third house in, stones stacked next to the door. Anne said that was what made her house different from the rest."

Rand stands there unable to speak. The old Indian stones she discovered in the yard, with indentations like small bowls in the middle. She stacked them up like a Scottish cairn, marking their new home as the end of a journey. He remembers Anne's elegant scrawl on a calendar square: *Strawberry Dinner. Get wine.* He remembers too what he said when he finally gave her the go-ahead: "Have it your way. Have people over. Feed them all the strawberries you want. I'll take a drive or something." These people never got the memo about the change in plans.

Fred and Judy are staring.

"She died," he croaks. "Two weeks ago."

He shuts the door carefully in their faces before their shock can turn to pity. He locks the door. Goes to the sofa, puts his head in his hands. All he can think is: Nothing can fix this. No walks no runs no birds *no Anne no Anne no Anne.* He's got to get away from these crowding memories, these crowding people. He wishes his damn heart would go ahead and finish it. Maybe it won't be long. Maybe he can do his short time. But Anne whispers in his ear: *Wherever you go, there you are. That's the whole problem.*

PART II

REBA'S FIELD

4

Friday afternoon, across the highway and down Field Road, Miss Reba Jones is sitting on her porch, staring at the new-green tops of the Gooley Pines, when she hears Reverend come flying down her gravel drive in his church van. The van scatters chickens, throws a cloud of dust. Miss Reba sees it on his face before he even gets out. Not a good day for justice.

Reverend's come to tell her of Tommy Jay's trial. Whiteman who killed her Danielle. Twenty-nine years old, sweetest girl there ever was, raised her from a child, nothing left of her now but ashes in a box and this lead weight on her heart.

Reverend walks across the yard, gives the side-eye to Papa's Black angels looming over on him. Reverend is not a tall man. But he has made peace with what she knows he thinks are pagan idols. He knows they stand for grief, mostly, but just in case they have powers, he stands tall in his black suit and tie, chest out, like a banty rooster standing up to the spirits bigger than him. Her own rooster darts out now, flaps and rasps his warning. Reverend diverts the attack with a firm nudge of his shoe.

"Good afternoon, Miss Reba," Reverend calls out in his smoothest, kindest way. She indicates the porch chair and he sits, wipes sweat with his hankie. Hot this afternoon. She offers neither water nor tea. She hopes he doesn't stay long.

"They had ballistics this morning," Reverend says.

"Don't tell me ballistics," she says. She knows what a bullet does.

"His boy TJ was set to testify, but the child has run away, they said. They're still looking for him."

"Eyewitness."

Reverend nods. "Our only chance, Miss Reba."

She knows about eyewitness testimony. She knows about circumstantial. She's watched *Matlock*, every episode, some of them twice. You can't get a murder conviction with circumstantial. Not if it's a whiteman.

She remembers the letter she typed to the DA before the trial. There's a carbon copy of it in the back of her Bible, tucked next to the other things.

Dear Mr. DA,

I can provide evidence of Mr. Snipes's poor character and his history of violent behavior against my niece, Danielle Esther Johnson. I would like to testify in the murder trial against him. Ask Sheriff Walter Pickett Jr., he knows I am a reliable witness.

Sincerely yours,
Miss Reba Jones
Cc: sheriff's office, the governor

Tucked next to her own letter is the reply they sent her six weeks ago, on Ambler County Court stationery. It says that character testimony such as she is offering is not admissible in this court, because she didn't see it happen with her own eyes. That's the law. But there's another reason they won't let her speak, she's sure of that: she's Danielle's witchy Aunt Reba, got Tuscarora blood in her, does spells and herbs and things, might be crazy.

"Summation was this afternoon," Reverend says.

"What they say?"

"Judge instructed the jury on manslaughter." Reverend is full-on sweating now.

"Don't hang for that."

"No." Reverend looks up. "Sure you don't want to sit?"

"Just tell me."

"Jury's gone home," he says. "Deliberation next week. Won't take long, I expect."

Next week. That's how it is on *Matlock*. Takes the jury a few days at least.

"Miss Reba," Reverend says, "we can always pray."

Reverend's been making her pray since the day her Danielle got shot, close range, by Tommy Jay Snipes, eighteen months ago, while the girl was cooking his dinner in that ratty trailer across the river, his boy TJ watching the whole thing.

Miss Reba is tired of praying. She prayed when Danielle moved in with Tommy Jay, ten years ago, the girl a scant nineteen years old. Girl thought she'd be good for that whiteman and his boy. Thought she loved him. "Somebody to take care of, Auntie," she said. Girl so full of love, it was like she had too much and had to burn it. Miss Reba prayed every day that scrawny, no-account whiteman would somehow become worthy, or Danielle would run home to this house, where it was safe.

Every day she regretted that she never told Danielle any of her stories about whitemen and their ways, stories that could have warned her away from such as Tommy Jay. She hadn't wanted a girl that sweet to know what whitemen do.

"This is a time that tries men's souls," Reverend says. He closes his eyes. "Jesus, open the hearts of the jury members to deliver us justice next week, as you have not seen fit to deliver it today. Jesus name, Amen."

Maybe they'll find that runty little whiteboy TJ. Only eyewitness. Maybe they'll have to start the trial all over again. For a moment, hope rises in Miss Reba like a small green leaf on a crooked stem. Then she remembers that TJ is the son of the man who killed her Danielle. He'll lie like a rug.

"You coming on verdict day?" Reverend says.

"I'll be there."

That night, Miss Reba sits in her porch chair, gold foil box of Danielle's ashes in her lap, dusk settling around her, Black angels leaning close. Three of them still standing, all in a row, eight feet tall, blacker than black against a pale bowl of sky. The cedar trunks have lasted more than seventy years, bottoms buried deep like fence posts. Papa put these up, one by one, for children dead or gone away. Big sister Sheba with her big blue eyes full of wrath as a coming storm, mouth open, wings spread, right arm raised. Little sister Pearl, getting silvery the way old cedar does. Gem Junior leans over to one side, like grief has weighted him.

Night breeze catches in the sycamore tree, snags at Reba's arms and neck like cobwebs. Seeds to plant, garden to weed, Mama's flower bed gone to ruin, and all she's wanted to do since Reverend left is sit here with Danielle.

Reba closes her eyes. Sees Danielle a little girl. Always wanting to sit in her lap. Always wanting to hear the old stories.

Are you a Indian, Auntie? she would ask, those small hot ribs pressing against her chest like bird bones.

I guess I was, for a time.

All your herbs and potions, they Indian things?

Old Lucy taught me. Reba had told her about Old Lucy.

Old hermit lady.

Yes.

And when Reba would take her to the Field for gathering, the girl would run around just like Sheba, pretend she was dancing an Indian dance, those big colored birds flying over her head, like in Old Lucy's day. The child was certain that one day the Indians would come back. Huts and cookfires, birds and singing. But Danielle is never coming back. And it's all because of Tommy Jay Snipes.

A rustle in the sycamore tree, caused by no breeze. *Avenge her,* Old Lucy whispers.

Sycamore leaves clap in applause.

Old Lucy loved vengeance. That is the Tuscarora way.

Something murky flaps in Reba's chest. How to make this feeling go away? Get up and do.

Miss Reba goes inside, lays the box with Danielle's ashes on the mantel next to the pink one for Mama and the blue one for Papa. She washes her town dress and pressure stockings. She hangs them on the line in the dark. She polishes her Sunday shoes. She pulls the Charles Chips can down from the high cupboard. Pulls out her father's old solid-steel service revolver. She sits down with a cotton ball and toothpowder, cleans the rust off as she's seen her papa do. Then she lights a kerosene lamp, carries the gun and the lantern out to the fence, shoots at cans. She gets used to the hard pull of the trigger, the weight and surprise of the gun in her hands like a slug of iron with a spark of hate inside.

5

Through the woods at Spill Creek Farm, Jolene Blake steps out on her screen porch, brushing her long black hair. The porch wrens fly up and make a fuss. She waves them away, and they settle in that old boot where they're making a nest. *Boom...Boom.* Somebody's shooting deep in the woods, past the goat barn. That familiar tug in her belly: *Where's Bobo?*

Last she checked, he was in bed, dead asleep.

Boom...Boom. It's coming from way across the creek, near old Miss Reba's house. She should call. But these days Miss Reba hardly answers the phone. She can barely stand to look at people. Even Bobo.

More shooting. Jolene thought she knew the sound of every rifle and shotgun belonging to every fool who ever tried to poach her woods. This is a new sound.

She pads down the hall and opens Bobo's bedroom door. There. Safe. His old transistor radio playing somewhere under his pillow. Snoring as loud as a man. Hair still silky and wayward as a child's. He's getting so big. A growth spurt. He's suddenly taller than her. Nineteen years old, and he's finally getting his delayed adolescence. The doctors said it would come around now. "That's how it works for Down syndrome," they said. They have the answers to everything except how to pay the bills. And how to keep Bobo safe now that his ancient dog, Ace, has died. That big white puff of a dog, like a giant milkweed. Ace protected the goats, the farm, and Bobo from all kinds of dangers for more than fifteen years. If Ace were here, he would be barking a fierce warning, fur puffed around his neck like a lion's mane.

The shooting has started up again. Jolene slips on her sneakers, walks out to check the pregnant goats in the barn. Amanda is halfway to standing, making snorts of alarm. Chloe is calm, staring at her with slotted eyes. Folly is dead asleep, one ear twitching. Jolene runs her hands over their taut swollen bellies. She rests a palm on Amanda's back. "Settle down, mama. Nothing to worry about." Amanda nestles back into the straw. Jolene scratches the white patch under Amanda's chin.

"Good girls," Jolene says. "Sleep tight."

On the way back to the house, silence. The shooting has stopped.

Who in the world could it be? Jolene has an awful thought: *Maybe*

Tommy Jay got out of jail. Impossible. And if he did? Miss Reba might kill him with a garden rake.

Stop, she tells herself. Don't borrow trouble.

Jolene sits at her kitchen table, works her hair into a sleek fat braid down her back, sets the brushings out for the porch wrens to line their nest, sees there's more than one silver hair snarled in with the black. She makes her list of chores. The late weather report comes on the radio. *First hurricane of the season has formed in the Atlantic near Cape Verde, the earliest hurricane in recorded history.* More strange weather. But nowhere near here, thank God. She's got to plant beans tomorrow. She doesn't need to check last year's weather log, the season's moved up by at least two weeks. Everything is getting earlier and earlier. It's hot as late May. The farmers at the market know, but they don't talk about it. If they talked about it, they'd have to admit something is shifting in this world.

Jolene writes down her income from the farmers' market today: $265. Some of that for Miss Reba. It would have been more, lots more, but the strawberry truck came and stole everyone's customers.

Jolene checks Bobo one last time: still snoring. She checks his windbreaker pockets. She loads Juicy Fruit gum on the right side. Finds a spoon on the left. Not one of hers. Since Ace died, he's been picking up things from farmers' market tables. Shiny things. A red apple. A tiny gold frame with a dried flower arrangement from Miss Phoebe, that woman's only income since her husband died. Once he came home with a plastic diamond ring, a child's toy. She'll just have to track down the spoon owner at the market next week, best she can.

Jolene flings her sweaty tee and bib overalls in the pile of laundry. She rubs udder balm into her cracked hands. Luke used to call them "lady hands, so white and slender," and he would kiss her palm. Now they're farmer's hands, stained around the fingernails with red earth, calloused and hard with planting, hoeing, milking.

She brushes her teeth, crawls into bed, and for a moment tries to conjure Luke beside her. The man-musk and fresh-grass smell of him. The way he pulled her to him. Kissed her ear. Then other parts. Eight years gone. Eight years since the last time they made love in Indigo Field, and he told her, *You have to put on a show for God sometimes, by having even rows of corn, painting the roof blue, or loving, right out in the Field.* She thinks about him all the time, but she barely misses him anymore. It makes her terribly sad.

The shooting starts again.

In the morning, after first milking, Jolene bags up produce from the garden, bread and muffins from the farmers' market. "We're going to see Miss Reba, Bobo," she says.

"Weba!" The name he gave her as a child, before he could say his *r*'s. It stuck. Miss Reba doesn't seem to mind. He runs off to pick clover and field daisies for the old lady.

They take the farm road that goes through woods and fords Spill Creek, and Bobo hangs out the truck window to watch the splashing. They enter the clearing—those big black statues, leaning at crazy angles, chickens roosting at their feet, the tidy brick house. Miss Reba sitting in her chair.

Miss Reba's got hands in her lap, tufts of hair coming askew from the side braids she usually keeps neatly pinned into her bun, eyes closed into slits behind those big glasses. That smooth blank expression. That old scar like a crescent moon on her cheek. She barely turns her head as they roll up.

Miss Reba has never exactly been a friendly person, but for many years they've had a kind of understanding. Jolene could talk to her, and Miss Reba advised, while maintaining her distance, her dignity, her separation. But since Danielle died, Miss Reba has clammed up completely. It's the grief, Jolene knows. But there's something else, something that scares Jolene a little. It reminds her of when Luke took her to meet Miss Reba for the first time, back when she was pregnant with Bobo. Luke said Miss Reba had been a midwife when she was younger, and she was all business that day, running her long brown fingers over Jolene's belly, checking the baby, feeling its position. Telling her which herbs to use on which days until the baby came, which herbs to use after. Looking at Jolene with judging eyes.

Jolene knew she and Luke looked like free-love hippies. *We're married!* she wanted to say. But that wasn't it. Miss Reba looked like she was making a decision: a decision about whether or not the nineteen-year-old girl before her was dangerous.

It's back to that look now. Jolene can almost understand it. The whole world would seem dangerous if a child you raised was murdered. "Stay in the truck, Bobo," she says.

"Why, Mama?"

"Just stay."

Jolene steps up to the porch and hands Miss Reba an envelope of cash, forty dollars for the twenty pounds of Reba's sweet potatoes Jolene's now got piled in her own pantry, another twenty for the eggs she sold for her. Miss Reba's eggs are popular. But nobody buys sweet potatoes in the spring. What's left is a little runty, a little soft around the edges.

"You sold out, Miss Reba," she lies.

Miss Reba takes the envelope and places it in her lap. Next to a big heavy gun. *Oh dear Lord.* "Miss Reba, you got critters after your chickens?"

Miss Reba shakes her head slow.

"I heard some shooting last night."

"That was me."

Jolene wants to say, *Are you okay, are you in danger, why do you have a gun in your lap?* But the look on Miss Reba's face stops her.

"Dora sent some bread and things," Jolene says. "Miss Phoebe sent you a jar of piccalilli." She places the paper bag on the porch. "People asked for your cakes and flowers." Those melt-in-your-mouth pound cakes. Those wild bouquets, all kinds of crazy flowers mixed together with things Miss Reba cuts in the Field. Larkspur and wheatgrass, daisies and mullein stalks, wild asters and roses. Reba called them "Mama's posies." Jolene glances at the flower patch. It's choked with weeds. "You need any help?"

Miss Reba gives her a look that could freeze a bird in flight.

Bobo jumps out of the truck and runs to Reba. Jolene sees her slip the gun into her apron pocket as she uses her cane to stand. Bobo's brought his jar of flowers. "Foh you!" Miss Reba sets the jar on the porch chair. He puts his arms around her. "Weba!" Miss Reba just stands there, arms rigid at her sides.

My God, what if that gun is loaded? It could go off. "Bobo! Miss Reba doesn't want to visit right now."

"I miss Dahn-yell," he says, and leans his head on Miss Reba's shoulder. Miss Reba sways and sags against him. Then she straightens up slowly, as if she were a wall being built brick by brick. Bobo wanders off to scoop scratch and feed the chickens.

"Trade for eggs?" Jolene says. "I've got new potatoes and sugar pods."

Miss Reba nods, trudges inside, comes out with a dozen and a paper sack full of thistle. Miss Reba never forgets to keep her supplied. Jolene makes rennet for her goat cheese from thistle. One of her trade secrets. But it's early May. Where in the world did Reba get thistle bloom?

"Thistle!" Bobo says. He starts pulling out the spiky flower heads.
"Ow!"

"Careful, Bobo!"

"Let the boy touch it," Miss Reba says. "He got to learn."

Jolene flinches. There's never been such hardness in Miss Reba's
voice, not toward Bobo. Miss Reba loves Bobo. They leave her standing
on her porch, staring at nothing at all, but so fiercely it might be an
invading army.

They're halfway through the woods when Jolene knows. The shooting last night—that wasn't hunting. That was target practice.

6

Tuesday morning, 10:45, Miss Reba Jones, legal name Ruby Queen Esther Jones, walks to the courthouse door, clutching her big black church bag. She's got her church Bible in there plus three tissues, half a stick of Juicy Fruit, a skein of yarn, crochet needles, and, wrapped in a double layer of afghan squares, the dead weight of Papa's solid-steel service revolver.

The deputy at the gate knows her. When she tells him she's afraid the new detector will ruin her knitting with electricity, he takes the bag, says, "What you got in this thing? A brick?" He peeks inside, pokes the Bible, the knitting, gives it back, and chuckles. Says, "Miss Reba, you are a hoot."

She glares at him. Everybody knows she's got no reason to smile.

Reba sits where she can see Tommy Jay's face from the side. *Look at him, laying back in his borrowed suit, like he's got all the time in the world.* Scrawny back and stringy hair. She can smell him. Bony whiteman smell.

Sheba spirit says: *You should have shot him a long time ago. Should have put Danielle in the car and drove to Baltimore, got her away.*

"Should-have can't help now," Miss Reba mutters.

Reba's church purse has got soft sides and she can feel the heavy handle of the revolver poking her thigh. Lucy's spirit rises, says: *Make sure he pay.*

Reba pulls a tissue from her purse. Looks around the room. There's Reverend, a few rows back. There's the churchpeople, in the back row. Like scared rabbits. Why don't they sit up front? Where they can be seen.

"All rise."

Reba stands. Tommy Jay stands. The judge sits. He's a new one. Young. Maybe there's a chance.

There is evil in the room. Reba stands like a rock against it, clutches her purse to her chest, the weight of it next to her heart like a second heart, a dead heart, next to her heart full of blood and grief. She stares hard enough to burn a hole in Tommy Jay's back, and he feels it. He turns, catches her eye, startles like a man caught in a noose, neck stretched out taut. He grabs the table and sits back down.

The jury comes in. Sits down. Stares at her. The bailiff announces the case number, says the names, the list of charges, but all she hears is, *murder of Danielle Esther Johnson*. Her dead baby sister Pearl's granddaughter, took her in when her mama got sick. Last of her kin. The very last. A happy child. Stayed happy. All through those years. Growing up. The little girl came to her in pigtails and a party dress, little white socks and black shoes. Big snaggletooth grin, eight years old, about the size of Pearl when Pearl was five. Brown saucy eyes. Curly lashes. Tight braids. Little yellow butterfly clips at the ends.

Miss Reba blows her nose, puts the tissue back in her purse, snaps it shut. Gun's still there. Eye for an eye, the Bible says. Justice might rain down like thunder today, right here in Ambler County Courthouse, but just in case it doesn't, she is not above killing Tommy Jay Snipes herself. She got off another practice shot this morning, hit too low for the can, blew the side out of the fence post, about knocked her arm off. Aim higher next time.

The judge says, "Does the jury have a verdict?"

The jury foreman stands. "We have."

"What is the verdict?"

"On the charge of first degree murder we find the defendant not guilty."

Churchpeople in the back cry out.

The judge rubs his eyes, asks to repeat. The whiteman juryman says it again.

Miss Reba opens her purse.

The juryman clears his throat.

"Go on."

"On the charge of intent to manufacture and distribute Schedule II drug methamphetamine, we find the defendant guilty of simple possession."

"Go on."

"On the charge of involuntary manslaughter, we find the defendant guilty."

They don't hang for that.

Miss Reba stands up. Power of Sheba rising in her legs. Voice of Lucy in her ears. She stands there like an oak, strong and solid-trunked. She stares at the judge. Stares at the jury. People from her own church sit there quaking.

The young judge looks at her, says, "Who is this woman?"

Everybody else knows who she is.

Miss Reba opens her mouth to speak but the veil draws across her eyes and now she cannot see the room. The purse is heavy in her hands, so heavy, her hand stuck to the gun, cool heavy metal, finger feeling for the trigger, a weakness in her legs, a loud bang. She can see nothing but Tommy Jay Snipes, eyes popped out and staring, red smear on his cheek, washed in his own blood like somebody shot him. *Was it me who shot him? It must be.* And then she sees nothing at all but smells the flowers.

When Miss Reba opens her eyes, the bailiff is fanning her with a yellow pad. The judge is calling for order. There's shouting all around. Reverend kneels next to her, his fancy pressed pants on the dirty floor. "You had a little fit, Miss Reba. You feeling faint?" Miss Reba feels around for her purse. "I got your purse, don't you worry about that." Reverend takes her arm, pulls her up to sitting. Reba's tongue is thick in her mouth. Where she bit it there is salty blood. It's been long years since she fell down. "Tommy Jay dead?" she says.

"No, Miss Reba. Nobody's dead. My goodness."

"Where is he?"

Reverend sops his brow with his handkerchief. "Miss Reba, they took him back to jail. We got to get you home."

But now EMTs come running, mess around checking heart rate, blood pressure, eyes. Finally Reverend waves them off, says, "I got this," and they stand back. Reverend puts her in his personal car, heads down Quarryville Road, crosses the Cedar River Bridge. Miss Reba listens to the thump of old tires on metal bridge joints, looks out the window as they turn down Field Road. Indigo Field is full of shadow, Gooley Ridge with the old pines gold and green, Jolene's farm all planted in spring crops. They cross Spill Creek, pull up into her yard.

Three things don't change. Chickens still peck. Black angels still stand. Brick house still here.

"Miss Reba," Reverend says. He sits behind the wheel like he's got all the time in the world.

"What," she says.

"I opened your purse. Just to see if you had your sugar pills with you."

"Mmm-hmm."

"Miss Reba," he says. "I saw the gun."

Miss Reba pulls her purse close. Still heavy. Still there.

"When you dropped your purse, it made such a noise I about jumped out of my skin."

Miss Reba knows for sure now. She didn't shoot anybody.

"Listen here," he says. "You know that ain't the way. Vengeance belongs to the Lord. You go around shooting people, you'll get all of us
in trouble."

Reba shakes her head, side to side.

"You got to find something to do. Stop stewing on Tommy Jay. Get
your mind off him. Help somebody. Like when you fostered those
boys."

"Ain't got time for that." She can't tell him all she wants to do is sit
on her porch and listen to the spirit voices rising up around her. Listen
for Danielle's voice to finally join them. He already thinks she tends toward pagan. He hasn't forgot the Tuscarora hiding under her Black skin.

"I'm praying for you every day," Reverend says. "Everybody's praying for you."

Reba tells him go pray for somebody else.

"You bring that gun to the sentencing," he says, "I'll turn you in
myself."

Miss Reba tucks the gun in a plastic bag and puts it back in the Charles
Chips can in the high cupboard. She makes herself some sassafras tea,
mixes in the last of the skullcap herb, sits down on the porch. It's hot
and steamy for May. Seems like twenty years since Danielle got killed.
All the rest of the family are dead or scattered—Mama, Papa, Sheba,
Gem Jr. , Thomas, Pearl, Airy, Little Gem—dried up and gone like dead
leaves after a high wind.

Sheba Angel's got a fierce eye, staring at her. *Why didn't you shoot him?*
Pearl Angel needs a coat of paint.

Gem Jr. doesn't say much. Tilted over so far, he's about to fall.

Whirlwind in the top of the sycamore tree. Old Lucy is here.

"I didn't do it," Miss Reba says. "I fell down."

Reverend comes by next afternoon while she's sweeping the porch.
He pulls right up next to Mama's flower bed, rolls down his window,
calls out, "Miss Reba. We got a sentence." He opens the car door, slams
it shut, stands before her.

"What," Reba says, sick at heart. That was too fast.

"Four years."

Four. Miss Reba knows that's low. Whiteman time.

"With credit for time served, that's thirty months."

Months.

"It's a sorry shame, Miss Reba. But the Lord works in mysterious ways, his wonders to unfold."

Miss Reba clutches the broom, holds it steady with effort, because it wants to rise up and whack Reverend in the head.

He steps back, glances up at the shadowy black figures in the yard. He leans in to whisper. "I'm not supposed to say this, Miss Reba, but we can always hope he dies in prison."

Friday morning, Reba sees it's rained and the world is a bright sparkly place, but all that bright just sags at her heart. She digs what's left of the chickenscratch out of the corners of the bin with her fingernails and flings the scrapings. She is slam out of chickenscratch.

Reba picks up the paper, finds the piece about Tommy Jay's sentence. She cuts it out with her kitchen scissors, writes the date in pen, folds it in two, and tucks it in the back of the big old family Bible with all the others. Bible's getting thick with papers. She pulls a new red rubber band from the kitchen drawer and slides it around the thickest part. That will hold for a while.

The phone rings.

It's that guardian ad litem from the courthouse. "Oh, Miss Reba. They finally found TJ Snipes under the Route 40 overpass in Morganton."

Miss Reba does not know why this is any of her business.

"Miss Reba, that boy needs a place to stay. I know it's a lot to ask, but—"

Reba holds the phone out from her ear, little tinny whitelady voice still talking, rattling on about how Butner Juvenile is no place for a boy like him, and you may not be blood kin, Miss Reba, but you are the closest thing to kin that boy has, and what a good foster mother you have always been in the past, and anyway it won't be for long, his daddy may get out on good behavior—

Miss Reba places the handset on the cradle and walks away.

She sits in her porch chair, thinks about Tommy Jay, and how she missed her chance. Thinks about Danielle, how she will never see her again.

She stands in front of Sheba Angel, asks, "What shall I do?"

Fierce blue eye says, *Shoot him.*

"Can't shoot a man in prison. Have to wait till he gets out."

Reba asks Pearl Angel, "How shall I live?"

Pearl's face, pale and gray, says, *My poor Danielle.*

Reba knows better than to ask Gem Jr. . He doesn't speak to her, never did.

Reba listens for Old Lucy. She's always got something to say. But all the voices in her head have gone quiet. Even the birds have gone still.

After Mama died, she lived alone in this house twenty years, something hard like a beetle shell covering her heart. Danielle broke it open when she came. The girl ran right up to her and put arms around her waist. *Aunt Reba!* Never been shy in her life. Reba took her to church, taught her to love her neighbor as herself. Even if he punch her in the face. Even if he shoot her in the eye. *Dear Jesus help me now.*

She was alone again after Danielle went to stay with Tommy Jay. Staved it off taking in Black boys to foster. But she has got too old for that. And now this. To be alone and know she has no kin in this world, no kin at all that she can find, so many letters written, so many false leads looking for Pearl's family, Little Gem's, Airy's, gone north, dead and homeless, dead in jail, died from drugs, shot, shot, shot—it's like looking into the dark sky and seeing no stars, just emptiness that wants to pull her in. Since Danielle's gone, she knows, for the first time, what it must have been like to be Tuscarora Lucy, the old hermit lady who lived in the Field for more than a hundred years, the last of her kind.

When Reba asked Old Lucy, one day toward the end, if she really was as old as people said, she said, *Here's why some people live so long. They ain't give up their misery. They hang on to misery like a worn out blanket. Only chance they know for joy is in this world, but they hang on to misery.* She looked at Reba with her glittery black eye and said, *You got to give away your misery.*

Misery doesn't feel like a blanket. No. It feels like her eyes closing, shutting out the sunlight. It feels like that beetle shell growing over her heart. It feels like her mouth rusting shut, nobody to talk to but the breeze.

Time to get up and do. She gathers up her trowel and her knife, some plastic bags to kneel on, others to carry things. Gets in the Cutlass and heads down Field Road. Parks at the gate, sagging on its hinges. Miss Jolene's got to take better care of that.

Reba opens the gate, walks the goat trail to the river, stares out at Lucy's island. Listens. She can hear Old Lucy's voice in the ripples of the water, telling stories of the old days, when she and sister Sheba ran in the Field, playing Indian.

Reba sets down her plastic bags, kneels, and digs around the roots of a little sassafras tree. *Dig when the leaves the size of a child's hand,* Lucy says. *Sassafras good for arthritis.* Reba cuts a bundle of thick roots, stows them in her bag. She finds the patch of skullcap in the shadows of the tall pines. *For your fits,* Lucy says. Reba digs wild carrots. Checks the stems. Hairy. *Smooth stem mean hemlock,* Old Lucy whispers. *Hemlock can kill a man.*

Miss Reba lets the hemlock be. She stares up at the Gooley pines. There were shadows up there last time she was here. Shadows that moved off into the woods.

She turns her ear to the ground, listens. There it is. The sound of earth sipping water after rain. Sister Sheba had a name for that. *It's sissipping,* Sheba says.

Miss Reba knows people say she communes with the dead. Her mama used to say, "It's one thing to hear voices. You know you're in trouble when you start talking back." Well, if all she has for people is these voices in her head, she will talk back. She's seen whitepeople have whole conversations with their dogs. At least she's talking to people.

Saturday, bright and early, Miss Reba goes to the mantel, says good morning to Mama in her pink foil box, Papa in his blue, Danielle in her church dress picture, all teeth and pigtails and smile. She walks out to the porch, greets the angels, chisel marks picked out in morning sun like somebody painted the edges gold. Hens come running, and she's got nothing to give them but corn grits from the bag.

A cloud passes, shades Pearl's face to black. The sun returns, makes a patch of light, a blank bright place on wood where Pearl's face was. Pearl says, *Let me go, sister. I am weary of sadness in this world. Let Danielle live instead of me.*

Reba lays her hands on the silvery grain and leans into the wood, holding it, smelling it, her heart against the heart of the old tree trunk, the memories clear: Pearl at four, dancing in the yard, at six, singing a church solo, "His Eyes Are on the Sparrow," such a big voice booming out that tiny chest, voice big enough to shatter and remake the world. When Pearl turned fourteen she ran off to marry a band leader in Rocky Mount. Papa said she was dead to him, and he made this as her grave marker.

Mama got news of Pearl from time to time. She went to Baltimore, then Chicago. She was a singer there. Had children. Grandchildren. One of them was Danielle—middle name Esther, like Reba. When Danielle's mama died, Pearl took her in. Then Pearl died from that cancer. They sent that little girl to her on a Greyhound bus.

How Reba yearns to see that child's face again. It's time to make a new angel.

Reba gets the paint cans, black, brown, white, and red. She picks up an old paint brush and washes a new coat of black on the wood. Paints new eyes wide and sweet and brown, with a kindly expression, makes her lips red and full. Danielle loved to crochet rainbows. Big afghans, little dresser scarves. She put them all over the house. Even the porch. *Look, Auntie,* she used to say, *rainbows on your queen chair.* Reba takes a piece of crochet in rainbow colors and pulls out the weave, cuts the crinkled yarn, and tacks long pieces to the body and wings.

The May breeze catches and twirls and raises the rainbow yarn threads up like wind in the wildflowers of the Field. Reba takes a cup of well water and a bundle of tobacco and sprinkles the face and body, arms and wings, says, "I bless you and protect you in the name of the Lord and all things holy. Your name is Danielle."

When Jolene comes to drop Reba's market money Sunday morning, Bobo looks up in wonder at the newly painted statue. "Dahn-yell!" he shouts, and he runs to hug it, then pulls back, sticky with black paint. "Put some mineral spirits on it," Reba says, giving Jolene the can. Jolene stops to look at the new face staring down at her. Her mouth opens. For once Miss Jolene got nothing to say.

It takes Jolene a while to scrub the paint off, and now Bobo smells of mineral spirits, so she makes him take a bath. When he's finally done, it's late morning. She sets him up in the goat dairy to make cheese with her. "Bobo making cheeese!" he crows. "First time!"

"First time," Jolene agrees. She has promised him this for a week. Since Ace died and there's no one to watch him, she's going to have to include him in this precise, patient chore, their income depends on it.

She's just pouring the first batch into the pasteurizer when she hears a truck pull up in the yard. "Hello?" a man calls out. *What in the world?*

Bobo runs to see. "Mama, Mama, Mama!" he calls. "The Big Tree Man!"

Oh good Lord, she forgot. Today is the day for the annual tree-fest on the Gooley Ridge. The Ambler County Society for the Preservation of Old-Growth Pines—a fancy name for a ragtag bunch of people whose annual meeting consists of hugging the biggest trees, followed by a picnic, and sometimes drumming. They spread their arms wide, hold hands, press their bodies against the trunks, and count how many people it takes to span their circumference. Then they actually write down this whimsical measure and give it to her on a little slip of paper.

"Mrs. Blake? Just wanted to let you know we're setting up." It's Justin, the spiky-haired guitar player who runs the meeting. He's got a big dog following him around, sniffing at her goats. "We'll stay about four hours. Have a picnic if that's okay."

"All right," she says. "Just keep that dog under control. And pick up the trash."

"Of course." The young man looks a little offended. As if nobody who ever loved a tree ever tossed a soda can.

"And don't park in the hayfield."

"Sure. We'll park down your driveway, like usual."

"Mama, Mama, Mama! Like Ace!" Bobo's got his arms around the dog's neck, and it's licking his face as if it's an ice cream cone. "Want to go, Mama. Want to go with Justin." The boy is happy as a sunny day.

"We'll see," she says.

"Yes see."

"Maybe see." Their little game.

"Mrs. Blake?" Justin says. "We're having a special ceremony for Mrs. Anne Lee. She loved those trees. And we'll bring him right back here after."

"Miss Ahnn!" Bobo says. Anne Lee was Bobo's tutor in special ed.

"I didn't know she was a member," Jolene says. How odd. She didn't seem the type.

"She came just once," Justin says. "After that she just gave money." Money. For what? Picnics?

"Want to go, Mama. Miss Ahn."

"I'll keep an eye on him," Justin says.

"All right, Bobo. Come straight home. By three o'clock." She holds up her fingers: three.

"No problem." Justin taps his enormous watch, which looks like it was designed for a *National Geographic* explorer.

The first year the Big Tree People came was the year after Luke died.

They seemed harmless enough. Bird lovers. College kids and professor types. A young woman informed her that the Gooley Ridge was a "four-point energy zone," whatever that means. The girl had a strange configuration of hair—blond dreadlocks scooped up in a scarf tied into a complicated knot, a lean body like a tennis player, and just as smelly. Her blue eyes seemed to have sparks in them. Was she high? No. It was just the way the sun shone through pine needles on her face, a wavering dance like the surface of a pond. "Mrs. Blake," the earnest young woman said, "it's a geographical spiritual center. A place where the magnetic energies in the earth keep people safe. Edgar Cayce was into it. You ever hear of him?"

"No," Jolene said. She didn't tell the girl she's a lapsed Mennonite.

"Some people say Eden was a place like this," the girl went on. "Or Heaven."

"Heaven, Mama!" Bobo said. Jolene had just told Bobo his father was in heaven.

"Walking in forests is supposed to be good for the immune system," the girl continued. "But I just like the trees. They make me happy."

Jolene feels the same. The big trees make her happy. It wasn't always that way. Luke had died not far from where the girl stood, his head split open, a white thick substance leaking from his ear. A branch had fallen while he was cleaning up after a storm. Going up there had frightened her after that. But when the Big Tree People came that first time, she found that hugging trees with them and with Bobo made her happy. "Papa is in Heaven," Bobo told the girl that day. He looked around, like his father might be hiding behind an enormous tree. Then he ran and hugged them all, Ace flying beside him, so full of joy.

Luke always told her that Indigo Field belonged to Miss Reba's people, back in history, and the Blakes cheated them out of it, so they should always give Miss Reba right of passage and right of use. If the Field belonged to Miss Reba and her people, no doubt these giant trees did too. She's never asked Reba's permission for the Tree People to come here. She wonders now if she should have.

Jolene watches her son shout and lead Justin and his dog and the Tree People up the goat trail to the Ridge—his favorite pink Oxford shirt glowing in the sun, his khakis still creased and clean—carrying a dried milkweed stalk high, like he's leading a parade.

Jolene briefly considers going ahead and making cheese without Bobo. But she promised. And what did Miss Anne always say at the school? "The more skills he learns now, the more he'll have for later."

Jolene's got another chore to do, one that must be done alone. A critter has been digging at the edge of Ace's grave during the night, in the soft soil under the pecan tree. Bobo hasn't noticed yet. She loads three empty buckets in the back of the truck and drives to the Field. She opens the gate and bumps over the rough pasture to the river. There are plenty of rocks here—smooth, river-worn, small enough to carry, big enough to hold down bones. While she loads river rocks, she listens to the drumming and singing up in the Gooley pines. She can hear Bobo's happy shouts. She wonders if Miss Reba can hear all this commotion. It's enough to wake the dead.

7

Monday morning Miss Reba reaches for her glasses, feels around for slippers, pulls her wrapper off the bed post, and scuffs to the bathroom. She washes her face, dabs on her Egyptian Queen hair oil, combs it through, fixes her braids, one fat cornrow on each side of her head, ends tucked under into a bun in the back. She's been pulling on her hair, and it's thinned out in the front. Well, she never did have good hair. She pours tooth powder into her hand and pokes the toothbrush in it. A child's voice comes right beside her: "Why don't you use toothpaste, Aunt Reba? Time to come into the twenty-first century. You can buy any tooth product you want."

Miss Reba drops the toothbrush, grabs on to the sink with both hands. It's like the little girl she raised is standing right here beside her. Not like the spirit voices in her head. This, Jesus help me, was right out loud. She looks down. No Danielle. She must have lost her mind. Had a little fit.

Miss Reba shakes her head and goes about her business. But there's a new zigzag in her heart like a crack down the side of an old clay pot. A jagged crack of hope.

She feeds the chickens, stands in front of her new Danielle Angel. Nothing. She goes back inside, cooks her eggs and bacon, pokes them with a fork, sets the fork down. Looks at her arms. A little girl's voice says, "Auntie, you got bones and ripples where your arms used to be." Miss Reba's heart stops in her chest. Believing. Not believing. She looks around. Nobody. But Lord have mercy, it's like eight-year-old Danielle's brought her little suitcase and moved right back in.

For more than a year, the space in her head that used to worry about grown-up Danielle—was she getting enough to eat, was that whiteman beating her, should she take her away to Baltimore—has been blank and dark, like the inside of a closed cardboard box. And now this. This child voice in her ear like a shard of light that hurts her eyes. Like a promise that can't be kept.

"Danielle baby," she says, voice catching in her throat, "have you come home to me?" She strains, listening for an answer. Believing. Not believing. She closes her eyes. A silence big as death surrounds her. Danielle is gone, if she was ever here.

Spirits talk, but they don't speak out loud like that. But then she wonders. All that drumming up in the Gooleys yesterday. Miss Jolene got her tree worship people up there again. Maybe they woke something that's been sleeping all this time.

Miss Reba goes about her business. Sweep the porch. Wash on the line. Brew tea. She's laying out herbs to dry on old newspaper, staring at the hole where she cut out the story more than a year ago, *Local Woman Shot in the Eye*, when she hears a rustle in the pantry. She goes to check the sweet potatoes for mice. No mice.

It's not till after lunch that she's got time to sit out on the porch with Danielle's box in her lap. Danielle Angel looks all bright and happy. Like she may have something to say. Miss Reba waits and waits. For a sign, a vision, a child's voice. Something.

Miss Reba dozes off waiting, dreams of two girls running in the Field.

When she wakes, the late sun is shining hard on Danielle Angel, looks like she wants to jump right out of her cedar skin. There's a rustle on the porch roof. A child's voice says, clear as day, "Auntie, tell me about Sheba. And the Indians in the Field." Lord God, Danielle really has come back to her, voice like a twist-braid, skip-rope girl! There is no denying it now. Reba can't see her, but she can hear her. Smell her. Smell of soap and a starched cotton dress and cut wildflowers she liked to make into tiny bouquets. The girl is here. And who knows what the rules of spirits are.

The child wants stories. But oh what sadness, thinking of the past. Sadness baked into the stories, like leavening. Miss Reba's heart falls. "No, child," Reba says. "I got no strength for that."

Danielle's voice goes quiet, like a sulking child. But later, when Reba's checking the new rows of corn, back where Sheba is buried, Danielle says it again. "Auntie, tell me about you and Sheba. Tell me about the Field." This is the price, it seems, for keeping this child spirit close and her own heart alive. She'll just tell the pretty ones. Maybe that will satisfy, for now.

"You there?" Reba says.

"I'm here," Danielle says.

Reba's body floods with joy and trepidation.

Miss Reba places her palms on the sides of the gold box sitting shiny

in her lap, like a birthday present. Bones of a young girl. .
Box light as can be.

There's a clatter in the sycamore leaves. Old Lucy's speakin,
Then all goes quiet like the silence on Papa's face.
Danielle is waiting.

Reba closes her eyes, opens her mouth, tries to speak. All that comes
out is a frog croak. Reba tries again, and the word that comes out is
"Danielle."

In the yard, the fresh-painted figure with rainbow threads on its
wings leans a little closer.

"Danielle baby, you remember this one, don't you. I know you do."

"Was a woman name of Tuscarora Lucy."

"That's right, baby. That's how it starts. Was a woman name of Tuscarora Lucy lived in Indigo Field. They say she lived a hundred years,
between the time they killed her people and time she died 'round 1954.
Sheba and me used to spy on her. Sheba ten years old, I was six. It
was hard times in Ambler County, people called it the Depression, but
Sheba and me, we didn't know no different. We had chores and picking
cotton and helping Mama, just like always. Then after chores, we had
each other and all the places by the river, the empty fields and cliffs and
ridges, and we was thick as thieves, spying on Old Lucy in her Field."

"Called it Indian Field."

"That's right. We called it Indian Field in those days, and everything
about it was a secret."

"Sheba could not abide a secret."

"That's right. Papa told us, 'Don't go to Indian Field, it haunted with
spirits, got a curse on it. And don't be messin' in Spill Creek either.'"

"Like to grab you and hold you down."

"That's right. I told you that too, didn't I, child? But Sheba wanted to
know about Old Lucy. So Sheba and me go looking."

"This is the good part," Danielle says.

"Yes, baby girl. It's about to get good. Hush now, let me tell it."

School's out, planting and hoeing done, we sneak out to the log across
Spill Creek—Sheba balances like a bird, I inch along on my hands and
knees, scared to fall off. We go past the old Blake farm. "Nobody lives
there but ghosts," Sheba says. We creep up the Gooley Ridge, hide
behind a big tree, sharp pine smell, big scabs of bark the size of our

ands, and we spy down on the Field below, new grass all trembling green between the rocks.

Sheba brings out her singsongy storytelling voice, the one that makes me shiver: "Old Lucy put traps out there for whiteman and colored alike. Snatch 'em by the leg." Sheba's eyes blue and round. I almost believe her. "She call snakes out their holes to slither around, case some-body come. She like to be left alone."

"She don't have snakes," I say. I'm afraid of snakes. I had a snake fall on my head one time. Right out the tree. Yes, that's the truth, Danielle baby. I look up. No snakes.

"She feed 'em on spiders and make traps outta spiderweb." Sheba's teeth tiny and white, like perfect baby teeth. Sheba's skin chocolate brown and shiny. Eyes the color of sky before dark.

"You makin' that up," I say. Sheba liked to make things up.

"You ever hear of anybody come back from Indian Field?" she says. "Nobody goes there. Nobody alive to tell the tale. She crazy. She got the powers." Sheba shivers her hands in the air and makes ghosty sounds, *Wooooo.*

"Why we come here?" I say. "Imma go home."

"Tell you a secret," Sheba says.

"What?"

She grabs my arm, pulls me down beside her. Leans close. "Papa say she make prime corn liquor," Sheba whispers. "She put in secret herbs, blackberry bramble, spring water, corn she saved from generation to generation, corn color like rubies, put a single kernel in the bottom of each jar, leave a tinge of red in the clear. Make whitemen crazy. That's what Papa say."

"How he know?" I ask, pulling out my braids. Mama made 'em tight. "Papa don't drink."

"He know lots of things," Sheba says. "Come on!"

She leads the way downhill, pine branch in her hand, whacking at spiderwebs, pulling me to hide behind a bush or a rock when she says she sees sign of Indians. "Papa say they call her Tussie Lucy, but the Tussie mean Tuscarora." She whacks a rock, then crouches down quick like she heard something, puts her finger to her lips: *shhh.* "She put a curse on whiteman," Sheba whispers, "'cause of what they do to her people. She the last of her kind."

"She must be lonesome," I say.

"We got to break the curse," Sheba says. "Find out the secret."

"What secret?"

"That's what we got to find out."

"I don't want to."

Sheba looks at me all impatient. "Shush, she gonna hear you. You got to be quiet."

Sheba keeps creeping along, whacking with her stick. If Tussie Lucy was around, she'd hear us pretty good, all that whacking.

Pretty soon Sheba throws her stick away, so we do our favorite thing: hold hands, twirl in a circle, fall down dizzy. Pretty soon we forget about Tussie Lucy, lie down, look at clouds. I'm pretty sure Sheba is making it up all about Tuscarora Lucy and her crazy ways. Sheba likes to talk big.

Sheba turns over, looks at me. "Wish I lived in the court of Queen Esther in the Bible."

"Why?"

"You named for her," she says, voice all dreamy. "Ruby, Queen Esther Jones."

"How come my name Reba then?"

"Silly," she says. "Because we sisters."

"So?"

"So it sound more like Sheba that way." Queen Esther, she tells me, stood up and saved her people from all being killed. "If we lived then, you would be my queen."

"No," I say. "That could not be true."

Sheba's been reading her Bible verses, but she mostly likes the stories about beautiful queens. Papa named her Sapphire, Queen of Sheba. Sapphire for blue eyes, Mama says, from Papa's side, way back. Blue eyes like sparkling gems, skin like silk, not ashy like mine, her hair all curls, not frizz. Sheba's teeth like tiny pearls. I got buck teeth, put one hand up to cover them if I have to smile.

Sheba pulls my frizzle hair away from my face, ties it with a stem of grass. "Most beautiful and brave." She puts hands on my cheeks, kisses me right on the forehead.

I know I am no queen. I'm a little girl. None too pretty. I live in world of cornshuck mattress and hair like hemp rope. Sheba dreams a world beyond the bone.

Now Sheba tickles my ear with a piece of foxtail grass. I wave her away. She jumps out at me, pretends to be an Indian, a crazy woman, a snake. She makes a bow and arrow out of twigs and loose thread from her dress. She tells me I got to play rabbit so she can shoot me dead. But all that time we're giggling and screeching, Old Lucy's watching us from all her secret places—up in her sycamore tree, on her island, in the brambles and vines by the river.

It's a hot summer day, we go down to the river bridge, a covered bridge in those days. We strip down to shimmies, hold hands, and jump off a rock into shallows. Laughing, splashing, Sheba swims like an otter in the deep, I flop and flap in the shallows like a snared bird. After a while, Sheba pulls me out. We crouch on the rock, shivering. That water's cold. We put our dresses on over our wet shimmies.

"She got a hut over there," Sheba says, dripping water. "On the island. She eat snakes and rats and little boys. Papa told me."

"Papa didn't say that."

"Oh yes he did. She kill and eat them and save their bones. Put them over a fire till they all dried out. Then she scrape the bones and suck out the juice. Just like Papa with fried chicken!"

Somebody snorts in the bushes behind us. "It's her!" Sheba says. "Run!"

We jump up, run like scared rabbits all across the Field, up to the top of Gooley Ridge. Look back, catch our breath. "She gone come out and capture us," Sheba says, and she sound right scared herself this time. "Tuscarora like to torture 'fore they kill."

I look down at the tangle of vines by the river. Something moving there. "Look," I say. A doe and two fawns step out to feed on scuppernong vine. "Tussie Lucy ain't going to eat us," I say. "She got deer and all that. I want to see her."

"Can't see her today," Sheba says, all business. "We late for supper."

Danielle baby, we was late for supper that day, our clothes all messed up, brambles in our hair. Papa give us a warning. But he don't tell what the punishment will be.

That night I wake up, hear a sound out the window. Howling and yipping from up in the Gooley Ridge. Gives me the shivers. I poke Sheba. "What is it?" I ask her.

"Wolves," Sheba says, in her sleepy dream voice. "Comin' to get us." She settles back into dreams, but I stay up all night, guarding her. I don't want any wolves eating my Sheba.

☙

Miss Reba hears the sound of ancient drums, drums made out of hollow logs, carried on the breeze from the Gooley pines. She hears a dog bark. She opens her eyes.

The sun has shifted, breeze is up. Danielle Angel looks alive. Sheba Angel's paying attention. Brother Gem never did have a lot to say. Danielle's box is warm, and heavier in her lap, the weight of a basket of eggs.

Reba rises slow, knees stiff, gold foil box gripped to her chest. Gold is for treasure. Danielle was treasure. But Danielle's spirit has slipped away again. Sheba too. Lucy.

It's time to feed the living.

Miss Reba makes her lunch, pokes at it. Turnip greens from the garden. Leftover chicken leg. Three small red potatoes from Jolene.

She can't believe Danielle has gone quiet again. She doesn't know what she expected. That the girl would come sit next to her at supper, eat a chicken leg, tell her how good it is, rub her belly? The girl has slipped away, leaving an empty place now filled with nothing but the memory of Sheba in the Field, but now Reba remembers all that came after, for Sheba and for Danielle, and she wants to fall right down on the floor. Where is the comfort that will put away this misery? This is worse than before.

After lunch, the phone rings. It's that guardian ad litem again.

"No, missy, I won't come to court," Miss Reba says. "I told you before and I'll tell you again. You keep that boy and his father too, better not hear you cutting them loose, either one."

Miss Reba puts the phone back in its cradle. *Click.* Heart shaking so hard she has to sit down and take a BC powder and brew some sassafras tea.

Eighteen months since Tommy Jay Snipes put a bullet in Danielle's head and now they're asking her. Eighteen months since she wrote the name *Danielle Esther Johnson* in her list of the dead and tucked the newspaper story in the back of her Bible with all the others. Whitelady's got a whole lot of nerve. This is one favor too many. She ain't going to family court. She won't take that killer's child into her home. She has never taken a whiteboy to foster and she won't start now. Black boys, yes. Not him. Lord have mercy. Tommy Jay's boy needs a place to lay his whiteboy head, and Danielle's smile is gone forever.

Reba puts her cup down, shaky, in the saucer. She folds her hands and raises her face. *Jesus, Lord, take these thoughts away,* she prays, but the thoughts rise up again and she has to grip the table to keep steady. That ratty trailer where Danielle tried to make a home with a crazy whiteman, where she cooked and cleaned and kept TJ going to school and doing his homework, she even brought the boy for supper on Sundays when Tommy Jay was off on a tear. Trailer slam next to a two-story pile of chicken droppings look like they might slide down one night and smother all inside, leave no sign of them in the morning.

Who knows what went on in that place, people said, but Reba has some good idea. Kudzu half covering one side, spreading on the roof like the poison spreading in the house from Tommy Jay's whiteman soul. Poisoned from his own drug mess, his back-room factory, crazy meth they call it, 'cause it makes you crazy and poisons the house too, just a breath of white powder drug gets in the floors and walls and you got to burn it down, there is no washing it clean. Crazy meth got in Tommy Jay and made him think he could make a million dollars and get away from his hellhole chicken-drop house, made him think he's all powerful, made him want Danielle to be all powerful Shee-ra Queen of the Blacks, but she never trucked with that, she never would marry him, she said time and again she was gonna leave and take little TJ with her, but she never could make it out the door. Ten years she got beat Saturday nights, holding back her check, holding back her sex. *Lord I should have gone and put her in the Cutlass and locked the doors and drove away, gone to Baltimore, but no, I had to let her find her own way, I had to pray and let Jesus do the work. Where was Jesus then, Lord? Your boy on earth? Left her dead in a pool of her own blood with TJ watching? Whiteboy getting training in how to kill a Black girl. Whiteboy hardly need it, with all that bad blood from his papa's side way back. Bad blood snaked all through the county now, wherever whitepeople acting up. Jesus been looking the other way for a long time. Lord, you hear me? This is the last straw. This burden is too big for Reba. Go find a whitelady to raise that child.*

Reba has been yelling at the picture of Jesus. The picture of Jesus and the little children. *Let the little children come unto me.* Oh no. Oh no. She steadies herself, heart pounding like a hammer. Maybe they'll put that boy in jail with his daddy. But she remembers TJ's smile when he was seven years old. How much Danielle loved to see him smile.

Reba remembers the last day she saw her, not knowing it was the last time, that beautiful young girl, turning her back, trudging to that ratty trailer, the boy slumping behind, pausing at the door, looking back as if he was about to turn into a pillar of salt.

"TJ's why I stay, Auntie," Danielle would say.

TJ's got a lot to answer for.

Before supper, Reba stands on the stoop waiting for a sign she will be struck dead for all her vengeful thoughts. She wonders how she will ever finish paying off what it cost to put Danielle's head back together for a proper coffin viewing. For the ash burning after. She wonders where Danielle's little girl spirit has gone.

Chickens squawk and scatter. Reba squints up, looking for that hawk. Tiny colored bird comes swooping, lands in the spirea bush. What the devil is it? Blue head, red belly, green wings. Old Lucy told of a bird with colors like this, but it was a big bird, two-foot wingspan, traveled in a multitude so great it blocked the sky.

Little bird eyeballs the chickens now, all gathered to peck. It swoops down, grabs grits, flies up to roost on Danielle Angel's head, just above those big brown eyes. Little bird cocks its head. Red eyes stare at her.

"What you want? You ain't getting my grits. Shoo!" Reba shouts, flaps her arms.

Chickens scatter, tiny bird flies up, dribbles a loose white stool down Danielle's head, into her eye. Oh *no,* you didn't.

Reba gets a wet dishrag and a stepstool, reaches up and scrubs the nasty off. Danielle's big brown eye comes alive, looks at her, says, "You best get ready, Auntie. TJ needs you. You got to go."

8

On the Gooley Ridge, the tender new branches on the giant pines lift and fall like palm fronds on a tropical breeze. They sense a change in winds far out on the ocean. Months early, loggerhead turtles are riding the super-heated Gulf Stream, returning to the Carolinas to plant their second nests of eggs. By dark of night, Green and Hawksbill and Leatherback scramble to shore in enormous flotillas, an invasion that chases beachgoers onto balconies to watch.

"Look at that," they say.

"I'll be damned."

"Never seen so many."

"Not all at once like that."

On Spill Creek Farm, while Bobo sleeps, Jolene Blake places river stones in a spiral pattern over Ace's grave. Sometimes something pretty will distract Bobo. And maybe it will keep that critter away that's been digging here. She checks Bobo's room. He's got that log drum that Justin gave him, and a stick to pound it with, and he's been pounding it all hours. She snags it to hide it in the barn. She checks his pockets. Finds a slip of paper. *Your biggest tree = 4 people plus one small child holding hands.*

At Butner Juvenile, TJ Snipes Jr., white male, fourteen years old, does not regret his life of crime. The Nabs and Mountain Dew were worth it. He got a whiff of freedom. He hitched as far west as he could, away from Mrs. Boyd's. But the cops tracked him down. And Mrs. Boyd wouldn't take him back.

It smells bad here. Worse than Mrs. Boyd's. Some of the boys pee on quarters and throw them out the window to the sidewalk, hoping social worker ladies will pick them up. Now they say they're taking him to court. He wonders what they're going to charge him with.

Eleven a.m., Tuesday morning, Ambler County Family Court, Miss Reba settles into a back row, purse in her lap. Danielle wants her to be here, she's here. That's it. Guardian ad litem glances around, sees her, looks nervous. That boy TJ standing there, arms crossed. That same jeans jacket. All of fourteen. Looks more like twelve. Freckles, red hair, pale eyes. They ain't been feeding him right. Boy's a little green around the gills, blood drained right out of his face. TJ looks around. Sees her in the back. Face lights up. Makes a saucy little wave.

All rise. Judge comes in. Same judge she's known all these years.

"I see the father's been sentenced," Judge says, leafing through his papers.

"Yes, Your Honor," Guardian says. "They went with involuntary manslaughter. And simple possession. Forty-eight months, credit for time served, so it's thirty."

A look comes on the boy's face like someone beat him with a plank. Boy's ashamed of what his daddy did. Maybe it's a streak of softness from his mother, Tracy Baffle, who was a kindhearted one when she first took a Snipes for a husband. That didn't last but five years.

Guardian stands up now, talks to the judge, gives the list of places that might take the boy: Baptist Home in Raleigh, Thelma Boyd who takes in homeless, but the boy was already there most of the year and she's the one who threw him out for stealing. Stealing what? Some gum out of her purse.

Lord help him, he's been staying at Thelma's all that time till he ran away. Thelma Boyd can't cook, everybody knows that. She feeds her people out of cans.

Judge says something about juvenile infraction. Stealing at the store all the way to Morganton. Took a bag of Nabs crackers and a bottle of Mountain Dew. Guardian says Butner's not really the right place for such a minor infraction, now, is it, Your Honor?

Judge shuffles papers. Is there any other option? Boy has no remaining family.

The boy turns his eyes to Reba. She is the only person he knows in the room. In the world.

"What about Miss Reba Jones?" Judge says. "Does she have an interest in this boy?"

Guardian cuts her eyes to Reba, looks back at the judge. "She's right here, Your Honor."

Take me, the boy's eyes plead, like a stray puppy whimpering in a box, saucy wiped clean from his face. Miss Reba's heart creaks open an inch. That boy's got no kin either.

Judge says, "Miss Reba Jones, will you take this boy?"

Reba stands up on her aching feet. She feels something rise in her throat, feels her mouth open, hears her own voice croak, "I will."

She is so surprised that came out, her mouth hangs open. She has to remind herself to shut it. *Someone speaking right through me, Lord. Wasn't my idea. Jesus said suffer the little children to come unto me. But Jesus never said, "Take in the son of the one who murdered your precious Danielle." Jesus never said that. Jesus or Danielle, one, made me say yes, and they're gonna have to take on the work. I'm too old, my spirit can't take more grief. I can only pray this little whiteboy will mess up so I can give him back. There he is, grinning like a fool, trying to come this way, but the guardian calls him.*

There are papers to sign in the office. She's signing papers for a whiteboy. She must have lost her mind.

In the parking lot, the boy stands there, grinning like he's about to split open. "'Bout time you busted me out of jail, Aunt Reba, I was about to starve to death without your fried chicken."

"You'll eat what I lay before you, boy," Reba says. "I am not your aunt."

"Call her Miss Reba," the guardian says.

TJ's wide-open face closes up. "Yes, ma'am," he says.

"You weren't in jail, TJ, you know that," says the guardian.

"Just like it," he says.

"You come to my house, you got to do chores," Miss Reba says. "Won't be any laying around watching TV."

"Yes, ma'am," he says, still buttering her up. That boy will say anything right now. She's seen this look before. Boys the court puts in her home. Black boys.

TJ follows her out to her car. "You still got this old car? This car's so old it's a classic!"

"Don't sass my car," Reba says, but that dark dragging inside her heart shifts. Boy makes her want to chuckle. This was what Danielle used to say: that boy will say whatever fool thing comes into his head. He's about to tickle me to death. Then Danielle would laugh her wide-open laugh.

"I won't sass it," TJ says. "I'll fix it up. I'll get auto mechanics in school and get my license and drive you around in style, Aunt Reba! Wait and see."

Reba is about to say, *Don't call me Aunt. I ain't your aunt,* but she gets that image in her head of riding around like a queen in the back seat,

TJ driving, car all shined up like a limo. She shakes her head so he can't see the smile sneaking up one side of her mouth. She settles her face and lays down the law: "You got to be sixteen to drive. And have the grades."

"Waaall, if you let me, I can drive all over your farm, it's private property." Boy's eyes shine just dreaming it.

Lord, what have you got me into? Danielle, this whiteboy going to be a handful.

Miss Reba takes the boy home. He gets out of the car and takes pause. He walks up to Danielle Angel. Looks at her with his head cocked to one side. Looks at Miss Reba like he wants to ask a question.

"Come on in the house, boy," Miss Reba says. She ain't got time for introductions.

TJ follows her inside. Boy came with a pair of socks, a T-shirt, and some packs of Nabs all rolled up together in a paper sack. He's wearing dirty jeans with big rips across the knee. A black T-shirt with some nasty writing on it. Sneakers that got doodles all over them.

She sees him looking at the mantel. Pictures of Danielle there.

"Miss Reba," he says.

"What?"

"What're all these boxes?"

All the times he's been here for Sunday dinner, he's never asked. There's a new one now. Maybe that's why.

"Never you mind," she says. "Go wash your hands. We're about to have some lunch."

She heats up her leftover field peas and turnip greens from yesterday and some hot dogs out of the deep freeze. Didn't expect to have to feed a boy today, no hot dog buns. She has biscuits left from breakfast. She cuts them in half, puts them in the pan to toast. Maybe they can make hot dog biscuits.

She puts out relish and mustard, a jar of piccalilli from last year's peppers, and a small bowl of fried apples. She sets down plates for each of them, napkins, forks and knives, and a serving plate with hot dogs and biscuits.

Boy sits down with his hat on, grabs up a hot dog from the plate in his fist, takes a big bite. Danielle taught him better than that. This boy left his manners at Butner.

"Wait," she says. "Take your hat off. We say grace."

Boy lays his hat flat on the table next to him, chewing.

Reba bows her head, thanks the Lord for His bounty and for good weather, the garden sprouting, summer coming, blessings abounding. She thanks the Lord for bringing TJ safely to this house and prays that he will be strong and smart in school. In Jesus name, Amen.

Boy staring at her, mouth open.

"You never said grace before?" she says.

He shakes his head. "She used to say it just like that."

He's calling Danielle "She." Like nobody can say her name.

"Eat your food," Reba says. "Use your fork and knife."

TJ grips his fork in one fist, his knife in the other, and saws away, putting big chunks of hot dog in his mouth and barely chewing before he swallows. Boy's all hunched up, elbows out, like somebody might steal his food while he eats.

Takes about two seconds for three hot dogs to go down his gullet. He looks around. Serving plate is empty.

"You got any more of those?" he says.

"You eat what I lay before you, boy," she says. She spoons some greens and peas on his plate, and a little dab of fried apple.

He looks at it with distaste. He stabs the beans and greens with his fork, puts them into his mouth, chews slowly, looks around like he's trying to find a place to spit them out.

He swallows. Pokes at the apples. What boy don't like fried apples?

Boy reaches under the table. Pulls out a pack of Nabs from his paper sack. Unwraps one end. He puts the packet in his open palm, holds it before her. Dirty fingernails and all. "Miss Reba," he says, "you want some Nabs?"

Lord have mercy. Only thing he owns in the world, he's sharing it with her. Maybe she misjudged him.

"Thank you," she says. She takes one and puts in on her plate. Truth to tell, she does not care for them, with their bright orange crackers and orange filling. She'd rather have a biscuit. But she nibbles on a corner, just to be sociable.

"Have another," he says.

"No, thank you."

He shrugs, crams two in his mouth and chews with his mouth open. Crumbs flying.

She zips her lip. She will teach him manners starting tomorrow. To-day she is paying attention, learning what she needs to know. Today is TJ's day. Tomorrow, whiteboy's whole world gonna change.

After lunch, she settles him in the upstairs room, shows him the dresser where he can put his things. She opens the window to get some air in here, so stuffy and hot. She shows him how to make his bed, tight clean sheets, hospital corners, fold the top edge. She lays out the bedspread, smooths it flat, tucks it around the pillows. She gives him a *People* magazine to read, tells him it's time for her nap, she doesn't want to hear a peep.

She heads back downstairs. Goes outside. "I did what you wanted," she says.

Danielle Angel stares down at her with a kindly eye.

"Come back," Reba pleads.

"Tell the rest," Danielle says.

So that's how it is.

Miss Reba goes inside, gets the gold foil box. Ashes want to hear too. She can feel the whiteboy up there, breathing.

9

TJ lies on the bed with his shoes on, turning the pages of *People* magazine and eating the rest of his Nabs. The easy life. This might be a good place to stay for a while before he goes to California. Aunt Reba isn't anything like Danielle, but at least she's not fake-nice like Mrs. Boyd. And it's a heck of a lot nicer here than Butner Juvenile.

Somebody is talking outside in the yard. Who's she talking to? First thing he learned at Butner: listen to what people say when they don't know you're listening. He gets up and sticks his head out the window as far as he can. He can't see anybody. He takes his shoes off, crawls on the porch roof to the edge, leans out to where he can see the top of her head. She's standing in front of one of those crazy black statues. It's like a totem pole with a Black person face on it. He's seen these statues before, when Mama Danny used to bring him here for Sunday dinner. But when he asked her about them, she said, "Don't pay those no mind. That's just some crazy things her papa made. He liked to whittle."

But these are more than whittling. And the one Aunt Reba's talking to looks brand new. There she stands, talking away.

What he wants to know is, *Is it talking back?*

He gets the shivers just thinking about it. He pulls back from the edge. But now the screen door slaps. Then creaks open. He peers over again. Aunt Reba's got something in her hands. One of those boxes from the mantel. The gold one.

He's heard kids at Quarryville Middle School talking about Aunt Reba. How she does secret spells like a witch, has Indian blood, and has buried treasure in the yard. Mama Danny said the Indian blood part was right. She never heard of no buried treasure. "All Aunt Reba got buried in the yard," she said, "is turnips and chicken bones." Then she laughed at her own joke. Mama Danny liked to laugh.

The guardian ad litem said he should celebrate her life by trying to remember the good times. He doesn't have to try. He remembers Mama Danny all the time, like she's standing right next to him. But when he tries to remember what she looks like, he hears screaming and a gun go off and blood everywhere, one big eye staring at him, the other one a hole full of blood. Then he sees it over and over again till he starts to sweat and can't breathe.

Don't think about it. Pinch yourself, hard. *Ow.*

Aunt Reba's talking again, but he can't see her. She must be sitting in her chair now. He listens as hard as he can. He can hear some of what she's saying. "Danielle...Indigo Field." Maybe she's going to bury her treasure in Indigo Field. Wherever that is. He scootches up, pokes his head over. Now he can hear.

"Danielle, now we're getting to that part you like, about falling in the river, down by Indigo Field. Hot day rising like a cathead biscuit in the stove. Yes, sugar, I know you like those. I'd make you a whole pan if I could. All right, settle down. You want to hear the story? Here it is."

TJ shivers and it's not the cold. Aunt Reba is talking to Danielle. But Danielle is dead. He wants to crawl back inside the window and hide under the covers. But he is frozen to the spot, ears wide open.

One day, me and Sheba find two cornhusk dolls with berry-stain faces on the big rock where we like to swim, down by the river bridge.

One's got big blue eyes like Sheba. Other's got brown like me.

"Look, Sheba," I say. "They so pretty."

Sheba picks up the blue-eyed one, turns it upside down, looks inside. "Old Lucy must be watching," she says. "Tryin' to capture us." Sheba makes it dance and twirl. Then she drops it off the side into the shallows.

"Why you do that!" I say. "You got to save her!"

Sheba shrugs. "Save it yourself. I don't like it."

Doll swirling in a lazy circle, closer and closer to the current.

I want it. I need it. I jump.

"Wait!" Sheba calls out. "You can't swim!"

But I am swimming. Bobbing and flapping, swirling into the river, sputtering and coughing and all caught up in my clothes, sliding down into green water after that doll.

Sheba hops rocks till she runs out of rocks, then she flings off her dress and jumps into green water and swims hard, but me and that blue-eyed doll are caught in the current and moving fast, twirling in a circle, sinking deeper now with every turn, sputtering, slapping water, I like to drown, but the air caught in my clothes holds me up from sinking.

Sheba catches onto a bramble, pulls up on a spit of land, tries to cut across to where I am caught in a whirlpool, green water deep over my head. Something catches hold of my dress, pulling me. Hot breath on my neck, I twist to see. Look right into the eyes of a wolf. I start to yell but my mouth fills up with water.

Danielle baby, Lucy watching us the whole time. From her island in the river. She hops out on a rock, reaches out one long bony hand, and plucks me out by my arm as I go by. Sets me on a sandy beach. The wolf dog comes up out of the water next to me, shakes, shows his big teeth. Old Lucy's got me with her pinching fingers. I want to run but I got no breath, wet clothes wrapped around my legs. Sheba yells, "What you doing to my sister, you old witch!" and comes charging out of the brambles to rescue me.

Sheba always was brave. So brave. She charges right past that wolf dog into Old Lucy, tries to knock her down. But Lucy is hard as iron. Scratchy old voice says: "You settle down. Your sissy going to be fine. Ain't hurtin' her none. She alive, see?"

Sheba saw.

I cough, spit, sit up. "Where my doll?" I say.

"You gonna get a lickin' for your clothes all wet," Sheba says.

Sheba, nothing on but wet legs and arms and shimmy. Old Lucy busts out laughing.

Sheba looks down. "Oh," she says. "Where my dress?"

Lucy and me laugh till Sheba gets mad, then she gets tickled, then she starts up twisting and flailing, making sounds like drowning: "This how you swim, Reba, *sink sink sink help!*"

"Stop that prancing," Old Lucy says. "Go get me some twigs, girl. We making some sassafras tea."

First time I ever seen it, Sheba does as she is told without any sass at all.

The witch lady takes me by the arm to her hut, tells me pull off my clothes. She takes them and puts them on a bush in the sun, puts a big bear skin around my shoulders. I know it's a bear because the head still on, eyes all dried up, snarly teeth. Where did she get that? Bear twice her size. She sets me by the fire pit, wisp of smoke coming up, and she starts scraping around, putting this piece of twig like so, that piece of twig like so. Wolf dog lays down beside me, fur the color of the red clay dirt where Papa grows his cotton, his big ears sticking up; he's eyeballing me, making whiny sounds like he can almost talk.

The witch don't look too crazy. But she do look strange. Hair all stringy down her back. Jay feather stuck in a plait on one side. Feather twitches in a secret breeze: *this way, that way, this way*. Lines so deep like cracks in her face. She's got a man's trousers on and a dress over top. Hands like claws, fingers black with fire cinders. Crazy long fingernails. She's got all kind of beads and shells looped around her neck on string that click when she moves.

I hunch down, shivering. "You her?" I say. "You Tussie Lucy?"

She nods.

Sheba comes back with her arms full of sticks. She sits beside me on the log, gets under the fur with me. We watch Old Lucy talk to herself while she moves around, builds up the fire. *Two little girls got no business coming out here, Gemstone Jones better keep them home.*

She knows our daddy.

Old Lucy plucks a hot coal out the clay pot with her fingernails. Tucks it in the twigs. Poof. Fire.

She puts some roots in a pot of water on the fire, watches it cook. She pours it in a gourd cup, puts honey in it for sweet. Sheba takes the first gulp, eyes light up. She loves the sweet things. Then she passes it to me, says, "You have it, Reba."

Lucy puts some river clams on the coals, they pop open, she picks them out with her long nails, sets 'em on a leaf. Shows us how to pry them all the way open, pull out the insides. They're chewy. We eat 'em cause we're hungry.

Lucy's dog whines and talks at her. "What's that?" Sheba says, shrinking away. "Look like a wolf."

Lucy gives the dog a clam shell to chew on. "No wolves around here," she says.

But I remember hearing that wolf in the night.

Old Lucy sits there smoking her clay pipe. We look around. Old Lucy's got feathers and dried weeds hanging from the branches all around her hut. She's got a sharp knife and a spear and baskets. She's got clay pots and clear jars. She's just like an Indian you hear about. But her skin is colored like ours.

Lucy gets our dresses from where she hung 'em up on a branch in the sun, she gives us a rag to clean up, shows us how to step across rocks to get home. "Don't tell where you been," she says in her raspy voice. "Might get in trouble."

So we don't tell. But we still get in trouble with Papa for messin' up our clothes. We take our whippin' and do our chores and plot for a chance to go back.

That's how we meet Tuscarora Lucy, we call her Old Lucy. She tells us her spirit name later.

❧

Miss Reba raises her head. The sun is low in the sky. Almost suppertime. Danielle has whisked away on the breeze. Nobody's here. Except that whiteboy up in his room.

That night Miss Reba watches TJ stab his plate full of potatoes, pork chops, and greens and swallow them down fast as he can. Boy must be starving to death.

Mouth full of food, the boy asks her all kinds of questions.

"Do ya ever find arrowheads?"

"I don't go lookin' for 'em. Close your mouth when you chew, boy."

"What's in that pot on the stove?"

"Sassafras root," she tells him, "good for the digestion." She doesn't tell about the skullcap she puts in for her fits, and the wild carrot for her sugar.

"You ever hunt?"

"Nope."

Boy says his daddy taught him how to hunt. Tells a whole happy story about learning how to use a shotgun when he was ten years old, killing his first deer, and how it was a doe out of season, and kind of by accident, branches made it look like antlers, you should have seen the blood pumping out, then he stops. Looks spooked.

Boy's thinking about Danielle.

Miss Reba has a system with boys. Wash up, new clothes, haircut, food. Bible study, church, and school. Then keep 'em busy with chores. Lots and lots of chores. It starts with washing clean. Who knows what kind of dirt is on that boy after being in that place. Lice maybe.

She stands up, clears plates, tells TJ he's got to take a bath. "Wash your hair too," she says. She sets him up with towels and soap and listens to the boy splashing for forty-five minutes, running her hot water, running up her bills. She sits at the kitchen table, paying her electric, her phone, her propane gas, licking envelopes, putting on stamps. When she gets to Quarryville Feed & Seed, there ain't enough. She has got to get her spot back at the farmers' market, or there just ain't going to be enough to make it till her fostering check comes, all this boy eats.

What has she got to sell? Turnip greens. Turnips. Boxes of runty sweet potatoes left from the fall. Eggs. A couple of strawberries. Not much else. She can make her pound cake. Jolene will have plenty of whey from her cheese drippings, gives it a tang. She could make fried apple pies. Got plenty of dried apples and spice and flour in the pantry. Butter in the deep freeze. Danielle's favorite, smells up the whole house with sweetness. Might bring Danielle's spirit back to her ear, saying, *Yum yum, Auntie, this is the best you ever made.*

Boy's stopped splashing. He comes out with her papa's old checkered bathrobe she gave him to wear. Heads upstairs. Tracking water. And mud.

How in the world can a boy take a bath for forty-five minutes and still have dirty feet? She checks the tub and sees dirty footprints on the wall. That's just wrong. He rested his feet up there, didn't wash them at all.

She is going to have to teach TJ how to take a bath. And how to clean a tub.

"TJ!" she calls out.

He freezes halfway up the stairs.

"You come back down here clean this tub. Never saw such a mess."

She stands at the bottom of the stairs, his damp towel in her hands. "What you doing with your feet up on my pink tile? You put your feet IN the tub and wash them too."

"Yes, ma'am," he says. But she can tell he is thinking, *I'll take a bath any way I want.*

She gives him Bab-o Cleanser and a rag and a plastic cup to splash the Bab-o off the wall. Another rag to dry it down. When he's done she comes and inspects. "Missed a spot," she says.

"Aw, man," he says, and mutters under his breath.

"Don't you be sassing," she says. "It's 'yes, ma'am.' Come back out to the kitchen when it's right. And wash your feet while you're at it."

TJ takes his time. Splashing again and Lord knows what.

Before bed, Reba makes him sit at the kitchen table and reads him the Bible Verse of the Day. Verse is about honoring your father and mother. Might not be the right verse for this boy to start out.

"Aunt Reba?"

She cuts him off. "Uh-uh. No, sir. You got to call me by my right name before I answer," she says.

"I mean, Miss Reba."

She nods. Boy's got to get that right away. She is not his aunt. She is not anybody's aunt. Not anymore.

"Miss Reba, do you believe in God and Jesus and all that?"

Boy takes her by surprise with that. "Yes, indeed," she says, but she looks away. She lost her faith when Sheba died. When Danielle came, that happy child brought it back. Now? Now she believes all right, but she is not sure she *likes* God or Jesus, either one. As Reverend says, there are gaps in her faith.

TJ looks like he doesn't believe her. So she turns tables. "*You* believe in God and Jesus?"

He shakes his head. She can see it plain as day on his face, the same question she has asked the Lord for a year: *If He's so all-powerful, how come He let Danielle get killed that way?*

"*She* used to," he says. "She used to pray all the time." He shrugs.

She catches a crumpled-up look pass over his face before he gets a chance to hide it.

"You got any Nabs?" he says. Face all pulled together now, chin stubborn, blue eyes blazing.

"Nope," she says. "But I got cake."

Miss Reba pulls a slice of her pound cake from the freezer where she had it wrapped up in plastic, saved for a someday snack. "It's good heated up," she says. She pops it in the toaster oven, gives it two minutes, till it's toasty brown.

She lays it down before him on a plate and he eats it with his hands, like toast, and between bites he tells her all about California, and how he wants to go there someday and see what it's like to surf in the waves.

"You got to finish school," she says. "After, you can go any place you want."

· He licks his fingers. Boy likes her cake. Good. She'll make that for the market next week and have leftovers for the house. You can make a boy do anything if you find out what he likes.

Reba says a prayer and sends the boy to bed. She pulls her cash box from the pantry where she keeps it, takes thirty ones for her purse, and hides the box behind the sack of grits. Boy's been known to steal. She tucks the Bible with all her family papers behind the other books on the shelf. She has another Bible she can use. She takes the shotgun shells, puts them in a paper sack at the bottom of the box of sweet potatoes. She pulls the Charles Chips can down, takes the box of bullets out, and the revolver, tucks them on a shelf back of the closet. Puts the Charles Chips can back in the high cupboard.

Sheba doesn't like him here. She don't like whiteboys. And Lucy might put a curse on him, set his feet to step on a yellow-jacket nest. Miss Reba hasn't heard the two of them since TJ came. And Danielle talks now only during stories. She couldn't hear the child spirit in the kitchen now if she tried. Boy's too blessed loud.

Reba wakes in the middle of the night to the *boom boom-boom* of what might be her heart and what might be some fool with rapper music coming down Field Road. The bed shakes underneath her and her heart shakes inside her chest. *Boom. Boom-boom.* Does that fool boy have a radio? She raises her head. No. The sound is from outside.

Reba gets up, puts on her robe and slippers, pads to the downstairs closet, yanks her overcoat on, gets out Papa's shotgun. Rummages in the sweet potato box. Puts two shells in her coat pocket. Tucks a flashlight in her other pocket. Steps outside. Full moon. Light spills over the yard, the driveway, the tops of trees like silver paint.

There it is, bouncing off the Gooley Ridge. *Boom. Boom-boom. Boom. Boom-boom.* Somebody's been leaving tallboys scattered down her road at night, and some days, in the morning, when she goes to get the paper, there's a little pile of ashes and butts at her mailbox. She doesn't know who it is, but she aims to find out.

She's about halfway there when a truck screeches tires and peels off toward the highway, *boom boom-boom* all up the hill. Rednecks. Only rednecks drink Red Bull and smoke Marlboros and screech their truck tires that way.

Reba turns to go back. But wait. There's a sound in the cornfield behind the house. If those blessed rednecks are in her corn patch, she's going to root them out.

Reba pulls a shell out of her pocket, slides one in, and heads to the cornfield. When she gets there, it's quiet. The smooth tilled field smells like fresh rain and worms. Her second planting of corn flares up like green hair ribbons, all in a row. That back corner rustles with dried-out yellow bells, shriveled up in the heat. Mama planted them there. Over Sheba's bones.

A breeze rises above her head in the hickory grove. There's a whiff of music. A woman's voice. It's not anything out of a radio. It is the singing of old voices.

She eases down, settles on a stump, listens. Closes her eyes. After a while, she begins to sing.

&

TJ jerks awake. *Somebody's outside. Where is he?* A place so dark you can't even see. Not Butner. Not Thelma Boyd's. Not home. Smells like lemons. Aunt Reba's house.

There's a white pillow under his head. There's pork chops and potatoes and cake in his belly. Aunt Reba can cook.

He's supposed to call her Miss. It's hard to remember, because Danielle always called her Aunt. Danielle was Mama Danny. Doesn't that make them related? But maybe you can't really be related if you're white and the other is Black. Anyway, he knows this much: Aunt Reba really hates him to say it: Aunt. Aunt Reba doesn't like him that much. She doesn't want him in her family. Probably because of Daddy. Who would want to be related to *him*, if you didn't have to be?

TJ squints in the dark. There's a breeze from the open window and a sound from somewhere far off, way out in the country. He kicks off the sheets, which have wound around his legs while tossing and turning and dreaming of running, running through the woods, chased by men, but he can't see who. There's a light flickering way off in the trees. Police? *Daddy escaped from jail?*

TJ pulls on his jeans and shoes. He checks for his pocketknife. He creeps down the stairs. Miss Reba sleeps down here somewhere. The floorboard creaks. He stops. He opens the screen door and steps outside. Those creepy statues stare at him. But there it is again. Singing. In the woods. A flickering light. A fire? He sniffs the air. It smells like wilderness.

A bat swoops out of the black sky, flutters around TJ's head. He ducks. *Shit shit shit.* He hates the country. Especially at night. He creeps through the woods, his eyes adjusting to the light, trying to walk like an Indian so he doesn't make any sound, but he has no idea how an Indian walks really, so he decides to just go slow. It doesn't work. Dry leaves rustle and twigs snap under his feet. Tree branches whack him in the face. *Ow.*

He stops. The noise is close now. Just ahead. There's a fire in a circle of rocks. Sparks fly up, swirling. Somebody's moving around, singing, raising arms up and down, throwing shadows on the trees. The words don't make any sense. *Ah ee ah ohhhh.* He crouches behind a tree. He sees her face in the firelight. It's old Aunt Reba dancing and singing like an Indian.

Maybe Old Lucy in that story is a real person. Maybe Aunt Reba learned it from her. Danielle told him there used to be Indians around here somewhere. The more hair you have, the more they want to scalp you, at least that's what he heard. TJ runs his hand over his head. It's been a while since he had a haircut.

Now Aunt Reba lies face down right on the dirt, arms spread, says, "Sheba, wake up. Come on out and talk to me. Remember when we were little?"

Is Sheba *buried* here? Aunt Reba's got a secret life, a life that only comes out at night, like bats, or vampires. He's got to get out of here.

He tiptoes away, eyes used to the dark by now. He can see everything. He never knew moonlight could be so bright. Everything looks silver-green. Moonlight shines on the ground in front of him. A path? Brambles stick to his jeans and hold him, like they want to drag him down. He struggles free, runs and runs until he reaches the open yard. He sprints past the Black angels, up the porch steps, into the house and up the stairs. He slides under covers, keeping his clothes on in case he needs to run. He lies there in the dark, heart pounding, listening to a loud new sound out the window. Crickets? Frogs? Birds? It's coming from all the trees and bushes, maybe from the ground and sky.

He really hates the country.

He's going to steal a car, get out of this place, and drive to California first chance he gets.

TJ pulls out his pocketknife, flips it open, holds it gripped in one hand, listens for the sound of someone coming. When he finally falls asleep, he dreams of Indians with hatchets, his legs twitching and kicking at unknown enemies.

In the morning Miss Reba goes upstairs, cracks TJ's door. He's asleep, arms flung wide, trying to take up the whole bed. Glinty red hairs on his head, sun picks them out like needles on a Gooley pine. Room's already got the stank of whiteboy. He's slept with his clothes and shoes on. Shoes all nasty with dirt, writing, and pictures. A heart. A skull and crossbones. No telling what dirt is all over her clean sheets. Don't he even know to take his clothes off in bed? She leans closer. A leaf in his hair. What has this boy been up to?

Another surprise: a shiny-blade knife in the bed, next to his hand, half-curled in a fist. Like he's ready to fight.

Oh Lord. What'd they do to him at Butner?

She picks up the knife by the handle. Snaps it closed. Slips it in her pocket.

A life can go either way at this age. What he's seen, what his father is. A life can be flattened or shaped round like a baby's head after birth. There's a lump in her robe pocket, an old charm she made once, a bird claw, a piece of turtle shell, strung together with red yarn, something she has carried around for many years. Reba fishes it out, places it on the windowsill where he won't see, behind the curtain. "Watch over the boy," she tells the charm. She doesn't know if it will work for him. It worked for her for a time.

Reba steps back to the doorway. "Rise and shine," she calls out. "Breakfast in fifteen minutes." Boy stirs in his bed, groans, turns over.

She goes down and starts the bacon. Nothing gets a boy up like bacon smell rising up the stairs. Worked for Black boys. She guesses it'll work for a whiteboy too.

The boy's quiet this morning at the table. None of that chatter and sass. Reba watches him eat, corrects his manners. "Sit up straight, boy. Nobody ever teach you how to hold a fork? Like this." When he's done, she shows him how he's supposed to take his plate, put it in the sink, wash it clean with hot water, soap, and a rag, and set it in the rack to dry. That ought to clean out his fingernails. "Let me see your hands," she says.

"What?" he says, suspicious. But he holds them out. Dirt still clinging under those nails.

"We're going to town," she says. "You got to spruce up. Clean those fingernails."

Boy looks scared for a minute, like maybe she's decided to take him back to the judge.

"We're going shopping," she explains. "Best get ready. Wash your face." She sends him to the bathroom with a fresh facecloth and towel. Lord knows the ones he used last night need washing.

He comes out five minutes later with his hair wet, formed into little spikes. Just a whiff of lemon soap over the boy smell. She checks him head to toe. Rips in his pants. Sneakers with holes, gray that used to be white, writing all over, mud streaks on the sides. Nasty-word T-shirt. *Lord, Danielle, this boy is a mess.* Reba makes him put the shirt on inside out so the nastiness doesn't show. "Better," she says.

He rolls his eyes. "Aunt Reba?" he says. "I mean, Miss."

"What?"

"You seen my knife?"

"Mmmm-hm. Yes, indeed. I believe I saw it in your room." She slips it out of her pocket, hands it to him. "That knife stays in this house," she says. "Don't be taking it out shopping or to school. You can keep it right here." She shows him a key bowl on the kitchen counter.

"But, Miss Reba," he says, "*everybody* has a knife."

"Not you," she says.

He puts it in the bowl. He picks up an arrowhead she keeps there. Puts it back. He picks up Danielle's yellow hair clips from when she was a little girl. Reba holds out her hand. He drops them in her palm. She slips them into her pocket. His eyes cut back to the knife. She can tell he's going to fish it out next chance he gets. She's going to have to watch him like a hawk. Boy with a knife in school is nothing but trouble.

In the car TJ fiddles with the radio, gets a country station. "You got a *pushbutton* radio," he says. "Cool." She does not know exactly what he means, but she lets it go. After a while, he asks her, "Miss Reba, how come you got a country music name? You named after Reba McIntyre?"

She's seen that white redneck lady on a TV show. Looks like a rabbit. "Nope." Not going to tell about her name. "They named her after me," she says to TJ.

Now TJ looks at her with his mouth open, then busts out laughing, little white fox teeth showing. "Named after *me,* she says. Oh, boy."

She remembers what Danielle said. *That boy's about to tickle me to death.*

At PTA Thrift, there are racks and racks of clothes. Reba pulls some black pants for church and some white button-down shirts. TJ tries them on behind the curtain. He comes out and models for her. Great day in the morning, he looks like a boy who goes to church and does what he is told. Except for that saucy look in his eye. He vogues for her, posing right and left.

"Stop that foolishness," she says.

TJ picks out a pair of jeans and a tee, tries them on, comes out the dressing room with a draggy butt and a shirt that has a picture of the devil on it, dripping blood from his teeth. "Awesome!" he says.

"Get that thing off you," Reba hisses. "You ain't wearin' no devil shirt." Chill running down her spine. Boy's so ignorant, he wants to invite Satan.

"Aunt Reba," TJ says, "it ain't the devil. It's Black Sabbath."

"You don't like it, Imma send you back to Butner. You ain't wearin' no draggy-baggy jeans to school. And I told you before. I ain't your aunt. You call me Miss Reba."

Boy shakes his head, goes back into the dressing room.

Reba picks out six T-shirts, size small. She picks out two pairs of jeans, size small. TJ is a small boy. Ain't got his growth yet. Boy don't even know. He's better off looking ordinary, bad as talk is going to be at his new school about what his daddy did.

At Family Dollar, she tells him to find a soda he likes and some chips. She needs some privacy with her toiletries. She picks up boy briefs and socks. Tussy roll-on, Egyptian Queen hair oil, Dr. Scholl's foam pads for her corns, tooth powder. She gets the boy a Mennen stick deodorant. Boy has a smell to him.

"They have Cheez Doodles," TJ says. "And Mountain Dew!" He puts a cold can on the counter. Reba catches the eye of the young Black girl behind the register. Her look says, *This a redneck for sure. Has a Black person ever touched a Mountain Dew?*

TJ grins at the girl, pops the top on the can, guzzles half of it down, rubs his belly. Burps. "That hit the spot."

Reba says, "Say 'excuse me,' boy."

"Excuse me, boy," TJ says. Miss Reba gives him the eye. "Just kidding," he says. "Didn't mean to burp. Not used to soda anymore, since I been in jail."

The girl shrinks back, and Reba pinches his upper arm, pushes him out the door to the car. "What?" TJ says. "I didn't do nothin'. Burping ain't against the law."

Reba releases him, crosses her arms, says, "You starting a new life here. You got to learn the rules. First rule: don't be talking about jail. Take the word jail off your list of words to say. Your daddy's in prison. You want to join him?"

Miss Reba takes him to the white barbershop. She doesn't know how to cut white hair or she never would set foot in this nest of vipers. There used to be a sign: No Colored. Now you're just supposed to know.

Whitemen turn, look at her, make a face and look at each other. She may not have stepped foot in this place before, long as she's lived in Ambler County, but she knows these men.

Barber gives her The Look.

She says, "Make it short. Clean up his neck." Then she settles in a chair to wait. She's going to sit here and make sure nobody talks nasty race talk to TJ. She sits, not moving, till the man's done, and TJ's hair is short and clean and not so crazy-looking. The barber puts some smelly stuff on his neck. TJ looks like a little banty rooster. Strutting around, checking the mirror. Hair sticking straight up.

She sets the five dollars on the counter. No tip. Not after that look he gave her. Man put pomade on the boy's hair, smells up the whole car with whiteman smell.

When they get home, Reba pulls over to pick up her mail out of the box. Six junk mails. Two bills. Pile of cigarette butts right in front the mailbox. She shakes her head, scoots down to scrape it up into a junk mail envelope. Lord, it stinks. Next time she takes the shotgun out to the road in the middle of the night, she'll blast away at whatever moves.

"What is it?" TJ says.

"Trash people," Reba says.

In the kitchen, the boy pulls up his jeans leg, scratches a scab on his shin. A thin line of blood runs down.

"What you do to your leg?" Reba says.

"It itches," the boy says.

"Let me see," she says.

He shows her. There's a line of fresh-picked scabs on his shin like basting stitches on cloth. Blood dripping down. Looks like blackberry cane got him. "You been running in the bushes?" she says.

"No, ma'am." He's started calling her ma'am. Like he can't remember she's Miss Reba.

"Sit here," she says.

Miss Reba grabs her kitchen broom, wraps a clean rag around the bristles, pokes a corner of the ceiling, snags a spiderweb. She shakes the spider out the door, says, "Go on your way, now. Plenty of flies for you out there." She pulls the spiderweb off the broom, rolls it into a ball between her fingers. Leans over TJ and pulls it out long, sticks it on the scratch. It stops bleeding.

"You put *spiderweb* on me?" TJ says.

"Old remedy," Reba says.

TJ stares at the sticky white web on the blood, now dried and pale. "Cool," he says.

He looks at her in a new way, like she's got superpowers.

Turns out, TJ knows how to chop wood. It's good for a boy to do that. Gets his boy energy out. He chops for two hours in his new T-shirt and jeans. She threw out the nasty ones. Not fit to cut into rags. When he comes in he's tired, hungry, sweaty. She sends him back out to the porch. "Go brush yourself off. Shake out that shirt. Get the wood chips off. Then come in and wash your hands. Dinner's on." After all that chopping, he's gonna appreciate his food.

Hard as it is with food on the table, the boy remembers to wait for grace. He remembers to take his hat off. *Great day in the morning.*

Over supper TJ starts up again, and this time he talks like somebody hasn't talked in a year. He tells her he likes fried chicken, baked ham, potatoes, and macaroni with cheese. He likes pound cake, just plain, and 7-Eleven cherry pies. He doesn't like showers, he likes baths. He doesn't like collards, greens of any kind, turnips, okra, or peas of any kind, including her prize Dixie Lees, saved over from last year in the freezer, cooked up fresh and tender with fatback. He doesn't like custard pie or coconut. He's got a thing for Mounds candy bars. She doesn't have the heart to tell him Mounds is all made of coconut. The boy is ignorant in so many ways.

He asks her all kinds of questions:

"Those statues. Do they have names?" She tells him the one that is Danielle. The rest are not his business.

"Can I drive your car down the driveway?"

When he gets one B on a quiz. And it's "May I."

"May I fix up your truck?"

She tells him he can start now by washing it, inside and out. The car too.

Boy lights up. "Can I wax them?" he says. Boy likes shiny things.

"Ain't got money for wax," she says. But then she thinks maybe she'll get some. Keep him busy. And maybe the wax will help hold the paint on. That car is old.

After supper she catches him staring at Danielle's photo on the mantel. The boy misses his Mama Danny. Jesus has got all his little children around him. *Let the little children come unto me.* Well, she let this whiteboy come into her house. But he's no little child. And in the picture, Jesus is Black, and all the little children are every color of brown, nary a white one among them. "Lord, Lord," she mutters, "I guess you didn't want the white ones either."

TJ looks up. "What?"

"Time for Bible study," she says. "Come sit at the table."

She reads the psalm about who may ascend the hill of the Lord.

> He who has clean hands and a pure heart,
> who does not lift up his soul to an idol
> or swear deceitfully.

"That means wash your hands. Don't tell lies. You hear me, boy? Jesus is watching."

The boy thinks hard for a minute. Then he says, "An idol is a statue?"

"Never you mind about statues," she says. "Go get ready for bed."

The Black angels aren't idols. She doesn't worship them. She talks to them. Only company she's had for a good long while. Danielle's child-spirit has gone quiet. This boy is taking up all the space in the house where Danielle used to be. But she's just too slam tired to tell the stories that might lure her back. *Danielle, this boy is trouble already.*

Miss Reba sleeps a fitful sleep that night, thinking about Tommy Jay laying back in his cell, doing his short time. His own boy laying up there in that bed, taking his ease. Miss Reba has the strongest urge to get up, root around in the sweet potatoes, find that gun. Make a plan to root that man out of jail. *You can wait until he's out,* Old Lucy says. *It won't be long.*

Upstairs, TJ listens to hoot owls, wonders if they are the voices of the statues she talks to.

Thursday, she teaches him how to hoe. New corn patch, grass growing up around the hills of squash. He weeds the squash right off the hill. "What are we going to eat, boy, if you kill off our food?" She picks up a squash seedling from where he flung it with his hoe, shakes it in his face: "This. Is. What. Squash. Looks. Like." He stands there looking crumpled. "Do better next time," she says.

For lunch she teaches him how to cook a grilled cheese sandwich.

He burns the first two. She can't afford wasting bread. She throws it to the chickens. She decides not to let him gather eggs. No telling how many ways this boy will find to crack them.

That night just before supper, Miss Jolene rumbles up in her big red truck. Goodness sakes, with all TJ's nonsense, Miss Reba has completely forgotten about the farmers' market.

Miss Jolene steps out, bib overalls, long braid coming loose down her back. With that hair and her green eyes, Miss Jolene could still get a man if she stopped hiding her figure. But those bib overalls and that sour face keep them away.

Miss Jolene spies TJ, squints like she's trying to figure out who he is, and then seems to see the resemblance to his father, Tommy Jay. Miss Jolene used to hire Tommy Jay for odd jobs. He always messed them up. Pulled the roof off her shed one time, went fishing, rain came and spoiled a whole season of hay. Then there's what he did to Danielle. Miss Jolene is not a fan of the Snipes family.

"This here's TJ," Reba says. "He's staying with me for a while." *Lord, Danielle, I hope it's not long.*

Miss Jolene nods at TJ, crosses her arms.

Bobo steps out, all dressed up in his pink shirt and red tie, smiling wide. Where that boy gets his taste in clothes is a mystery. He gives Reba a big hug. Then he turns and gives the boy a big hug. "TJ!" he says.

TJ pulls away, says, "Whoa, man, what are you, queer? TJ don't play that."

Jolene's eyes flare like green fire.

Reba tells TJ to apologize.

"Yes, ma'am," he says. TJ looks at Jolene, looks at Bobo grinning, something clicks. Bobo is different. "I'm sorry, man. But you sure are a big boy, ain't you? Miss Reba, how come he's so big?"

"He's big because he's almost a man," Reba tells him. "You best remember that."

"You the *man*," TJ says, grinning at the big sweet boy looming over him and swaying side to side.

"I the Man!" Bobo says, smiling to beat the band. "Want some gum? I have twelve rocks at my house. Twellllv." The boy rolls the word on his tongue. It is one of his favorite words.

"No way," TJ says, tickled.

Jolene's eyes say, *Don't you dare make fun of my boy.*

"Time for chitchat later," Miss Reba says. "You got work to do." She sends TJ and Bobo to the pantry to fill a bucket with turnips, and she pulls six full egg cartons from the cooler. She tucks cold packs around them. Stonehaven people think eggs have to be cold. But that's only if they're not fresh.

The two boys pass things up to Jolene, who slides them in the pickup truck bed behind the cab, wedges them in with boards, and ties bungie cords to cleats to keep them in place. Miss Jolene is the carefullest person she knows. She don't leave things to chance.

"Might come back to the market," Reba says. "Next week after this boy's in school."

Miss Jolene's sour expression wipes right off her face, like a beam of sunshine caught there. "My goodness, Miss Reba, it will be good to have you back."

Reba nods. It won't exactly thrill her to be there, but she'll make enough to get by.

Jolene gets a spring in her step, tucks an old quilt around everything to keep it clean overnight. Night air will keep it cool.

By the time they're done, Bobo has told TJ about his collection of arrowheads, his collection of rocks, his collection of feathers and bones, his dog Ace, who is now in heaven with Papa, and his baby goats Bebe, Charlie Angel, Spots, and mama goats Amanda, Chloe, and so on. That boy can run on.

TJ takes it all in. Grins. Leans back on the tailgate. Says, "Bobo, you are a trip."

Bobo laughs and laughs. "Mama," he says, "go see the chickens with TJ?" He has names for all Reba's chickens, which he no doubt will teach to TJ.

Jolene does not seem to like this idea. But Bobo is so happy, Jolene gives in. "Okay," she says. "But don't stay long."

Bobo yells, "Come on, TJ!" and runs off to the chicken shed, arms flapping,

TJ tries to be cool. Then he runs after.

Jolene leans on her truck, crosses her arms. "How's he settling in, Miss Reba?"

"He works hard. But he tends to mess up."

"He's lucky to have you," Jolene says. "I hope he knows that."

"If he forgets, I'll tell him."

"You got your squash in?" Jolene says.

"Two plantings," Reba says. Two because the boy killed the first. "How about your beans."

"One row. I'm behind on everything. Baby goats and Bobo take all my attention."

Miss Jolene is always behind. Maybe once TJ is better at hoeing, he can work for her. Hardest working white woman in Ambler County. She may not like the idea.

Now the boys come running back, Bobo all out of breath. TJ all flushed. Happy.

"The chickens do tricks!" TJ says. "Like jump up and flap. Turn around and peck. You teach them that, Miss Reba?"

"Nope," Reba says. "That's all Bobo."

Bobo's bounces up and down on his feet. "Mama, Mama, Mama!"

"Yes, Bobo?" Looks like Miss Jolene's patience is wearing thin.

"I like TJ. Stay with Weba tonight. Want to stay with Weba and TJ."

"Bobo," Jolene says, "you have chores to do. Market tomorrow."

"Mahkit Day!" Bobo shouts. TJ smiles, shakes his head.

TJ seems to like Bobo. The boy has brightened right up. Maybe Bobo will be a good influence.

Miss Jolene drives away. Bobo hangs his head out the window, waving.

All through dinner TJ chatters about chickens and making money at a roadside stand with chicken tricks, all kinds of foolishness. The Bible study that night is Proverbs: *a foolish man devours all he has.* It's as though Jesus picked the verse. Boy sits there, stomach full of her beans and greens and potatoes and biscuits, and there are no leftovers for Friday. *A fool and his money are soon parted,* she thinks. *I'm the fool. Taking in this whiteboy who eats too much.*

10

Sunday morning shines bright on the heads of the Black angels. Reba stands out on the porch in her navy-blue dress with white polka dots. Rooster crows and struts. Reba flings grits in the yard for the hens. "Danielle," she says. But there is no answer.

TJ steps out in his new white shirt from the Thrift. Black pants, black shoes, blue tie. Hair in those little red spikes he likes. Miss Reba sniffs the air. He's using her Egyptian Queen hair oil. She's going to have to jerk a knot in his head about that. Later. Today they're going to church.

Boy has surprised her this week. He says "please" and "thank you" now. He hasn't complained that she doesn't have cable, or a cell phone, or anything like that. And so far, he's left that knife in the bowl. He's almost ready for school on Monday. But the only way TJ's going to make it in Poolesville School is if the Black boys and church mamas know him. It's too much to ask them to take him into their hearts. But they've got to let him into church.

Reverend will be surprised to see them.

Reba walks right through the church door. Brandon, Tyquan, and Abednego, her young men from fostering, are here, sitting all together in the back row. They've all got homes and new families now. They rise to greet her. "Good to see you, Miss Reba," they say, all smiles and sweetness. "How you been getting on?" Then they see TJ behind her and clam up. Edge away.

All the way up the aisle, people turn and stare, raise hands in surprised greeting, for she has not been to church in eighteen months. Smiles halfway on their lips, their eyes shift and faces freeze and then they turn away, for behind her is the boy whose father brought down sin and terror on their beloved Danielle. Whispers and low chatter flow like ripples out behind her. *Did you see…can't believe she…bring a boy like that…what his father did…*

Reba leads TJ up to the pew she likes, halfway on the right. She points to his seat, has him scoot in first. Reba sits right next to the aisle, keep him from running out the door. The boy settles in, looks around. He's got that right leg jiggle, happens when he's nervous.

She can feel everybody staring at the back of his head, TJ's red hair sticking up like a knot of lighterwood about to set the place on fire. Church people have been talking about her before this, and they'll be talking about her after. She knows what they say. *Them Jones is some bad luck people.* Then there are those Black angels in the yard. People say they're graven images. People say they're black magic. People say they fly around at night, screeching like screech owls, setting evil spirits loose in the land.

They ignored it all while Danielle was alive. With Danielle by her side, all was forgiven, if not forgotten. But now, there's this: In a county where all the Black people are cousins, or second cousins, or cousins-in-law, Miss Reba Jones has lost her last blood relation. Her family stopped getting cakes and casseroles when somebody died a long time ago. Papa put a stop to that. When people die in her family, Black people stop on the street and speak to each other, but not to her. They're scared to death of her. And now here's TJ.

Bible verse, singing, prayer, Reverend's talking the longest time about wages of sin. Danielle would tell the reverend he's got it all wrong. *This is the time of year to talk about things being born. Birds, corn, even chickens know that.*

Don't think about it. Watch the whiteboy.

The boy stands up when she does, sits down when she does, looks scared. He pretends to hum along with the songs, doesn't know any of this, it seems. His daddy was never a big churchgoer. And he wouldn't have come to this church if he was.

Now Reverend's whispering in his husky voice. *Jesus loves you. This I know. 'Cause the Bible tells me so.* Fist hits the podium. *Whomp.*

Lord have mercy. He's using that little song Danielle loved. She would stand there in front, church dress on, little braids out to the side, big toothy grin so full of joy, mouth open wide and singing. Now he starts pacing, calling out scripture, talking about the cross. He died for our sins. We're supposed to forgive. *Whomp.* Reba's got no plans to forgive. Who can forgive a man who'd kill a child so full of joy like that? She can't see Jesus forgiving him either. Jesus is one fierce man.

Reba's read the whole New Testament and Jesus ain't the gentle man people think. He's out turning over tables and ruining people's lives, taking their good men away, walking around the countryside, tromping in people's fields on the Sabbath. Jesus scares her half to death the things he does. But sometimes—sometimes she wishes he would speak to her like he used to when Danielle was little. In the tenderest way. Like a big brother might, if you had one anymore.

Reverend finally winds up, church choir finally finishes the hymn. People start to crowd down the aisle to visit. On the way to the church door, Miss Reba checks the boy's hair and face and tie, then propels him in front of her toward the reverend, hands on both his shoulders so he can't squirm away. "Reverend," she says. "This here's TJ. Danielle's boy." Leave Tommy Jay out of it. Everybody knows that part.

She pokes the boy in the ribs. "Nice to meet you," TJ says, just like they practiced.

Reverend smiles at her, shakes TJ's hand, says, "Welcome." But everyone knows he means, *I've got my eye on you, boy.*

Miss Reba soaked the chicken parts in buttermilk overnight, baked the sweet potatoes this morning. She pulled and washed greens and turnips fresh and took snap beans from the deep freeze. Now she puts it all out and starts to cook, gets TJ to work stirring, yellow apron over his Sunday clothes. She hasn't cooked this much since Danielle was alive. She doesn't have an appetite, thinking about this boy and all the trouble he's going to be. It's clear from all those faces that churchpeople will blame her for anything he does.

"Miss Reba?"

The boy's finally got it right. "Yes?"

"Do I gotta go to church?"

She puts down the chicken leg she's been dipping in flour and pepper. Looks at him. Sighs. Boys hate church. She doesn't like it so much herself these days. But boys need to go. Especially whiteboys.

"Yes," she says finally. She turns back to the chicken.

"Everybody hates me there," he says. Boy ain't stupid.

"They don't even know you," she says. But he's right. Church people hate people they don't know. People they don't know are dangerous. Since Danielle died, and Miss Reba stopped going, there's no telling what kind of stories they've made up about her.

"You don't like it either," he says, sulking. He's hit a nerve.

"Never mind what I like," she tells him. Lord, give me some peace and quiet, this boy is about to wear me out. Jesus does not reply.

She has the boy set the table, put the food out, wash his hands again, say grace. TJ pokes at his snap-bean casserole with fried bacon on it. He eats a bite. Then another. Great day in the morning, he's found a vegetable he likes.

He puts his fork down. "Miss Reba?" he says.

"Yes?"

"Did you go to Poolesville School?"

She nods.

"What's it like there?"

Boy's asking if it's all Black people, like church. Like everything in Poolesville. "It's small," she finally says. "Those boys from church go there. Tyquan, Brandon, Abednego. They're nice boys."

He looks as though he doubts that very much. He hasn't touched his chicken leg.

"Does Bobo go there?"

"Bobo used to go to special ed. They shut that down."

Boy sits there stewing. His only friend. Bobo.

"Eat that chicken, don't let it go to waste."

He takes a bite. Sets it down. Looks a little sick.

"They're all going to know about Daddy," he says. "What he did."

"Might be," she says. "But you ain't your daddy. Hold your head high." How many times did her mother say that to her?

Time to distract with food he likes. She gets the next-to-last piece of pound cake from the freezer, toasts it, puts it before him. "Use your fork," she says.

He uses his fork. Eats it all. Then he licks his fork and presses it down on the plate to catch the crumbs. Then he licks the fork again. Danielle used to do that.

"Don't lick your fork," Reba says. "You can have another piece."

"No, thank you," he says, all formal. "May I be excused?"

Not just yet. "You going to church now," she says. "You got to learn how to pray." This boy's going to need Jesus on his side. He's going to need all the prayers he can get. Boys at school are going to want to fight him.

"I know how already," the boy says, his chin all stubborn, freckles popping out, face red. "She taught me. But it don't do any good."

"You never know how or when a prayer may be answered," she tells him, something Reverend is always saying. She's been waiting for her prayers to be answered for a long time. Her prayers for Jesus to put Danielle's head back together and make her come back alive. There was

that child voice talking right next to her elbow last week. Maybe Jesus
had some part in that. But then He took it away.

"I can pray for whatever I want?"

"Yes. As long as it's something good." She shows him how to fold his
hands, bow his head. "Start with saying thank you," she says. "Then tell
anything you did you're ashamed of. Ask forgiveness. Bless the people
in your life. Then ask for things. Then say 'in Jesus name I pray Amen.'"

"Can I pray for more Nabs or cake?"

"Yes," she says. "You can pray for any food you want. Try it now."

The boy folds his hands, squeezes his eyes shut. "Thank you for this
good cake."

He's supposed to say "Dear Lord." She lets it go. "Go on."

"I wish I hadn't...put my fork on the crumbs."

"Okay. Now say you're sorry."

He opens his eyes. "Who'm I saying sorry to, you or Jesus?"

"Jesus," she says. And even she knows that sounds ridiculous. "Now
bless people."

He closes his eyes again. "Bless Miss Reba and Danielle, even though
she's dead." He winces, like he's in pain.

Oh Lord, he thinks about that girl almost as much as she does. She
clears her throat. "What else?"

"Oh yeah. Jesus, I need more Nabs. Amen."

Close enough.

"May I be excused now?" he says. Boy looks tired. Worried.

"Go outside, sit on the porch," she says. "Get some sun on your
head." Might do him some good. It surely will do her good to have
some quiet.

She watches out the kitchen window. Boy is standing in front of
Danielle Angel, talking to her. Wonder what he's saying. Maybe she's
talking to *him* now. Instead of her. She's been too tired to tell Danielle
stories most days this week. She misses that girl's voice in her ear, the
sad small heft of the gold box in her lap, taking the place of a little girl.

Boy's going to school tomorrow. She wonders how long it will take
him to get into trouble. Thunder rolls over her head, rattling the tin
roof. Rain pounds down. Last thing she thinks before her head hits the
pillow: you're out of chickenscratch and grits, both. Those chickens
going to stop laying eggs.

11

Monday morning TJ rolls out of bed, takes his shower, brushes his teeth, dips his fingers in Egyptian Queen hair oil and pulls his hair in little spikes. He swipes the steam off the mirror with the palm of his hand. Looks cool. He puts on the green T-shirt and jeans. He sniffs his underarms. He smells like Mennen and soap. He pulls on his lucky sneakers, white Converse High Tops with writing all over them, slits in the sides. Danielle found them for him at the dump, and they were just his size, with a little more to grow on, already broken in. Somebody had started the doodle. He just kept it going. Added snakes and hearts and lightning bolts. Colored them with markers. Cut side slits with his knife when they got too small. Aunt Reba tried to throw them away, but he pulled them out of the trash. No way he's wearing church shoes to school. His lucky shoes help him make it through the day.

He puts on his jacket—it's hot out, but he likes his jacket. It looks cool.

He gets to the kitchen before Aunt Reba is done frying bacon. On the kitchen table is his backpack, trapper keeper, punch-hole paper, pens, pencils. Everything he needs for the first day of school. Except his knife there in the bowl. He reaches for it. Aunt Reba looks up. He picks up the arrowhead instead, inspects it carefully, puts back.

"Look at you, all bright and early." She looks him up and down. She nods. "You clean up good." Just what Danielle used to say.

Maybe Poolesville School will be different. Maybe they never heard of his daddy and all he did. He eyeballs the pocketknife in the key bowl again, but he sees her watching and looks away.

He eats a biscuit and half a piece of bacon, but it rolls on his stomach. He can't eat the eggs.

"Scrape it in the bowl," Aunt Reba says. "I'll give it to the chickens."

Aunt Reba drives him all the way to school herself. "First morning is special," she says.

He nods. Will she pick him up after? She doesn't say. TJ hates school buses.

She drives him right past Daddy's trailer, right past the bus for Quarryville School. Kids on that bus used to yell at him, sing a nasty song when they dropped him off. A song about how bad he smelled. He catches a whiff through the window. There it is. Whole trailer park smells like chicken shit from the farm next door. TJ swivels to watch the Quarryville bus grind its gears. He hopes they get stuck in the mud. He knows how to pray now, so he prays in his head: *Please, God, let them get stuck and have that chicken shit stink in all their clothes for the rest of their lives. Jesus. Amen.* He feels himself starting to sweat. Maybe Miss Reba will get him some Man Spray. This Mennen ain't enough.

Miss Reba takes a hard right down the River Road toward Poolesville, crosses the river, drives up to the squatty building that looks like it's been there a hundred years. She walks with him to the office, makes sure they remember who he is, shows his papers. She asks where to catch the bus home. She's not picking him up.

The social worker is all smiley face. She walks him to homeroom. Hands the teacher a note. The teacher reads it. "Tommy Jay Snipes, Jr?" she says. Everybody looks up. Tommy Jay is Daddy.

"No, ma'am," he says, "it's TJ."

But it's too late. They all know who he is now. He can tell by their faces. They've heard all about his daddy. What he did. But at least it's not all Black. It's about half and half.

The social worker cuts out. The teacher tells him to sit in the back, where there's an empty desk. Right next to those Black boys from church, sitting all in a row. White shirts, khakis, one even wears a tie. Brandon, Tyquan, and what's-his-name Abid-Negro. Not supposed to say Negro to people. But that's what it sounds like, and he can't get it out of his head.

TJ raises his hand in greeting. They all look the other way, except for Abid-somebody, who raises his hand back and says, "Hey."

"Hey," TJ says. He almost smiles. But Black boys don't like you unless you're cool.

It goes like that all day. English, math, social studies. The teacher calls out his name. Tells him to sit in the back. All the kids stare. The Black boys kind of edge away when he sits down. Every once in a while, Abid-somebody nods in his direction.

There's a girl in his classes with crinkly blond hair. Looks like a cheerleader or does batons or something. Short red skirt, little tank top, and a shiny white jacket with a big red horse on it: Home of the Mustangs. She likes cars.

He watches her from his seat in the back. Thinks about how it would feel if he were standing next to her outside somewhere, maybe waiting on the bus, and a little breeze made that golden hair fly up and tickle his face.

The girl drops a pencil, bends down to get it, catches him looking. Gives him a little grin.

He thinks about how nice it would be if she'd just say, "Hey, TJ," in that sweet voice girls use. But then the bell rings and they have PE.

After they run around the track about eight times and everybody's falling over in the locker room, gasping for air, a white kid the size of a semi-truck comes up to him and says, "I know who you are."

"So what?" TJ says. He thinks about punching him. But this kid is huge.

"You need a gang," the big kid says. "You're kind of puny."

TJ's face gets so hot, it feels like his freckles are popping out of his skin.

Miss Reba told him not to fight the first day. She has a surprise for him after school.

"And you're kind of big," TJ says. *Jesus, don't let him hit me. Amen.*

It tickles the big kid to no end. He goes haw-hawing down the lockers, snapping his towel at butts.

"Kind of big," TJ hears him say. "I guess so."

Abid-negro is standing next to him. "We call him Bully Angus. Best leave him alone."

TJ nods, cool as a cucumber, like he doesn't want to hug the skinny Black boy standing next to him for just even talking to him. If he can just remember to never say his name.

At the end of the day, when TJ steps on the bus, he closes his eyes for an instant and prays for the girl to be on it. *Make her my girlfriend,* he prays, *and I'll never get in a fight again. Jesus Name Amen.*

The girl's not on the bus. People move their backpacks over to take up empty seats. When he finally finds a clear place, it's next to the nerdiest boy in school. Glasses and braces and everything. Pocket pens. TJ doesn't even look at him when the boy says hey. He can't afford to hang out with somebody worse than he is.

TJ sees her out the window. She's getting picked up by her mom. Girl is all smiles. Calling out bye-bye to all her friends. "Bye, Leora," they call out. "See you in practice."

Her name is Leora.

She even smiles at her mama when she gets in the car, happy as can be.

The girl smiles at everybody.

The bus goes by Daddy's trailer again. TJ holds his breath as they go by.

Kids might know what Daddy did, but they don't know what really happened. Nobody knows what really happened because he never testified. He wanted to. He wanted the world to know just what an evil motherfucker Daddy was, so they'd put him in jail forever. He didn't do it, and now Daddy can get out in a couple of years, sooner if he escapes. And the first thing he'll do is come looking for him. Because he told Daddy, "I'm going to tell the whole thing. I hope you fry." Daddy said he'd kill him if he did. Said, "I done it before and I can do it again." So when it came time to testify, TJ chickened out. He ran away from Thelma Boyd's and lived under a bridge for a week where nobody could find him.

Here's what people in school don't know: he's the reason Daddy got away with murder.

12

With TJ off to school, Reba collects eggs in her bucket—six brown and five white, should be twice that. Chickens swarm around her, peck-peck-pecking the ground, looking up at her like hungry children. Three hens come all the way on the porch, and the rooster even tries to head in the screen door, like he's got plans to raid the pantry. She kicks him out the door, roots around for some dried-up-looking sweet potatoes, cuts them in pieces so the rooster doesn't get it all, and tosses them around the foot of Danielle Angel. Time to break down and go to Quarryville for chickscratch.

Before she can get dressed for town, here comes Reverend, rumbling down her driveway. He's going to have a lot to say about her coming to church. He's going to be just a little too happy about that.

"Miss Reba," he calls out, "so good to see you in church yesterday."

"Mmmm-hmmm." Now he'll be asking her to teach Sunday school. He steps out of the car and stands before her.

"Miss Reba, I am troubled in my soul," he says. "I have prayed and prayed. And I have to tell you the nature of my concerns." The man proceeds to tell her, standing right out in her yard, that she may not understand how that whiteboy's going to bring trouble. Church people are all up in arms. "Why not help a Black boy," he says, "like before?"

Seems Reverend and Jesus both are not fond of whiteboys. But it rankles her. She'll be done with this boy in her own time. She can't just give him back, out of the blue, for no reason. Much as she wants to. "You don't want him in church?" she says. "Then you don't want me either."

"Now, Miss Reba, that's not what I meant. I'm just concerned." He looks at her with his most sincere eyes.

"Reverend," she says, "Danielle would be ashamed of you."

It hits him like a body blow, his hand goes to his heart. "I will—I will pray on it."

Miss Reba eyes the porch broom. Reverend walks slowly to his car, past the looming statues, the rooster nipping at his heels, but he pays them no mind at all. Man is thinking about Danielle.

Miss Reba puts on her town dress, takes the net off her hair, puts on her pressure stockings and town shoes. She picks up her pocketbook and keys and gets in the Cutlass, clicks her seatbelt, fingers her bead necklace. Says her usual prayers plus one for having enough gas to get there and back, plus another one for TJ. *Lord Jesus keep that boy out of trouble, and when he does get into trouble, keep it on the mild side.* She puts the car in gear and heads into the world, full of dangers and whitemen. It's not half a mile before she sees one: a jogger out on the highway. Old man with skinny legs. Must be a Yankee from Stonehaven. Nobody around here would run for no reason. Not in this heat.

At Quarryville Feed & Seed, they've got what's left of the baby chicks all piled up in wire boxes, yellow fuzz turning into pinfeathers. Danielle used to love when these came in every spring. She'd say, "Auntie, I need one of those babies." Owner always opened the cage, smiled at the little girl in pigtails, holding yellow fluff in her small brown hands.

"Danielle baby," Reba would tell the child, "we got chickens at home." She didn't tell her there wasn't much chance of fluffy yellow chicks hatching out of her eggs. She always sold or ate them. Reba listens now for Danielle's voice in her ear. Nothing but yellow chicks peeping.

Miss Reba goes to the counter to order scratch, fifty pounds, and the man says, "You got behind a bit, Miss Reba. Got to pay each time now." She pulls out twelve flabby ones and some coins from her change purse.

When she gets back to the car, the new stock boy has piled her bag of scratch in the trunk. Whiteboy's got no manners, didn't ask, *Where you want it, Miss Reba?* Supposed to put it on the passenger seat, sitting up, so she can slide it onto the porch. How the blue blazes will she haul it out now, her back the way it is? That is one deep trunk.

Miss Reba's made it this far, so she decides to get all her shopping done at once: a pack of hot dogs, more grits, and a bag of rice from Piggly Wiggly. You can make things stretch with rice. She pays and gets her bags. Near the door, a bunch of churchpeople are standing around the newspaper stack, gossiping. They look up and see her, jump like they've seen a ghost. They nudge each other, hush their children, mouths fallen open or slammed shut. "Didn't see you standing there, Miss Reba." Nobody says, *Have a blessed day.*

Churchpeople loved Danielle. But now Miss Reba is bringing that whiteboy. They're afraid he's going to kill their children.

Miss Reba heads home and it starts to drizzle. She turns on the wipers, the windshield smears with bugs and dust. She grips hard to the wheel to keep from going into the ditch. With a load of chicken scratch in the back and the road wet, this car rides heavy and wants to veer.

The road swoops down to Cedar River Bridge. River's high after last night's rain, the color of slick red clay, like they have up in Burlington, then a stream of blue-gray where the soil from the Field mixes in.

What's this? Sheriff's car parked in the Field where the trail goes to the water. Wonder what mischief young Walter Pickett Junior is after. Maybe Jolene knows. Her land.

Up ahead, there's that whiteman in the red ball cap again. Jogging in place in front of the Sunrise Gas N Grill, skinny white legs sticking out his shorts, talking on a cell phone. Old man should have more dignity than to run around half naked like that. She's looking at him so hard that for the first time in her life she misses her turn onto Field Road.

Now the man goes to cross the highway, not looking where he's going, still talking on that phone, and her with bald tires, road wet, got to jam on brakes and slide to stop. Man runs *into* her car, hits it hard, goes down, cell phone flying, and she can't see him.

Lord Jesus, has she killed a whiteman in broad daylight, right here in front of the Sunrise Grill?

But no. She can see him crawling around in her side mirror, picking up his phone, pushing up off the ground, looking surprised to see her sitting there, like where he comes from there are no cars on the roads. Man puts his hands up like he's under arrest, mouths "sorry." Miss Reba shakes her head. Man wasn't hurt at all. Her heart may need repair.

Man ducks past the Stonehaven sign, limps in that way.

She sits there, frozen, and in her little eye she sees a man, a whiteman, a different man, lying in the road, and the memory makes her legs tremble. Lucy says, *That whiteman out on the highway? Tell the truth. You sorry you slammed on brakes. You wish you'd run him over.*

Jesus Lord help me now. Jesus Lord bring me back to this world.

Sunrise Grill. Blinking lighthouse. Here.

No sign of the whiteman.

Miss Reba pulls across the highway into the Sunrise parking lot, circles the pumps, pulls back on the road heading the other way, then turns right on Field Road. The glory of the tall pines, shining gold as the sun peeks through the rain, pulls her home. And here's Miss Jolene's tidy garden on the left, that house with Mr. Luke's crazy blue roof. She's out planting a new row. Woman working herself to a nub out there, wet to the bone, trying to keep that boy happy. Trying to keep him alive.

Miss Reba crosses Spill Creek, pulls across the road to the newspaper box, plucks the paper out, turns left into the long drive. It always feels just right to be here: her farm, her chickens, old truck needs fixing in the side yard. Mama's flower patch by the porch. Black angels with their wings open wide. But today, her legs are too weak and trembly to get out of the car. So she sits and waits till her strength returns.

House made of brick. Papa built it on a strong foundation. Mama used to say, *Wise man build his house on a rock. For the stormy day.*

When Miss Reba gets the strength back in her legs, she steps inside and picks up a kitchen knife, carries it back outside and opens the trunk of the Cutlass, stabs a hole in the feed bag, slices it open. Feed spills all into her trunk. She scoops and flings with her bare hands. Chickens come running.

There's a dent where the whiteman ran into her car, right there on the left front fender. She looks closer. The dent is the size of her hand. Bigger. The size of a whiteman's thigh. How could a puny little whiteman like that dent her car? This car's built solid. She looks closer. She can see light through the dent. The whole blessed fender is rusted through, under the black paint. She picks at the edges and a chunk comes off in her hand.

When a whiteman sold her this car six years ago, she never noticed till she got home that the bottom was rusted out. She had to put thick mats down to keep from pushing through. She taps her knuckles along the other fender now, the side, the top. Should be hard and tight. But it's not. The black paint is all bubbles. Whiteman must have spray-painted right over rust, and now it's coming up. No money to fix that. No money to fix anything. The whole car is going to crumble around her while she's driving down the road.

Whiteman who sold her the car is long gone.

But there is the one who made the dent just now.

Miss Reba wipes her hands, walks inside, pulls out her typewriter from where it's gathering dust in the pantry, puts it on the kitchen table. On this day, there is one whiteman won't be getting off scot-free.

Miss Reba tucks two pieces of paper plus a carbon into her typewriter and composes a letter, just the way she learned in Poolesville Secretarial School.

Dear Mr. _____:

On 10 May, at 9:45 a.m., in front of the Sunrise Grill, you ran into my car and left a dent in the left front fender. Then you ran off. This was a hit and run.

I know you live in Stonehaven Downs. When I find you, I will report you to the police. To compensate me for my lost time and worry, my suffering and my dent, you may reach me at 15 Field Road, Poolesville, NC.

Sincerely, Miss Reba Jones

She types "cc: sheriff" at the bottom. Then she finds an envelope, stares at the blank space where a name and address should go. How will she ever find that man's name? How will she find out where he lives?

Miss Reba sits with her Bible, closes her eyes, lets it crack to a random verse, looking for guidance. But when she puts on her glasses to see, all the clippings slip out the back and onto the floor. She gathers them up, puts them back in order, new to old, no need to read them, she knows them by heart, going back to her papa's time, all the crimes committed against her kin by whitepeople up to and including the man who shot her Danielle in the eye, point blank range, left half her head in a pot on the stove. How to make this feeling go away? Get up and do.

Miss Reba folds the letter, puts it in the envelope. She licks the edge and seals it with the flat of her hand. Then she drives up to Sunrise Grill to find out who that skinny whiteman is. The one who dinged her fender and walked away not a care in the world. Sunrise boys are nosy. They know everything about everybody who goes in there.

Whitemen all gathered around the grill, gossiping about tractors.

Miss Reba steps up to the counter. Asks Mr. Joggins if he's seen a whiteman with a red ball cap, was here this morning. Old man. Shorts on.

The boys all turn to look at her.

"Sure," Mr. Joggins says, "I seen him here. He likes our sausage biscuits. We call him The General."

"He's got that West Point cap," Joggins Junior explains.

"You got business with him?" Joggins says.

"He owes me money," Miss Reba says. She holds up the letter.

Sunrise boys look her over. What kind of money could a man like that owe a woman like her? "He dinged my car," she says.

"Dang, I saw that!" Junior says. "We was all watching from the window. That was you, Miss Reba? He had that cell phone out his pocket, y'all remember?"

"Ringtone like a parrot," Joggins says.

Miss Phoebe's redneck nephew chimes in. "We thought there was a bird in his pants!" The boy hoots, biscuit pieces fly out his mouth. No manners at all.

"We watched him go out the door," Joggins says. "He ran right into a car. That was you, Miss Reba?"

"Mmm-hmmm."

"Well, I'll be. We didn't see it was you."

"It was me."

"He left a dent?"

"Big one."

They all go out to see. Joggins puts his whole hand in the dent, it's that big. He fingers the edges, looks like he wants to pull a chunk, doesn't.

Joggins Junior pipes up. "He was limping when he ran away. You dealt a blow, Miss Reba!"

Joggins says, "Miss Reba, he should fix it. He comes in every day. I'll get it to him, don't you worry."

Miss Reba is none too sure about that. A letter should go through the US mail to have the weight and force of law. But she gets a pencil stub out of her purse and writes *To the General* on the envelope and hands it over. Joggins has got a car newer than hers, but he can't afford a dent either. Not from a Stonehaven Yankee. He'll do it.

"I'll give him hell for you, Miss Reba."

"That is not necessary," she says. "Just give him the letter."

The minute she's out the door, she sees them all laughing. Whitemen stick together. That General will come in here, open the letter, read it out loud and they'll all get a big chuckle. She's going to have to write another one. Track him down herself.

Miss Reba drives home. Rolls two pieces of paper plus carbon into the typewriter. *Dear Mister General.* She barely hears the squeak of the school bus brakes, stopping at the end of the drive.

"Whatcha doing, Miss Reba?" She startles, sees it's only TJ. Lord God, she has completely forgotten about the boy. "Never you mind," she says. "Put your things down. You got chores to do." She sends him outside to chop more wood. She tucks the new letter in an envelope, seals the edge, writes *To The General* on the front, sets it in the key basket. She hasn't done a lick of chores today. She hasn't put away the hot dogs she bought. She hasn't got dinner. She promised the boy a surprise. She has one last piece of cake. That will have to do.

Miss Reba checks the answering machine. No blinks. Nobody called to tell her the boy's in trouble. He's made it through the day.

At supper the boy tells her about his classes when she prods him. "The church boys don't like me," he says. "But Abid, Abid—"

"Abednego."

"Yeah, that one. He's okay."

He doesn't want the cake. She's already toasted it. "Give it to the chickens," she says.

She sends him outside. After a while, she looks out the screen door. He's talking to Danielle. She wonders if the girl is ever going to speak in her ear again that way—out loud. Skip-rope little girl. Her belly twinges with yearning. Oh, to hold that child in her lap once more.

Stories might bring her back. Even if the child doesn't speak out loud, Reba can always feel her there, the weight in her lap getting warmer as the stories fly into the air. When the boy's in bed, she can try.

She sets the boy down to do his homework. He complains and fiddles, chews the eraser right off his pencil. She wonders if Reverend was right, that TJ's going to bring all kinds of trouble, syphoning evil toward her. Like that whiteman and his dent. Like whatever wickedness the sheriff was finding, out there in the Field.

She sends the boy to bed. Pulls the gold box off the mantel. Weight in her lap warm and heavy as a laying hen.

TJ's creeping out the window when he sees it: a claw tied to a piece of something, like a voodoo charm. He's read a story about a magic monkey paw at school. But this is not a monkey paw. He doesn't know what the heck it is. Something of Miss Reba's. He pokes it with his finger. It doesn't zap him or anything. He pushes it to the corner and crawls outside, dragging the quilt behind him.

He's just settling in, trying to hear what Miss Reba's saying, when there's a scuffling sound behind him like the claw's come alive and now it's creeping up the side of the house. He jerks away, looks up. There's a mama raccoon and three babies hanging on to the drainpipe. "Shoo!"

TJ hisses. But they just hang there looking at him. He hunches his jeans jacket tighter around his ribs, turns the collar up, wraps the quilt over his head, and pretends they aren't there. *Dear God,* he prays, *please don't let any raccoons bite me in the ass.*

❧

Miss Reba settles the box in her lap. Listens. There's some rustling on the porch roof.

"Danielle baby, you there? I never told you some of this before. I know you're listening." There is no answer. Reba opens her mouth. Begins.

❧

That spring is so hot and droughty, we have to water all Papa's garden with buckets and sometimes his cotton too. But every day we can, me and Sheba run to the river to see Old Lucy.

Everywhere Old Lucy goes, that wolf dog follows, but we ain't scared of it anymore. She tells us his name, but we can't say it, so she says, "Call him Yellow Dog." He seems to like our company. Lucy shows us where to dig clay by the river and the dog digs beside her. She teaches us to make clay pots and the dog lays at our feet, panting. Here's how you do it: Make a snake of clay, circle it around your lap, small and pointy at the bottom, then bigger and bigger and smaller at the top. Smooth it with wet fingers, inside and out.

"Why make it pointy?" Sheba says. "Don't it fall over?"

"Tuck it in a fire, heap the coals around. Point helps you dig it in."

While she works, Old Lucy keeps her eyes closed most the time. Sheba asks, "Old Lucy, why you close your eyes like that?"

Old Lucy says in a spooky voice, "See with my little eye. Spirit eye. All that needs seeing." Then she laughs, and it sounds like a rope rasping on a pulley. "Eyes get tired. Got to rest sometimes."

Sheba and me watch Lucy walk over to a shed she's got, with a bundle laying on long sticks up in the air. She rests her hand on the bundle. "What's that?" Sheba says.

"The Old One," Lucy says. We don't want to ask if it's a dead person. But it looks about the size of a man.

We come home scratched and brambled, miss our chores, and Papa flails our legs with blackberry cane till they bleed. Tussie Lucy sees the next day and she gets mad. "Ain't enough people getting whupped in this world without doing it to young girls."

"Don't tell him we been here," I say, "he'll kill us for sure."

A look comes over Lucy's face, like she's deciding something. "Your daddy don't drink liquor."

"Nope."

"He like to eat, though, don't he?"

"Yes." He likes to eat and we're getting scarce with no rain. Been cooking dry peas with nothin in 'em but old hog grease. Garden scorched, chickens stopped laying.

"How about you bring him something today. See if he like that."

"He won't eat it," Sheba says. "He don't like you."

"We'll see what he do," says Lucy. She loads us up with three shad for me to carry, a skinned rabbit for Sheba, all wrapped in leaves and tied with scuppernong vine. Old Lucy puts her hands on her hips, gets a look on her face like a proud mama. "See if he don't like that," she mutters, like she's talking to herself.

When we get home Papa says, "What man give you that?"

"Not a man, Papa," Sheba says. I cut my eyes at her, *No no, don't tell.* But she's already got her mouth running. "Tussie Lucy give it to us. She nice. How come you don't like her?"

"That where you been all this time? That where you go? Heathen Indian, make corn liquor?" Papa's face gets black-red when he's mad.

"It's just some food," Sheba says. "She had extra." She lays her rabbit out on the plank table and I lay my fish and Mama touches the bundles, pulls the vine away, places her hand on the silvery fat belly of a shad.

"Been a long time since I had shad roe," she says. "Just what this baby need." She turns to Papa. Says, "Gemstone, we need the food. Besides, you know I'm related on my mama's side. Girls ought to know where they come from."

Sheba looks at me. I look at her. We're related to Tussie Lucy?

Papa's face clouds over like a thunderstorm, but he pinches his mouth tight and says, "Huh. She got Indian blood? Tell her to make it rain."

Mama lays down the law about keeping up chores, hoeing in the morning, keeping clothes clean. "Back by suppertime, hear? You got to help with supper." We keep the bargain most days that summer—we hoe early, and fast, so we can run to the Field. Old Lucy gives us skins and moccasins to wear while we're with her, we set aside our clothes to keep 'em clean. And Mama gets stronger from all Lucy's snares.

Sometimes we beg Papa to let us spend the night down by the

river—so we can night-fish with the fire, Sheba tells him—but the real reason is so we can hear more stories, dance around in our pretty moccasins. Old Lucy had some stories in her.

He always says no. Till one night he says, "Bring back some fish."

Danielle, that night Lucy builds a fire on the rocky point at the breeze side of the island, sets us down to watch.

Fish rise around us on the cool silver of moon water, fireflies rise in the thickets like slow sparks, ripples look like eels wiggling on the black surface. Old Lucy wades in. Reaches down. Pulls up a basket full of fish flapping their tails.

She sets some to smoke, roasts some on sticks, and we eat those whole, burn our tongues. Once the fire's gone to coals and our bellies are full, Lucy tells us *hush*, and even the crickets go quiet. She closes her eyes, lifts her head high, and opens her mouth.

"My name is Tuscarora Lucy, Keeper of the Bones, Born of Whirlwind, Voice in the Sycamore Tree, and my people are the Tuscarora of Catechnea Creek, the proud ones of the great war, the first war, the ones who rose up and set on the whites of New Bern, they who stole our children, sold them for slaves, poisoned our men with rum and pestilence, killed our deer..."

She tells how Tuscarora killed every whiteperson in that place, set them up in positions—priest like he's been praying, soldier like he's shooting—for somebody to find. She tells about how their women stuck pitch pine splinters all over one whiteman, their leader, John Lawson, set him on fire until he is just a pile of cinders. She tells about how new whitepeople come, bring guns and soldiers, kill so many of so many nations, put the rest on reservations. Some of her people go north to the Iroquois. But some of her people fight and run and hide in the woods and follow the rivers, and find the others still living, Cheraw and Saponi, Eno and Santee, even the Old One, who is Croatoan, and they settle this place together. A safe place between two rivers.

She tells us about the fields of tobacco, peach trees, beans, and corn. She tells us how the sky fills up with *amimi*, the pigeons who darken the sky for days while they pass over. And the colored birds, what they call *estatoah*, who mate for life, and who love to raid the fields. When she was little, Old Lucy says, she got the job to pound her stick on a hollow log to scare the birds away, but she put down her stick and just stood and watched them raid the Field. She picked up their feathers, orange, yellow, green, and put them in her hair.

"At night," Old Lucy says, "the many small cookfires of my people spread along the water. For a time, whitemen forgot the people who lived in the land between two rivers."

I close my eyes. I can see them. Birds overhead like a feather sky by day. At night, fires all along the river, mamas and babies and men cooking supper. Telling stories. Singing.

I open my eyes. Lucy's gone quiet, fiddling with white shell beads on a string around her neck.

"What's that?" Sheba says. "Your mama give it to you?"

Lucy lifts up the string of beads. They shine gold in the firelight. "This here from my people. Nothing left of them but shell beads and bones and stories." Old Lucy stares into the fire, then at us, with coal-black witch eyes. "And you," she says. "You still here."

Sheba finally says what she's been itching to say: "Old Lucy, Mama say we related."

Old Lucy just looks at her.

"We Indian?" Sheba says. "Don't look Indian."

Old Lucy holds up her arm. Puts it next to Sheba's.

They're the same color. Old Lucy's a Black Indian.

Next morning, Lucy takes us to the top of the Gooley Ridge cliff, points her bony finger. Yellow butterflies, one by one, passing across the river. Ten. Twenty. A hundred. They keep coming. I try to count them.

Sheba stands at the cliff edge, raises her arms. "Someday I'll fly away from here," she says. "Someday I'll go where they going, free and high and fluttery." She makes her skinny arms swoop in circles around the top of the cliff, and a butterfly swirls around her. Yellow Dog lays down and watches her.

Old Lucy regards her for a moment, sitting on her haunches, then turns to watch the river of fluttering yellow. "You don't know where they going," she says. "You don't know what they see."

"I will see far-off lands," Sheba says. "Kings and princes of many nations will come to see me dance." Sheba's been reading *Arabian Nights* from Mama's shelf. She twirls and twirls, closer and closer to the cliff edge. She flings herself down on the ground, stretches her arms out past the edge. Yellow Dog scootches close, whimpers. "This wind will lift me up," Sheba says, "far, far away. To my secret land."

"Miss Lucy, tell her she got to stay here. She got chores to do."

"You do 'em," Sheba says. "I got business to attend to." She watches the butterflies so hard, seems like she might find a way to turn into one.

Old Lucy looks at Sheba with a hungry look. Like she knows she can't make her stay. "They come to see you dead at the bottom of the cliff, you don't settle down," Lucy says.

My eyes go blank and I can see it: Sheba laying dead, white cloud around her head, trickle of red down one side of her face. I cry out, I fall down, the air around me smells like flowers. I open my eyes. Yellow Dog licking my face. Lucy snaps her black eyes at me. She saw what I saw.

That day Old Lucy gives us our animal names. Sheba is Yellow Butterfly that Flies Away. I am Little Turtle who Stays in the Field.

Lucy gives Sheba a sack of river clams to take home to Papa, and gives me a sack of herbs for Mama, to help bring the milk when the new baby is born.

&

Miss Reba raises her head. What's that sound? Rustling on the porch roof. "Danielle?" Now it stops. "Who's there?" she calls out. No answer. That boy spying on her? One thing she can't abide, that's a snoop.

She walks up to Danielle angel. "When the boy's in school," she promises, "I'll tell you the rest." Danielle's eye gleams. Miss Reba stares into the pupil of that eye. Something is moving there, drawing her in. A small bone face, arm and leg bones crossed, shifting under ripples of red and gold.

&

TJ lies in bed, his eyes squeezed closed, quilt pulled up to his chin. He can still see the people in the Field. The fish in the river. Sheba dancing. The butterflies that take you far, far away. He wonders if Old Lucy is still alive. Living there on her island. He wonders if that piece of claw and shell on the windowsill belongs to her.

Aunt Reba's coming up the stairs. He keeps his eyes closed and holds completely still. She's standing next to the bed. He lets his mouth gape open like he's asleep.

She steps to the window, pulls it shut. She tromps back down the stairs.

Old Lucy is a Black Indian. Aunt Reba must be a Black Indian too. *Little Turtle That Stays in the Field.* That's hilarious. He can almost see her head poking out of her shell, with her glasses on.

In the morning, he wakes early, runs to the window, hoping to see

the colored birds that feather the sky. No such luck. He wonders if
Miss Reba is making all that up. He would like to see the many small
cookfires of the people. And he would like to catch fish like that, you
just scoop them up with a basket. That Field has got to be somewhere
near here. And that island.

He grabs the claw thing off the windowsill. Tucks it in his pocket.
School kind of sucks. Miss Reba won't let him take the knife. He's going
to need all the voodoo he can get.

Miss Reba drives him to the end of the driveway. Watches him get on
the bus. Like he's a criminal or something.

13

Early Thursday morning Jolene and Bobo are elbow deep in the potato-washing buckets on the porch, rubbing off dirt and sand with their fingers, when they hear the school bus go grinding up the hill. Bobo lifts his head. "Late foh the bus!" he says. "Miss Ahn at school!" and she has to remind him, "School is closed. Miss Anne has gone to heaven." Bobo puts down his potatoes. "I miss huh."

But now a car comes bouncing over ruts into the yard, and the slurred double toot that is Ambler County for *hello, come out, no harm intended.* Bobo runs to see and Jolene jogs after, wiping her hands on her overalls. Maybe it's one of those Tree People, lost a drum or something.

It's the sheriff, already stepping out of the car. "Mrs. Blake." He tips his hat.

"Yes?" What in the world is he doing here?

Bobo gives him a big hug, leaning in. "Want some gum?"

"Hi, Bobo," the sheriff says, blushing and uncomfortable, not quite sure how to negotiate his gun and all manner of equipment on his belt under this assault. He settles for turning his gun side away, and patting Bobo on the back. Good Lord, with his pink face, buzz cut, and big ears, Sheriff Walter Pickett Jr. looks so young, how does anybody take him seriously? But he's the one who found Bobo and Ace last year when they got lost. Credit due for that. Instead of telling Bobo the truth, that she'd sold his beloved baby goats to that Mexican butcher in Siler City, she told him they ran away. So he and Ace went looking for them, wound up tangled in briars down by the river.

The sheriff's still patting. "Bobo, that's enough," Jolene says. Bobo steps away, puts his hands behind his back, sulks.

Finally released, the sheriff coughs, turns to Jolene. "You heard, ma'am?"

"Heard what?"

"About the Indian bones. Bridge crew found them, in the cliff next to the river."

"Oh my goodness." Luke always wondered if there was a burial ground there.

"Bones, Mama!" Bobo cries. Bobo loves animal bones. He keeps a collection of bird and animal bones in that old shed, things his father gave him.

"Hush, Bobo," Jolene says.

"Looks like the rain washed it out," the sheriff continues. "Your land, I believe?"

Jolene nods. "My land."

"Looks like a pretty old burial," the sheriff says. "We got to call in the state archaeologist. He'll want to have a look. Just standard procedure," he says, "nothing to worry about. You'll get a letter. Some forms to sign."

"Goodness," Jolene says. She wonders if the letter is in the pile she hasn't read. "An Indian burial?" she says.

"Indians, Mama!" Bobo shouts. Luke told Bobo about the Indians who used to live here.

"From what-all I could tell, yes, ma'am. But I'm no expert. Looks like a baby buried in a pot. Nothing left but bones."

She feels a snag in her belly. The miscarriage she had years ago. She buried her up in the Gooley Pines and never visits. *Shake it off. Try to listen.*

"We kept it out of the paper for a few days, keep people from tromping around. But it's coming out this week."

"Tromping around?" That doesn't sound good. She does not want people tromping around.

"Want to see the bones, Mama!" Bobo is practically jumping up and down.

"Ma'am." Sheriff Walter Pickett Jr. gives her a stern look. "That's what people like to do sometimes. Come and see things like that."

"I don't want people messing up my pasture. Can't you put a guard out there?"

"I can drive by," he says, "from time to time. I put some tape out, but nobody can see it unless they're already down by the water. The more tape you put out, it seems to me, the more people want to see it."

"Want to see it!" Bobo crows.

"Bobo!"

"And Mrs. Blake?" The sheriff pauses, looks around. "Division of Archaeology may want permission to look into it further."

"Look into it?"

"To dig."

"*Dig a Hole in the Meadow*, Mama!" Bobo shouts. His favorite book.

Tiny frogs popping out of holes, mice, rabbits, children, hole-diggers all.

"I can tell you they already have somebody across the highway, the Stonehaven land next to the river. They got permission there already."

"To dig?"

"Yes. In my experience…" young Walter says. He clears his throat. "I mean, what I hear, the sooner you go ahead with this kind of thing, the sooner it blows over."

"Does Miss Reba know?" Jolene says. If what Luke said is true, these baby bones might belong to Reba's people.

"She does if she reads the paper."

Miss Reba reads the paper. And she is in no shape to hear about more dead relations. "Son of a gun," Jolene says.

"Mama! You swoh!" Bobo loves to catch her swearing.

Sheriff Walter Pickett Jr. holds his lips tight together, like he's trying not to laugh. Then he puts his hat back on, tips it to her, serious as a heart attack, gets in his big car, and drives away in a cloud of dust and yellow pollen.

That night Bobo insists on reading his favorite book with her.

"This one!" he says, opening to a random page in the middle.

"A rabbit can dig a hole for her nest," she reads. "Now you." The next picture is his favorite, small children with big bowls of mashed potatoes, making holes for gravy.

"A boy can dig a hole in mash potatoh!" He turns the page. "You read!"

"A big dog can dig a BIG hole for his bone," she reads.

"Like Ace," Bobo says.

"Yes." Oh dear.

"Miss Ace, Mama."

"I know. I miss him too."

It rains again that night. Good for the beans. In the morning, she can almost hear them sprouting.

14

Spirits have been restless all morning. Old Lucy sent a fly to buzz around TJ's head at breakfast. Sheba brought yellow butterflies to circle her angel statue in the yard. Seems like the story last night cracked open the earth and let them out. But still there is no child voice, and the bright noise of birds and bugs and breeze in the leaves might drown her out if there was. Reba strains her ears to hear, wills the crickets to be silent, like Lucy could do. A dim memory from last night: A world in Danielle's eye. A vision of child bones, rippling black and red like river water after sunset.

TJ is off to school. The dent is still there. The new letter is sitting in the key basket. Lucy says, *Don't let that whiteman do you that way.*

Miss Reba leaves the breakfast dishes where they lie.

Up at Sunrise Grill, Miss Reba backs into a parking space, sits there facing the highway, the letter on the seat beside her, waiting. The General comes here every morning. Isn't that what they said?

After a while Mr. Joggins comes out, taps on her window. "Miss Reba, you need anything? Pump you some gas?"

She never buys gas here. It's too pricey. She can hear that high whine rising in her voice as she tells him, "Just resting my bones, Mr. Joggins." She hates that voice. But you use it, they leave you alone.

People drive by. No joggers. No General. Around lunchtime, Joggins Junior brings out a bacon biscuit, the kind she has been known to purchase here from time to time. But she has no appetite for a biscuit. And he'll be wanting to charge her for it. "You find that General, Miss Reba? He pay for your dent?" He's staring right at it. He can see nobody has paid for this dent. Red streaks seeping down the side, after that rain last night. Looks like somebody put a fist in the side of her car, came up with a bloody hand. "Not yet," she says. "But he will." Junior shuts up and goes inside. She can almost hear them gossiping about her. Let them talk. Finally Junior comes back out again. "Daddy says to tell you The General ain't been by. He gave your letter to Miss Phoebe. She knows everybody."

Miss Phoebe is a big busybody at the farmers' market. With her frilly apron and bun, she acts sweet as blueberry pie, but that whitelady

knows everybody's business. Wonder if she knows The General. She
don't socialize with Stonehaven folks. Most likely she dropped it in the
mud.

Hot as blazes in this car. Sweat rolling down. She is so tired of sitting
here, stewing.

Now Mr. Joggins comes out again. "Miss Reba," he says, "you want
me to give you an estimate for that dent? We can do the work here if
you want."

Whiteman trying to make more money than he already has.

"It's free," he says. "The estimate, I mean. Just take a minute."

Couldn't hurt to know how much that General owes her. Miss Reba
nods. Gets out of the car to watch, make sure he don't knock any more
holes in the car.

Mr. Joggins gets his clipboard and a sheet of paper. He taps her car
with his knuckle, in all different places. Shakes his head. Writes things
down. He even gets his rolling cart and scootches under. Pokes around
with a screwdriver, just his legs sticking out. Miss Reba gets a shiver
down her arms. What if the whole car falls on his head while he's down
there?

When he's done he adds it all up. "Miss Reba. You got to replace
the whole fender. It's rusted through. Try to smooth over the dent with
anything, the whole thing might fall off the frame."

"Whole fender," she says. Sounds like money.

"It's $45 for parts, if I can find it at the junkyard. Forty-five for
labor."

But he ain't done.

"Thing is," he says, "the frame ain't too good either. I can't guarantee
the fender would stay on that frame. You got to get a new car sometime
soon. It ain't safe to drive."

Been driving it all this time, floorboards rotted out, may as well drive
a little longer.

"You let me know when you're ready. I'll keep an eye out for something good. I got a friend sells used in Sanford."

Another whiteman ready to cheat her. That's just what they do. They
can't help themselves.

She makes Joggins write the numbers down on a piece of paper and
sign his name.

She's got an estimate. She's got the letter. Both on the seat beside her.
Now, where is that whiteman General?

Miss Reba stares across the highway at the fancy rock-pillar entryway to Stonehaven Village for Yankee Whitepeople, willing him to come out. *Come out come out wherever you are.* Sheba's voice in her ear, playing hide 'n' seek.

Miss Reba has never passed through those fancy pillars. When she goes to sell at the market, there's a back way on a gravel road the farmers are supposed to take.

Sheba would go right in the front way.

Miss Reba rises up in her seat, checks for traffic, puts it in gear, crosses the highway, and drives the Cutlass right into the place where Yankee whitepeople live.

She passes whiteladies out in the sun, colored gloves on, big hats, rooting around their flower beds. They don't know you've got to get your hands in the dirt to know a flower bed. Some stand and stare as she goes by. Like they've never seen a car this old. Or a Black lady.

One lifts her hand to wave—or to flag her down?

She gives it some gas, and the car blows out black smoke. The ladies fan the smoke away, like they're flapping away a swarm of bees.

She keeps going. She dare not stop and ask. She knows what would happen. Little old whitelady'd pull out a cell phone and call 911. *There's a Black lady in the neighborhood, driving around, she might steal our flowers. Our ugly houses. Our hats.* Young Sheriff Walter would laugh and shake his head, say, "Miss Reba? Gosh sakes, she's got to be eighty years old." But his deputies are just as likely to get out the cuffs and drag her off to jail. One of her foster boys, Tyquan, got in trouble that way, all of twelve years old, mowing a whitelady's lawn. Somebody didn't like the way he looked next to whitepeople houses.

No sign of a whiteman running down the road. Nobody much out in this heat. She needs a different plan. Reba tucks the letter and the estimate in the glovebox, on top of the registration. She can bide her time.

She drives the Cutlass home, going extra slow in case the sides decide to fall off.

General owes her ninety dollars. But ain't nobody going to give her a new car.

When she gets home, Reba can't settle down enough to sit with Danielle. Can't read her book. Can't stand to watch her soaps. Can't read her Bible, with all the slips of paper in the back she has tucked in over the years. *An Account of Crimes Against Our People.* It used to be just her family. Then she expanded the list to things she saw on the news. The last one was Trayvon. She stopped watching the news after that one. They let that whiteman in Florida hunt down a young Black boy, cold-blooded murder, in broad daylight, in this day and age. They set that whiteman free. Now they've done just about the same for Tommy Jay.

That whiteman messed up her car. Just got up and ran away. With his fancy house. People in Stonehaven living all high on the hog. On the land where Lucy's people used to be. Lucy whispers in her ear: *Get your money. Take it out of his hide. Set his house on fire.* "Hush up, Old Lucy, I can't do that." Lucy came from Tuscarora, and they are a vengeful people. But they had plenty to be mad about. Whitemen stole their children.

Reba touches the yellow hair clips in her pocket, finds no comfort there.

She used to be alone in this house, and it was quiet enough to draw Danielle's spirit out, make that child's voice speak right in her ear. But now it's whitemen running into her car, and trying to sell her bacon biscuits, and that boy talking her ear off, sleeping in Danielle's bed. Boy will be home in an hour. Time to get up and do. That child voice always comes when she's just going about her business.

Miss Reba putters in her kitchen, washes the dishes she left this morning, goes to set the paper in the stack in the pantry. She doesn't want to read whitepeople business today. But a headline snags her eye: *Indian Burial Found by the River.*

Miss Reba parks the car, walks through the gate, finds the goat trail.

Here's the swimming rock. One bird calls. Then a jay, loud as day: *Here here here.* Lucy pointing the way. Car tracks in the sand. Man shoe tracks. Then a mess of yellow ugly police tape all zigzagged across the riverbank.

Jay squawks and flaps to the top of the cliff and there it is, dim in the shadow, a clay jar, cracked open like an egg, pieces crumbled down the cliffside. What Papa called a heathen burial. In the hollow shell, a tiny skull and ribs and little leg bones of a baby folded up the way they used to do. Reba shuts her eyes. Sees what Old Lucy taught her to see: the orchards and the gardens, *the many small fires of my people.* She lifts her eyes to the great pines, the tips gold and green in the afternoon light. But here is this sadness kept in a pot. Something opened that should stay closed. Whitemen have no business coming here. This is sacred ground.

A rustle in the bushes. A scratching sound. A whimper. A yellow dog rises up from the scrub and looks at her, panting. Lucy's dog is long dead. But this is the spittin' image. Wolf face, long tail like a question mark over its back. Eyes glaring like it knows her. The dog's lip curls. Lucy speaks. *Whitemen coming no matter what you do.* The dog turns, slips away into the thicket, disappears like a puff of pine smoke. The jay calls from high up in the pines. *Jeer jeer jeer.* Deer graze at the clifftop, turn their heads to watch her. She can feel snakes moving under the ground. Lucy's got all her creatures watching these bones. Reba breaks out in a sweat, a trickle down her back.

She takes her stick and whacks at the police tape till it falls away, then she clumps what she can reach of it into a ball and throws it into the river, watches it float downstream.

Breeze on her skin. Coming from the wrong direction. Feels like someone stripped her naked, took her clothes, and threw them in after.

When she gets home, there's a message on her answering machine. TJ has been caught stealing. "An iPod," the message says. "From Tyquan Alston. You better come pick him up." Miss Reba gets back in the car. This is one kind of trouble she's been expecting.

PART III

FIELD OF BONES

15

In the eternity that trees know as growing season, the Gooley Pines, the Great Trees, *Tatcha na wihie Gee-ree*, have watched the rain slither down the cliff and chew away at the clay, leaving a slide of pebbles and sherds, mud and slurry. They sense the clay pot loosening from its nest of roots. They shift their roots and try to cover the bones.

When men come, the Great Trees throw shadows down the cliff, shifting the light with their branches. In the thicket below, a wild dog suckles her young.

Three days ago in Chapel Hill, Charles Mathers, PhD, poked the young man who's been crashing on his couch since his mother died, unable to get it together to find a job, apply for school, or shave his face, and said, "Jefferson Lee, get up off your ass. I've got a job for you."

"What?" Jeff rubbed sleep from his eyes, sat up.

"They found some bones in a cliff in Ambler County. I need a digger."

While he waited for permission for access to the land, Mathers has done some fast talking to set up a test dig across the highway, in a ragged corner of the floodplain owned by developers of Stonehaven Downs. It was a place they could neither develop nor use in any way. "Might be good publicity," he told them. "Could be a significant find. *New York Times*, *National G*, all that."

And now, Friday morning, Jefferson Lee, aspiring archaeologist, having worked for two mornings alongside Chuck marking a four-square area with string and stakes, setting up a tarp and plywood tables, troweling out weeds, rocks, and topsoil, has been left in charge while Chuck goes off looking for funding and newspaper interviews.

Jeff sits by the river, smoking his one cigarette per day, watching the first light of morning skim across intersecting ripples that shift and slide over hidden rocks below. He can't believe his luck. It's almost as if his dead mother reached down, yanked him up by the shirt collar, and plopped him down in the middle of the life he always wanted, the life she believed he could have, if he only put his mind to it.

The giant pines on the steep cliffs west across the highway shift and toss in the breeze, birds shouting their mating songs. The oaks and sycamores by the river seem to speak in return, bowing and bending and lifting. He picks up a cluster of tiny oak leaves cast to the ground in last night's storm, thumbs their fragile green skin, tender as a woman's breast. It occurs to him that every spring when the leaves come out here, there must be a day when the rushing sound he's hearing, a sound like a happy ocean roar, is brand new. It is the sound of new leaves all talking at once. He wonders if the ones who lived here had a name for that.

At the funeral his father had been so lost. Barely able to stand up straight. Spit and polish in his dress whites, the stiff collar straining his neck, trying to stand at attention, but slipping to one side, finally leaning on Carrie as they stood beside the grave. Carrie told him later she found him on his knees in Mom's closet, smelling her clothes. Jeff saw the wounded expression, the tremble in Dad's hand. The colonel. The tough old bird. Jeff promised his dead mother then that he would watch over his father. But he hasn't even called. Now there's no escaping the obligation, he's camping a scant mile from the house. *Your father will be so glad to see you,* he can hear his mother saying, the usual well-meaning lie. Maybe tomorrow, he thinks.

He's already found potsherds, clay pipes, turtle shells in the dig section nearest the river. He's got to mark what he's found and lay it out on the tables for Chuck to inspect. He's got to do it right. *Don't fuck up.* This feels like more than a second chance. This feels like his big break.

He's wanted to be part of this kind of work, this kind of life, for so long now. The only question always was: *Are you good enough?* Maybe not. He's already dropped out of two grad programs. One night, after a long conversation with Mom, she'd finally called him on it, said: "You think you aren't any good so you quit before you even try."

He thinks about his last project. Not his best moment.

He had joined up with Noah Benson's spring break dig in New Mexico, to prove Mom wrong. Noah was a big deal. He was lucky to get the slot. But after the first three days, Jeff hadn't cared how it came out, he'd loved it so much—the searing light, the soft colors at dawn, the tent life. The easy camaraderie in the mess tent; the serious, focused, painstaking work during the hot afternoons; the burnt-sugar sky at sunset; the thrill of connecting to a lost world. Noah Benson called them Midwives for the Sacred Dead. They were bringing the dead back to life, back to the light of day.

Noah Benson had seemed to favor him, had begun to take him under his wing. He had hopes of getting his name on a published paper. That could be the ticket for grad school.

Marietta was another one of Noah's protégés. She was sad and self-contained and extremely efficient by day. At night she crept into the tents of sleeping grad students and fucked them silly. First one. Then the next night, another. Noah didn't seem to notice. The men on the site began to hate each other. Jeff watched the goings on, swore he'd stay out of it, then one night, having flung himself into a dreamless, exhausted sleep, he woke up to her body pressed against his, his erection already damp from her juices. He jerked back, startled, but she was kissing him now, all over, covering his mouth with hers when he tried to protest. He saw she was crying as she kissed him, whispering, "Please, please," and something in him was deeply stirred. Marietta Semple needed him. He couldn't resist a woman who needed him. He knew it was a mistake but he did it anyway.

Noah had finally figured out what was going on. Noah had tracked her down and spied through the tent flap as she worked her charms on Jeff. Noah threw both of them off the site and banned them from work on any of his projects ever again. That meant pretty much all of New Mexico, for the foreseeable future.

He'd hiked into the midday sun, parched and sweating salt, drank hot plastic-tasting water, and hitched a ride to the outskirts of Tucson. He hunkered down on the shady side of a gas station, drank six cold Lone Stars, and swore to himself he would never ever get involved with a woman again, not while on a dig. Women always screw things up.

"You were right, Mom," Jeff said on the phone the next day, when he finally got the courage to call. "I'm a total fucking loser."

"I *never* said that." His mother's voice was fierce, angry. "I only said you were afraid. Everybody's afraid. *I'm* afraid." The next time he called, a week later, the neighbor Bess answered the phone. Mom was dead.

Now, squatting next to the cliff, watching the sky-fire rise over the river, Jeff finally wonders what his mother ever, in a million years, had to be afraid of.

16

At ten a.m., Col. Randolph Jefferson Lee, retired, buckles his seatbelt, stops at the highway, and stares at Sunrise Gas N Grill with longing, wishing he had time for a sausage biscuit before his cardiology appointment. He turns the other way, toward Chapel Hill.

The doctor, as usual, is going to tell him he's screwed up his heart and there's nothing to do but eat poached salmon and dry chicken breasts and take slow, shuffling walks around the neighborhood for the short time that remains to him on this planet. Since Anne died, there's no one to enforce these rules. The colonel plans to go down in a blaze of homemade pimiento cheese from the Sunrise Grill and forbidden runs. Still, he has a morbid curiosity to find out just how bad it is.

When the checkup is over, the doctor turns to him with look of wonder on his face. "Your heart is strong," he says. "I've never seen a recovery like this. You're practically a medical miracle." Rand doesn't believe it. The doctor doesn't seem to either. "Your previous diagnosis must have been wrong. Look," he says, and lays out the EKG. The lines go up and down in a perfect rhythm, strong and clear. "Have you been following diet and exercise?"

Rand nods. Well, he was until Anne died. Since Carrie left, he's drinking too much. Maybe it was the running. He wasn't supposed to run. He sits there, the pure pain of his new health radiating from his heart like a sore layer of muscle, a new muscle, one he has never used before.

The doctor is more concerned about the enormous bruise on the front of his right thigh. "What happened here?"

"Had a little accident," he says. No way he's telling that tale, the woman coming out of nowhere, bouncing off her fender, the cell phone dropping, a spiderweb of cracks in the screen, Anne's face frozen and discolored under the cracks, *dead dead dead,* because of course Carrie had been calling from Anne's phone. She'd taken that along with a pile of clothes and who knows what else. Behind the windshield, the woman's face was blank and black, her glasses magnifying her eyes. *Why didn't she look where she was going?*

"Any pain when you walk?"

"A little," Rand says. Actually it hurts like hell. The bruise has bloomed into a rosy swelling, purple in the center, the shape of California. When the doctor pushes hard, Rand yelps.

"Rest, ice, elevation," the doctor says. "Stay off that leg for a few days, and come back if it doesn't start to fade in a week. We'll shoot an X-ray."

Rand's been lying around the house for days, with a pack of frozen peas on his leg, medicating with bourbon and ibuprofen. He'll go crazy if he doesn't run soon.

Back in the car, Rand starts to turn toward the hospital to visit Kip, a habit for so many months. But then he remembers Kip died. Poor Kip. *Poor me.* No one to run with anymore.

Rand gets discount gas and drives through the car wash to get the crusted pollen off. The damn car looks derelict with all that yellow oozing and dripping down the sides after last night's rain. Another thing he's learned here: if you don't park your car in the garage in the spring, you will be punished. He's sure the neighbors are talking about him. *The poor colonel, he just doesn't seem to be able to keep up with things these days.* But there sure seems to be more pollen this year than last.

Rand has one more stop before he goes home. He drives to the bank in Carrboro, the one where nobody knows him. He takes out $250, cash, drives to the post office, pays for a money order made to cash. He slips it in an airmail envelope, red and blue borders all around. He prints the familiar address, JOHOR, MALAYSIA, with a blue ballpoint pen, pays the postage. These days people send money through Wi-Fi. He prefers the old-fashioned way. He likes to think about where it's going for just a moment, before he lets it go. He likes to say to himself: *I am a citizen of the world.* He likes to remember a time when he was doing important work in far-off places, secret work, work that would somehow save the world from blowing up for a while. For the first time ever, he also allows himself a remembered whiff of curry, a woman with golden skin and black eyes, a smile meant just for him. Then he walks away and remembers who he is. US Army colonel. A man bound by duty.

It's two in the afternoon, steamy hot, by the time Rand lays out his running shorts and shirt and heads out, bum leg and all. It's time. He'll go stark raving mad if he has to lie on that couch another damn day. The hell with ice and elevation. With any luck, the neighbors will all be off playing tennis or taking naps, not watching out their windows, scrutinizing his terrible slow gimpy jog: *The poor colonel. I can't believe he's running. After all he's been through.*

Rand crosses the highway to the land that nobody seems to own, the broad rocky field and the steep hill with tall pines. He nixes the sprint, grabs low branches to pull himself up the slope until he reaches the crest, the spongey pine duff, the sweet air, warm and thick. Then he follows the crest to a side trail that overlooks the abandoned field below. Across the highway there's something new in Stonehaven, in the rough flats near the river. A truck, a man with a shovel, a tarp over four flags marking a small square. Is he building a house? It seems an odd place for it. It would be a very small house, barely room to stretch out to sleep.

Rand bends and inspects his thigh, which is sending shooting pains into his knee. The whole thing has become a strange green-black-yellow color the shape of a southern continent—more Africa than South America. He taps his fingers on a wide yellow swath at the top that mimics the shape of the Sahara desert. There's still a terrific lump in the center.

Maybe he can walk off these shooting pains. He wanders a little farther in, something he hasn't done for a while. The big pines sway over his head, shimmering the light on the forest floor. He rests his forehead against one of the giant trees, closes his eyes, and inhales: *sandalwood, pine, vanilla, amber.* A jay calls from somewhere near the river.

He remembers the day he heard those sirens. *Another man bites the dust.* His heart is fine. It was Anne's brain that exploded.

Rand leans back against the pine bark and looks up. The enormous crowns sway in the breeze, showering pollen on his head, into his eyes, his mouth. He blinks and spits. Rubs his eyes. There is a rough warmth emanating from the trunk of the great pine and he lets it soak into his back, a momentary comfort.

Rand stumbles to the place he likes to spy on the tidy little farm below. The blue farmhouse roof seems to be peeling now. But there are perfect new rows of tiny green plants. Beans? Some kind of vine trellised to a fence. The slender woman carries buckets to the barn, followed by that big boy. He hears the faint *maaaa* of a goat. Can he picture Anne milking goats? No.

It's clouding up. Rand gimps to the Sunrise Gas N Grill, sausage biscuits, all day long. He'll sit among men, listen to men talk, pretend he isn't even there.

He wipes the sweat off his face with paper napkins, eats his biscuit.

The farmers who hang out in the mornings are nowhere to be seen. He finishes, limps down the aisles, finds BC powder and a tub of home-made pimiento cheese.

He pays at the counter, and the fellow hands him a box of Tampa Supremes. "You left these before," he says. Rand remembers all too well. That day he was here, heading for the door, and his cell phone rang like a squawking parrot—Carrie must have downloaded that ringtone, it scared him half to death—and he tried to root the phone out of his pocket, dropping everything, including the phone, that squawking getting louder and louder. The Sunrise boys laughed their asses off. Of course it was Carrie, who had ideas for what he should do that day, and he tried to listen as he backed out the door, then began to jog, trying to get up some speed, because he had promised he would always take the cell, yes, always answer it, because *where were you when Mom was dying on the tennis court and they couldn't find you*—and that big black car came out of nowhere.

The man behind the counter hands him change. "Miss Reba ever get up with you?"

Who's Miss Reba? Rand wonders. "No," he says. Maybe Miss Reba is the lady who makes the pimiento cheese. He put in an order last week. They finally have some.

Back home, Rand sits on the couch, glass of bourbon in hand—as Anne would say, *It's five o'clock somewhere in the world*—ice clinking, curtains closed, no one to spy on his bad habits. The cockatiels are quiet in their cages. Anne's lovebirds scold, then go still. The house crouches around him, full of shadows.

He thinks about calling his daughter. He's sure she's been trying. But she's calling a dead phone. Jeff never calls. Last he heard, his son was crashing on some college buddy's couch in Chapel Hill. He may as well be in Timbuktu.

This house needs some noise and light. Rand turns on a lamp, grabs an apple from the fridge, limps to the den. King Philip and Queen Philippina mutter and churrip as he approaches. *Oh bloody hell,* one of them says. Anne taught them that. In an English accent. She thought she was being funny. Rand pulls the cover off. Released from darkness, the two of them perk up, fluff their pink crests at him. Philippina says, *Happy! Appul!* Philip says, *Awwk!* He's the slow learner. Rand checks their water, cuts the apple into slices with his pocketknife, feeds the slices through the cage wire. They clutch them with hungry talons, peck and tear with such enthusiasm they have to flap for balance, pink down puffing through the cage wires into the air around him, settling at his feet.

"Want out?" Rand says. "Want to fly around?" They freeze. Queen Pia cocks her eye. King P drops his apple, lifts one claw like a question waiting to be answered, lets loose a stool.

"Bird party," Rand says, but even he can hear that his voice does not sound like a party, not like the brief escapades he used to arrange, when Anne was out of the house. He opens the cage anyway, and they creep slowly toward him, as if they don't know him very well.

Rand limps to the kitchen, gets a fresh bag of frozen peas. The cockatiels flap after. He lies down on Anne's powder-blue Chesterfield sofa, the birds alight on the sofa back. There's something wrong with the painting of Anne over the mantel. He gimps up to the portrait, gives it a nudge. There. It was crooked.

She always wanted to have a portrait made of him in his uniform. "Dress whites," she said, "bring out your eyes." "When I make general," he would say. "Soon then," she would say, smiling, as though she had all the confidence in the world.

Anne seems to be staring right at him now, trying to tell him something. God, she was a beauty. And that dress. She always wore that color of blue. Satiny gowns, gowns with enormous fluffy skirts, slender sheaths with long gloves. She wore that color the first time he saw her, a lowly enlisted man, working kitchen duty at an officers' club party in Germany.

"Who's *that?*" he remembers asking the cook that night. The girl shimmered with life, and joy, and mischief. "The general's daughter," the man said, and his tone said, *Not for the likes of you.* She was a beauty, but not aloof at all. She seemed to talk to anybody, kids, old ladies, waiters. So there was hope. But he knew one thing: he needed to be different from who he really was to have a chance with her.

He stares up at Anne's face. Even in this dim room, the painting catches the light in Anne's eyes, the bloom on her arms and shoulders, as if she's breathing, alive, right here. He's had four days of lying on the couch, icing and elevating, to consider the facial expressions in Anne's portrait. Some days she seems wry and amused, some days loving and full of joy, some days she bears a penetrating gaze that makes him want to beg forgiveness. For sabotaging her social plans, for not knowing how to help their wayward son, for never rising in the ranks.

He is not going to die. He is going to live. And it is the worst possible thing that could have happened to him. A long life with no Anne in it. A long life to consider all the ways he made her miserable. A long life to make it up to nobody.

17

Saturday morning Rand wakes late to the sound of the cockatiels screeching from the den. He rubs his eyes, winces at the mid-morning sun blasting through the living room window. He's still in his rumpled clothes, cattywampus on the couch, a bag of melted frozen peas fallen to the rug. He stumbles down the hall, sees he forgot to put the cockatiels in their cage last night, and the pink-crested birds are screeching and flapping at the window. They're so territorial. Is it the mailman? He peers out. It's that little bird Anne saw in the yard a few weeks ago: blue head, red chest, green wings. Rand remembers her paging through the *Peterson's*. She'd paused at Carolina parakeet. "Extinct? Rand! Give me those binocs!" He'd said, "It's not a Carolina parakeet. Is that what you thought? My God, Anne, extinct means there aren't any more of them."

She conceded the point and kept looking, settled on painted bunting. *Not endemic to this area. An accidental.* Which meant blown here in a storm. He wonders now why it's still hanging around. Shouldn't it fly back to the coast where it belongs? The cockatiels screech at a higher pitch. "Settle down," he says. "You could take him out if you had to."

Now the colorful little bird flitters in circles on the ground, zooming its wings like a hummingbird, skittering here and there on the grass like a June bug. Is there something wrong with it? There's a small greenish bird in the bush nearby. June Bug hops on top of Greenish Bird, and they...*Ah.* Well now. He turns away, checks the food and water in the cage. They've scattered seed all over, hulls on the rug, water gone. *Get it together, man.* He goes to find the bird food.

Now there's a knock at the kitchen door. *Oh, for crying out loud.* Maybe whoever it is will go away. The knock comes louder. A muffled voice. Rand limps to the door. "Rand? It's Bess." He opens it a crack.

"What is it?" he says. He hopes she hasn't brought more casseroles.

"We're headed over to the Bistro for brunch. Thought you might like to join us."

Brunch? He hasn't even had his coffee. George has the Jag out, rumbling in the driveway. "No thanks," he says. "Got some things to do around the house." Bess peers over his shoulder, sniffs the air, sees the cockatiels perched on the back of the sofa. She seems to know he had pimiento cheese and crackers and bourbon for dinner last night. Anne's best friend has a nosy side.

"The maid will come next Tuesday," she says. "You can get her twice a week now if you want."

"Who?"

"The maid, Rand. I was able to get her back on a schedule with you."

"Don't need a maid," he says. "I can do fine without a maid."

Bess closes the door and leaves, George waves from the Jag. He must have polished that thing all yesterday, it gleams so brightly. The Accord is already covered in pollen.

After they leave, the kitchen phone rings, a sound he hasn't heard in weeks. The cockatiels screech and jump into the air. The lovebirds flap in their cage.

"Hey, Dad," Carrie says, "I'm home. Finally. My flight got delayed. Why haven't you called me back? I've been leaving all kinds of messages."

"I'm sorry, honey," he says.

"They've got me flying all over, New York, Memphis, Chicago, for depositions on this case," she says. "Thunderstorms over Chicago, we had to land and just sit on the plane for an hour. Then it started *snowing*. Do you believe it? It's *May*." She continues the litany of her trip, the man who sat next to her, his line of business, his new iPhone, an app that tells you if someone you're dating is a felon, and on and on, and he lets his daughter's voice wash over him in a drift of comforting chatter, while he strolls to the kitchen for his first cup of coffee. But there is no coffee. "Goddammit, Anne!" She's the one who makes the coffee. Made the coffee. *Christ on toast*, he's out of coffee. He forgot to get some.

"Dad?" Carrie's voice tinny in the receiver.

"It's fine," he says. "I'm fine. No damn coffee in this house." He pours the dregs from yesterday in his cup, puts it in the microwave. Presses buttons.

Carrie has gone silent. Then she says, very casually, "What did you have for dinner last night, Dad? Did you try that chicken marsala I left in the freezer?"

He says, "Chicken, sure, it was great. Delicious."

Carrie pauses, and he knows he has not convinced her, and when the microwave beeps, he doesn't know how to open the door, so he stands there, pushing buttons, pulling at the door frame, muttering. He finally manages to open the microwave, pull out the coffee dregs. Take a sip. Awful.

"Hey, Dad, just thought of something," Carrie says brightly. "Do you ever do FaceTime?"

FaceTime. He knows what that is. Everyone wants to see each other these days, spy on each other, on every detail of their lives.

"Never did that," he says, clearing his throat, then coughing. "Those apps are too complicated for me." A total lie. Back in the army, he was always videoconferencing, and that was before civilians ever heard of such things. Sitting up at a conference table, wearing a pressed uniform, reporting to authority. It was his job. No way he's doing that anymore.

"You just tap the icon on your phone," she says. "The rest is automatic."

"It broke," he says. "I dropped it." May as well admit it.

"You dropped your phone?"

Anne's face cracked like a ghost caught in a spiderweb. "None of the buttons work."

"Dad." There's silence on the line. Then clicking. "I've got an extra. I'll send it to you. Be there tomorrow."

"Don't send me a phone!"

"Too late. It's on its way." Carrie says her "love you" and "bye," and clicks off without giving him a chance to argue.

That afternoon, Rand musters. He cleans out the birdcages and gets them all settled in with fresh seed, fruit, water. He makes a list for the grocery store: Coffee. Filters. Bread. His leg is acting up, and he sticks on pain patches, doses with BC powder. Pours his first bourbon of the day—*it's late enough in the day to consider a civilized drink,* Anne would say. He's dozing on the couch when another knock comes on the door. He sits up, tries putting weight on his leg, and it seems a little better. He staggers to the door, planning to ream out Bess or George or whoever the hell is interrupting his quiet. "Who is it?"

"Dad?"

Rand opens the door. "What are *you* doing here?" he says, and immediately hears what Anne would say: *Good Lord, Rand, act like you're glad to see him.*

Jeff breezes in, newspaper in hand—is that a pine needle in his hair?—his shirt filthy, and he's got a ridiculous vest on, like a fly fisherman's, with a thousand pockets, and a big grin like an eager twelve-year-old. Jeff plunks a gallon bucket of strawberries on the counter.

"Hey, did you know there's a farmers' market here on Fridays?"

"No. No, I didn't know that," Rand says. But then he remembers. *The Cutest Farmers' Market in the World. Spring Gala. Croquet.*

Jeff is picking through the bucket. "Most of these are still good," he says, as if he's admitting that his peace offering is defective. "Hey, Dad," he says, looking up with those wide blue eyes, "I got a job."

"What? Where?" Rand knows he should be saying, *That's great, son, congratulations,* but the truth is he doesn't quite believe it.

"Here," Jeff says.

What possible kind of job could this boy get in Stonehaven? Lawn mowing. Waiting on tables. "At the Bistro?"

"Not at the *Bistro,* Dad. Whatever that is." Now Jeff's unfolding the local paper on the kitchen island, pointing to a headline: *Indian Burial Found by the River.*

"That's me," he says. "I mean, I'm assisting the archaeologist. Chuck Mathers. We're setting up a dig. They found some bones."

"Well," Rand says. "This is a surprise." It's a surprise that the boy got a job and it's a big surprise that it's somewhere near here. He wonders if Jeff is getting paid anything for his new "job." It doesn't sound like more than digging ditches.

"Where exactly is this?" Rand says.

"That's the thing." Jeff's blue eyes shine with excitement. "It's right here. The developer is letting us do a test site right in Stonehaven. The flat place next to the river. We've been setting up there."

Rand blinks, unable to reconcile the man he saw today with the boy before him.

"When we get permission from the landowner, we'll check out the cliff burials, and that field across the highway next to those big pines. It's called Indigo Field."

The big pines. The abandoned field that nobody owns. It has a name. That's *mine,* Rand wants to say.

"Chuck says it could be the biggest Tuscarora find in a century." The boy's eyes shine.

"Chuck's sold you a bad pony," Rand says. "The Tuscarora are all in Upstate New York."

"That's the thing, Dad. They are now. They started out right here. They moved up there after the wars."

"What wars?"

"The Tuscarora-Yemassee Wars."

"Never heard of that."

"Twenty nations in the Carolinas besides the Cherokee." Jeff plunks down a book. *A New Voyage to Carolina,* by John Lawson. "It's all in here. It's a university press, Dad. All the sources you need."

Rand turns the book in his hands. It does say UNC Press on the spine. He sets it down. But the South has never quite been a reliable source of history. Look what they call the Civil War: *The War of Northern Aggression.*

"It's going to be huge, Dad. Just the ticket I need for grad school."

Jeff was always talking to his mother about grad school. Becoming an archaeologist. But *Christ on toast,* does he have to do it here? He can hear Anne's voice in his head: *He just needs a little encouragement. I have faith in him. You should too.*

Rand knows he should try. He picks the book up again. "I'll check it out," he says. "It's great you have a job, son."

Jeff plunks his rucksack on the couch, what he has that passes for luggage. It appears that his son needs a place to stay. It appears that his archaeology friend has loaned him a ramshackle Ford pickup and he's parked it in the driveway. He's got a bag of clothes and a bedroll, and he could use a shower.

"I just need to crash here tonight," Jeff says. "Didn't sleep at all last night. I'm not used to all the noise."

What noise? Rand wonders. "Sleep upstairs," Rand tells him. "There's a bed."

"I sleep better on a couch," Jeff says. "Don't worry, Dad, I'll be out of your hair soon as I set up a tent at the dig."

Now the boy's opening kitchen drawers. "Dad, have you got any batteries?"

"Try the junk drawer." Rand points. Too late, he remembers what's there, right on top. The dead cell phone, the cracked screen saver, Anne's face smudged and dark as if it's underwater.

Jeff picks it up. "What the—" The boy stares at his mother's ruined face. He places the cell back carefully and shuts the drawer. Looks at his dad with devastated eyes. Turns away, coughs, squares his shoulders. "I almost forgot," he says. "I saw Bess at the farmers' market yesterday.

She said somebody there gave this to her." Jeff pulls a crumpled-look-
ing envelope out of his pocket and hands it to him.

It has a penciled address: *To The General.* Is this some kind of joke?

"Bess said nobody knew of any generals here, but she thought you
would know."

"There aren't," Rand says.

"What about that friend of yours? The navy guy. Would he know?"

"He died."

"Hey, Dad, I'm sorry." The boy looks mortified.

Rand looks at the envelope again. It looks strangely familiar. The
letters are blocky and all caps. Someone has pressed down hard to make
the pencil marks. It looks like his mother's writing, on letters she would
send him. Rand folds it in half and moves to put it in the trash.

"You aren't going to read it?" Jeff says. "Hey, maybe it's for you."

The crack cuts him like a knife. No army man jokes about rank.
Rand knows this letter is not for him. But he is curious. He slips it into
his pocket. Maybe there *is* a general here. Somewhere.

Jeff sprints upstairs, two steps at a time, to take a shower. Leaves his
bags all over the living room carpet like he owns the place.

Rand changes into proper clothes, grabs the keys, heads to the store
for coffee. He'll stop by the Sunrise for a bag of sausage biscuits. More
pimiento cheese too. The boy's going to be hungry.

When he returns, Jeff is nowhere to be seen. His truck is gone. His
bedroll is still here. No note. No nothing.

Rand looks around and sees the room is still a mess, and it's his own
doing. He cleans up dead coffee cups and bourbon glasses. He takes out
the trash. Surely the boy will be back today. The kid has never missed
dinner in his life. At six-thirty, Rand pulls out one of the casseroles and
heats it up. Will it be enough? He waits, silverware and napkins set at the
kitchen table. The boy never shows. Now he starts to worry. It's raining
cats and dogs out there now. What if Jeff is in some kind of trouble?

He remembers this feeling. Teenagers. Waiting up half the night for
them. He dumps the casserole in the trash. He hates that kind of food.
The boy can fend for himself. If he ever comes home.

Jeff sits in the truck, engine cranked, heat set on high. It's fucking
pouring out there. He pulls off his soaked-through shirt and pants,

rummages in the back for a wool blanket, drapes his clothes over the vents. His dry clothes are at Dad's. He wonders if Dad even noticed he's gone. When he got out of the shower, Dad had disappeared, as if his only son wasn't even there. Maybe he was doing one of the Stonehaven widows Mom told him about. *They travel in packs,* she said, *hunting spare men.* No, even Dad, with all his crappy past, wouldn't do that, at least not so soon after Mom died. Would he?

Now that's just mean. "I know," Jeff says out loud. "I didn't really mean it."

Your dad is a little hard to get along with sometimes, Mom would say. "No kidding, Mom." It occurs to him that it's weird that he's talking out loud to his mother. But for a moment it felt like she was really sitting there beside him.

When he got back this afternoon, the site was already fucked. The rain is making it worse.

The first thing he'd seen was the tarp flapping in the breeze. Some kind of animal had dug out the corner stake. The neatly marked sections had been clawed at, artifacts scattered, his cookstove knocked over, and his pot with clumps of burned Chef Boyardee from last night scratched and chewed. There was a single paw print big enough to be a dog—or a coyote. Whatever it was, he knew he had to get it out of here.

"If you see critters around, scare them off," Chuck had told him, pointing to the pellet gun in his toolbox. "If that doesn't work, shoot 'em."

In Navajo stories, coyotes showed up at dawn and dusk and played tricks on you. This animal, apparently, came out in the middle of the afternoon. Jeff had tied the flapping tarp to a fresh stake, set about picking things up. The second worst thing to happen at a dig site is rain. Around six, the sky cracked open. Water came down in buckets, like a monsoon in Malaysia. The tarp held. But water poured off one side, ran across the dig site and into the midden-rich section. He grabbed the shovel and scraped a shallow diversion ditch as fast as he could, sending mud and artifacts shooting toward the river.

Then he crouched under the tarp, rain blowing sideways, and picked up whatever he could from the slurry at his feet, tucking bits of pots or points or whatever in his vest pockets.

Now he's been sitting in the truck for twenty minutes. This rain isn't going away. He should call his dad. Let him know he'll be stuck here for a while. But he doesn't have a phone.

Dogs and rain. *What's next,* Mom would say, *the plagues of Egypt?*

He's half dry and mostly warm when the rain stops, and the sun breaks through just in time for sunset. He steps out of the truck. The sky has gone gold-pink, with swirls of black clouds. There's a rustling in the thicket by the river. A boulder there. It shifts, rises, stands on four spindly legs. Then two small rocks rise. A mama deer and two fawns. They turn to watch him. Then they slip into the mist rising along the river.

He wonders if the critter that chewed on his cookpot is crawling up the cliff, chewing on those bones Chuck told him about. A baby in a pot. He hasn't actually seen it yet. They don't have permission. *Don't fuck this up.* But he has to go see.

The sky has gone magenta, the river is on fire with reflected light, but in the shadow of the cliff beyond it's full dark. The sand is smooth and damp under the bridge. The only tracks are some kind of bird—a heron? Jeff turns on his flashlight, slips under the bridge, and checks the wet sand beyond. Deer hooves, adult and tiny both. Then, fresh paw prints. They track along the edge, then veer into the water, as if whatever it is turned into a fish. Jeff pauses. He's about to cross the line into Widow Blake's property. That's what Chuck called her, the lady who owns this side of the highway. "The Widow Blake," Chuck said. "I'll be sending her a letter. Hope to God she gives permission."

He remembers that Chuck told him this damp soil next to the river is a no-man's-land—a state right-of-way under the bridge, and beyond that, a riparian zone, owned by the Widow Blake, but accessible by canoeists and other water users according to state regulations, "based on English common law and the edicts of Emperor Justinian," Chuck had told him, with a wry grin. "Just consider yourself a water-user," he'd said, "in the tradition of the Roman emperors." So it's okay to walk here—sort of—but not in the field above.

Jeff's flashlight beam catches on a wisp of torn yellow police tape. Where's the rest? Chuck told him the police blocked the whole area. Here are washed-out smudges that might be sneakers. Small ones. Not his or Chuck's. Somebody paused and looked around here for a while. No shovel holes. No beer cans. But right by the water the flashlight picks up fresh paw prints again. Jeff follows them until his shoes crunch on a pile of small rocks. The flashlight beam picks out arrowheads and potsherds fanned out from the base of the cliff. This is the marker. He looks up, flicks the beam along the tangle of vines and bushes above his head until he sees it: a mudslide. Above it, a shadowed indentation in the cliff wall. Look closer: a pot hollowed out like an Easter egg. The LED flashlight sparks on the spindle of ribs. A skull like an alien's face. The sacred dead. It's all still here, just like in the pictures. Then he sees that it's not just like in the pictures. No. The mudslide has gotten bigger, exposing two more pots in the cliff, one to either side. One cracked, one still intact. *Holy shit. Wait till Chuck sees this.*

When his heart stops racing, he sees that the dog prints go right into the thicket, an impenetrable mass of briars and vines. Jeff scouts around for an entry, finds none. Did the dog dig around those pots? It doesn't seem so. It looks like the rain just slid off the field and poured down the side of the cliff, washing more soil away.

Jeff retraces his steps to the truck, grabs a plastic tarp and a blanket from the stash behind the truck seat. He tucks a few cans of Vienna sausages in his vest for dinner, along with a sleeve of crackers. Then, under the protection of Emperor Justinian, Jeff lays his tarp right below the new gaping hole in the cliff. He builds a smudge fire out of pine cones and needles to keep the mosquitoes off. *Good thing Dad made me join Boy Scouts. Good thing I've got a lighter in my pocket.*

A great silence surrounds him, a silence thick with river sounds— ripples, plonks, frogs calling to their mates, pine resin crackling. Full dark now; a howl from somewhere high on the clifftop tingles his spine. Coyote? Wild dog? The crickets and frogs have gone silent. There it is again, a broken downturned note, mournful and solitary. *I know how you feel, pal,* Jeff thinks. The next howl seems to come in response to his thought, and the sound, echoing, seems to rise up into the air just above him. Jeff piles more twigs and pine needles on his fire.

He will guard the sacred dead all night from this interloper. But he wants to see just what kind of critter it is. He lays out a row of Vienna sausages from the thicket to his fire.

Just before dawn Jeff hears a scraping sound. He opens one eye. A small dog is creeping along its belly, gobbling the sausages as it goes. It's a puppy, the color of Carolina clay, with upturned ears and a curling tail. The puppy's head jerks up, stares him down with yellow eyes. Jeff stares back. The dog's eyes hold his. It flattens its belly to the ground. A growl from the back of its throat. There's one more Vienna sausage. "Shoo!" Jeff says. In a flash of bright fur, the dog turns and is gone.

It's going to be hard to scare away a hungry puppy. He doesn't want to shoot it. He's going to have to figure out another way. Maybe he can trap it. Find some kind of feral dog rescue to take it. The good news is so far it has not dug out any new bones.

New bones. He's got to call Chuck. Tell him the news. He'll go to Dad's, catch some *z*'s, use the phone. Get Chuck to drop off the field phone he promised.

Sunrise glimmers in the mist above the water. The smell of the river rises, thick and green and heavy. Birds zoom overhead, going about their important morning business. He banks the fire with sand, grabs the tarp, gets in the truck, turns the key. This is going to be so great. He hopes to God he doesn't screw it up.

18

Sunday morning early, when Rand heads to the kitchen for coffee, he finds Jeff snoring, feet hanging off the couch, mouth open, unshaven. When did his son become this giant, muscled person, with enormous feet? There's something about those bare feet that deeply annoys him, they take so much for granted, and there's something about the snoring that stirs a strange tenderness. This is his son. Whom he barely knows.

"Rise and shine," he says, thumping his son on the shoulder. God knows what he was up to last night. Jeff doesn't tell him much. Never did.

The boy groans and turns over. Rand gets out the coffee grinder. That'll get him up.

Jeff puts a couch pillow over his head.

Now the lovebirds are chattering at him. "Hang on, hang on." Rand takes their cover off, feeds them, waters them, pours his coffee. They keep talking. Louder. Maybe that will get the boy up. Rand drinks coffee and regards his son, who is now lying splayed open, his arm over his eyes. Rand hasn't watched him sleep since the boy was ten years old.

After army base American schools all over Asia, Jeff went off to boarding school at twelve, and since college, he's been home for Thanksgiving with regularity, for Christmas some years, sometimes Anne's birthday, and sometimes for a week or so in summer. But what Rand remembers is the sight of Jeff leaving. Going out to see friends. "See you later, Dad."

When Rand suggested the army, the boy blanched. Like the army was the last thing he would ever do. "It was good enough for me," Rand remembers booming. Truth is, he hated the army. It was just a way of staying alive at first. And then it was a way of keeping Anne. He was good at it—the running projects part—they needed him. But he never rose the way he'd expected to. The way Anne had expected. Poor Anne.

Jeff's still snoring. Rand sets a clean mug next to the coffee machine, heads out for his gimpy jog to see the glimmering lights in the Gooley pines in morning, his secret places about to be invaded by his son—that is, when the kid finally gets up. He walks the path that leads to a view of the field. The field has a name. *Indigo Field.* Rand squints at the flats beyond the highway. There it is: A brown tarp, staked with ropes, not sagging a bit, tied off to trees on one side. A plywood table. A neatly arranged camp. That four-square hole marked with string. Compact piles of dirt. His son's new job. He's a little bit proud. The boy seems to know what he's doing. Digging is hungry work. He'll bring back another sack of biscuits. He already threw out the others.

When Rand gets back, the tub of strawberries is still there, but Jeff's truck is gone again. There's a note:

> Sorry I had to stay on-site last night. I need to get back out there to meet Chuck. He's giving me a field phone, so here's the number if you need me. 919-555-6798. Jeff

If you need me. Does he need Jeff barging into his life, taking over the couch, leaving his things lying around? No. But there's a new hollowness in the house that can be filled only with the expectation of seeing Jeff.

Rand sits there with his bag of Sunrise biscuits and the half-eaten tub of strawberries, feeling like the air's gone out of him. Then he sees that Jeff has folded the *Ambler County Argossy* just the way Anne used to do for him with the *Times*, with a circle around the article of interest. *This is it,* Jeff has written on the paper, above a blurry black-and-white photo. A baby buried in a clay pot in a cliff. The gaping shadows that are eyes seem to be looking right at him. *Christ almighty.*

Rand slumps against the counter, shooting pains radiating like spokes from the front of his thigh. Jeff barged in, then disappeared—*where's he gone now, for Chrissake?*—his nosy neighbors, Carrie calling, Anne's face on the wall, even that haunting bone face looking at him from the faded photo in the paper, they're all crowding in, no peace possible in this place. He slips both hands in his pockets, a habit from when he was a smoker, always fishing for matches as a prelude to a smoke. There's a wad of folded-up paper. The letter. *To The General.* He slips a paring knife along one edge. Reads it. *What the goddamn hell.* It's for him.

> ...I know you live in Stonehaven Downs. When I find you, I will report you to the police. To compensate me for my lost time and worry, my suffering and my dent, you may reach me at 15 Field Road, Poolesville, NC.
>
> Sincerely, Miss Reba Jones

Her suffering and her dent! He couldn't possibly have damaged that old clunker. The woman has decided he owes her money. A knot of fear, then fury, rises in him. Somebody figured out he's from Stonehaven and decided he has a lot of money. His leg throbs. Pain and suffering. Hell, she's the one who owes him. And what the Christ is she doing calling him The General? As if she has taken a sharp stick and poked him, said, *"You'll never be a general, will you? The one thing Anne asked of you."*

He will find 15 Field Road and set this woman straight.

Rand washes his face, brushes his hair, and brushes his teeth. He shaves. He checks his leg. The swelling is strangely mottled now with yellow, green, and black. He sticks pain patches on, puts on a fresh cotton shirt, clean khakis, and black shoes. He puts the letter from Miss Reba Jones in a file folder and places it in the front seat. He wipes pollen and bird doo off his windshield. Everything spit-polished. Ready for battle.

He sits in the car, hands gripping the wheel, knot in his belly getting tighter and tighter. *What are you afraid of?* It's ridiculous. He starts the car. He passes the stone entry pillars, turns left onto Quarryville Road. Then right on Field Road. He runs across it every day. The old biddy must be down here somewhere.

There's a faded red mailbox on the left with a picture of a goat on it. Spill Creek Farm. #10. That's not it. He keeps going. But the road feels strangely familiar. The asphalt cants one way, then another, rounding corners and gentle hills. The road crosses another creek. There's another driveway on the left. A black mailbox: #15. His heart begins to pound.

He heads down a long drive toward a small brick house. He parks in the yard. There's an ancient pickup by the barn, one wheel missing, strangely shiny. Chickens pecking. No car that he can see. Is he in the right place? He turns toward the porch, sees three tall shadowy figures all in a row. Taller than him. *What the Sam Hill are they?* He looks closer. Rough-hewn faces, painted black, arms and legs carved out of tree trunks, like totem poles. Wings made of boards. One is freshly painted, with a red-lipped smile. One has an arm raised high, mouth open, faded blue eyes staring. One is faded to gray with some kind of military jacket and hat.

A breeze tickles the trees in the yard, makes a rattling sound. *Someone here?* He looks around. No.

The colonel straightens his shoulders. Sucks in his gut. He steps up to the porch, knocks on the door. He has practiced his speech: *Let's see that dent. Looks like that's been there a long time. It will be a cold day in hell when you get any money out of me.*

He knocks again. "Hello?" No answer. No one's home. Just a broom leaning up against the porch wall. No car in the yard at all. Maybe this isn't the right house. It's Sunday morning. Maybe the old biddy goes to church.

He turns and sees those crazy statues again. The light glints and shifts on the raised arm. There's a screech and a flutter of wings, the chicken flock bursts up, feathers flying, and a rooster comes charging at him across the yard, all the way up to the porch. His mama used to say, *A rooster's spurs can rip you to pieces.* He remembers one who tried, when he was five. Rand grabs the broom and fends it off as best he can. Then he leaps off the porch and runs to the safety of his car. He sits there, thigh throbbing, heart pounding. Then he puts it in gear and heads home. *First round, the old biddy.*

Rand is icing his thigh, thinking about Miss Reba, how she's somewhere out there, festering with malice against him, possibly a crazy person— those statues looked like the product of an inflamed mind—when Jeff bursts back into the house and plunks a grocery bag on the counter. "Look what the cat dragged in," Rand says, a lame attempt at Dad-humor, saying the kind of thing Anne used to say, but it falls flat.

"Yeah, Dad, I know I look like shit," Jeff says.

"Language," Rand says. Your own boy shouldn't swear in front of you. It's a sign of disrespect. What would Anne do? He's got what's left of the coffee. He could offer some. But before he can get it out of his mouth, the boy grabs the mug and pours his own. Making himself right at home.

This is *his home,* he can hear Anne saying. "No, it's not," Rand says.

"What's that, Dad?"

"Nothing." Rand watches as Jeff pulls out heavy cream, flour, buttermilk, sugar. What the hell is he up to now? Before Rand can ask, Jeff abandons his groceries on the counter, pulls off his muddy boots, sticks them next to the kitchen door, then runs upstairs for a shower, taking the steps two at a time. Then Rand hears him rooting around up there in the closet. What is he doing up there? There are going to have to be rules. *Call if you'll be late. No swearing. Mind your own business.*

The kid has drunk all the coffee. Rand dumps the grounds, makes more.

But when Jeff comes down sparkling clean, in a T-shirt that looks like it's been living in the bottom of a backpack since the Mesozoic Era, he goes straight to the lovebirds, takes them out of the cage into his hands, says, "Sweet bird, sweet bird, sweet bird." The lovebirds chirp and fluff and peck at his lips. Bird kisses. Just like Anne. It almost makes him stagger with sorrow.

"Hey, Dad," he says. "I'm going to make it up to you, all this mess. I'm making you strawberry shortcake. Your favorite, right?"

Rand stares into the open trash can. It's full of strawberries. "I threw them out."

"What the fuck, Dad?"

"Language," Rand says again, out of habit, but he's remembering the moment he decided to toss them. An enormous bucket of ripe red berries, squatting on the counter like the party Anne never had. Like an accusation. He'd stayed up half the night worrying about this boy, then he thought, *Hell, we've never really gotten along, and maybe the kid doesn't plan to stick around. He'll be out the door as soon as possible.* And his heart dragged in his chest. Just like now. "I thought you weren't coming back," he says, and he can hear the quaver in his cantankerous old voice.

Jeff comes to stand beside him. He looks into the compactor. "Gee, Dad. I think some of them are still good." And he starts picking strawberries out of the trash. Washing the coffee grounds off them, one by one. Laying them on paper towels to dry.

The shortcake is pretty good. More than good. It's so good that he wishes Anne were here, to see the sweetness of her son, making his father something good to eat. He slips another bite in his mouth. Silky whipped cream—from the health food store, Jeff said—some special kind of sugar that's a little crunchy on the berries, and sweet biscuits made with buttermilk.

As he watches Jeff fill the sink with soapy water to wash the dishes, massaging the sponge in slow circles on the plates, rinsing each plate, one by one, washing dishes exactly the way Anne used to, it's all he can do to keep from saying, *Why don't you use the dishwasher, like people in the civilized world?* Rand gets a jagged panicked feeling, almost like a heart attack coming on. He can't stand people walking into his life right now, throwing him off, breaking his heart just by washing dishes, making strawberry shortcake. He needs to go someplace to be alone, to figure out what's next, before this kid completely takes over his life, making his new healthy heart hurt in a brand-new way. *I tried, Anne. I just can't stand it.*

The boy is chatting him up now, filling the air with talk, just like the lovebirds in the morning, telling him about new bones, he found them himself, Chuck was amazed. Finally, the boy pauses. "So, what's up, Dad? Bess said you haven't been going out much."

"She doesn't know what I do." He went out this morning. She doesn't know about that, apparently.

"You're still running, right?"

"Sure. I always run."

"Carrie wants to know what you're eating."

"It's none of her business what I eat!"

"Gee, Dad, it was a joke." The boy looks hurt now.

Rand remembers an idea Anne had some months back. "A trip to the mountains," she said. "You'd love it, darling. A little like home? I'll call some places, make a plan." The North Carolina mountains are nothing like West Virginia, he told her. But mountains are a good place to be left alone. He can think away from all these interruptions. He's got to make a plan for the rest of his life, whether it's months or years, stretching to the far horizon like a ship going nowhere.

"I'm thinking of taking a trip," he says.

"A trip? Really, Dad?" The boy looks so surprised. As if his father must be too fragile to get in his car and drive.

"I still know how to drive," Rand says.

"Sure, Dad," Jeff says. "I didn't mean it that way." But he has a funny expression on his face. Like he knows Rand can't stand to be in the same room with him. *I didn't mean it that way, either,* Rand wants to say, but of course he doesn't. Because the truth is, he really can't stand it.

By noon, Jeff has gone back to his job site, out of his hair. Good.

Rand feeds the birds, recycles his empties, packs some clothes, ibuprofen, pain patches. His binoculars, cans of sardines, a cooler with bread, baloney, and pimiento cheese. Crackers, RC Colas, and bourbon. Field rations. He throws in *A New Voyage to Carolina*. He'll need something to read. He writes a note to Jeff, puts it on the counter. *Feed the birds. I took your book. Back in a few days.* He makes a list of daily duties. Then he calls Jeff on his field phone. The connection is terrible, all static.

"What?" Jeff says. "I can't hear you... *crackle crackle crackle.*" It sounds like someone is crumpling up paper and hissing into the phone. "Dad? Is that you?"

"This is your father. I'm going to the mountains for a few days."

"Where...*crackle crackle*...going?"

"The mountains, Jeff. The mountains. I told you before. Can you hear me?"

"Mountains?...*Crackle crackle crackle*...mountains? I don't get it."

"I want you to take care of the birds," Rand says.

"The birds? Is there something wrong with...*crackle, snap, pop*... Dad, are you okay?"

"I left a note on the kitchen counter," Rand says.

"Kitchen? *Crackle crackle pop*...kitchen? Dad, are you having a heart attack?"

No, he's not having a heart attack. He's going to live for twenty more goddamn years.

"I'm fine," he says. "Feed the birds."

Nothing but static now. "Hello? Jeff?" Rand hangs up. Jeff will come by for his shower, find the note, he'll know what to do. The birds will be okay for a few days if he doesn't. Jeff was never the most reliable kid.

He will drive from overlook to overlook like a tourist, smoking cigars and blowing smoke out the window. He will stay wherever he finds a Vacancy sign, drink beer and bourbon, eat fried foods and eggs for breakfast, pack a sandwich for lunch, and find places to stand and stare at mountains. Rand grew up among mountains. He figures if he stares at mountains long enough he'll know what to do. Where to go. How to live.

&

Jeff squats next to the river, watches the sun sink into the water, breathes in the dank smell of the earth beneath him, wonders if what he's hearing is the sound of plants growing.

Dad's gone, the house deserted. There was a note on the counter about how exactly to feed the birds. As if Mom hadn't taught him years ago. Why did Dad run off like that? Carrie's going to freak. He won't tell her about that call, how he thought Dad was having a heart attack, how he dropped everything, got in the truck, tore down the highway to the house. Nobody was there but the birds. There was a cardboard box, Amazon delivery, on the stoop. He put it on the counter. He went to check the cockatiels, cleaned up their cages, filled the water and seed, gave them half an orange to peck. Stood there muttering, "Fuck. Fuck. Fuck you, too, Dad," until Queen Pia muttered it back to him: *Fuck*.

Crap. He forgot how fast she learns.

Now he wonders where Dad's gone. Mountains could mean anyplace. He wonders just how depressed Dad is. There's no way of knowing. But losing somebody like Mom? So suddenly like that? He's got to be a mess. Anybody would be.

Then Jeff wonders if he's ever coming back.

19

The colonel takes an exit for the Pisgah Forest, ends up on a narrow two-lane road shaded by enormous hemlocks. He slows the car to a crawl to follow tilted hairpin turns that seem to want to shunt him off the mountain.

He stops at a sagging tourist cabin, and the owner, Mrs. Patel, shows him to his room. She tells him, in a strong immigrant accent, "Room has two beds, just use one." Rand considers the two narrow beds, with their thin blankets, as chaste and hard as army cots, and he wonders how it has come to this: A narrow bed in a musty room. A brown-skinned woman from India, hands on hips as if daring him to complain.

He sleeps fitfully, wakes to a sound, lifts his head to the open window. There it is again. Barred owl. *Who cooks for you?* A sound so lonely it makes him want to weep.

He lights a cigar and steps outside. The moon illumines a place where clouds stream upward, the nighttime exhalations of thick greenery. He watches the mist slide up one side of the mountain to a place where it flattens and curls away down the other side.

He remembers watching clouds like these for hours. His pa would find him where he'd laid down the hoe beside a row of corn. Pa said, "Idle hands is the devil's workshop." Every time Pa caught him looking at the sky like that, he beat him with a strap, until one day Rand was big enough to run away and hide where nobody could find him.

Morning rises in the North Carolina mountains bright and chill. Rand sticks a pain patch on his bruise, wraps his thigh in an Ace bandage—that seems to help—and looks around his bare-walled room, not even a picture of a mountain or a bird. There's something strangely soothing in it, in the hard bed, the thin shredding towel and washcloth. At the office, he gets a bad cup of coffee and tells the owner, "Another night." The woman nods and looks at him with suspicion, asks for cash in advance. Rand peels off some bills.

"No sheet change," she says. "My boy will straighten up."

"Sure," Rand says. The ice is behind the counter. "A bucket of ice?"

"The boy will bring."

Rand packs a lunch of cigars, RC Cola, and a baloney sandwich, and when he opens the door to head out, there's a boy, about ten years old, arms and legs like brown sticks, holding a tiny plastic baggie full of ice. "For you," the boy says in a high voice.

"Okay," Rand says. He tucks the baggie in the cooler and turns to the door. The boy is still standing there. Does he want a tip? No tip, dammit, for bringing a handful of ice that should be in a machine in the hallway.

"Mister?" the boy says.

"Colonel," Rand says.

"Colonel, you want a guide? A mountain guide? I know many places."

"No thanks," Rand says. *Jesus H. Christ*, the last thing he wants is company.

"I have a map," the boy says. His big eyes liquid and brown. His spindly arms hang out of an enormous T-shirt. For a moment, the kid reminds him of his big brother Decker, when they were boys, wearing hand-me-down clothes way too big for them, running through the woods, sunburnt and scraped by briars.

The boy is watching him with pleading eyes.

"Let's see that map," Rand says.

The boy pulls it out of his back pocket, unfolds it, points to something. "This," he says, "goes to the top of the mountain."

Rand looks around. He doesn't see a trail anywhere. "I'll show you," the boy says. He gestures with his arm. "Come with me." He leads Rand across the parking lot to a place where the dirt shows through the grass, a trail leading into the woods.

"You need the map," the boy says.

Ah, so that's his game. "How much?"

"Five dollars."

"How about one dollar now, the rest when I make it home." For all he knows, the boy could be leading him into a den of thieves, or off a cliff.

"Kamil!" The boy's mother's voice calling from across the parking lot. "Come here now."

The boy dashes away, no dollars at all in his pocket. Rand turns the map in his hands. It's a topo map, with every detail marked. Here's where the road is. The highway. The cabin. The trail. Someone has marked five *x*'s on it. Five trails. Five mountains. It's a good map. He folds it up and puts it in his pocket.

As he walks, the thick cool air floods his lungs and heart like a second chance. He remembers running in hills like this with Decker. Making owl calls, cougar calls, and their own special signal, owl-cougar-hawk-bobcat-chicken.

"Do it without laughing," Decker told him.

Rand never could. He stops and tries it now, cupping his hands around his mouth. "Hoo-hoo-hoo. Rrrroooow. Kee-oh-ree. Screeeeeem. Squawk buck buck buck." Well. Turns out it can be done. "I win," Rand says.

Kee-oh-ree! A hawk calls back to him. He can't see it for all the trees.

The trail gets steep. He keeps walking.

Finally he steps, panting, thigh aching, into a grassy clearing. The sky expands overhead, a blue bowl. Stunted trees and enormous rocks cast shadows on the grass. He checks the map in his pocket for the first X. He's here, "Up Top." Decker's name for the wide field of grasses and huckleberry at the peak of their mountain, the place where they would go to look at blue sky and clouds passing overhead, away from Pa's angry voice, his strap.

Rand wonders what the boy with the map comes here for.

Rand walks to the highest spot, tests the grass—dry—lies down under the silvery gray snag of an enormous dead tree. He spreads his arms wide on the warm dry grass and watches the clouds flow through dead branches for hours, and nobody comes to tell him not to.

Something tickles his ear. Just like Decker poking him with foxtail grass. Maybe that kid followed him. Rand opens his eyes, sits up. No kid. No Decker. Just a patch of shooter weed. He pinches one off, twists the stem into a loop, and pops the top like a small missile. Three-foot firing range. Not bad. He and Decker used to have entire wars based on these weeds, and on bombing each other with sticky burdock seed pods.

Rand inspects the smooth trunk of the dead tree. Bark long gone. Texture under his fingers like rippling muscles. Like Decker's "brother trees" back home—two old chestnuts, long since struck by blight, bark stripped off by wind, one leaning, caught in the branches of the other.

"See?" Decker would say. "One holds the other up. Like brothers." He would put his arm around Rand's shoulders, and that skinny warm grip made Rand feel rooted in the ground. Like the two of them were trees and would always be trees, alive and growing toward the sky. Then Decker would hook his foot around Rand's, lean and push against him, and Rand would push back, to see who could get the other to fall over first. Decker always won, though sometimes he pretended for a while that Rand could beat him.

Sometimes they clambered up the leaning tree to the standing tree, climbing as high as they could go, looking out on ridge after blue-green ridge, and imagining they saw castles and kingdoms glimmering in the far distance. One day Rand climbed the highest and turned to say, "I won!" But Decker wasn't looking at him. He was poking at a small branch that still sprouted green leaves. "Look," his brother said. "The heart is still alive."

In that tree they felt free of the way Pa looked when he came back from the mine—blackened and red-eyed, stooped and weak, and the way Ma looked when she saw him: anxious and wondering if he had brought home his pay, or if it had all gone to the white liquor jar concealed in a brown paper bag held close to his chest like a gift he had no plans to give away. Rand's heart twinges with the memory: Pa died in the Bartley Mine.

Decker ran off to join the army, leaving Rand to figure out how to feed his mother on a patch of corn and some cabbages. Rand was eleven. About the size of the boy back at the motel. He remembers being hungry. He remembers being so hungry his stomach was tight and hard as bone.

It's only ten-thirty, but Rand pulls out his lunch, unwraps his sandwich. Wolfs it down. He drinks his RC Cola. Saves the cigar for later. He's still hungry.

In his room, Rand wolfs down crackers and cheese, unwraps his leg, checks the bruise: it's got a purple-black edge to it now, shaped like a giant eggplant. He pops some ibuprofen, checks the ice—melted—and pours a short one. He picks up Jeff's book, *A New Voyage to Carolina*, flips around, starts reading. The Tuscarora were indeed in the Carolinas. Plus the Sewee, the Cheraw, the Eno, the Saponi, the Waxhaw, the Croatoan, the Hatteras, it goes on and on, with this young Lawson fellow describing every turn like a paperback novel—lightning, floods, panthers in the woods, funerals with much wailing, and the stripping of flesh off the bones of the dead. The man came to Carolina during a golden age for birds: *The Parrakeetos are of a green Colour, and Orange-Colour'd half way their Head.* It's extraordinary. So that's what Jeff is working on. Rand wishes he were here so he could ask him more about it.

When Kamil brings him his ice that evening, it is a full gallon bag of square cubes, as if made in an old-fashioned ice tray. "Where did you get these?" Rand says.

"I made them for you by myself," Kamil says. "And I brought you a magazine."

The kid is really buttering him up. The kid likes cash. He gives him the five dollars he owes, and an extra dollar fifty for the ice. "Good map," he says.

"Take me with you tomorrow," the boy says. "You need a guide."

"Your mother needs you, Kamil. And besides, I have your map." The boy looks like he's about to cry. His mother must work him hard. "Listen, kid," he says. "Hard work is what makes you a man."

The kid scowls. "A man like you? A man who is all alone?" A mean tone has come into his voice.

"That's enough," Rand says. "You can go now."

After he's gone, Rand flips through the magazine. It's an ancient copy of *Cosmopolitan*. Ridiculous tests about how to please your man. Ridiculous advice about taking care of your complexion. Anne never read those magazines. She was more of a *Ladies Home Journal* gal.

Now here's a story: *Five Ways To Be Happy!* He scans to number one. *Close your eyes. Think of a time when you were happy as a child.* With Decker. Running on the top of that mountain. Look how that turned out. Rand scans to the end: *5. When's the last time you were really really happy. So happy you could shout for joy?*

Was he ever so happy he could shout for joy? He can't think of a time. He closes his eyes. *Thick jungle splashes shade and light. Birds call from giant trees. Zara, her big dark eyes gleaming back at him. Her even white teeth, her wide smile. Her shoulder touches his, round and strong and smelling faintly of curry. She is pointing to something. Something so beautiful it makes him cry out,* "Jesus Christ, is that it?" *It can't be. But it is.*

20

It is not quite daylight when a hot tongue wraps around Jeff's fingers, still greasy with Vienna sausages. *What the fuck?* He cracks one eye. The puppy is licking him.

All the bait he put out next to the river last night is gone. The pup makes a move toward the almost-empty Vienna sausage can, and Jeff snags it by the scruff of the neck. Needle teeth in his thumb. *Shit shit shit.* He traps the pup in his sleeping bag, extracts his hand, and stares at the wound, pinpricks of blood in a half circle. *Dumb* shit. The thing could have distemper, or rabies. He sucks the blood out, spits, wipes it on his jeans, all the while keeping the pup squirming, whining, inside his sleeping bag.

Jeff fishes into the Vienna sausage can, pulls one out, holds it in front of the wriggling lump, releases the lump. The pup sticks its head out, seizes the sausage, and wolfs it down, looks around for more. Jeff doles out small pieces, lets the pup eat until its tummy is distended and it falls into a doze.

The pup's skin is loose on its bones, ribs sharp under his fingers. He names the puppy Usen, after the Apache god Noah Benson told him about. A god who lives in the sky. Because this pup came out of the blue. Where is its mother? *"O ha le,* Usen," he sings. *"O ha le."* He rubs the pup's belly. The pup groans contentedly. Jeff checks. It's a boy. No fleas.

Jeff remembers reading, in the stack Chuck left for him, something about a breed of dog that lived with Native Americans in the Southeast. Curled tail. Up ears. Yellow-red. Like this one. Maybe this is a descendant of that breed. A "Carolina dog." He wonders, belatedly, whether the local Tuscarora spirits will take kindly to a pup named for an Apache. The pup opens one eye. Bares his tiny teeth.

Jeff washes up with the hose from the water tank in the back of the truck, ties a length of clothesline around Usen's neck, and surveys the day. Light floods the Field through new leaves, and a piney breeze freshens the world. It's a good day to dig. He slips on his heavy gloves. Usen helps him scrape loose earth from a square yard of subsoil. Jeff piles it into buckets. He heaps the soil gently onto the screen he's made with hardware cloth and mosquito netting. Turns the hose nozzle on, rinses the silty earth away. Small rocks. Pieces of turtle shell. Nothing much. On the third section, Usen noses a spot, and Jeff finds a bumpy layer of potsherds and clay pipe fragments. He scrapes them gently into a bucket, feels something hard and rounded underneath. He leans back to let more light in.

Sunlight sparks on a small unbroken pot, still half buried. The pup yips and settles on his hind legs. "How'd you know?" Jeff says. Jeff loosens the earth around it with a dental pick, then brushes the soil back carefully. He steps away to get the measuring tape. When he turns back, Usen has dug all around the pot and is trying to drag it away with his teeth. "No, Usen!" Usen sits. Jeff measures. Then he lifts the pot carefully, shakes it gently. A rattling sound. Seeds.

Chuck had told about a site where a farmer plowed over a cache of Cherokee pots filled with squash seeds. The farmer planted them on the remote chance that the seeds were still viable. They grew like crazy, produced enormous orange squash. "Candy roaster." That's what they named it. Chuck didn't know the native name.

Jeff holds the pot close to his chest, pulls a survey flag from his back pocket and marks the spot. He needs a camera. He needs a cell phone to mark GPS. No cell phone. No camera. Usen bites and snaps at the flag and tries to pull it out. "No, Usen." He grabs the dog by the nape, it wiggles and scratches like a rabbit caught by a hawk. Jeff drops the pot. It cracks from top to bottom but holds together. The pup sits. Looks at him with round eyes, grinning. It takes Jeff a minute to see it: The pup is humped and straining. Pooping in the hole. Then he noses loose sand on top. *Fuck*. So much for science. He can't keep a dog here, even if he is a Carolina dog. He'll have to find him a home. He saw a vet's place in town. Maybe they do rescue. He's got to run into town anyway for supplies. *Don't fuck this up.*

Jeff calls Usen to get in the truck—the pup has already learned his name—but Usen veers off and runs into the culvert under the bridge, then into the thicket, and up into Widow Blake's field. When the pup comes back, he's got a bone piece in his mouth—what might be Kentucky Fried Chicken and might be a human finger bone. *Jesus H. Christ.* Jeff spends twenty minutes fruitlessly searching along the riverbank for where the pup might have made his discovery. All the pot burials along the cliff seem undisturbed. He stops at the edge of Indigo Field. Could there be a disturbed grave in this field? He can't go there to find out. They still don't have permission.

Back at the truck, he slips the bone into a Ziploc, marks the date, tucks it in the glovebox for safekeeping.

He can't pretend it didn't happen. It could be what Chuck calls "the keystone find." The thing that makes sense of all the other things. The thing that pulls it together. Chuck had been so excited when he showed him the new bones. "You're going to get your name on my paper," he said. "You deserve it. If I don't hear from the Widow Blake this week, I'm going to track her down and charm it out of her. We've got to document this before it all washes away."

Usen sits beside him now in the truck, sniffing at the glove box and grinning. "You're awfully proud of yourself, aren't you?" Jeff can't be sure, but he thinks the puppy nodded.

The cool thing about little towns like Quarryville, Jeff thinks, is that you can walk into almost any place and they will talk to you as if you were a long-lost cousin, even if you are a complete stranger. That hadn't happened much in New York, or California, or New Mexico. Maybe this is what his mom liked so much about the place. The downside is that everywhere he goes, they already seem to know who he is and exactly what he's up to. Jeff has been trying to keep things cool, stay under cover, like Chuck Mathers said to. "If they ask you questions, just nod and say, 'Yes, ma'am.' Then shut up." But word's gotten around.

"Mister Injun Digger," says the man at Sunrise Gas N Grill, where he gets cigarettes and Slim Jims. "You dig anything good yet?" Jeff only smiles. The man points at the Slim Jims. "Those for you or him?" Usen barks and wags.

"You want a dog?" Jeff says. "He'd like it here."

"Nope."

At the Cedar River Diner, the waitress pours his coffee-to-go with cream and sugar, the way he likes it. "Hey, how's it going with those bones, hon? What a cute pup!"

"You want him?" Jeff says.

"Already got three."

Then at the dump, the man waves him in, says, "Mornin', chief." Jeff wonders if it's a little joke—like since he's digging them up, he must be one of them. But how does the man know? At the side of the recycle hut, there's a lady with a box of puppies she's trying to give away. He wonders if she'd mind taking one more. But no. He wants to personally know whoever takes the little guy. He might be a Carolina dog.

After picking up more tarps at Quarryville Feed & Seed, he pulls in at Quarry Large and Small Animal Clinic. The girl behind the counter says, "Rescue Clinic is Friday. But we do shots." She pulls a syringe out of a packet, a vial out of a small fridge, and next thing he knows, he's got a rabies tag. *They let secretaries give the shots here?* He knows the South is behind the times, but this is weird. She hands him her card. *Joyce Locklear, DVM.*

"Oh, I know what you're thinking," she says. "She's too young and *pretty* to be a vet. Hmmm?" She raises an eyebrow at him.

"No, ma'am," he says, "I mean, I didn't think that, but, I mean—" *Busted.*

"Where'd you get this dog?" She's pulling Usen's tail up, letting it spring back into a curl. She's checking his teeth.

"He's a stray."

"But I mean, where did you find it?"

"By the river." Chuck will have his hide if he tells the whole story. *I'll let you know when we can go public,* he said.

"This is a special dog," she says. She examines Usen's ears and under-belly, his dewclaws and paws. She pulls a collar off a rack. "Free collar for any rescue. You've got to keep the tag on a collar." The collar is pink and sparkly. "Sorry," she says, "that's all I have in his size."

Now would be the time to tell her Usen is not a rescue, he's a nuisance, and does she know anyone who will take him *now*? But she's taking in his T-shirt—University of New Mexico Archaeology Team, *oops,* no wonder everyone in town knows who he is—and starts talking about the Tuscarora who lived in Indigo Field, but really they were Lumbee, and Lumbee people are the kind who let in just about anybody—runaway slaves, moonshiners, and even Cheraw. "Of course some say they're connected to the Raleigh colony, but that seems a stretch to me."

What the hell is she talking about? When he tells her Usen's name for the rabies form, she makes a crack about Geronimo. How in the world does *she* know the connection? Is she in an anthropology program?

"Are you a…historian?" he says.

"I'm a Lumbee," she says.

"Wow." He doesn't know what Lumbee are, but clearly they are a nation. *You don't look Indian,* he wants to say, but that is the number one stupid thing to say, he knows that much.

"You're not from around here, are you?" Her round blue-green eyes ready for him to spill. Jeff can't help it. He tells her his cover story: Yes, he isn't from around here, his mom just died and he's helping his dad out. Over in Stonehaven.

"Stonehaven, right. I am so sorry about your mama," she says, shaking her head. "I know what it's like when your mama dies." Suddenly he wants to tell her everything—how his dad has gone off somewhere, and how unfair it is Mom died without any warning, as if struck by lightning in the middle of a clear day, how much he misses her voice on the phone, her steady, husky voice. He misses Mom's stringy, tennis-muscled arms wrapped around him, her short frosted hair tucked just under his chin, smelling like lemons. Her cornflower-blue eyes that looked at him and saw something he never quite could see: a young man full of promise.

Jeff takes the rabies tag, tucks Usen into his vest.

"Here," the lady says, handing him a crinkly bag. "Free treats with each shot." She tucks a flyer in his hand. "And get that hand looked at. Immediately."

"Thanks." It isn't until he's sitting in the truck that he realizes he never asked her about finding a home for Usen. Rescue clinic on Friday. Maybe he'll come back.

Usen noses at the crinkly bag of treats, the flyer in Jeff's hand. Jeff tosses him a treat and opens the flyer: Carolina Dog Breeding Association. The picture looks just like Usen.

Maybe this vet knows the secret story of Indigo Field and will tell it to him. He tucks her card in his inside vest pocket with the flyer. He examines his thumb. The puppy bite is red and swelling. Sore. *Crap.* He sits in his truck for a minute, breathing. Remembering Mom. The small hot body of the puppy feels like a second heart, pressed against his chest.

21

In three days, Rand has limped up three mountains, thinking of nothing except the sky, losing all sense of time. Every night he eats a guilty greasy burger at the diner next to the motel. He sips bourbon in his room and thinks about calling Jeff and Carrie to check in. But the phone in his room is turned off. When he asked her to turn it on, Mrs. Patel said, "You don't have a cell?" The woman looked at him with deep suspicion. As if she knew that he's the kind of person who runs away from trouble, who ran away from the searing eyes of his dead wife over the mantel, eyes that seemed to be burning his skin off, layer by layer, to see into his faithless heart.

Anne never knew the work he did all those years. He wasn't allowed to tell. Special projects in Germany, then Fort Barry, California, where he first learned about the rough tangle of Nike Missile sites in the Bay area—a tangle that was only the newest iteration of centuries of battlements along Pacific cliffs, going back to the Civil War. Finally, by the time he was in Malaysia, Salt II had happened and the job was to decommission the missile sites, take apart the missiles, and store the nuclear material in places where it would be safe. It was dangerous work. Secret work. If the Russians knew how many damn missiles they had pointing in their direction. If China knew. Well, maybe they did know. But he couldn't tell Anne about it. "Dammit, Anne," he says. A wife should have known. But he was honor bound. And for a social butterfly like her, the secrets would out, no matter all her good intentions. They told him to tell her he was in charge of ordering base supplies. Not very heroic.

Oh, she was loyal, said things like, "He's the one makes sure we all have food to eat, clothes on our backs, and bourbon or beer, thank God," her smile bright and cheery. "My hero." *But I* am *a hero,* he wanted to say to her, *I'm saving the world. I'm saving you.*

He could not stand the whiff of disappointment in her eyes, her wry accommodation of his mediocrity. So every weekend, he ran off with Peet, his driver, chasing after rumors of tropical bird sightings in the high places. Peet had high ambitions to build a hotel for foreigners who loved birds. He chatted away as he drove, confiding that he knew of a secret place where paradise birds lived and bred, a bird that didn't belong here. That's how he met Zara. Peet's niece. A beautiful, strong, warm-skinned girl who looked at him with shining hope. Another thing he could never explain to Anne. But now, even more than when Anne was alive, she seems to require an explanation.

I was lonely. I was stupid. I was already living without you.

The boy, Kamil, brings him bags of ice twice a day now. Rand tips him two dollars a bag. The boy comes, stands in the doorway, says things like, "You like my mountains?"

Where did this boy get the idea these were *his* mountains? Little runt. But truth to tell, Rand kind of likes the kid's larcenous impulses, his grandiosity. *His* mountains.

"Sure," Rand tells him. "There's another two dollars in it if you bring me a better towel."

A couple of times, Rand has been dozing in his bed, window open, and the scolding voice of Kamil's mother, and the piping voice of Kamil, the smell of curry spice and oil, bring a flash of memory, a face and a place very far away, Malaysia. He dwells there in a dreamlike state, allowing imagination to converge with memories that have been tamped down, shut out, pushed away for years. *Birdcall, wild parrots. Stormy rush of monsoon. Children laughing, splashing puddles, a village on the side of a mountain, up a red mud road. A warm brown face, a young woman's face full of laughter and confidence. A face that believed in him. A face he has not allowed himself to remember when sending his airmail letter, not until last week. Anne wouldn't like it. Now it comes back in full flood.*

When he wakes from these drowsing moments, his dick has swelled against his thigh, half mast. There is no painting of his wife in this barely furnished room. Her voice has gone completely out of his head. In its place is Zara. He finishes off in the bathroom, door closed, locked, in case that nosy kid barges in.

When he's done, showered and shaved, and poured a drink with Kamil's ice cubes, it hits him: The child would be about the same age as Kamil by now. Maybe a little older.

On Thursday, Rand unwraps the Ace bandage around his thigh and sees his bruise is changing again. Strange red and pink and yellow streaks have spread out from a center that has now turned an angry blue-green. He is sore all over, scrapes and bug bites, and the tendons in the backs

of his legs feel like tight rubber bands about to snap. He's not moun-
tain-hard the way he was as a kid. He remembers a Bible quote his ma
would recite while nursing him after a tumble or scrape: *From the sole of
the foot even unto the head there is no soundness in it; but wounds, and bruises, and
putrifying sores: they have not been closed, neither bound up, neither mollified with
ointment.* "See now?" she'd say, and laugh. "You're fixed. The Bible ain't
right about that part, anyway." Rand slaps on more pain patches and
rewraps the Ace bandage.

He still has no idea what to do with the rest of his life.

Kamil comes with his ice and his good towel. "Two dollars," Rand
says, counting out the bills.

"Four!" Kamil protests.

"Three-fifty," Rand says, just to see what he'll do. The boy sulks.
Rand gives him the full four.

"Take me with you," Kamil says, as he does now every day.

"You belong here," Rand says, "with your mother." And of course
that's true, but part of him wishes those skinny brown legs could run
up the trail before him, that happy young voice shouting with the joy
of boyhood.

The boy has finally confessed where the map came from. A hiker
and journalist had come to hike five mountain trails, take photos of all
of them, for an article for a famous magazine. "He left his map," Kamil
said. "I have never even been to those places, except for this one." He
pointed to the trail at the far end of the parking lot. "My mother did not
like that I was gone so long."

"I guess not," Rand said.

Rand packs a lunch, gets in the car, and heads to the fourth of five
mountains. Halfway there, he pulls in at an overlook to take a leak. He's
just settled into it, next to a tall shrub, when a Subaru pulls in and two
peppy birders clamber out with scopes and tripods, floppy hats and
pocket shorts. They set up in a rush, point and exclaim at something he
can't see. He zips, walks over.

"Peregrines," the lady says, pushing her spectacles up on her nose.

"Courting," the man says, leaned into his scope, adjusting.

"They were here last year," the lady explains. "But they never come
this late. Everybody thought they'd lost their way."

Now three other cars pull up, pocket-pantsed birders pile out and
set up, and the man begins to lecture: "Peregrine means 'wanderer,'
and these birds are known to travel fifteen thousand miles in migration

during the year. They mate for life. Frieda and Jesus have been returning here to nest for three years. This year we thought they'd been poisoned or lost. But finally, here they are. We're seeing more of this. Just as the population has begun to thrive, migration patterns, courting seasons have become disrupted. We suspect some aspect of climate change. Perhaps the fact that prevailing winds have shifted during the spring and fall, not providing the loft and speed they're used to."

Another messed-up bird migration. Rand knows about those.

"There's another pair courting on Bennett Mountain," the lady tells him. "I can draw you a map. But you'll have to walk a ways."

He takes the map. He wants to see the birds.

Rand lies prone on a rock outcropping, binoculars focused, and he can see it all. The dips and lifts, the crosswind zooms. Light as air. The peregrine lands on a ledge just below him. There's a female there. The male bows and screeches. The female bows and screeches. They peck and screech and it's so loud and annoying that Rand presses his thumbs over his ears. So this is how they court. He prefers the human methods—officers club dances and women in silk dresses. Anne in blue. And just like that, Anne's rosy shoulders, freckled face, deep blue eyes are there, just as if he's staring at her portrait in the living room.

The female pecks the male and he tumbles off the ledge, starts looping and zooming again. The bird just can't help himself.

On his way down Bennett Mountain, it starts to rain. The radio picks up a scratchy country station, a woman's voice, a high lonesome sound, cutting in and out where the mountains block the signal. *I'm just a poor… wayfaring stranger / Traveling through…this world of woe….* Anne used to sing that to him when he got the blues at a new posting. She knew he loved the travel, and also hated getting used to a new home. Where she got the song, he had no idea. It was his mother's favorite. It wasn't the kind of thing Radcliffe girls learned growing up.

The song turns into crackling and hiss. Rand's just about to turn it off when the voice comes in high and clear through the crackle:

I'm going home to see my mother. She said she'd meet me when I come. I'm only going over Jordan. I'm only going over home.

His legs go weak, and he can barely press on the gas. He pulls over on a narrow ledge, sets the brake, and lets the sadness roll over him like dark water. His mother, skinny and bent over, grubbing in the cold for creasy greens. Dandelion greens. Something to eat to fill their bellies. Rain pounds his car roof and slides down the windows, making the world a green smear.

He pulls out the bourbon and takes a swig. All these days he's been emptying his mind, letting go of his life, letting go of a future with Anne, and now he remembers all the things he never wanted Anne to know. That winter he and Ma ate seed corn, and drank jars of white liquor sweetened with elderberry jelly, their only sustenance in a four-day blow. They huddled together under every quilt they had, and three cats too. Two cats froze. Ma got drunk and told him stories of birds—the ones she called The Wandering Souls: warblers and snow geese, woodcocks and swans. And the ones that stayed the winter: cardinals and finches, towhees and robins, hawks and owls. She told him all about the print of the tropical bird on the bedroom wall, set in a thin bamboo frame. "Ma gave me that," she said. "It's a bird of paradise. See how he does his tail like that? It's a love dance. Showing off for his girl."

The bird had a tail like a golden fountain over its head, a green throat and yellow eyes, and rust-red wings halfway spread, as if about to fly. Ma told him it was from far-off Asia, and there was only just a few birds like this, on a special island where no white man went. Tucked under quilts and shivering, her arms around him, Ma vowed that if she ever got off this mountain, she'd find a place where tropical birds of all kinds and colors lived, and she would live with them, and eat goat milk and honey, like in the Bible. Rand felt the same.

She slept for a time. Rand looked at her lined face, the veins in her eyelids, as she slept, barely breathing. He wondered if Ma was telling these stories because she wouldn't get another chance. They were going to die.

When she woke, Ma's voice had turned into a silvery whisper, like the ice outside was seeping into her throat. She was fading. But she kept telling stories. She told him of her courting days with Pa. Told him of her wedding dress, lace arms and throat, pearl beads at the bodice. Her parents were respectable town people who shunned her when she married a miner. "My pa hated your father so much. But he sends us that ham every Christmas," she told him. "Only way I know Ma's still alive."

Rand always thought his own pa bought that ham. He hadn't wondered why it kept coming after Pa got kilt. How he wanted a mouthful of salty ham right then, cold seeping into his bones, his hungry stomach a hollow place that felt fragile, like an empty eggshell. His ma had fallen silent. Was she breathing? Rand could feel his strength slipping away. Surely Decker, if he ever came home, would find them curled up and frozen solid, being pecked apart by crows.

A poison rose in Rand's half-frozen heart against his brother that night, kindling like a small green fire, flaring up from time to time, then banked and waiting like those coal-mine fires deep in the ground. *You left Ma and me alone. You left us to die.*

He and Ma woke to sunshine and ice dripping, still alive, still hungry, but now with blinding hangover headaches. The squirrels and birds seemed to have all blown away in the storm. There was nothing to shoot. Rand went out on the stoop, down into the cornfield, and pulled some left-behind short ears with a few kernels to chew on. He knew then it was either go into the mines, become one of those black-grimed, red-eyed boys who planned to die young, or go ask his ma's people for more than an annual ham.

The sun shone so hard that day, it thawed the ice, and the air became balmy over the chill. The day after the weather cleared, he told Ma he had to go to town, barter for supplies. He hitched a ride on a timber truck, and the man gave him a cigarette. Taught him how to smoke. At first the cigarette made him sick. But then he noticed the raw emptiness in his belly had soothed. He wished he had another one.

Rand knew he had to spruce up to visit his ma's people. He'd never met them before. It was a sunny, windy day. When he got to the outskirts of town, there were shirts on the line in every backyard. He plucked one off and ran and ran, sure he'd be shot. But he wasn't. He put the shirt on. Tucked it in. Went looking for his grandpa. He knew his last name. That was about it. He asked around. Someone pointed the way.

When he finally stood at their front door and blurted out his name, the lady looked at him. Called out, "Raaan-dolph." He hadn't known he was named for his grandpa.

"Want yer ham early this year, that it?" An old man stood before him, red-haired and freckled. Blue eyes searing. Face red as a boiled tomato.

"Pa died," Rand said. If they hated Pa so much, that would surely make them happy.

"Drunk hisself to death, I reckon."

"No, sir. No, sir. It was the Bartley Mine." He stood up straighter. A mountain killed his pa. Not drink.

"Reckon the drink softened the blow."

His grandpa was trying to make him mad. Just like Decker used to. Hoping he would blow up, so he could kick him off the stoop. But Rand had practice holding it in.

"Your pa was a hard man," Grandpa said. "Well, I'm a hard man too. Tell your ma she can come home. But spawn of that man ain't welcome here." The man put an enormous cured ham on the stoop, stepped back, and shut the door in his face. In the crack before it shut, he saw the frantic eyes of his grandma, wanting him, wanting something. But her husband was a hard man.

Rand slept in the rain that night, under the big rhodie where he'd stashed his ragged overcoat. Somebody had nipped it. It was only fair.

He went home and stood before his mother, in the wrong shirt and no overcoat, and told her they wanted her there more than anything. He wanted to stay here and keep the farm running. Ma looked at him, her lower lip curled under, the way it did when she knew something you weren't telling. "I got no reason to leave this mountain for that miserable little town. I'm a-staying."

They ate creasy greens that night, with big slabs of ham. The ice had brought out the greens in the corn patch. Ma said they were a gift from God. With every bite of ham Rand could taste the bitterness in his grandfather's eyes. But he ate it. They had food to last for a while, through the hard season of early spring. When they finished dinner that first night, though, they both went out on the porch and were sick. Their stomachs weren't used to food.

Rand learned to trade. He traded a chunk of the ham for cornmeal. He chopped wood for seeds. Fixed a roof for a couple of jars of snap beans. Repaired a shed for seed potatoes and onions. When frost cleared the field, he planted his potatoes and onions, then corn and beans and squash and okra. Ma picked and canned and stored things away in the root cellar with the vengeance of someone who would never be hungry again if she could help it. But Rand knew they'd never make it through another winter without money. Over the summer he chopped enough firewood to last, sold part of his corn crop to man with a still, and bought a broken-down donkey and cart Ma could take into town. All that time he kept thinking his brother might send word, send money, send something to help them hang on. But one day he knew his brother wasn't coming. He made a plan to leave too. It was the only way.

He was way too little to lie his way into the army the way Decker had planned to. He had to find more work. Rand made a bundle with an extra shirt, a scrap of blanket, his pa's hat and knife, and left one morning before Ma was up. He wrote a note for her, said he would send money when he got his pay. He would let her know where to write to him.

He spent four years wandering from town to town, doing odd jobs, sending money, learning that the poorest people will feed you, the uppity ones like his grandpa will turn you away. When Ma wrote him that Decker was back, that his brother had been in jail all that time, Rand sent Ma all his money and went and joined the army.

Years later, when he and Anne were in Malaysia, he got a letter. Ma had died in a house fire. Decker buried her on the mountainside.

Rand could have gotten home leave. "We should go," Anne said. But he didn't want to. He couldn't stand to see the human wreck that was his brother.

Rand's belly fills again with the slow green fire of bitterness. And twisting around it like greenbriar, this thought: *If I'd stayed, I could have saved Ma. If I'd been with Anne that day, I might could have saved her.* He closes his eyes and sees what he's seen every day since that terrible morning: *Anne stands on the tennis court, sways, drops her racket, sinks to her knees. Falls to the side, knees skinned, hair wild, tennis dress askew. Mouth open. Not breathing. Blue eyes staring.*

He shudders, gulps breath, gulps water, rests his head on the steering wheel. He's got to rid himself of these awful imaginings. He must do what he did when he left Ma and those West Virginia hills behind. He must cast his thoughts of Anne into darkness, like a mine collapsing into dust over the bodies of living people.

Rand wakes in his motel room with a plan. He rises from his narrow bed, stretches, goes to the door, opens it. The cool mist of mountain night fills his lungs. A barred owl calls, then another. He walks to the near edge of the parking lot, where the land falls away into misty valleys. He feels an excitement like electric current pulsing in his heart. Anne's voice has come back to him, giving clear instruction: *Time to write your bird book, dear.*

Uncommon Bird Migrations. The boxes of notes, the maps of travels, the discoveries—African parrots were in Rome. Rose-ringed parakeets were in London. The paradise bird, the bird who'd lived only in New Guinea, was in Malaysia now. He'd seen it with his own eyes. He could do it. He's got value in the house. He's got a pension, a payout from Anne's life insurance, some stocks he cashed out, setting up for his own demise. He could sell the house and do what he's always wanted to do, what he gave up when Anne decided she wanted to settle in Stonehaven. He could travel the world, track down that elusive bird of paradise again, the one Zara showed him, defying all of the theories of the experts.

He can see it like a battle plan on a gigantic war-room map, with pins in it: He'll fly to LA, visit Carrie there. He'll zip up to San Francisco, visit the wild parrot colony there as a kind of send-off—yet another surprising place for tropical birds. He'd discovered them one day on a challenge run across the Golden Gate, to the Ferry, then looping back to the Presidio. One, then six, then fifty rose up from the giant eucalyptus grove there and began to zoom over his head. It was as if the jungle had traveled thousands of miles and settled like a feathery cape over his shoulders. Such screeching life! Such articulation of the air, such strange animation of a misty American hillside.

The thought of that rowdy flock of bad boys makes Rand rise up on his toes on a rock ledge and breathe deep, flooded with freedom and purpose. He will go to Papua New Guinea. Australia. Indonesia. Then, back to Malaysia. Every place on the long list in his notes. He might even track down Peet, his excellent guide and driver. Maybe stay in Peet's Birdland Hotel, the man's dream of a tourist attraction, just a pile of cinderblocks and a bamboo cage of birds last Rand saw it. Maybe Peet's finished it by now. He will travel to places he's been, and places he's never been, because he can't stand to be where he is now.

Rand remembers the feeling of leaving it all behind, Zara and the baby. The deep, frozen sadness, Anne's orders: no contact. Above him now, the leaves dance and sway in the dark, like an invitation to rise and fly. *Maybe you'll see the boy in Malaysia.* His heart swells with the surprise of hope, like sun after an ice storm.

That night, Rand persuades Mrs. Patel to let him use the desk phone by giving her ten dollars. Exorbitant. The woman must be making a fortune off this place.

Carrie doesn't answer. He leaves a message. When he hangs up, turns out Kamil has been eavesdropping. The boy follows him back to his room.

"Why do you leave us, Colonel?" he says.

"Not leaving yet," he says. "I've got one more mountain to climb tomorrow. Remember?" He holds the map up, points.

"My mother will be sad."

"Oh, she'll find another tourist," he says. There is no love lost between him and Mrs. Patel.

"Where are you going?"

"Home, my boy," he says. "Then, to faraway places." Saying it out loud makes it real. He can't wait to go.

"Take me with you," the boy says.

22

Friday, early, Jeff stands on the stoop, peering in his dad's kitchen window. Nobody's home. He uses his key, flips the light on. Usen scrambles into the house, trailing his rope leash. The house smells like pale blue carpet and bird poop. No coffee cups, no bourbon glasses, no TV on. The place is exactly how he left it last night. Dad's not here.

He should have come home by now. "A few days," he'd said. Maybe he fell off a mountain. Maybe he had a heart attack. Mom was always talking about his heart. *Crap.* He's supposed to be doing research in Chapel Hill today. But it's time to call Carrie. *And maybe the police.* He picks up the phone.

"He called me," Carrie says. "Left a message."

"What? When?" Jeff says.

"He wants to come to LA."

"He's in *California?*"

"No. But he said he's got a plan now."

"What plan?"

"How the hell should I know?" she says. "That's all it said. Oh, and he'll be home today. Or tomorrow." She's got that snotty *I'm his favorite, he tells me everything* voice.

"Carrie, I was about to call the cops."

"Well, you don't need to now."

"Jesus. Nice of you to let me know. I thought—"

"Dad's just being Dad. And hey, I get up early. I called you twice already today. If you'd turned on Dad's answering machine, you would know." *Click.*

Usen runs ahead to the kitchen, trailing his rope. Jeff puts a bowl of water down for him and scatters some Cheerios. That will keep him busy for a while.

While he's feeding the lovebirds, Jeff sees that the catch on their cage door is bent. They've been pecking at it. Trying to get out? Maybe they're bored. For sure they miss Mom. *Birds need company,* she always used to say. *They miss their flock. So we are the flock.* He's never seen Dad actually pet them.

Jeff pulls them out of the cage one at a time, strokes their feathers, rubs their cheeks against his cheek, talks to them. "Good bird. Sweet bird." Bird kisses. They perk up nicely, *peet peet peet peet, chatter chatter chatter,* O'Mally grooming Molly, *all lovey-dovey,* as Mom used to say.

But when he checks the cockatiels in the den, they haven't eaten their food. They're hunched up in the corner of the cage. Mom used to play classical music for them. "Let's try something new," Jeff says. He fiddles with the ancient stereo, tunes in a station with booty music. Ludacris is all trash-talk, and King P raises one foot, then another. Queen Pia bobs her head and squawks in time. Pretty soon it's a party.

Jeff lets the birds out and they crab up his arm to his shoulder and peck at his hair, still dancing and bobbing to the music. They freaking love this music.

"What the fuck, Queen P. Dad in LA? That doesn't sound like Dad, does it?"

Happy appul, she says. Usen leaps up and snaps at a tail feather, and Pia goes bouncing around the room, screeching at the top of her lungs. King P squawks and flaps and dive-bombs the pup.

"Usen!" Jeff grabs at the pup, spills birdseed all over the place. By the time he gets everybody back in their cages and settled, there's bird poop, feathers, seed, and shredded newspaper all over the den. Then he sees the recliner. Usen's chewed a small hole in the base at the back and is contentedly ripping apart a flap of leather. Holy crap. Maybe he can glue it back. There's got to be some superglue around here somewhere.

He extracts the piece of leather from Usen's needle-teeth. Usen bites at his shoe, tugs his shoelace. The dog has blue-pile-carpet fuzz all over his muzzle. What has he been doing with the rug?

Jeff ties Usen's clothesline to the kitchen table leg. Finds glue in the junk drawer, under that cell phone with Mom's face on it. He glues the patch of leather in place and smooths the edges. Finds a needle-nose pliers and bends the lovebirds' door catch back so it will close. He scrapes up the seeds and litter and blue carpet fluff from the den floor as best he can. He leaves the radio on. Who knows, maybe they'll learn some new words and piss off Dad. *Bonus.*

In Chapel Hill, Jeff ties Usen's rope leash to the bike rack in front of the Wilson Rounds Library. It's too hot to leave him in the truck. But Usen is so cute, all the coeds will be "rescuing" him. He pens a note on a hot-pink Post-it: *I belong to JEFFERSON LEE,* and tucks it into the D ring on the sparkly collar. *Just do the best you can in the circumstances,* as Mom would say. "Wait for me," he says. Usen squirms and whines.

Jeff follows signs to the North Carolina Collection and asks to see a manuscript Chuck told him to check out. "The Johnston Blake file?" he says.

The curator nods. "Dr. Mathers told me you were coming." The man shows him where to stash his pack, gives him cotton gloves, and leads him to a special room.

"This just came in from Ambler County," the curator says. "The part you want is about ten pages in." The man opens a heavy cardboard folder to some yellowed pages covered with faded quill-pen script. "Someone should write this up," he says.

Jeff turns the pages carefully until a line of faded ink catches his eye:

> Many years after the Indian Wars that killed off Red Men in the Eastern part of the State, there were a dozen women and children of mixed blood, calling themselves Tuscarora, living by the Cedar River, in a Place people called Indian Field. They were left behind when their few men went North to make a home for them with the Iroquois. There had been great battles over the hundred years preceding but now their numbers had dwindled and they no longer felt safe living among White People. Some of our so-called Christian townsmen came on horses one day and attacked and killed them all—defenseless women and children—except for two survivors: an Old woman, and a Baby set floating in a basket. A storm blew up out of nowhere and there was a double Tornado, so the story goes, that twisted over Indian Field like the Fist of a vengeful God raining down upon the men committing these despicable acts on defenseless women and children. Those Men who witnessed, and returned to the town, mostly came on foot, telling the tale that their horses had been pulled up into the air by Pagan spirits and Devils. People became afraid of the Field from that time and left it alone. But sometimes they saw smoke as if spirits of Tuscarora still lived there.
>
> This is the story as I know it, as Told by my Father Johnston Blake, a Truthful Man of Great Integrity and a Friend to the Indians.
>
> —Sardinia Louisa Blake, September 1869, daughter of Johnston Blake, deceased. I attach my seal and avow its Truth.

Holy shit. Jeff marks the place with a slip of paper. He's got to make copies for Chuck. He'll never believe it. *Someone should write this up.* This could be his big chance, original research, his first paper with his own name at the top. *Pagan spirits and devils. A baby in a basket.* The backs of his arms prickle. Indigo Field was *Indian Field.*

There's a commotion in the hall. Usen is barreling toward him, trailing a chewed-through clothesline across the marble floor. The curator takes the cotton gloves and points to the door, a stern expression on his face.

By the time Jeff gets Usen back outside, it's eleven o'clock. He doesn't have time to make copies. Chuck is coming at noon. He's got so much to tell him. He's got to stash Usen someplace. Dad's garage? That will have to do.

Jeff's got all the finds labeled and marked. He's got handwritten notes on everything. He's got so much to say.

Right on the nose of noon, Chuck roars into camp in his red Chevy Blazer. "Nice tight camp," he says, admiring the tarp, the toolboxes, the plywood worktable. Jeff shows him the Ziploc bags with marked artifacts: incised pottery, bones of deer and birds and turtles. "And this," he says. He lifts a cardboard box to reveal the cracked pot. "The crack is my fault," Jeff confesses. "I dropped it." No way he's telling about Usen jumping up on him. "But listen." He shakes the pot gently. "Seeds."

"Hey," Chuck says. "There are advantages to a cracked pot." Chuck wedges his fingers gently along the crack, pulls out a kernel of dusty red corn, grins like a bad boy. "Let's plant one of these suckers," he says. "Just a little unscientific experiment." He walks to a sunny damp spot by the river, pokes a hole in the soil with a stick, and drops the seed in. He pats the earth down around it and marks it with the stick. He squats, drizzles his water bottle on the earth, gives it a good soaking. "Maybe we'll have something to show when I bring the reporter by."

"Reporter?"

"*New York Times.* Maybe next week." He wipes his hands on his jeans. "Those new burials you showed me. That's making this a big story. Let's go see what's going on there."

Jeff leads the way. They stand in no-man's-land, staring up. Tree roots cling to all three pots, as if cradling them from harm, but now two more pots have emerged from the cliff face. The shadowed eye sockets of two new skulls stare back at them.

"Holy crap," Chuck says. He snaps a picture with his cell phone. "If this doesn't get us funding, I don't know what will."

They walk back in silence. Something has been opened up to them: a gift, a mystery, a sadness, a loss.

"Better get on with it," Chuck says. "I've got something to show you." He clears a spot in the back of the pickup truck, pulls out a roll of drawings. "Nineteenth-century maps call it Indian Field," he says. "When it belonged to Johnston Blake."

"I've seen that name," Jeff says.

"On a historic marker?"

"On that manuscript at UNC. I didn't get a chance to make a copy."

"Too bad." But Chuck is unscrolling the next thing that has his full attention: a drawing. Faded ink on parchment, bark huts nestled beside a protective cliff, people gathering fish in baskets from a stone weir in the river, peach orchards and tobacco rows. There are people dancing in a circle of carved poles with faces on them. People dancing before the glory of the big pines that crown the hill marked Gooley Ridge above them. Chuck leans in, his face flushed red with feeling, his Scots-Irish showing. "Can you see it? A village spreading all the way to the Gooley pines. That's where the mother lode will be."

"Wow. Who drew this? Where did you get it?"

"Johnston Blake again. Apparently he was quite the scholar of Indians in his day. At one point he owned all the land from here—" Chuck sweeps his arm to include the camp, the river, Stonehaven—"to there." Chuck points across the highway to the swath of giant pines. "And a thousand acres beyond. Indigo Field is the part owned now by Mrs. Blake. Still haven't heard from her." He pauses. "There may be descendants in the county," he says. "Anybody you meet could be Native American. Maybe even the widow lady. She's a Blake, of course. The story goes, there was some intermarriage. A polite way of saying it."

Jeff remembers that the vet was Lumbee. But that's a completely different nation. He decides then and there he'll be the one to find a Tuscarora descendant. To talk to someone like that? That would be the mother lode.

Now Chuck lays out two later maps, one from the 1890s, one from the 1920s, and tells him about his theory of name erasure in historical documents. "Still Creek," he says, "in 1890 probably indicated a whiskey still." He shifts to the later map: "See? Now it's 'Spill Creek.' Someone made a typo. Or didn't want you to know where the still was." He shows

Jeff where Lucky's Crossing was, then the covered bridge that replaced it, then the current bridge, which has no name at all. Buffalo Creek is now Smith Creek, erasing the historical presence of woods buffalo in the Carolina Piedmont, and so on. "See," Chuck says, "where this map calls the place next to the river Indian Field? The next map calls it Indigo. The last Indigenous people had been gone for a generation or two. And there was some story made up about an attempt to grow indigo here. Never happened. The landowner wanted to erase the Indians." As Chuck flips from one map to the other, Jeff can see that names shift and disappear as if written in invisible ink, whether by intent, carelessness, or mapmaker whimsy.

"It's the things that are written down that we remember," Jeff says. "Even if they're wrong."

"Now you're getting it," Chuck says. "Well done." He rolls the maps up. "Now," he says. "Tell me what you know about Johnston Blake."

Jeff tells him everything.

"Wow," Chuck says. "What else?"

He tells about the dog he found on site, how it could be a Carolina dog.

"Not just a common everyday yellow lab mix, run off from the back of a good-ol'-boy pickup truck?"

"Well, maybe," Jeff admits. "But what if it really is?"

"Did you shoot it?"

"No!"

"Where is it?"

"In my dad's garage."

"Your dad's taking care of it?"

"Not really." Jeff wonders what Usen has chewed up in there. "I'm trying to find a home for it." He pulls out the flyer about Carolina dogs.

"We haven't got funding for DNA tests," Chuck says. "But who knows, we might get some from these guys." He hands the flyer back. "Call them. Tell them what you've got." He grins, raises his index finger as if he were a teacher in class. "Optimism," he says, "is the fallback position of archaeologists."

Chuck chugs the rest of his water. He's already sunburnt. "Hot here," he says. He moves to a camp stool in the shade. "Now about that massacre. Sounds like a made-up story to me. Doesn't match up with these organized burials we're seeing. But the claim that it's Johnston Blake's story gives it some credence. We've just got to get access to that field across the road. The cliff burial. The mother lode." The afternoon sun sparks the red hairs bristling on Chuck's face, on his eager smile, lighting him up like a Scottish thane showing off his lands. "The mother lode," he says again.

Chuck takes more pictures with his iPhone, including one with Jeff holding the cracked pot. "You better see this too," Jeff says. He reaches in the glovebox and pulls out the Ziploc with the finger bone in it. He waits for Chuck to say, *How did you let this happen?*

"That's no chicken bone," Chuck says, holding it up to the light. "Tooth marks. Where was it?"

"It was just lying around." A total lie. "I think the feral dog was chewing on it before I got him off the site." That part's true.

"I'll take it for testing. For now, it's a chicken bone. I really don't want the sheriff coming out and shutting us down." Chuck slips the baggie into his pocket. He checks his watch.

"Listen," he says. "One more thing. The curator called me. He did not take kindly to a dog crashing his dust-free, climate-controlled collection. It took some fast talk to keep you from being banned for life. And if you're going to be an archaeologist, if you want to be taken seriously, you've got to make copies."

"I know. I fucked up. It won't happen again."

"You're an asshole not to tell me. There are fifty grad students who would grab this job."

"I'm sorry." *Sorry sorry sorry sorry.*

"It's okay. I've been known to be an asshole. Just don't fuck this up. It could make your career, but it also could make mine." Chuck turns away, looks at his phone. "I've got a conference call, and the reception here is lousy. I've got to go. But here." He pulls a check out of his notebook. "I scared up some more expense money. Get a burner phone. And a service that covers out here. We've got to be able to stay in touch. That field phone is crap." He loads up his Blazer and takes one last look around.

"Good work," he says. "Go have a beer." He pulls out a couple of twenties. "And something to eat besides Vienna sausages. You're looking a little rugged."

"Thanks, man."

"I'll be up at Carolina for a week or so, if you need me. I've got to weasel some lab space to store all this. Wouldn't want it to get washed away in a storm."

"Okay."

"Keep an eye on those cliff burials. Call me if more get washed out. And take a shower," he says. "You got some bone-digger stink on you."

Jeff, embarrassed, checks his pits. They are pretty bad.

"Hey," Chuck says, "it's the badge of honor of the bone digger. You're in the club for sure now. And truthfully?" He looks around with relish at the Field, the Gooley pines, the dusty camp, the dig. "Truthfully, I really miss this part."

Jeff doesn't have time for a spit bath. The Stonehaven farmers' market closes at two. He desperately needs some veg to round out his Vienna sausage dinners. And strawberries for Dad. Dad will be home tonight. Maybe. Time to get Usen out of garage.

Usen eyeballs the crowd, yanks the clothesline out of Jeff's hand, and goes scampering from booth to booth, peeing at will on tufts of grass that have the most interesting new smells—truck wheels, people's shoes, gum wrappers, and feathers.

The pup catches sight of a flock of Canada geese wandering on the far side of the green, near a pond. He tears off, ignoring Jeff's calls. He runs circles around the panicked birds, herds them into a tight huddle, then scatters them by barking. Now they hiss, heads lowered, and charge the pup.

"Usen!" Jeff calls. He grabs Usen by the scruff and tucks him in his vest, but now there's a big young fellow standing before him.

"Let me see," he says to Jeff. He pokes a finger in Jeff's vest, touches Usen on the nose. "Pomise to be good?" the boy says.

"That's Usen," Jeff says.

"You-seh?" the boy says. The puppy licks his finger. "Like Ace!" he crows. His face squeezes in delight, and he throws his head back, face flushed, neck cords straining, in the most complete display of happiness Jeff has ever seen, outside of a kachina clown mask in a Ute ceremonial dance. Jeff can't help but smile. "He likes you," Jeff says.

The kid is tall, fuzz on his upper lip, and he's got a blue UNC windbreaker, pink-striped Oxford shirt, khaki pants, short red clip-on tie, big arms and tummy filling out the oversize boy's clothes. A happy yuppie.

"I am Bobo," the happy yuppie says.

"I'm Jeff."

"Want some gum?" Bobo carefully unzips his windbreaker pocket and brings out a stick of Juicy Fruit, extends it in his direction.

"No, thanks," Jeff says.

Bobo unwraps a piece and pops it in his mouth. Puts the gum wrapper back in his pocket.

"Can I play wih yoh puppy?" The boy is tickling Usen's tummy now, making the pup play at biting his fingers.

"Uh." Jeff glances back at the geese, who have retreated to the safety of the pond.

"On a *leash*," Bobo says.

"I guess so," Jeff says. "Just for a little while." He sets Usen on the ground and offers the frayed end of the rope to Bobo, who kneels down and fingers the dog's collar.

"Spahkles!" he says. His big hand grips the leash tightly. "U-seh!" he calls, tugging the rope. Usen trots alongside Bobo, wagging, not even looking back at Jeff, all the way to the circle of farm trucks.

As Jeff watches, Bobo makes Usen sit. Then, palm up, says, "STAY." Usen stays, his fat tail thumping. Then Bobo pats his chest, says, "Come, boy!" and Usen runs to Bobo, leaping onto the boy's ironed khaki pants with muddy feet. Bobo reaches down to pet him, crowing, "Goo boy! Goo boy!" then kneels down to hug Usen, then rolls to his side as Usen crawls up onto his large belly and begins a game of alternately nipping at his red tie and licking his face.

Jeff hunkers down to watch them play. In minutes Usen the wild dog is completely socialized. Usen watches the boy's every move, understands its meaning, and acts accordingly. Bobo is the leader of the pack. Bobo is the head puppy. This dog belongs with Bobo.

Jeff's heart twists at the thought. He doesn't want to give Usen away. Usen is company. But he must give him away. As if suddenly remembering his existence, Usen bounds toward Jeff and leaps for his face. Bobo follows, whooping, dancing in a circle around them. Jeff springs to his feet and tags the pup lightly on its rump. The chase is on. First Usen, then Jeff, then Bobo, each chases in turn, then tags, then whirls and is chased, weaving through the crowd, returning to the clear space at the center of the green, circling again, jumping the rope, tagging, returning the tag, jumping the rope again, muddy, paw-printed, ecstatic, finally tripping over the leash, falling to earth, laughing and panting for breath. None of them notices the glances of growers, one to another, the nods, the murmurs.

"Just like old times, before that boy lost his dog."

"A new pup?"

"Just what he needs."

"Wonder who that is with him?"

"That's the digger, out in Indigo Field."

"That so?"

The village church bell rings one-forty-five. The strawberry truck has a big sign: SOLD OUT. Bobo and Usen stand before him, winded, panting. "Come see!" the big boy says. "Come see Mama!" He takes Jeff by the hand and begins to tug him along. The joy in him is contagious.

"Okay, okay, I'm coming!" Usen dives into the crowd, seeming to know exactly where he's going.

"Mama!" Bobo calls out. "Look! Here is U-seh! Here is Jeff!" A woman in T-shirt and baggy overalls is reaching into the back of her truck. Now she turns around. "Look!" Bobo plunks Usen on the produce shelf, next to a picked-over box of sugar snap peas. Usen looks up at the lady and wags. "Sit!" Bobo says. Usen sits. "Shake," Bobo says.

Usen lifts a paw.

The lady takes the muddy paw between two fingers and shakes. "Nice," she says. "Polite."

"Like Ace!" Bobo says.

"Yes. Like Ace." The woman peers around Bobo's wide shoulders to take a look at Jeff. "Your dog?" she says.

"Yeah," Jeff says. Jeff can barely breathe. This is Bobo's *mother*? Her pale green eyes stare right through him. Her dark hair hangs in a thick braid down her back, sweaty strands stuck to her flushed cheeks, and her chin has a cleft like an Irish girl's. Bobo's mom is *hot*. He slicks his own sweaty hair back from his face. He wishes he'd shaved. Or at least changed his shirt.

"I see you've met my son," she says.

"Yes, ma'am," he says, grinning stupidly. *He ma'ammed her. Crap.* Bobo's mom looks him over as if he were some new breed of prize ass.

Finally Bobo's mom smiles, a brief brilliant flash of light in her eyes, a small curve of her lip. "I'm Jolene. Thanks for letting him play with your dog. He's been missing his dog since..." She doesn't finish. That serious look back on her face.

God, if he could only see that flash of a smile again. "I should thank *him*," Jeff says. "He saved Usen from a terrible fate—being pecked to death by a pack of geese."

An old lady across the way in a frilly apron suppresses a snort.

"This is Miss Phoebe," Jolene says. He shakes Miss Phoebe's hand.

People like to know who your daddy is in the South, right? "Uh," he says. "My folks live here. Rand and Anne Lee? Well, it's just him now."

Bobo's mom looks sad, and an old Black lady walks over from the next booth, stands beside her.

"This is Miss Reba," Jolene says. The old Black lady looks him up and down.

"Hi," he says. "I'm Jeff."

"Hmmm," she says. She looks at Usen as if she's about to introduce herself to him. No, it's not that. It's as if she knows him. Usen whines, then makes a sound halfway between a bark and a laugh.

"Did you want something?" Jolene says. "Market's closing."

Jeff stares at Jolene's mouth, then drops his eyes to the peas.

"Peas would be great," he says. "I love peas." He feels like he's about fourteen. Everything he says sounds dumb.

"What else?" Jolene says. "I've got some chard, a few early beets and new potatoes. Reba's got turnips and turnip greens, a couple of strawberries. She sold out her fried pies and pound cake first thing. Then there's this lonely tub of goat cheese needs a home, and one last sad little bunch of oxeye daisies from the back field. Bobo likes to pick them."

"Great," Jeff says. "Perfect. I'll take it."

"The daisies?" Jolene says.

"I'll take it *all*," he says. Like he is King of the Nile. He's got cash in his pocket. He wants it all.

Jolene weighs and bags, writes down numbers. Miss Reba bags up turnips and greens.

"Just like Miss Anne," Miss Reba says.

"What?" Jeff says. Like *who?*

"Just like your mother," Jolene explains.

"You knew my *mother?*" Jeff says.

"Your mama," Miss Reba says, "she loved her spring flowers. Daisies and irises. She used to buy up my whole table, by the bucket. Hard to forget your mama."

Jolene nods. "Bobo knew her too. Didn't you, Bobo? Miss Anne? From school?"

"Miss Ahn!" Bobo cries out, happy. Then his face sobers. "She gone."

Jeff is flabbergasted. Bobo knew his mother. Miss Reba too. Jolene.

Now Bobo's face crinkles up in pain. He's crying. Bobo is crying about Miss Anne. This boy, so full of joy, loved his mother.

Jeff stands there, stunned, his arms full of produce. He feels the known world expand around him, the way it does when sunlight sparks the surface of a lake, then suddenly shoots clear to the bottom. He sees the tiny hairs on the pea pods, the down on Jolene's cheek, the faded red of her pickup truck, the soft red of her curved upper lip, the bright red of Bobo's tie, the red of a strawberry Miss Reba is holding out for him to taste. *Things are going on he knows nothing about, all around him. Mom's life moves under the surface of the world, like fishes glinting under the surface of water.*

Bobo moves to be comforted by his mother. Jolene's arms wind around the big boy's soft belly, one hand strokes his hair. Jeff takes the strawberry from Miss Reba. Hears her say the words: "I am so sorry for your loss."

He misses her terribly. Mom was the only person in the world who understood him. But he had never loved her quite the way this big strange boy had loved her. Or known her the way Miss Reba knew her—as somebody who would buy a whole table full of flowers, for the pure joy of it. He had scarcely known his mother, truth be told. *Shit.* He feels like crying too.

Jolene clears her throat, tells him it will be eighteen dollars, please. He counts out the money, places it in her lean, earth-stained hand, the color of her palm like the smooth skin of a butternut squash. Miss Reba rummages in the back of her truck and hands him a pint of strawberries. "Half price. Dead ripe. Got to eat 'em today." The other trucks are moving out. The market has a dusty, empty look. Jolene tells Bobo to give the leash back to Jeff and help her load up.

"Mama," Bobo says, "I want Useh. I want Jeff. Come ovah and play."

"We'll see," Jolene says. "Get in the truck now."

Jeff can't bear to see them go. "Listen," he says, "I'm making strawberry shortcake tonight. Dinner too. Why don't you come?"

Miss Reba and Jolene pause, look at each other.

"I'm a good cook, really, it'll be great. There's plenty of room," he says, realizing as soon as he says it that he doesn't actually know if Dad is coming home tonight, but what a riot it would be to have these people—Miss Reba and Jolene and Bobo—what a good time they could have sitting around his mother's dining room table, he could make Swiss chard stuffed with rice and golden raisins in a goat cheese sauce, sugar snap peas on the side, baby beets and new potatoes halved, steamed and buttered, the handful of daisies on the table in a jelly glass. Maybe Miss Reba will tell more about his mother, and maybe he can get serious Jolene to smile again.

Miss Phoebe is whispering to Jolene, and Jolene is shaking her head violently. Miss Reba goes back to her table to finish packing. Jolene looks at Jeff. "I thank you for your offer," she says. "We just can't today." Those sad-serious eyes.

"Maybe some other time?" Jeff says, crestfallen.

"Maybe," Jolene says. She turns away, shoving baskets and crates into the back of her truck, helping Miss Reba load hers too. "Thanks, though. Thanks for making Bobo...happy." That flash in her eye. That curve of her lip.

He has made her smile again, if you can call something that vanishes so quickly a smile. Now she is pulling up the stakes for her shade canopy.

"Here, let me help." Jeff bends beside her.

"No!" Jolene says. "No, I'm sorry, it's just so much easier to do by myself."

"Okay." Jeff watches Reba get in the truck, Bobo lumber in beside her. Apparently Jolene doesn't let them help either.

Jolene pulls the canopy down, folds and stows it. She folds the tablecloth and stows it on top. Then she folds up the two tables and slides them into the rack above the produce. She loads in Reba's baskets and buckets. She has a neat, compact system, like a long-distance hiker, for breaking camp and moving out fast. Jeff has a guilty feeling that she wouldn't approve of his slapdash cold-water camp by the river, his pickup truck full of old tarps and miscellany.

Jolene slams the creaky tailgate shut with a bang. "Well, goodbye," she says.

Bobo leans across Miss Reba and waves his hand as if his life depended on it. "Bye-bye!" he calls out. "Bye-bye, Useh! Bye-bye, Jeff!"

Jeff waves back. Jolene cranks the engine and pulls away.

"Son of a bitch," Jeff says out loud. He's got to see her again.

The old lady with the frilly apron turns and looks him up and down. "I think she likes you too."

And just like that, everything else goes out of his head.

23

As they drive home, Jolene asks Bobo about Miss Anne. She hadn't realized he was still grieving. Or maybe it's just mood swings, like a teenager. Doctors said this would happen more now.

"Miss Anne was nice. You miss her."

"Miss huh," he agrees cheerfully. "She have blue eyes." He gropes in his pocket for gum. "Her boy is Jeff." He sneaks a look at her to make sure this is right.

"Yes," Jolene says. "You remember. Good."

"Like you and me. Miss Ahn and Jeff."

"Yes, that's right." Bobo's way smarter than most people give him credit for.

"Jeff is nice. He's a big boy."

"You're my big boy," Jolene says, and pokes his tummy with a finger.

"No, Mama. Not your big *boy*. Big *man*."

"Okay. Big man." TJ had said that to Bobo. *You the Man.* He probably thought he was being funny. She's going to have to keep him away from Bobo. Bad influence. Jolene changes the subject. "Bobo liked Usen?"

"Cute!" Bobo says. "A baby dog, like the baby gohs."

They drop Miss Reba, and Bobo helps her unload from the back of the truck.

The rest of the way home, Bobo talks about Jeff and Usen. "Jeff can come ovah?" he pleads. "Jeff can come ovah with U-seh?" Bobo pants like a dog, his new thing, pretending to be a member of the dog family. He licks her arm and whimpers. "Puh-leeeez?"

"You are not a dog," Jolene says, buying time.

"Yes, a dog."

"No."

Jolene would rather have TJ over, a known quantity at least, than this Jeff person, who makes her feel—strange. Guilty for being unfriendly. Longing to be younger herself. His reddish hair, unshaven freckled jaw, his—enthusiasm. His sweetness with Bobo. Luke had been like that. Sweet, almost like a child himself sometimes. And something else. Jeff had a hungry look in his eye that almost made her blush.

She pulls up into the yard. "How about TJ?" Jolene says, backing into the barn to unload her gear. She regrets it the minute she says it.

"TJ has a girr-friend." Bobo squints his eyes and puffs out his lower lip.

Oh dear God. TJ has a whole list of things that Bobo wants. She's been hearing about it ever since the two of them went off to see the chickens in Reba's barn. They covered a lot of territory in that short time. Jolene turns the truck off, tucks the key in the ashtray. Here it comes.

"He drive a cah. Weba let him."

"I doubt that very much," Jolene says. "That might be a big story."

"TJ get a dog," Bobo says.

"I don't think Miss Reba's going to let him have a dog," Jolene says firmly. TJ must be crazy if he thinks Reba will let him have a puppy around her hens. "You have the goat babies," she reminds Bobo, a little desperately. Goat babies that she steals from him each year and sells to the butcher. What does Bobo have, really, that can compete with girlfriends, and driving cars?

"Mama, I want U-seh and Jeff. I want Jeff! I WANT JEFF." Bobo is banging his fist against the door panel, hard. Ace used to press his weight against Bobo to calm him when he got like this. But Ace is not here.

Bobo bangs his head on the dash, yelling. "JEFF AND U-SEH, JEFF AND U-SEH."

The doctor says if she lets him do this it could lock in patterns in his brain. Sometimes it works to yell. "BOBO. LISTEN TO ME, BOBO." Her voice sounds high and hysterical.

The newborn kids in the pen now set up a cry, "Maaa! Maaaa!"

"JEFF AND U-SEH, JEFF AND U-SEH."

"STOP, BOBO, STOP, YOU'RE SCARING THE BABIES."

Now he pounds his head harder and God, there's blood on the dash, she reaches to grab his forehead and he yells NOOOO and pushes her arm away so hard his fist connects with her chin and her head cracks against the window and for a moment her vision goes white and she is faint with fear. This is the moment she's expected since Luke died. Bobo has finally gotten bigger than she is and she cannot control him and he will hurt someone and be taken away.

Bobo's face now looms over hers, his eyes big and worried, he reaches a pudgy finger to touch her face and pet it. "Hut?" he whispers.

"Mama hut?" She squeezes her eyes closed, smells his breath on her face, Juicy Fruit gum and peanut butter, mixing with the pain of a knot on the back of her head and the sense that her brains have been flipped over like a fried egg. She opens her eyes and makes her mouth into a smile, but cannot help the tears of relief slipping down her face. Her dear sweet boy. He's still here. "Mama's okay," she says. "Mama fine." They sit there, patting each other's cheeks, as the evening birds begin to call.

After late milking and feeding, Bobo becomes very quiet. In the kitchen, Jolene pulls out the Flintstone Band-Aids and covers the bruise on Bobo's forehead.

"I like Pebbles," Bobo says.

"Which pebbles, Bobo? In your collection?"

"No, Mama, Pebbles *Flinstone*. A girl." He picks at the Band-Aid. "Ow."

She does not understand, but there's no reason she should understand everything in the world.

"Ace got rocks," Bobo says. He's peering out the kitchen window at her river rock spiral. He hasn't said a word about it before.

"Yes," she says. "Ace got rocks."

"He run away?"

"No, Bobo. He's right there."

"Dint go to heaven?"

"His bones are there, but his spirit is in heaven." Oh dear Lord. It doesn't make any sense to her, why should it make any sense to him?

"I want Ace. I want Jeff. I want Useh." The sadness in his voice breaks her heart. For the first time in his life he knows he's not getting what he wants and he will never get what he wants. No crying. No tears. Just a great sadness spreading.

She wraps Bobo in her arms and he sighs and leans in. She decides then and there to call this fellow Jeff first chance she gets. There is no reason the boy shouldn't have a few of the things he wants, in his great big yearning heart. "Don't be sad, Bobo."

"Not sad," he lies.

"I'll call Jeff," she promises. Maybe her customer Bess has his number. Bess knows everybody. Maybe this Jeff person would be a good tutor for Bobo, like his mother. She could trade for veggies. She feels her cheeks flush, remembering the way he looked at her. Not just hungry, but eager. Inviting her to dinner that way. *Don't be ridiculous. He's way too young for you.*

It's been a very long time since she had a man in her life.

It was embarrassing what she did that first year after Luke died. She would ask Reba and Danielle to watch Bobo while she went out galivanting with the county agent, or the Registrar of Deeds, or Frank Ridley, her banker. The county agent took her on a tour of his favorite farms and leaned her up against his truck, pushed up her skirt, and put his fingers in her panties. She let him do it more than once. Her body was so lonely for Luke, she did all kinds of things. Got drunk with the Registrar on white liquor. Let him do things to her that Luke used to do, and her body responded. That went on for weeks. She didn't really like him. Finally she felt so awful about it, she broke it off and didn't go to the county offices for a year.

With Frank Ridley, it was more a matter of going out for pizza or spaghetti, which she always managed to get on her blouse, then going to his house and watching videos on TV in his den. He was very sweet to Bobo. Confided in her that he had a beloved baby brother who had Down syndrome. "The sweetest boy in the world," he said. Told her the whole sad story about his parents putting the boy in a home some- where, keeping it secret. Since they died he was spending untold sums trying to find the boy. She liked him for that. And for how he was with Bobo. Kindly. Generous.

Sometimes he kissed her. During reruns of *Designing Women,* he would crawl on top of her and paw at her breasts. The most embar- rassing thing was, her body responded. He came to the farm a few times. Stood in Indigo Field, gazed up at the Gooley pines and said, "Beautiful. A wonderful site for a hotel and spa. Stonehaven people would love it. It would have to be tastefully done, of course. And up there—" he pointed to the Gooley Ridge next to the river—"a cell phone tower. Stonehaven people get terrible reception." It shocked her that anyone would think like this. Couldn't he see that the great big trees and the field below were a kind a miracle? A place so full of peace. Like that Big Tree girl said, a place that keeps people safe.

That was the day he asked her to marry him. He made it sound like a kind of business proposition, and she imagined it would be something like this: a world with no worries and plenty of sleep and Bobo safe, with a kindly father figure. *Frank would be at work all day and she'd run the farm as usual, but he'd drop by at night and give her money and—*oh good Lord, share her bed. Would he even fit in her bed? Frank was a large man. She couldn't picture it. She doesn't want it. But there was one temptation— the chance to have another child. A little girl this time.

She said no. She couldn't be with somebody who didn't love the Field. There had been a connection between her and Luke that was all spark and fire, the deepest pleasure she had ever known, and it was all wrapped around a love of this place that went deep as the tap roots of the Gooley pines—as deep as they are tall. There was no replacing that.

The offer's open, Frank told her. As if he were considering how to sweeten the deal.

At his camp, Jeff watches the sun set, eats his raw veggies and goat cheese and strawberries, and thinks about Jolene's lips. He tosses a few strawberries to Usen, who bites them out of the air then yips for more. How is he going to get her number? He wants to make her dinner— feed her strawberries one by one.

Dad didn't come home. No strawberry shortcake for him.

He's supposed to check in with Chuck tonight. It's almost time. He and Usen sprint down to the river's edge, then wade around the thicket. Usen zags, gets caught in briars, and Jeff has to pluck him out, thorns ripping scratches through his shirt. Then it's up the cliff to the Gooley Ridge, to a place under a hollow sycamore tree, where he's not supposed to be, but he's learned gets the best reception. Jeff leans against the tree, looks up at its white-gray spotted trunk, its reaching white arms, muscled and smooth, catching the sunset light, leaves shifting, making whispering sounds. What secrets do they know? The tree's got to be two hundred years old. He can't reach all the way around it.

He dials. Chuck answers.

"Your pot with the seeds," Chuck says. "*Crackle crackle*...big hit."

"Great," Jeff says. Usen is screwing around with the rope leash, making little yipping sounds. Jeff twists this way and that, hoping for better reception.

"...private benefactor...wheels of bureaucracy...too slow..."

"Excellent," Jeff says cautiously. He got most of that. He hopes. Why didn't he go to town, get a cell phone? *You wanted to sit and think about Jolene.* Now the dog is running circles around the tree, dragging his leash behind him, shaking it in his teeth as if it were a snake. Jeff hopes Chuck doesn't ask about the dog.

"You still...*crackle crackle*...goddamn field phone?"

"Getting the cell in the morning," Jeff says. *First thing in the morning. Promise. Dammit.*

"Everything all right there?" Chuck's voice sounds tired.

"Sure," Jeff says. Usen's got a tangle of rope around his feet and ankles. *WTF Usen?*

"I saw...Noah." The reception is suddenly clear.

Jeff straightens. "I thought he was in New Mexico."

"He needs funding too," Chuck says. "He says good luck to us."

"Great." Jeff feels suddenly happy. Chuck said *us.* The puppy yips.

"What's that?" Chuck says.

"Birds," Jeff says. "They're all over the place."

After Chuck rings off, Jeff sees that Usen has wrapped the rope around the tree and his ankles. He can't move. "Usen! Crap." He reaches down to pull the rope free, but Usen has pulled it so tight, he's kind of strangling himself. *What the actual....* The field phone rings. Chuck again? He presses ON. "Is this...*crackle snap*...Jeff...?" A woman's voice.

"Bess?" Maybe Dad is home.

"*Crackle crackle*...Jolene Blake...farmers' market...Bobo loves your dog...*crackle crackle*..."

"Jolene?" He can't believe it. She's calling *him?*

"Tomorrow...ten...goat cheese?

"Um, yes, okay." He can't quite grab the rope. "Where do you live?" Usen is making choking sounds at his feet.

"Ten Field Road. Spill Creek Farm." It's suddenly so clear, it's as if she's standing right next to him. At his ankles, the goddamn rope is cutting off his circulation. He reaches down again with his free hand. Loses balance. Teeters sideways off the tree and into the duff. Drops the phone. He reaches around for it frantically in the leaves. There it is. "Yes. Yes. Yes," he shouts at the mouthpiece. Is she still there? He hopes to God she can hear him.

"Bobo needs a tutor...*snap crackle pop*...worksheets and games."

"Yes," Jeff says, *Oh my God yes.* "I'll be there." The line goes dead.

He's got a mouthful of leaves. He can barely move. There is a dark, thick smell in the dirt here, like a dead animal. He struggles to sit up.

Usen has pulled out of his sparkly collar. The dog sits there, head cocked, as if he's more than slightly amused by the ridiculous creature before him.

In the morning, Jeff checks the site with Usen, then drives into Quarryville to the Family Dollar, leaves still clinging to his hair and clothes. He picks out a burner, buys a load of batteries, makes sure it works by calling Dad on the home phone. It rings and rings—Dad's still not there—but then it picks up, Mom's cheery voice: "You've reached Anne and Rand Lee. We're so glad you called, but we're off tripping the light fantastic...you know what to do."

"Mom," he says. "I met a girl."

Back at the site, Jeff pours warm bottled water over his head, washes his face and armpits with Dr. Bonner's Peppermint Soap, combs his hair, and puts on deodorant and a white dress shirt, the one he wore at Mom's funeral, but now it's an extremely wrinkled white dress shirt. Oh well. Jolene wants to see him. He and Bobo will be friends. He will see those lips, those green eyes, that schoolgirl cleft in her chin, and he will have to keep cool. A tutor is not a boyfriend. At least not right away. *Chill, man. Just see how it goes.* He wishes he had time for a real shower at Dad's. He needs to feed the birds. But there isn't time. It's nine-thirty. He hasn't figured out the GPS app on this phone, so he's left some time to try to find her place. A new tutor needs to show up on time.

"Truck, Usen," he says. Usen jumps in, rests a mud paw on his jeans and grins. "So much for making a good impression," he says to the pup. The pup looks him up and down, like *you in your wrinkly shirt. Ha.* Usen paws at the shirt now, but Jeff fends him off, ends up with a muddy sleeve. "I'm going to have to find a home for you, dude." Usen looks out the window.

Jeff tears down Field Road and finds Spill Creek Farm. It's not far at all. He's way early. He pulls up into the yard and Bobo comes running.

Jolene pauses at the bottom of the porch steps, watches Jeff get out of the truck and look around. There is a moment as he stands there in the sun—his big boots muddy and his hair awry, as if he combed it wet and then went driving in his truck with the windows down—when Jolene feels like she knows him from somewhere long ago. "The big trees," he calls out, walking toward her, gesturing over his shoulder to the Gooley Ridge, where a breeze is sparkling the pine needles.

"Yes, "she says. "The light in them this time of day." The wren that's been nesting in Luke's old boot on the porch releases loud silver notes from the rafters. *Teakettle teakettle teakettle!* Such joy in those small throats.

The pup puts his muddy paws on her overalls. "Usen! Get down!" Jeff says. Usen veers off to run circles around Bobo.

"No worries," Jolene says. "These are work clothes." Before he got here, she rubbed in some of Miss Phoebe's rosewater hand cream. Now she's standing in a cloud of rose-scent. She smooths the front of her bib, brushes straw from her hair. What is she doing? It's as if her body, under her overalls, wants to flirt with him.

"Useh!" Bobo calls. "Come here." Usen runs to him. Sits. "Good dog!"

"He really likes you," Jeff says. He looks around the yard, as if for a ball they can throw. "What's this?" he says, looking at the spiral of stones she placed over Ace's bones.

"Ace," Bobo says.

"His dog," Jolene says. Good Lord, she hopes Bobo doesn't take this moment to burst into tears.

Bobo kneels down and pets the stone that goes over his old friend's head. Bobo looks up at Jeff. "Ace went away."

Jeff thinks about this for a moment. "You miss him."

"Yeh."

"I miss my mom," Jeff says.

"Miss Ahn!" Bobo crows. "I miss huh too." Bobo stands, puts his arms around Jeff, and Jeff puts his arms around Bobo, and Bobo cries a little. It is a miracle day. Bobo understands death today. And Jeff understands Bobo. Jolene can't believe it. But it is so.

"I can't stay," Jeff says to her. He looks like he'd like to. "I've got to go feed my dad's birds."

"Birds, Mama! Jeff have birds."

"Well, my dad does. You like birds?" he asks.

"Yess!" Bobo says. "I have feathers. Come see."

"Maybe I can take you to see Dad's birds sometime."

"Let's not get ahead of ourselves," Jolene says. Lord, she's going to have to keep an eye on this one. He doesn't know boundaries.

"Oh yeah, of course, sorry. With your permission, of course."

Okay then.

"Let's go!" Bobo is bouncing up and down.

"Later," Jolene says. "We have chores now."

"I'll bring Usen back sometime," Jeff tells Bobo. "Would you like that?"

"Yesss!"

"And I could do worksheets with you. Your mom says you have a lot of those. And maybe we can play games."

"Games, Mama!"

"And read?"

"*Dig a Hole!*" Bobo crows.

Jeff looks at her quizzically.

"His favorite book," Jolene says.

"Ah."

Usen is tearing around the yard, and suddenly his nose quivers. He stops. He smells the goats. "Show him the gohs, Mama!"

"Next time, Bobo," she says. "Mr. Jeff has to go."

"Just Jeff," he says. "No Mister."

"Okay," she says. He writes down his new cell phone number and hands it to her, and his fingers brush her palm. The touch sparks her whole arm, and down her back and legs. What in the world? He's just a boy.

"Wait!" she says. "I forgot your veggies!"

"My veggies?"

"I can't really pay," she says, "but I can supply you with the world's finest green beans. And goat cheese. And so on."

"Perfect," he says, "but this was just a social visit. No need."

"I've got them all bagged up." She hands them over, a bagful of sugar snaps, baby beets, and arugula. She hopes he doesn't invite her to dinner again.

"Let's say Tuesday? Ten a.m.? Maybe more if it works out." She can finally do some errands. She's got to ask Southern States for an extension. What she made last month didn't cover it. Frank Ridley can wait for the mortgage payment. He'll get it when she gets it. He never seems to mind.

"That'll work." Jeff grins at her, happier than he has any reason to be.

She watches him go. Bobo runs alongside the truck, "Bye! Bye!" until Jeff sticks his arm out the window, waves goodbye, and takes the turn down Field Road.

Jeff astonishes her. He *connects* with Bobo. And he may be young, but he is no boy. The look on his face warmed her whole body. And maybe she does want him to make her dinner. The way he described it before, it sounded delicious. With Bobo to chaperone, of course.

24

Saturday morning, early, Rand pulls on his running shorts—the only clean pants he has left—and hauls his bags to the car.

He loads his cooler, only one warm RC Cola remaining and a flabby piece of baloney, which he consumes. The boy has forgotten to bring ice today. When he looks up, Kamil is sitting in the front seat, facing forward, a stony look on his face. *For Chrissake, the kid was serious.*

"Look, Kamil," he says. "Why do you want to leave here, anyway?" he jokes. "These are *your* mountains."

"She's not even my mother," Kamil says. "My mother sent me here. To pay off her debt. She lives in Ahmedabad."

Could that even be true? His ice boy living in servitude. That can't happen in this country. Can it? He gives the boy a twenty. In the rearview mirror he sees the boy's face streaming with tears. Or maybe it's a trick of light, so bright now that it blinds him.

At 11 a.m., Rand turns the key and pushes the kitchen door open, but it snags on something. He bends over to see. Green feathers. Red beak. Jesus. It's one of Anne's lovebirds. He picks it up. Limp body. Claws curled and hard. That mark over the eye. O'Mally.

He clutches the bird to his chest. *Oh bloody hell.* Jeff was supposed to take care of them, dammit. He flicks the light switch. There's the note he left on the table. All instructions clear.

The cage door is open, and Molly is huddled inside, chattering weakly. Full food dish, full water, hulls scattered all over. "Sweet bird, sweet bird, sweet bird," he calls, and she stops, cocks her head, looks at him. Takes a step toward him. Cocks her head the other way. Sees the dead bird in his hand. She shrieks and flaps away, beating her wings against the cage until green feathers go flying. Then she sits there, quivering.

"Sweet bird," Rand whispers, his voice cracking. He wants to reach all the way in, bring her outside the cage and hold her against his chest. He wants to feel that quivering hollow-boned body, that fast-racing heart, fluttering against his. But he's never done that before, and right now it might scare her to death.

He tops off her feed and water, but she has no interest. She only quivers. He does the only thing he can think of to calm her. He covers the cage, darkening it so she can sleep.

Then he picks up the phone to call Jeff and ream him out. But there's no answer.

A knock on the door. Jeff? No. Bess pokes her head in, says, "You're back! How were the mountains?"

"To hell with the mountains. Anne's damn bird is dead!"

"Oh no, Rand. What happened?"

"O'Mally got out." Rand says. "She'll probably die too." Anne always said lovebirds don't do well in singles. They are sold in pairs.

Bess goes silent. Sees the bird on the counter. Rests her fingertips on it for a moment as if she could bring it to life with touch.

"I'm so sorry, Rand," Bess says. "Are the other ones okay?"

The other ones. Rand turns and sprints to the den.

King P dances at the sight of him: *Oh bloody hell!*

Queen Pia says, *Fuckfuckfuck!* Pia's got a new word. There's some kind of filthy rap music on the stereo. Without a doubt, Jeff's been here. He turns it off. *Damn him. Irresponsible. Always screwing up.*

The birds have plenty of food. The rug beneath needs vacuuming. He stands there, watching them eat and shit, watching them perk up. These are sturdy birds. Strong birds. They can survive a lot.

He stands close to the cage, rests his forehead on the wire. King P fluffs his crest and pecks at Rand's hair. Pulls out a few strands and eats them. *Yum,* King P says. *Yum, yum.* He goes back to the seed tray.

Queen Pia opens her beak and grips one of Rand's fingers through the wire. She bites hard.

"Ow!" Rand says.

Happy appul, she says. *Fuck.*

"Yes. Exactly. Fuck."

Pia looks him in the eye, cocks her head, awfully pleased with herself.

"Won't be able to invite any polite company over," he tells her. "Not with your potty mouth."

For the first time, he really looks them in the eye, first Pia, then King P. They eye him and twist their heads around and coo with unrepressed delight. Do birds love? All he knows is that in nature, ones like these travel in enormous flocks, ravaging the countryside in a raucous gang. Men could shoot whole flocks, because when one died, they all came back—to save him? To grieve? Maybe birds get lonely in a cold empty house with its dim light and smell of blue pile carpet. Maybe they missed him. Her. They're staring him in the eye, and for the first time he feels an attachment like a fishhook pulling on his heart.

Rand raises his head and sees Bess standing there.

"They're okay," he says, but it comes out like a sob.

"Goodness sakes, Rand, what happened to your leg?"

He looks down. The bruise is a spiderweb of black and pink. There is something really wrong with it. "It's fine," he lies. "I'm fine."

Rand sends Bess home, unpacks his bag, loads his dirty clothes into the washer. The house is hot, smells like birdshit and wet newspapers and something else that stinks. He puts three pain patches on his leg, takes three ibuprofen and one of Anne's Xanax for good measure. He turns the thermostat down to sixty-five, pours a glass of bourbon on ice. It's eleven-thirty in the morning. What the hell. Be like George.

Get it together, old man. You've got to bury a bird.

Rand gulps his drink down, goes to the garage to get a shovel. Using his good leg, he digs a small square hole under the azaleas close to the kitchen alcove where Molly roosts. Worms and beetles in the damp soil. He goes back inside to get the bird, cradles him in his hand. The red beak has dulled, as if it's covered with a thin layer of ash. That eye, half closed. He can't put O'Mally in the dirt like this. He needs a container. Just like when the kids buried their pet hamsters and mice. A shoebox.

Rand pokes around the closet floor, finds a box of Anne's pumps, red, still in the store tissue. He dumps the shoes on the floor. She loved this damn bird. She would want something of hers in the box with him. A scarf?

A glint of gold catches his eye on the Berber rug. A ring? No, an earring. One of those tiny hoops Anne was always wearing. And losing. It's just the right thing. Half a pair of earrings, like a pirate's treasure, buried with half a pair of tropical birds.

He slips the hoop on his finger and takes the box with its tissue to the kitchen, picks up the brilliant green bird with the red beak, strokes it awhile with his finger. "O'Mally," he says. "O'Mally Boy." He remembers Anne singing that old Irish Danny Boy song to the birds, changing the words. He tries to sing it, but his voice cracks on the second line. Something about pipes? Hills? Well, he can't remember. It's pretty sappy, but he always liked the way it sounded in Anne's scratchy, husky voice.

He hears a rustling, muttering behind him. Molly. She remembers the song. He can't sing it anymore. His throat has completely closed up. What did Anne used to say? *They mate for life. They are never unfaithful.*

Rand moves Molly's cage into the den with the cockatiels. Maybe company will help. And some apple slices.

King P starts whistling "Let Me Call You Sweetheart," and walking back and forth on his perch, crest fully raised. Is he flirting?

Pia screams in outrage: *happy appul!*

"Jealous?" Rand slices her a piece of apple too. "Everybody settle down."

Molly mutters, slumped and guttering, in the corner.

Rand sits at the desk and starts his list. First order of business: Call Carrie. Set up the first leg of his trip. He connects on the first ring.

"Dad?" she says. "Are you home? We've been trying to reach you all week."

"I went to the mountains. What do you mean, 'we'?"

"Jeff and me, who else? I thought we agreed you would keep in touch. At least tell us if you were traveling."

"I called you," Rand protests. "I left a message."

"Yesterday," Carrie says. "What about when you left on Sunday?"

"I told Jeff. I left a note. Everybody knew."

"Jeff was about to call you in for a missing person. He thought you fell off the mountain."

"What? That was completely unnecessary. I wasn't missing."

"You never check the answering machine. That's one," Carrie says. He can see her starting a list of complaints on her fingers, the way Anne used to. "Two," she continues, "you don't answer your cell phone. Three, you don't call back when we leave messages."

"I told you, the cell phone broke," he says. *Plus I didn't want to talk to anybody.*

"I sent you one, Dad. Didn't you get it?"

"I wasn't here."

"Well," Carrie continues, "you actually talked to Jeff. Not me. Does that mean you no longer feel it's necessary to talk to your only daughter?"

"No, honey, that's not it at all. I just needed to get away—"

"Dad, you're making it very hard to keep track of you."

"Who says you need to keep track of me?"

"Dad. We agreed."

"I never agreed. I do what I want." This is not going well. He is supposed to be buttering her up, so he can come visit.

"What's this about coming to LA, Dad? And selling the house? You're not supposed to make any major decisions for two years after a spousal death."

Spousal death. He hears the words in his head like a mocking song: *Anne died, Anne died. Anne's favorite bird died.* Rand sags into Molly's cage. She rubs her face against the wires. "Poor Molly," he says.

"What's that?" Carrie says.

"Nothing, honey." Carrie's still talking. Something about her new reality show about the Grieving Process. Three families, three deaths—a mom, a kid, and a beloved golden retriever. Rand slumps into the recliner. He should tell Carrie about O'Mally. She always loved that bird. "Honey," he says, "I'm sorry. I just buried one of your mother's birds."

"What? Oh, Dad. What happened?"

He wants to tell her how he found him on the floor. How Molly is all alone now. He opens his mouth to say the words. That's when he sees it: a tiny dog turd in a pile of blue fluff, under the library table. "What the *hell*," he says.

"Dad?" the tinny voice comes out of the phone. "What's going on?" He pushes a button to make it go away.

25

Jeff ties Usen to the truck bumper in the shade, tells him to stay. He roots in his vest pockets for a smoke, finding one in a squashed pack with a wad of field-stripped filters. He lights it. Dad's somewhere inside, making his strange plans. Drinking. It will be a short visit. He'll have to confess about the recliner. There will be yelling.

He finishes his smoke, field-strips the butt, and puts it one of his many vest pockets, pinching and sprinkling loose tobacco around his boots. A blessing he learned somewhere. *Beauty all around me.* He doesn't know if it will work here, but it calms him.

The door flies open and Dad charges out, almost running him over. He's got a paper towel clutched in one hand, a spray bottle in the other. Usen yips. Dad spies the dog. "You!" Dad shakes the paper towel at Usen.

"What?" Jeff says. "What's that?"

Dad opens his hand. Nested in the middle of the paper is a dog turd with blue fluff stuck all over it.

"You killed your mother's bird. You put dog shit in my den. If you didn't do it on purpose, you're a bigger fuckup than I thought." Dad thrusts the paper towel at him. "Here," he says. "You can have it back."

Jeff takes the paper towel and stares at the dog doo. "Killed a *bird?* Dad?"

His father's face is red, contorted. The yelling commences. "I ask you to do one thing for me, one simple thing, and you fuck it up. O'Mally was your mother's favorite. You've been a fuckup your whole life and you're a fuckup now. Get the hell out of here. I don't want you coming in this house." Dad slams the door in his face.

Jeff stands there, breathing. He knows the drill. His ears pound. He's used to the yelling. Usen has slipped his pink sparkly collar and stands beside him, teeth bared. Jeff reaches down, settles the pup. O'Mally's dead. *Poor bird. Poor Dad.* He wants to push the door open, find out what happened, see if he can help. But Dad's in one of his "States of Wrath," as Carrie calls it. There's no talking to him.

Jeff tosses the dog shit into the woods. Pops the paper towel in the trash bin. Rescues the collar and leash, opens the truck door.

Usen leaps inside.

"You screwed up, Usen." But the dog was only doing what was natural—going where other animals had gone. There was bird poop all over the damn place. Dad seems to like it that way.

Usen crawls into his lap. "O'Mally died," Jeff says. "Dad hates my guts." Usen licks his nose. "Dad thinks I'm a fuckup," he says. "I *am* a fuckup." Usen bites his hair.

What would Mom say? Mom would say, *Try again tomorrow. You're not dead yet.*

Usen seems to be laughing.

PART IV

SPIRITS RISING

26

In Indigo Field, bees madly scramble from honeysuckle to blackberry vine, pokeweed to dogbane to sourwood. In Jolene Blake's bean patch, they fight over the choicest flowers, loading up on nectar and fertilizing as they go, returning to their sycamore tree hive in Miss Reba's yard, where worker bees seal trickles of nectar into wax pots of liquid gold. There is so much honey already this season, Miss Reba can see the wax cells bulging out of the hive. She sits on the porch and decides: she'll take the honey early this year. If she can ever find the time. That boy TJ is running her ragged.

In Stonehaven Downs, the colonel is mapping his escape plan, pricing plane tickets. He wonders how his son is doing. Sometimes he spies on the boy from the shade of the Gooley pines. He seems to be digging a lot of holes. Rand wonders what he's finding. He wishes the boy would barge back in the kitchen door, bringing strawberries, but he knows what he said is unforgivable. And he is no good at apologies.

At the dig Jeff has found so many new artifacts, he's had to go buy more Ziploc bags. He can't wait to see what they find across the highway, when they finally get permission. It seems to be taking a long time. And he's got to find a home for this dog, before the *Times* reporter comes. Leaving him in Dad's garage is not an option.

High up on the Ridge, a hot wind comes, and the Gooley pines drop last year's needles, last year's cones. New cones fatten to the size of small apples, clutching their seed in early green hearts. Something is coming. They'd best be ready. Their branches sprout a second round of blooms; the blooms dangle and drift more pollen, more cones.

Along the coast, in the damp sand nestled between the dunes, sea turtle eggs incubate, waiting for the right tide, the perfect night, the ocean's call to safety.

❧

Monday, after dinner, Miss Reba catches the whiteboy standing on the porch running his mouth again, talking to Danielle Angel, making excuses no doubt about that iPod. Boy's still mad about having to apologize. And all the extra chores. Hasn't talked to her for most of a

"Selma," Papa says, "we got to pay the taxes or we lose everything we got."

Mama sends me and Sheba off to get kindling, Gem and Thomas out to chop more wood, we can hear her grumble about spending money on oranges and candy when we need the wood for keeping children warm.

Me and Sheba set down our stacks of kindling wood and stand at the top of the Gooley Ridge. We got Christmas for Lucy in our pockets, been a long time since we seen her. We each sewed something pretty on a square of cloth, told Mama it's for the teacher when school starts.

Mine is red cloth with a golden fox head on it. Sheba's is blue with a yellow bird. The water's low in the river, looks icy cold, but we see rocks sticking up in a straight line toward the island. Lucy's fish trap shows when the river's low.

Sheba skips and hops across, I step slow and scared I will fall. We step on sand, weave through vine and bramble, come to Lucy's hut. Her fire's banked, coals covered up with sand, a wisp of smoke seeping out. No Yellow Dog. We call out. Nobody answers. "Must be out visitin'," I say.

"She not the visitin' kind," Sheba says. She looks around. She points: Next to the hut, a row of jars. Clear water tinged red. "Bet you five pennies she out bringin' white liquor to people. Whitepeople put it in the Christmas punch."

I look at the jars. So what Papa said is true. Old Lucy makes white liquor.

"Don't you want to taste it?" Sheba says.

"Nope," I say. "Papa say it make you crazy."

Sheba grabs a jar, twists off the lid, takes a big gulp. She almost drops the jar, she chokes so hard. She puts the lid back on, puts it back in the row. "Hot going down," she says. She rubs her throat and chest and belly with her hands. "Never be cold, you drink that jarful."

I watch Sheba for signs of being drunk. She don't act any more crazy than usual. She just gets real quiet, and I can tell she's thinking about something. We leave our cloth squares on the log where Old Lucy likes to sit.

When we get home, we pile our sticks by the house. Sheba tells Mama I got too cold, but she saw a big branch she could tote back by herself. Mama nods. Sheba goes. I stand there mouth open, but then I shut it. I know she's run off to see a boy she likes from school, give him a Christmas kiss.

Next night, Mama's in labor, and when she's done, Papa comes out, face like thunder, and says to me, "Those herbs you brought have killed the baby."

I run in to see.

Mama's got no strength left. Water leaking from her eyes. Small bundle next to her. I can't look. I sit and hold Mama's hand. Pearl is crying. Thomas is crying. Gem Junior stares at his feet. Sheba has run off somewhere. Papa yells at Mama, says he better not hear she let Old Lucy bury that child the heathen way. Then he goes outside, whittles his stick down to nothing. Then he does another.

Mama sleeps. I pick up the bundle that is a dead sister and wonder what Papa means about heathens. I peek inside. How can anybody bury a sweet thing such as this? Sweet skin so soft, fingers so tiny you can see the lamplight through them. Eyes shut, rosebud lips, tiny face *dead dead dead*. Just what I saw in my fit. Back when I ruint Christmas. I pull the baby close to my heart. I close my eyes to see her alive again, but the fits don't work like that. I rock and rock that dead baby like I have the power to bring her back.

27

Tuesday morning, second period, TJ sits in an orange plastic chair at the school library. He's next on the computer. Poolesville School doesn't have enough, he has to wait his turn.

He's supposed to be finding an unsung hero from history for his English paper, but all he can think about is what Bully Angus did. That day in gym, Bully Angus took his backpack, held it over his head. "Zip zip," he kept saying, zipping and unzipping the pockets.

"Cut it out," he told Bully, and of course that just made Bully laugh and empty the pack in the trash. Then Bully said, "Look, isn't that Tyquan's iPod? Right on top." Everybody thinks he stole it. Abid-somebody won't even look at him anymore. Tyquan jumped up and punched him.

Miss Reba made him go and apologize to Tyquan. Even though he didn't do it. At least she didn't beat him like Daddy would.

"Fifteen minutes," the teacher says now. It's his turn. He wants his hero from history to be Old Lucy, because she knows how to make corn liquor. He wonders where her island is.

TJ Googles *Old Lucy*. Nothing. *Indians*. Too many things. But at the top of the list is *Indigo Field*. He clicks. Here's a newspaper article. It says there are Indian bones buried there, and they're digging them up. So Aunt Reba's stories are true. He scrolls down. The article has a map. The bones are right next to the river bridge, in the cliff. There are comments at the bottom of the website.

> This is just what my daddy always said, it's Indian Field.
> Those bones should be left alone, it's sacrilegious to dig them up.
> My granpa told me there was a massacre there. That's why so many bones.
> If you screw in a Indian boneyard the girl won't get pregnant.

TJ thinks about Leora. He doesn't want to screw her. He just wants to touch her hair. And maybe kiss her.

On the map, there's a big island in a river. Maybe that's Lucy's island. Sheba jumped across on rocks. He wonders if Lucy's still alive. He wonders if Leora would come with him, live on Lucy's island, wear a deerskin and cook fish on a stick.

He checks the clock. Ten more minutes. He looks up prisons.

Last night he woke up in the middle of a dream. Daddy had escaped and was coming to kill him. Daddy was on the porch roof, scratching to get in. To kill him for what he said. *I'm going to tell the whole thing. I hope you fry.* TJ sat there in the dark, clutching his pillow, fear churning his belly, wondering whether to bolt or fight. Then somebody scratched at the window for real. TJ picked up his shoe. He could hit Daddy in the face, roll him off the roof. He opened the window. A claw reached out. He about had a heart attack. But it was raccoons.

Those cute little guys wanted him to come out on the roof with his quilt and play. One of them kept pawing the air like it wanted him to give a high five. It was so funny. But his heart was still pounding. What if Daddy was in the yard, hiding in the bushes? *I get out of here, Imma come wring your neck.*

"Sometimes a bad dream is just something you're worried about," Danielle used to tell him. "Sometimes it's a warning." This one felt like a warning.

TJ scrolls down to read the description of Daddy's prison. Blue Creek Minimum Security. Minimum security means they let them out to clean the roads. He's seen the white buses and the men in orange suits out on the highway. Always a bunch of guards with big-ass shotguns watching. But people escape all the time that way.

TJ writes down the number for the prison. Who has a phone he can borrow? He has no friends.

Leora smiled at him once. She's just across the table. He passes her a note. *Can I use your phone? Emergency. My aunt is sick.* He puts a little sad face at the end. She takes the note. Reads it. Looks surprised, then makes a little frown at him. Writes down her answer. Passes it.

At lunch. In the hall.

He smells the note where she touched it. She catches him doing it. Smiles. Glimmering hair all shining in the sun.

At lunch he opens his paper sack to see what Aunt Reba made him. Bully Angus swaggers up, leans across the lunch table, grabs the paper sack and reaches in. Pulls out a chicken leg, apple, and a piece of pound cake, and eats them right in front of him. "Hey!" TJ says. "What the hell."

Bully licks his lips, folds the paper bag, unzips TJ's pack, and tucks it back inside. "Bring more chicken next time," Bully says. "Or else."

Tyquan's right behind Bully, smirking. Abednego looks away.

TJ stands waiting in the hall, stomach growling, staring at the flyers taped to the wall, Junior Prom coming up, plus all the things to do this summer when school's out. Cheerleading camp. Baseball camp. Lumbee pow wow. There's a picture of a boy covered in red, blue, and yellow feathers, some sticking out of his head, some like wings flying out to the side. Cool.

"Is your aunt okay?" Leora stands beside him in her cute cheerleader outfit.

"It's her heart," he says.

"You live with her?" But there's a question in her eyes: *What happened to your mom and dad?* She doesn't know.

"My parents got a divorce," he says. "It's just temporary. Until I can go to California."

"Oh. Tough luck." Leora hands over her phone, says, "You're not going to steal it, are you?" She grins.

"Nope."

"I know it wasn't you," Leora says. "Bully Angus told me what he did. Do you believe that? What a jerk."

TJ is so surprised that she would care that he can't say anything. Then he says, "Thanks." One person in the world knows he didn't steal Tyquan's iPod—Leora. And maybe Danielle. But Danielle's dead. He pulls out his notebook, finds the phone number, realizes he can't have this conversation in front of Leora. "Uh, Leora?"

"Yeah?" She's been staring at the flyers on the wall.

"Can I take it over there? It's kind of private."

She looks at him like, *Your aunt is private? What the heck?*

"Sure." She shrugs. "But don't steal my phone."

"I won't."

He makes the call and they ask if he's a relative. "I'm his son," he says, and just saying it makes him feel like throwing up. The man confirms Daddy is incarcerated there. Then he tells him when visiting hours are.

"When do they get out to clean the roads?" TJ says.

"I cannot release that information," the man says. *Click.*

He hands Leora her phone.

"Thanks, dude," he says. Did he really say that? She's a *girl.*

She looks at him like she wants to laugh, but doesn't. "No problem, dude."

The bell rings. She tucks the phone in her pack, flashes him the peace sign, and floats down the hall on clouds of golden hair.

After lunch period, TJ walks right out of school and heads for the highway. He stands there, looking up and down the road. No white buses. No cons in orange suits. No guys with big-ass rifles. He's sure his dream was a warning. But Daddy could be anywhere. Maybe he should just run while he has the chance.

TJ looks at the sun, tries to figure out which way is west. He thinks about California, Tennessee, and Hawaii. He's seen all these places on the big map in homeroom. He's spread his hand wide across the miles to see how far they are, then held his hand up to the mile key. Tennessee is pretty close. About three hundred miles. He almost got that far before. Hawaii is the farthest, and you'd have to have a boat. His stomach is growling like a bear. If he's going to run away, he needs supplies. He learned that last time. And cigarettes. Cigarettes make the hunger go away.

TJ roots in his pack for his lunch sack, hoping there's something Bully missed. Some Nabs in the bottom? He can almost taste them. Nope. He wads up the bag and throws it in the ditch. Then he goes and gets it and stuffs it back in the pack. Aunt Reba has this one paper bag she uses over and over again. And she hates litter. He wonders if she's making country steak tonight. Just like Danielle's. Maybe she's not cooking at all. But he knows she keeps Nabs in the Charles Chips can.

TJ sticks out his thumb toward home, gets a ride right away. The guy talks for solid ten minutes, gives him two Marlboros and some matches, takes him right past Daddy's trailer and heads across the river bridge.

"You know where Indigo Field is?" TJ asks. He lights up. *Ahhh.*

"Sure, kid. It's all that over there." The man points at the other side of the road.

TJ looks. Scrubby weeds and an old fence. "Here's good," TJ says. The man pulls over. But he won't stop talking. He tells a long story about how he brought his girlfriend to the Field last Saturday, and she thought it was so romantic. Finally TJ says, "Cool, man. I gotta go." He gets out, runs across the highway, jumps the fence, and heads down to the river to look for Lucy's island.

TJ picks up a stick and whacks away at weeds down by the water. There's a big rock. He climbs up and looks out. Sun blasts down on his head. He shades his eyes. There. Rocks in the water like stepstones. A bunch of tangled vines and bushes. Lucy's island? One way to find out.

TJ jumps down to the water's edge, and a bunch of yellow butterflies swirl up, flutter around, and settle back down in the mud. He squats and pokes one with his finger. It flutters up and comes back down, rests on his hand. It's got a long black tongue sticking out. Tickling him, tasting his sweat. Cool. It flutters up and flies back to the sand.

He sets his pack down, puts his cigarettes and matches in his jacket breast pocket, and steps out on a rock. He's always had good balance. He steps to the next one, and the next. On the fifth rock, it feels like someone pushed him. He slips and falls nuts-deep in the river. *Shit, it's cold.* The ripples around him sound like somebody laughing. The current's pushing him out into the deep. He can't swim.

TJ tries to stand, but his shoes slip on the lumpy river bottom. The next rock isn't too far. He reaches, stumbles forward, grabs the rock. His nuts are about frozen. He makes his way the last few steps to a patch of sand. Vines and trees and bushes. He listens. Nothing but the river making those laughing noises. Nobody's been around here in a really long time. The breeze is hot. His wet jeans grab at his legs.

He finds a trail into the bushes, and there's a clearing. He looks around for a hut, for feather charms hanging from poles, for a big bear-skin, for jars of corn liquor tinged red, but there's nothing. Vines cover something that might be a shed, or just a bunch of fallen-down trees. He stubs his toe on a rock, looks at his feet. The rock is part of a circle. He crouches down, claws at the sand with his fingers. Black cinders under sand. *The many small fires of my people.*

When he was little his mom took him to a party where there was a bonfire. A man put down a pile of pine needles, leaned sticks against each other, then built four stick walls around it. "Tepee in a log cabin," he said. TJ puts a clump of pine needles inside the circle of rocks, piles small sticks on top. He gets down on his hands and knees, lights a match, holds it in his palms till it catches, then pokes it into the pine needles. Poof. Sparks. Flame. He watches it for a while. A puff of wind makes it cave in and go out.

He gets a stick and pokes around some more in the dirt. Maybe there are arrowheads or bones or something. He loses his balance and steps in a fire-ant nest and they come swarming up his shoes. He tries to scrape them off with his stick, then he jumps in the water to drown them, but one is stuck under his sock, biting and biting. He has to dig it out and squash it with his fingers. Now his foot itches like crazy.

He looks around for snakes. He pokes the bushes with his stick. His stick hits something hard. It's a jar full of clear liquid. He holds it up to the light. It's got a tinge of red in it, a puffy-looking thing at the bottom. Lucy's white liquor with the red corn for color. He tries the lid. It's rusted on solid. He's found Lucy's island. He could live here. Catch fish in baskets. Roast them over the fire. Daddy couldn't find him here. But now he's really hungry. He looks around for some clams to eat. But they are all either popped open with the inside missing or closed tight. You need a fire to open a clam. Or a pocketknife. But his pocketknife is in the key bowl.

TJ holds the white liquor jar up, sun glints in the clear like diamonds. He wishes he could show it to somebody. He wishes he could have a taste. Daddy was bad to drink. But he's never even had a sip of beer. He tucks it in his jacket, buttons the jacket all the way up. Jacket's so tight, no way it will fall out.

By the time he's back on dry land, the sun is pretty far down in the sky. He skipped school. His jeans are soaking wet. Now he's got to make up a story for Aunt Reba. She's going to be mad. Really mad. Danielle said, *If you feel like you have to lie, try to tell as much of the truth as you can stand.* That ain't gonna fly with Miss Reba. Maybe he should hitch to California. But he's so hungry. She might be making her country fried steak. That's just a fried hamburger with gravy. He'll go back for dinner. If she tries to send him to Butner, he'll run away to Lucy's island.

TJ looks up. There's something glimmering in the cliff. The low sun makes it shine like gold. He walks along the water, to see it better. When he looks up again, it looks back at him. The internet was right. There's a baby in the side of the cliff. Holes where eyes should be. Dead dead dead. The way the light flickers through the trees, it looks like it might be moving. He blinks. There's more than one. There are two babies in the cliff. No, three. More. *Is it multiplying, like the Pod people?* A howl comes from the top of the cliff. *Lucy's dog? Jesus Christ.* He backs away, falls on his ass into the water, and the jar slips out onto wet sand. He scrambles to his feet and starts to run.

28

Miss Reba stands on her porch, hands on hips, watching TJ trudge up the drive. Since he's been here, this boy has stolen Tyquan's iPod, broke it in half, apologized only because she made him. He's messed up her mama's flower bed, her squash bed, her corn. Yesterday, she went up to close that window he's always leaving open, saw her mama's quilt bunched up on the porch roof. She got a hammer and nailed the window shut. And now here he is, late from school, soaking wet, covered in sand and mud, smelling like tobacco.

Miss Reba reams him out good. He wasn't on the bus. When she called the school they said he was absent all afternoon. His clothes are wet and muddy. Sticks and weeds in his hair. Shoes ruined. "Where'd you run off to? Best tell the truth."

"I went to Lucy's island. I wanted to see if it was true, all what you said."

It stops her dead.

She stands there squinting at him. "You been spying on me?"

He nods. "I like the stories, Miss Reba. I like Indian stories. And all about Sheba."

She stares at him some more. *What does he know about Sheba?*

Finally she opens her mouth. "Don't spy," she says. "And don't you ever lie to me."

"Yes, ma'am."

Miss Reba skewers him with a look. She sends him upstairs to think about his ways. Then she goes to talk to Danielle. That angel face bright and kind and lively.

"This boy's always going to lie. That's what whiteboys do. It's in the blood. Danielle, something don't change, Imma have to give him back."

"He told the truth just now, Auntie," Danielle says right out loud, her brown eyes gleaming. "It's good he likes Sheba and Old Lucy and your stories. I like them too."

"He needs to stop using my Egyptian Queen," Reba says.

"Tell him," Danielle says.

"Boy needs something to keep him busy. These chores ain't enough."

Danielle goes quiet, like she agrees. But maybe she's gone away again.

Reba scoops chickenscratch from the trunk of the car, flings. Chickens come running. Dent still there. Whiteboys and whitemen dogging her on every side.

"Jolene needs help," Danielle says.

"That's right." Miss Reba nods. "And she would make him work. No lazing around at Miss Jolene's." Let the whiteboy leave her in peace a few hours.

"Tell me a new story, Auntie," Danielle says. "Tell me the story you don't want to tell."

Miss Reba's heart sags in her chest. She knows just the one she means. But not with the boy spying. That boy's going to go work for the hardest-working white woman in Ambler County, soon as she can arrange it. She picks up the phone. Calls Jolene. Who seems to need help more than pride right now.

"Saturday?"

Yes. Saturday.

29

Saturday afternoon at Spill Creek Farm, Jolene is up to her elbows in the kidding pen with Folly. There are two new kids with silver dapples on their flanks. Bobo has named them Wiggles and Kicks. But Folly, her oldest goat mama, is exhausted. She hasn't been able to feed them. And now Bobo's out in the yard somewhere, calling, "Mama! Mama! Mama!" until she comes out of the barn.

"What!" she says, exasperated.

"TJ here!"

Jolene plucks her birthing gloves off her hands, lays them on the sink counter, and heads out to face the son of the man who killed Danielle. Bobo will work in the barn. TJ will work in the garden. The two of them will not be left alone together. Miss Reba waves. TJ gets out of the car.

Bobo cries out, "TJ!" Gives the boy a big hug. Bounces up and down on his toes, all smiles.

"Hi, Miss Jolene," TJ says. "How you doing?"

"Fine, TJ," she says. "Just fine." Looks like Miss Reba has taught him some manners. She hopes he doesn't have his father's work habits.

"Show TJ my babies?" Bobo is practically hopping in place.

Jolene nods. "But after that, TJ has to work. Bobo has chores to do."

"Okay, Mama!" Bobo says. "Come see, TJ!"

TJ looks at Jolene, grins at her. He likes Bobo, Jolene can see that. Maybe that's a good thing. Maybe not.

She follows the two of them to the barn. She will need to keep an eye on them. Her plan is to keep them apart as much as possible. Besides, Bobo already has a new best friend, and as far as she knows his father isn't a murderer.

Jolene watches as Bobo kneels in the straw, and the flock of new kids stumble over to nuzzle his overalls, looking for a meal. "Stick out yoh finger," Bobo says. "Like this." One of the kids latches on and sucks.

"No, man. TJ don't play that." TJ stays on the other side of the gate. Then he tries it. The baby sucks hard. TJ laughs out loud. "Whoa, there, little buddy." The goats seem to like TJ. But Jolene knows goats will attach to anything. If there aren't any other goats around, you will be its herd—you, or a duck or a dog, or whatever living thing is handy. TJ, for instance.

"All right," Jolene says. "Time for TJ to work. Time for Bobo to do chores. Feed the mamas so Mama can milk."

TJ looks at her quizzically. She knows how she sounds. Like she's talking baby talk. But it's what Bobo responds to. It's his special language. He likes to hear his name.

"TJ," she says, "come with me." She grabs two hoes and her garden gloves. She's got to set him up chopping weeds so she can get back to Folly, check her and the kids, then start the milking. The girls do not like to be kept waiting.

TJ follows her to the bed of French filet beans. They look so terrible, already overrun with crabgrass and amaranth that have thrived in this heat. She's a little embarrassed for him to see them. She never mulched. She's behind on everything.

She shows TJ a pointed hoe. "This is for the deep roots, like amaranth," she says. "See here? You have to chop deep, then pull the root out."

TJ takes it. Tries it out. "Like that?"

"Yes."

She shows him the half-moon hoe. "And this," she says, "is for the surface weeds. Henbit, chickweed. Those just scrape off like this. Miss Reba says you've done this before?" She hands him the hoe.

TJ nods. "Yes, ma'am. I know how to chop weeds." He looks a little insulted.

"Don't get too close to the stem. Don't dig in near the roots. You've got to get in there with your fingers to get what's close." She forgot to bring him gloves. She pulls hers out of her back pocket. "Here," she says. "You'll need these."

"Thanks," he says. He pulls them on and flexes his fingers. They're a little big on him.

"Pile the weeds onto the tarp here. Just drag the tarp along the row. We'll mulch it all out when you're done."

TJ picks up a hoe. Starts to chop. She watches him for a minute or two. Then she says, "Come see me in the barn when you're done. Bring your tools with you."

"Yes, ma'am," TJ says. The boy looks insulted again. Like she thinks he would steal her hoes or leave them in the dirt.

God, please don't let him kill my prize filet beans.

TJ shows up just as milking is over, hoes balanced on his shoulders, blades scraped off clean. Bobo is done hosing down the feeding buckets for the kids. Folly has settled down. No bleeding, feeding normally, no need to call the vet. She's the oldest doe. Jolene was worried. Bobo cuddles the babies in his arms.

They can all mulch together.

The tune of an old hymn from her childhood comes to her, one her mother used to love. How did it go? She hums, fills in her own words in her head.

> Let us all mulch together, on our knees.
> Let us all mulch together, on our knees.
> When we mulch on our knees, with our face to the rising sun,
> Oh, Lord, have mercy on me.

She would sing it for Bobo if TJ weren't here. But she doesn't want Miss Reba finding out she makes fun of church singing.

TJ takes the pitchfork, hoists the flakes of spoiled hay, drops them every few feet in the paths in a row. He's done a good job weeding. And he catches on quickly. She and Bobo spread the hay by hand, three inches thick, next to, but not touching, the stems of the tender plants. TJ is better at hoisting than Bobo. Bobo gets distracted and drops things in the wrong place.

Bobo holds up a worm for her to see. "Look, Mama! Wiggly!"

"Nice, Bobo. Put it back." Worms mean good soil. She's been working on this strange blue clay for eight years, adding composted goat and chicken manure. It is finally producing beautiful crops.

The French green bean plant before her is covered with healthy blooms—purple and folded, pale on the inside—and some of the blooms have fallen and left behind tiny beans like green needles. She'll have to pick in three days. It's only mid-May. Everything is so early this year. If this weather holds—warm during the day, rain at night—the second planting might make it before summer heat burns it to a crisp or grasshoppers start chewing.

The sun's been in and out of the clouds all day, and now it streams across the hayfield from the west, lighting up the tops of the Gooley pines above her, the dark green humps of potato plants, the purple flowers on the young bean plants and the bright straw under their knees. *When I fall on my knees, with my face to the setting sun.* She hums the hymn and feels the light on her shoulders. The farm is beautiful this afternoon. Bobo is happy. TJ may be a blessing after all.

30

Miss Reba settles into her chair. Afternoon light caught in the sycamore. Danielle's box in her lap. Black angels leaning in to hear. Place seems so quiet without a whiteboy rustling around, getting in trouble. Box heavy as a bowl of peaches in her lap now. Danielle is coming alive.

"Danielle baby," she says. "The hard part is coming."

❧

That winter after the baby died, we live in a house of sorrow. Seems like Papa's mad all the time. Mama's so quiet. The house is so cold. She sleeps with coats over her, the young ones curled around.

Sheba's acting up. Papa acts like it's my fault she's gotten to that age where she likes boys. She's always hankering to get away.

"She's your sister," he says to me. "You got to watch her. Make sure she do right. You hear?"

"I can't make her do nothing," I say, and he slaps me across the face.

"Lissen here," he says. "You follow her. Don't let her go to the Field and that crazy Indian woman. Don't you go there neither. And if she go to Lucky's Tavern, or she go with a boy, you run back and tell me."

So I do it. Maybe Papa will like me if I do. Maybe I will save my sister. But Sheba likes to do what she wants.

I follow her into the Gooley pines. I watch her kiss a boy. I watch her with a boy she says she loves. They lie all over each other. He pushes on her. Then he tells her go away, he don't love her. I follow her all the way down Spill Creek Road to Lucky's, watch Sheba drink so much she falls down and Papa has to come.

I tell Papa some. I don't tell everything I see.

Papa punishes her, but she don't care. She mostly gets mad at me.

"Why you tell on me?" she says. "Papa don't need to know every little thing I do."

Me and Sheba have slept in the same cornhusk bed since we were babies. I am used to having a warm Sheba back to lean on, the sweet-musky girl smell helps me sleep. But now Sheba pushes me off with her elbow, her foot, her knee.

I lie there, pretending I live with Lucy's Indians in the Field. Sleep in a hut by the river.

Next fall we are back picking cotton. Sheba won't tell the Indian stories anymore as we go down the rows. She wants to tell me about boys. Kissing. Love. But I don't like to hear it. I hum Indian songs so I can't hear. I pick faster so I get ahead. Sheba stays behind, mooning, looking at the sky for signs of boys.

Mama has another baby. Papa names her Mount Ararat, for the place of safety in the Bible. We call her Airy. I don't like to hold her at first. I remember the other baby. *Eyes shut, rosebud lips, tiny face dead dead dead. Papa say the herbs I brought have kilt her.*

One day in October, I tell Mama I know where there are hickory nuts. I run off to see Old Lucy.

She's sitting by the fire, smoking her pipe, like she's been waiting for me. She looks up, then she looks around, as if to say, *Where is Sheba, the one I like best?* But then she nods and takes me by the hand and leads me into the hut. She never let us all the way in before. Old Lucy's hand is like a claw, dirty nails curling under, but warm and strong. It's dark inside. She got hides on the wall. Hole for smoke. Pallet for a bed with rags and skins.

Old Lucy kneels down before a trunk, opens the lid, pulls out a bundle wrapped in skins and a piece of soft quilt. She opens the skins, one flap, then another, till I see what it is. It's a book. A big book with a crackly dark cover and spine, pages that look rough and yellow. Like a Bible. "Can I touch it?" I say. Old Lucy nods. I put my palm on the crusty dark leather. It's cool and bumpy to the touch, and it smells like old tobacco. Lucy cracks the book open to the middle, and a groaning sound comes from the spine.

"What's that!" I say.

"My people speaking," Lucy says.

Old Lucy turns the book so I can see: black ink pictures of Indian huts and gardens, women and babies, ships and maps, fish traps and fire pits. People gathered around. Making supper. Goosebumps rise on my arms. It's just what I saw when I closed my eyes, listening to her stories by the fire.

"Who made that book?" I say, for I have never seen one like it.

"Johnston Blake," she says. "And others."

"These your people?" I say.

"Some of them," Lucy says.

Old Lucy turns the page. On one side, there's a man with shell beads around his neck, a bird on his head, arms up, looks like he's about to fly up into the sky.

"This here," Lucy says, and points a bony finger at the next picture. "This how we do the bones."

It's a hut with a raised floor made of poles. Just like she has. But this one in the picture has dead bodies laying side by side. Eyes closed. Skin all shrunk to the bone. On the ground underneath is a small fire, and smoke drifts up through the floor to where they lie.

"Those dead people?" I ask.

Lucy nods.

Her bundle in the pole shed must be one too. "How they die?"

"Pestilence. War. Sorrow."

I remember now what Sheba said, a long time ago, about Lucy scraping people's bones. Sucking out the juice. "What happens to the bones?" I say. Maybe she's about to kill me. Maybe it's all true what Sheba said. *What Papa said.*

"Don't eat 'em like people say. We tell that so they scared of us." She chuckles deep in her throat. "Scrape and clean. Wrap up in deerskin." Old Lucy pets the fox skin next to her hand. "Fox if it's small. Pots for babies."

"Sheba say in India, people turn into animals when they die. Your people turn into animals?"

"Sometimes," Lucy says. "But mostly they spirits. We wrap 'em up and fold the bones a secret way nobody knows but the Keeper of the Bones. We put 'em where we stay. If we have to move, we take 'em with us. That way we can talk to spirits wherever we go."

I think about that. So this is the heathen burial Papa's so afraid of. I've seen Lucy make a clay pot big enough to bury Mama's baby who died. But Mama and Papa buried that baby themselves, under the sweet-shrub.

Miss Reba raises her head. Phone's ringing. She can't tell any more of it now. It's just too sad.

"Danielle," she says, "I'll tell the rest later."

31

Jolene opens one eye. It's the dead of night. The electric lantern casts a dim light. She is lying next to Folly in the straw, her arm flung over Folly's ribs, the sweet-sour smell of mama goats in her nose, the tangle of dreams catching at her like wisps of hay stuck to her face and hair. In her dream, someone was kissing her. Luke? No. Frank? *No.* Someone with blue eyes and freckles. Someone who smells like sweat and earth. Bobo's new friend Jeff. *What's he doing here?* Jolene sits up.

When he came last Tuesday, Bobo was so excited. It's hard to admit, but so was she. It's how much Bobo likes him, she'd told herself. But it was more than that.

Bobo and TJ are dead asleep in the kidding pen with the newborns, covered with old quilts. Bobo asked if TJ could stay the night, and since they were doing so well, she called and Miss Reba said yes. Now Bobo's sprawled big as a grown man in the straw, sleeping with his mouth open, a tiny baby goat tucked against his side. TJ's curled in a tight ball, a peaceful expression on his face, clean and innocent, his arms around his kid, holding it to his chest.

The boys did great last night. TJ made PB&Js and coffee, Bobo showed him how to bottle feed. TJ looked sweet feeding his kid, saying things like, "There you go, little buddy, drink all you want." She could hear them talking for hours and it was a new sound in the goat barn— boys fooling around. Maybe Bobo has another new best friend after all.

Maybe TJ doesn't take after his father. Maybe he takes after Danielle, who was sweet to the core. A beautiful young woman. She was like a mother to TJ. It makes sense that he would have a piece of her inside him.

Jolene steps over the gate and rests her hands on each of the tiny kids, one by one—first TJ's, then Bobo's, careful not to wake the boys. The first baby is sleeping hard, belly full of warm milk. But Bobo's is cold and stiff. She pulls the body gently from beside Bobo. Holds it to her heart. Smooths the silver-dappled rump. So beautiful. She remembers Luke declaiming his favorite poem, back when he was an assistant professor and she was a wide-eyed college girl. *Glory be to God for dappled things....* He bought Folly, their first goat, for those lacy circles like impressions of silver coins on her tiny flanks.

Jolene rubs her cheek against its cheek. Sweet baby goat smell. Then she wraps the newborn in an old towel, places it in the back of the truck. She'll bury it next to Ace, to keep him company.

She leaves the boys and remaining kid sleeping soundly. Time for coffee. A full day coming. There is no time to dwell on the sadness that comes with any animal death. She's up an hour early this morning. Maybe she can finally read her mail.

The dial on the kitchen radio glows green in the dark. The porch wren is making its raspy warning call, *Stay away, stay away.* Little brown eggs must have hatched.

She fills out her work log for yesterday:

Temp: 56/80.
Rain: none.
Births: Folly—two—1 buck, 1 doe

She draws a line through "doe." Writes "deceased."

Garden: weeded and mulched—¾ of row 1, filet beans.

Did TJ leave the pitchfork out there? It's supposed to rain later. Rust is the enemy of the well-worn tool.

She refills her cup from the percolator on the stove. She picks up the first letter in the pile, one from the Division of Archaeology. She slits it open with a paring knife.

Dear Mrs. Blake, I'm writing to ask permission to conduct archaeological surveys on your land. It's a long letter from someone named Charles E. Mathers, PhD, about how her land could contain the find of the century, and so on. He describes what he believes is under the soil: a Native village spread all along Indigo Field, next to the Gooley pines. He describes what she could expect, how long it would take. There would be a man on-site at night to protect and guard the area.

Jolene sets the letter down. The sheriff told her about the cliff burial. But she hasn't paused long enough to imagine the rest of it. Indigo Field has lain there, producing her thistles for rennet and forage for goats, and Reba's herbs all the way back to when she was midwifing, and all the time, underneath, there's been a secret world. Remnants of a village full of people. Something Luke hinted at. She can almost see it, rising out of the mist by the river: people cooking on open fires, tending gardens, the Gooley pines shimmering above. Dr. Mathers wants to bring all that to light. It gives her the shivers. She's always thought of Indigo Field as a lonely place, her special place, haunted only by goat trails and memories: making love with Luke on a warm patch of grass between the rocks.

Turns out she has neighbors there. Dead ones.

Bobo would love the activity, the people nearby, the arrowheads and discoveries. He was so excited when the sheriff came and told them about the bones. Maybe Bobo could be a helper. Maybe that's another skill he could learn. Bobo is very careful with his collection. And what did Mathers say? There would be a man there, guarding it.

Jolene counts off the pros on her fingers: She doesn't need the pasture till winter. As long as they're done by then, it could work. Bobo would make even more new best friends. She is about to pick up the pen and sign when she remembers that Miss Reba's people used to own the Field, the pines, everything. Maybe she should ask her first.

Jolene refills her coffee, prepares to dig into her pile of bills.

She pays Southern States and Electric, and a vet bill from two months ago. She reads an article in the Organic Farmers Association newsletter about solutions to fire ants. No, chickens won't eat them. There's a big creamy manila envelope from the bank with two envelopes inside, a bank letter and a Frank letter. She opens the bank letter first. It's from a bank she never heard of. *Dear Mrs. Blake, I am sorry to inform you....*It says that since her bank was purchased by Family Home Mutual in Charlotte several months ago, the rules have changed. She's in the "red zone," which means the collateral she put down will be seized if she does not pay up within sixty days.

Sixty days. She checks the date on the letter—five days ago. So, fifty-five. No problem. There's extra milk now. She'll catch up and pay off in time. She always does. But there's more. The letter reminds her that the collateral she gave *hereinafter called Indigo Field,* was a twenty-acre parcel bounded by the river and the highway on one side and the Gooley Ridge on the other, the line drawn to include all those enormous pines. There are numbers at the bottom. What she's paid, what she owes, the amount due now: $40,000.

She blinks and looks again. Dear God. They want her to pay in full. Not just what's past due. All of it.

Son of a jigsaw sailor. She's got nothing worth that kind of money.

She tears open the other envelope, the one from Frank.

Dear Mrs. Blake, I know this notice must be a blow. I know how difficult it is to make a living farming these days, and on top of that you face the struggles of raising a special boy. I believe I can help. Would you like to meet for coffee?

No. No, she would not like to meet for coffee. Every time she does bank business, she can see him thinking: *If you married me, you wouldn't have these problems.*

It's impossible. She can't lose the Field. She can feel her heart sinking into a familiar panic. She shakes it off. There are boys to feed, goats to milk. As far as the money, she'll think of something. Later.

Jolene cooks up fifteen whole-wheat blueberry pancakes, piles them up on a plate, covers the plate with a cloth to keep warm in the stove, brings out a Mason jar of last year's honey from the wild bees in Miss Reba's sycamore, heats some in a saucepan on low, and heads back to the barn. She checks on Folly. The mama goat gets to her knees. Groans. Lurches up, stumbles to the water bucket and drinks. Jolene throws her arms around her, presses her face against her warm neck, closes her eyes, drinks in the smell of life. When she opens her eyes, light is flooding through the barn from the tips of the Gooley pines. How is it possible that she could lose them? Jolene finds the pitchfork illuminated with sunlight, leaning against the wall. TJ brought it in after all. And her gloves too, laid out on the rail.

Time to wake them up. Time to start the day. What is it Miss Reba always says? *Time to feed the living.*

She wakes the boys, laughs at the pieces of straw stuck to their hair. Bobo looks around. Where's the other one? "Mama! Theh ah two!" TJ looks at her as if he knows. But she just can't bear to see Bobo cry this morning.

"Mama's taking care of the littlest one," she says. "Go make a bottle for this one. TJ can help."

Jolene sets out feed, milks the does, strains and chills the milk, then she heads to check on Folly, squirts some vitamin molasses mix into her mouth. Then she looks in on the boys. Bobo has the remaining newborn between his knees, bottle tilted just so, the way he's been taught. He's crooning a song to his little one, eyes closed in pleasure. TJ looks up, says, "Miss Jolene, how's—" and she knows he's about to say, *How's the other one?*

She shakes her head, puts finger to lips: *Shh.* TJ looks at her, confused. Looks at Bobo. Then shrugs. Let him think she's lost her mind. "Breakfast soon," she says. "Blueberry pancakes."

"Pancay!" Bobo cries. "Yum. You will like them, TJ."

"Stay with this baby, Bobo," Jolene says. "I'll feed the other ones."

When she's done, Jolene surprises the boys, brings the pancake breakfast right into the barn. They eat in their laps, sitting on a straw bale, while the newborn stumbles around between Folly's legs. The boys laugh and joke and don't ask once about the missing one. She sends them ahead to carry the dishes to the kitchen. She stands to follow, then pauses in the yard. There's such a shimmer in the new pecan leaves overhead, she has to take a moment. Watch the cloud-mottle in the pink wisp of sky. Listen to the shouts of so many birds calling out their breeding songs at once, feel everything stop for the earth to spin. *The microbe dance,* Luke used to call it. The sense that your own arms and legs, your own breath and heart, are part of a dance that includes newborn spiders floating on silk in the new green timothy, sparkling and dewy, a mystery held in the safety of farm fields below and skies above. What was that Hopkins line? *Landscape plotted and pieced—fold, fallow, and plough.* She can't lose the Field, the farm, the Gooley. It is impossible. She remembers how a deep part of her said "home," when Luke first showed her the fields, the small house, the Gooley Ridge in sunlight. Life without this place would be a dark cave.

She stops to peer at the brood of just-hatched wrens in Luke's old boot on the porch, their tender pink necks straining upward, beaks wide open, gaping gullets. So trusting that they will be fed. So vulnerable.

She'll have to drive TJ home soon. Maybe it can wait till afternoon. Bobo is having so much fun. And she hates to leave a newborn alone. Anything can happen. Coyotes, for instance. She's heard yipping from up on the Ridge. She raises her head and listens. It's awfully quiet. What are those boys up to? She doesn't see them anywhere.

TJ can't believe he just slept in the straw with a baby goat. He wishes there were somebody he could tell. Danielle would get it. She always liked animals. "Our furry friends," she called them. "I draw the line at bugs." But now Bobo is motioning him to follow.

"Come see!" Bobo says.

"What?" TJ says. The big kid is such a trip. He's not too smart, but he knows everything about goats. Like how to hold a milk bottle so bubbles won't get in a baby goat's stomach.

Bobo leads him to an old fallen-down shed behind the barn, shows him a table with a small box on it. Bobo opens the box. "Papa's things," he says. "Look."

There are all kinds of nature things inside. Dead beetles. Yuck. But some bugs are pretty.

"Buh-fly," Bobo says. He points to orange and black, yellow and black, and pale green butterfly wings dotted with what look like golden eyes. "One-two-three-twelve," he says. The kid is beaming with pride over his bugs. "Touch it!"

TJ pets one with his finger. Orange dust sparkles on his fingertip.

"Soft!" Bobo says. He pets it too.

"Yeah. Soft," TJ says. He wipes the dust on his jeans. But now the big kid is showing him the next thing, emptying out a cloth bag.

"Mista Rid give me pennies!" Bobo lines them up, all twelve of them, shiny and new.

"Okay, sure, man, nice pennies." If it were him, he'd ask for quarters.

Now Bobo opens a glass jar. Empties it out.

"Awwoh-heds!" Bobo says. There must be a hundred of them.

TJ picks one up. "Where'd you get this?" He thinks about Old Lucy on her island. Maybe these are *her* things.

"Papa find that one," Bobo says. "In the *snow.*"

"In the snow?" Can you find an arrowhead in the snow? The kid's making it up.

"Papa in heaven. In the pines."

Bobo's dad is dead? *Well, you don't see him around here anywhere, do you?* TJ wishes his daddy were dead. For sure his daddy never gave him arrowheads and shit.

"Shahp," Bobo says. "See?" Bobo sticks the point in TJ's palm.

"Ow," TJ says.

"TJ hut?" Bobo looks so worried.

"No, man, I'm just kidding."

Bobo puts it back in the jar.

"Look, TJ! Feathahs." He opens a metal box, points to a dried-up dead bird. Holes for eyes. Faded orange and green feathers. It looks really old. And it looks like something's been chewing on it.

"Papa say Cah-linah pah-keet. Last one. Want to pet it?"

"No thanks, man." The bird is dead. Who wants to pet a dead bird?

Bobo closes the lid. Points to the dark end of the shed.

Looks like there's an old tractor back there. Maybe something he could fix, once he takes mechanics. But it also looks like it's full of spiders, cobwebs hanging down like vines.

"Se-cwet." Bobo puts his fingers to lips. "Shhhh."

"Sure, okay. I can keep a secret." TJ hopes the secret isn't just another pile of bugs or pennies or dead birds.

"Be cahful, TJ! Spi-dah!" Bobo is waving his arms around, whacking at his head like he's got spiderwebs caught in his hair, and he's making little "Ah! Ah!" sounds. But the kid keeps going. If Bobo isn't afraid of spiders, then *he* can't be.

TJ steps over rusty tools, axe heads, rakes, and tractor wheels. Spiderwebs snag his face and arms. Bobo stops in front of a wooden table. There's a big box on it, and sun peeks through a knothole, making it shine like gold.

Bobo puts fingers to lips. "Po-mis not to tell?"

"I promise." It looks like the kind of box that might have pirate treasure in it. Gold coins and shit.

Bobo steps on a milk crate. Opens the lid. "Look, TJ."

TJ looks. The sun flickers on a bundle of deerskin. Soft fur on the inside edge, glistening white in the ray of sun. "Pet it, TJ," Bobo says. "Soft!"

TJ pets it. It must be a white deer. His daddy told him about the white deer, how they show up like magic charms in the woods. "Where'd you *get* this?" TJ is suddenly so jealous of this big strange kid, whose daddy gave him things like this.

"Look," Bobo says. He opens the bundle.

"Whoa. Dude. What is *that*?"

"The Bone Man."

TJ stares at it. It is a man. Folded arm bones, folded legs, backbone like a long white snake, then at the top, a skull. Smooth and yellow. Bobo reaches in and wiggles a tooth. "Look, TJ, it wiggles."

"Bobo, this is some crazy shit you got here."

"Crayzeee shih," Bobo says, beaming. "Papa say he old. Don't touch!"

But Bobo is touching it, petting the head. He lifts the skull carefully, hands it to TJ.

TJ holds it up to the beam of light above his head. Looks inside the nose hole. The back of the skull is round and shadowy, like the dark side of the moon. A spider falls out on his forehead.

"Shit shit shit!" TJ drops the skull, slaps at his face to get the spider off.

"Uh-oh, uh-oh, uh-oh!" Bobo flaps his hands. "Spidah!"

Bobo's making little high-pitched cries of distress. "Bobo," TJ says, once he gets the spider off, "it's okay now." But he can't see where the skull went.

Bobo points under the table. "Get it, TJ!"

It's totally spiderwebs under there. But TJ gets down on his knees. He reaches into the dark. Picks up the skull with his fingertips. There's a crack where it used to be smooth and yellow. "Sorry, dude," he says, and he's saying it to the Bone Man as much as to Bobo.

TJ puts it back in the box. What is Bobo doing with something like this in his shed? He wonders if somebody murdered it. He wonders if Miss Jolene even knows the bones are here.

32

R eba wakes up Sunday morning and TJ's not here. Jolene called. A goat died. She wanted TJ to stay a little longer. The place feels empty of life. Death hangs in the air on a morning like this.

She goes out on the porch in her slippers, looks around. Feeds the chickens out of the trunk of the car. Puts her hand on the dent. It's gotten bigger. The whole fender is crackled with red rust now, spreading out like a spiderweb from the dent the whiteman made.

Little breeze in the sycamore tree. Danielle is standing by. Gem floating in his watery grave. Sheba Angel looks at her with a sad worn-out face. It's time to do something she's been wanting to do for a good long while.

Reba gets out the paintbrush, opens the can, puts black paint on Sheba, spruces her eyes up blue and white, lips red. Mouth open, like she might speak. Little white teeth. She finds Sheba's sword, fits it into that raised fist, paints it silver. Lord, Lord. What has she done? Now Sheba looks like she wants to bellow out her story.

Danielle Angel got that pleading eye. "What happened to Sheba?" she says.

Gem leans in. Seems like he wants her to tell his story too.

Reba goes inside and pulls down the gold-wrapped box with Danielle inside, wishes she had a box with Sheba's ash and bones. But Sheba's bones are back in the corn patch, where the red corn grows. For reasons Reba understands only in her arms and legs, like poison or fear, Papa wanted to hide the evidence. Evidence of a crime so terrible it could come back and kill them all just by the telling.

The box in her lap feels heavy as a toddler. Sun bright in the sycamore tree. Little breeze comes. Reba closes her eyes. Fat green leaves make noise like hands clapping, like the rhyming song Sheba liked to sing: *Sally Jones went to the fair, found her little boyfriend there, punched her boyfriend in the nose, 'cause he was with Alice Mose.*

"Lissen here," Reba starts. Everything goes quiet. Her little eye opens and she sees it all, Indigo Field and all that happened there, rising up like fish in the river. Sheba rises too, says, *Time to tell my story.*

Miss Reba opens her lips and lets her words fall like a child falling into a cornhusk pallet full of sisters and brothers, and she is suddenly no longer alone. Danielle's here. They're all here.

It was war time then, Danielle. Gem Junior wants to sign up. Papa says he's too young, but Gem runs off to join. He writes Mama a letter, says he gonna be serving his country on a far-off tropic isle in the Pacific. Thomas hears that and he wants to go too. "You too young," Mama says. "All of twelve years old." Her lips press together: *No.*

Gem's ship never gets to the tropic isle. Gem and his boat sink in blue deep water. Midway, they call it. When Sheriff Walter Pickett comes to tell Papa, Papa stands on the doorstep trembling. After, he sends me for a jar of Lucy's hooch, gets drunk the first time I ever seen. Crying and yelling and singing songs in the yard. Falling down. Mama has to drag him in the house. Papa's right, I reckon. *Drinking make you crazy.*

Sheba turns sixteen, starts running off to Lucky's Tavern by the river every night now, a place churchpeople visit on Saturdays, talk bad about on Sundays. At Lucky's, Black and white alike drink, play cards, jitterbug, listen to jazz. Earl Hines Orchestra got a new song on the radio, Sheba's all crazy for it, sings it to me in the bed, all about being lonesome, and it rains and rains.

Sheba got a taste now for Lucy's hooch, sold by the jar and by the glass from behind the counter at Lucky's. She got a taste too for playing tricks on the Hooper boys—two big dumb whiteboys still left in that family after the youngest run off to war. Sheba say Billy Hooper got a crush on her, "dumb cluck." She say he and Cletus got out the draft 'cause they Daddy on the draft board. She never liked these Hoopers, even more since Gem Junior died that way, so she cheats them at cards, puts bugs in their drinks, tells them lies about places to go fishing in the river, catch the biggest fish in the world. "Walk out on the rocks," she says, knowing they can't swim. She hopes they drown.

Sheba comes home and tells me her tricks on them, liquor breath on her lips, sister-girl smell warm in the bed. I close my eyes, see Lucky's clear as rain, though I never been inside. I see Sheba looking for a way out of sorrow, like a bug fighting its way out a spiderweb. I have got my first blood and want to ask her about it, feels like snakes in my belly. But I don't. "You 'bout to grow up, Reba," Sheba says to me, breathing on my head. "Imma go away soon. You come too."

I want to say, *Don't go away, don't don't don't*. But looks to me like Sheba finally seen her chance to fly up with those yellow butterflies and dance for the kings of many nations. Almost makes me want to go. But I am the Turtle Who Stays in the Field.

Papa switches Sheba's backside with a briar when he hears about where she's been at night, Mama reads her Bible verses. Sheba only laughs and says, "Wait and see. Imma go to Norfolk, Virginia, where the sailors go."

August 6, 1945. Danielle, you learnt this in school. In Japan that day, people eat rice for breakfast, walk to work, send children to class. They look to the sky, hear a strange sound. A great light shines, lights up their bones through the skin. Buildings and people and every living thing turn to ash.

All over Ambler County, people hear it on the radio. They run and tell neighbors. Run and tell us. Mama and Papa sit there, don't eat their supper. "It's a sin, Selma. That's what it is. A sin. Our own son fought for those whitemen." The children and me, we look up in the sky, wonder if something like that might set the whole sky on fire, all the way to here. Sheba shivers when she hears it, takes to her bed. It takes her a week to gather up her courage again. Then we hear about Nagasaki. Seems like the bombs are getting closer to where we live.

Not long after, Sheba packs to leave.

I was eleven that day, all bucktooth and ashy-skin, Sheba seventeen, all chocolate skin and curves. She puts her things in an old sack, says, "You coming? Train stop down in Quarryville tonight. Train to Norfolk. Somebody at Lucky's give us a ride." I don't want to go. But I can't stand for her to leave me behind. I put my church dress into a pillowcase and follow her into the woods, down to the river. Outside Lucky's, she stashes her bag behind a tree. "Wait here," she says. I stare through the smudgy window, watch Sheba's smooth body sway, watch her flirt and dance, watch her sapphire eyes glint and flicker, watch her rule a kingdom of men not worthy of someone named for a great queen in the Bible.

So many people that night at Lucky's, they spill outside. Music louder than ever. I creep to the doorway. See better that way. Music stops. Man's voice comes on the radio. "It's over!" the voice say, all crackle and spark. "The war is over!" Bells ring, people shout. Everybody in the room looks so happy. I feel happy too. Maybe nobody else will have to die. Maybe Sheba will stay home now.

Old Lucy must have brought a fresh batch of hootch, because now they're all drinking whole glassfuls of clear liquor, tinged blood red. Drinking to the death of the enemy, drinking to the power of the US of A. Hooper boys talking about how the power of the A-bomb proves white minds is smarter, and how they wish they been there, just to watch Japs fry. A few more drinks and the Hooper boys cry over their little brother who got killed in the Pacific, Battle of Midway.

Sheba drinks down a glass of Lucy's brew, steps up on a table, cries out, "Here's to my brother and yours! Dead in the same battle, fightin' the same war. Brothers in arms!"

Everyone turns to Sheba. Something twists inside her to say what she said next. Sheba always been brave. But now all the fear is burnt out of her by that Hiroshima fireball. That Lucy hooch. She turns to Lucky behind the bar, says loud enough for everyone to hear, "Bet that little runty Jimmy Hooper too chicken to fire off a shot 'fore he drowned." She looks around to see how this has landed.

"Sheba, now settle down," Lucky says, all nervous. "Hey," he calls out, "drinks all around. War's over! I'm buying."

But the Hooper boys is scowling.

"Don't talk about Jimmy like that!" Billy says.

"Traitor!" the big one, Cletus, yells. "Your brother got drowned by the Nazis! Blown to smithereens!" Now he's yelling about how the Nazis is better than the Negro race, how colored soldiers don't even fight, they such cowards.

I feel the heat rise in me. *Hooper boys so ignorant, they don't know nothing about Gem. They don't even know Nazis different from Japs. Japs are the ones killed him.*

Now the Hooper boys stare up at the bravest person in the room, decide to take her down.

Sheba stands over them, her skirt flares out at their noses, hips sway with the music. Eyes half closed, but glittery, like blue ice, and the two Hooper boys move toward her. Queen of Sheba Jones puts hands on hips, stares them down. "What you two boys lookin' at?"

"Let's celebrate!" Billy yells. "C'mon down here and give me a kiss."

The half-drunk, happy whiteboys at the bar laugh. Radio says over the world soldiers are kissing women on the streets, in Paris and New York and San Francisco. Whiteboys thinking, *Why not here?*

"Hell no," Sheba says to Billy. "I'm dancing. Go kiss your brother."

Billy pushes his shoulder into the back of Sheba's knees, grabs her around the waist. He pulls her down to the table top and sits on her belly while Cletus holds her arms. Billy leans down to kiss her mouth. "Just a kiss, Sheba," Billy says. "Just a little kiss." Sheba pulls away, kicks and heaves, bites Billy on the ear. Billy rears back and screams like a woman.

I start to tremble, smell something sweet in the air. I close my eyes like Old Lucy taught me. I see what will happen next. I see Sheba, running, blood and rocks. I see her face in a cloud of white.

My eyes spring open. I run right at Billy, push hard as I can. "You get away!" I yell. "You get away from my sister! Go on outta here!" My voice gone high and screechy.

Hooper boys turn, look at me and laugh. "She wants a kiss too!" Cletus says. He lunges at me, I run around the table. Big ugly whiteboy, all belly and a big head. Cletus grabs me, fat hands on my waist, my ribs. Nasty wet lips next to my cheek. Tongue wagging. He lift me up and make a smoochy noise. "Got the little one!" Cletus yells. "This one too ugly to kiss."

I kick him hard with both skinny legs, yell bloody murder.

Sheba pushes Billy off, scrambles up. She pulls a tiny sharp blade out her garter, reaches out and slashes Cletus' arm. Blood spurts on his chest, my face.

"She cut me, Billy!" he says, as if it ain't possible for a woman to hurt a man. A Black woman. A whiteman. "She gonna get it now," he says. Face curls up with hate.

"Wha'd you do that for, Sheba?" Billy says.

"Teach him to mess with my sister," Sheba hisses.

"Y'all settle down," Lucky says. "No fighting in here. Go on outside if you gonna fight."

Sheba kicks her way free, yells, "Go home, Reba, run," and she runs out the door the other way, into the woods.

Billy follows Sheba.

I run after.

Cletus follows me.

I run and run and cry and the fit is on me, I am lost in the woods but I can see: *Sheba runs and flies like a bird into the Field. Sheba flies around rock and snare. Billy flies behind. Sheba hears him catching up. Sheba turns to fight.*

Billy loves Sheba.

Sheba hates Billy.

Billy picks up a rock, tells her to put the knife down.

Breath at my back.

Hands pull me down.

Cletus has found me.

He breathes on me his stank breath, hand over my mouth, I try to yell, to bite his hand, but he pinches my nose so I can't breathe. I kick and kick and pull his hair. He grinds himself on me, slaps my face, punches me in the belly. Pulls my panties, rips them down. Pulls my legs apart. He shoves his nasty hand inside my privates, feel like animal paws, I shut my eyes. I rise up high in the Gooley pines, look down on the whiteman who put his face next to the face of a skinny Black girl. *Too ugly to keep,* he says. He holds her down. Bites her cheek. He shoves and shoves, hate pushing inside, like poison spurting. Then he leaves her in the Gooley pines and runs down into the Field. Black girl turns her face to the bark of a tree. Pale green moth there, wingspread the size of a girl's hand. She puts her hand on the tree bark, feels something warm and strong seep into her palm, gathers strength. She watches the moth rise up. *Where is Sheba?* she asks the moth. Moth leads her to the top of the Ridge. Indian Field below.

I open my eyes. I see everything.

Blood moon in the sky above the river.

Stars like eyes full of fire.

Down in the shadow between the rocks, Sheba and Billy.

Sheba slices across his belly, blood spurt.

Billy puts his hand on his belly. Falls to his knees. Looks so surprised. "Why'd you do that, Sheba?" he says. "I just want to kiss you."

Cletus comes up behind, cracks Sheba's head with a rock. Billy cries, "Stop, stop," but Cletus don't stop. He cracks her over and over and she falls like dead weight to the ground.

Cletus drops his rock. Looks up. Sees me watching, frozen, on the Ridge.

I could have run to stop him. I could have flown down like a bird and pulled him away, cracked his head with rocks. But my whole body has froze solid and all I can do is watch. Watch Cletus Hooper kill my sister Sheba.

A sound rises from my belly that I never heard before.

A sound like the world ripped wide open.

Old Lucy's traps and lies and snakes and spells have not kept this day from coming. All her power and skill. But she hears me calling, raises her head from her bed of rags and skins. She makes a new spell. Calls forth her serpent friends.

Snakes rise and slither and swerve and curve around Billy's legs and arms and trunk and strike and strike and strike, pumping poison. Then they come for Cletus.

Cletus looks down, snake twining his leg, face full of fear. He jumps and leaps and flies over rocks and snakes, leaves his brother there to die.

Lucy walks across snakes, all slither and glint in the Field, to the place where Sheba lies. She kneels down, lifts Sheba's head, peers into her white-blue eyes. Shuts them with her thumbs. No herbs nor healing needed.

Lucy looks up. Sees me watching behind a tree. She hiss at me, "Get your papa."

Papa and I come fast as we can, riding on his mule King, till King balks at the edge of the Ridge, snorting. We look down. Field all lit up with the light of the blood moon. There below, Billy twined in snakes. Head, arms, legs, belly, private parts. Beside him, Sheba, washed and clean, wrapped in white doeskin like a present.

Papa drops the rope and runs to her. I follow.

Sheba's face looks black and cold. White fur around her head like snow. Eyes half open, mouth open as to speak, to sing, to yell out a taunt or whisper a secret. Trickle of blood slips down her cheek. One blue eye gleams between half-closed lids, stares straight at me.

Why didn't you come help me? her eye says, loud as day. *We sisters.*

Papa stands over Sheba and his face goes blank and terrible, like he can see all the terrible world in Sheba's half-shut eye. He crouches down, wipes his finger across her cheek, comes up blood. He makes a sound like choking. Then he hoists Sheba in his arms, staggers across the Field, won't let me help. He heads up the Ridge to the Gooley pines, his shadow black and flickering like moth wings in the moonlight on the path. When he gets to the top, he says, "Hold that mule, Reba," and I hold the rope harness and press King's nose against my dress, for everyone knows that a mule hates the smell of death and won't move in pure stubbornness if it don't like what it smells.

Papa loads Sheba bundled in her fur across the blanket on King's back like a sack of peanuts, but gently, and takes the harness. But King will not budge. Papa grabs up a clump of moss and earth from the ground, presses it into King's snout. King snorts and takes a step. Stops. Papa yanks a blackberry switch from the ground with his bare hands. Hands it to me. "If he balk, switch him. Switch him till he bleed."

Oh, Papa, I want to say, *your beautiful white King.* Papa loved that mule, cared for him and groomed him, called him King Pharaoh and fed him corn sometimes, sometimes oats. I have never seen him switch King. He is always gentle as a lamb with him.

I cannot do it. I cannot switch his King. So Papa takes the blackberry from my hand and switches and switches till black blood slides down the white rump and legs, flies from Papa's bramble-rip hands. I hold King's nose and cry. I don't make a sound. I hold King's nose against my chest and pull. He comes to me, sad and slow, like an animal whose heart is broken.

Miss Reba does not see the chickens settling around her feet as if to comfort her. She does not see the bees swirling around her head. She does not see the honey dripping down, sweet with thistle nectar and bitter with the pollen of Queen Anne's Lace. She does not see the yellow butterflies that sip at Sheba's newly painted lips, then swirl and rise as if some spirit has broken free from earthly bonds to fly. Miss Reba blinks her eyes and sees what is next, and after that and after that, and she sees it all as if from the top of a whirlwind. Old Lucy taught her to send her heart up into the sky to see down on it all and now she sees it: Indian Field below. The Gooley Ridge with its burden of bones. The Great Trees, *Tatcha na wihie Gee-ree,* bending and swaying like women, grief tugging at their tap roots, dropping cones as if a great storm sweeps their branches. But there is no storm. There is only the groaning and cracking of branches. The past breaks through, rises like a flood of tears.

33

J olene pulls into Reba's yard, sees the old lady sitting in her porch chair as usual. But what's that in her lap? Bobo jumps out, runs to her. TJ moves to follow.

"Wait," Jolene says to TJ. She opens her change purse. "I can't pay you for the whole day and night. Just for a few hours."

"No problem," TJ says. "You fed me and everything. I liked the goats. And Bobo—he's a trip."

Jolene counts out twenty one-dollar bills from her market cash, then adds two more. "Well," she says. "You were a big help."

"Yes, ma'am," TJ says. "I was glad to do it."

He seems to mean it. Will wonders never cease. Maybe she will hire him again, help Miss Reba keep him in line. Get some help at the same time.

But now Bobo is yelling, flapping his hands in distress. "Weba!" he calls out. "Weba!"

Jolene looks up. Miss Reba's still sitting in her chair, but her eyes are staring in a strange way, her face frozen and blank—*and good Lord*—tears running down her cheeks.

"Aunt Reba," TJ says. He jumps out of the truck and Jolene follows.

"Miss Reba?" she says. "You all right?" She puts her hand on Reba's shoulder. But Reba is rigid, only the seep down her brown cheek shows she's alive.

TJ makes a sound. He's staring at something. Jolene turns to see. *God in heaven.* Those black statues. The middle one looks like it's alive, and angry, and wants to fly up in the air, sword in hand, smiting things.

They put Miss Reba to bed with a cup of hot sassafras tea. "She gets funny when she tells her stories," TJ says. He has picked up the gold foil box that was in Miss Reba's lap and now he places it on the mantel.

"What stories?" Jolene says.

"About Sheba and the old days."

Who's Sheba? Jolene wonders. *Some Bible thing?* But she lets it go.

"Boys, go find something to do. I'm going to sit with Miss Reba for a while."

She pulls a chair up and sits beside the bed. Miss Reba lets her pull the glasses from her face and set them on the night table. Miss Reba looks at her with her wet blind eyes and Jolene can barely stand it, there is such a deep hole there, such pain. Shouldn't someone apologize to her for the terrible thing that happened to Danielle? Tommy Jay never did and never will.

"I'm sorry," Jolene says. "So sorry." Jolene picks up Reba's hand. It is warm and strong and strangely small. Jolene always thinks of Miss Reba as a powerful woman, but her hands are so small. They smell of Miss Phoebe's rose lotion and earth and sorrow. Jolene pats that hand gently, says, "I know, I know," and Miss Reba turns her head away and closes her eyes. Jolene checks her pulse. Slow deep beats. Then she takes Miss Reba's hand again, holds it in both of hers.

She's never been this close to Miss Reba. She's never touched her this way. They are not touchy-feely friends. But Reba's hand in hers feels just right. *You are very dear to me,* she thinks. She dares not say it out loud. Miss Reba might pop up and pull her hand away. Miss Reba does not allow familiarity. Maybe because she's been alone so many years. But Miss Reba was the one who birthed Bobo, who wrapped him and put him in her arms, who said, "Miss Jolene, Mr. Luke, this is a special baby." She knew before they did exactly how special. And after Luke died, Miss Reba is the one who picked her up and told her she had to work. Got her a slot at the farmers' market. Sold for her on days she could not face the world. And most of all, Miss Reba was Bobo's first best friend, even before Ace. They seem to get each other in a way nobody else can. Miss Reba lets Bobo hug her. Until this year, she hugged back.

The boys are hovering outside the door, whispering.

Miss Reba still hasn't spoken. She may have had a stroke. You're supposed to ask a person to smile, check for uneven expression. Miss Reba never smiles. Jolene wants to call a doctor. But Miss Reba doesn't like doctors. She doctors with herbs from the Field.

"Mama! Want to stay with TJ and Weba! Want to stay ovah!"

"Miss Reba is sick, Bobo. She can't watch you right now." She hasn't asked Miss Reba to watch Bobo since Danielle died.

"Want to stay, Mama. I watch HUH." He reaches out to pet Miss Reba's hair.

"I'll keep an eye on her," TJ says. "Don't worry. You can go."

There is a rustling from the bedcovers. Miss Reba raises her head from the pillow, heaves a sigh. She pulls her hand out of Jolene's and pushes out of bed.

"Where's my cane?" she says.

TJ hands it to her.

"Miss Jolene, you go about your business. You got goats to care for," she says. "Bobo can stay."

Jolene hesitates. But Miss Reba is firm. "Go on now. Bobo's going to keep me company. Keep TJ busy. Chase my blues."

Miss Reba's speaking clearly. No slurring. She didn't have a stroke. She's just caught in sorrow. And Jolene really shouldn't leave Folly and the new baby alone for long. "Okay," she says. Let Bobo take care of Reba. There is a certain justice in that. Reba's been taking care of him for years.

Bobo jumps up and down with glee. Jolene kisses him on the forehead and goes.

Jolene is sitting alone in the dark, straining to hear the night birds through the open kitchen window, when a vision comes to her of ruin: The farm foreclosed, the goats sent to a rendering plant, the Gooley pines cut down, she and Bobo living in a small apartment in Quarryville with beige walls and streetlights blocking out the night stars. Bobo is a bagger at the Piggly Wiggly and people make fun of him. She works in a horrible office somewhere, wearing skirts and lipstick, typing. She knows how to type. She does not know how to run a computer. Such a life is impossible and yet it seems inevitable.

If they foreclose and take the Field, the Gooleys, she can't keep Bobo safe here on the farm. Without the Field for winter pasture, there is no dairy. And the first thing the bank would do is clear-cut the great pines. Joggins showed her a cutting operation once, with enormous machines screeching and whining through the trunks, and the trunks finally breaking, then falling, side branches cracking like bones the whole way down until the earth shook with death. Then silence. She could not bear it.

Forty thousand dollars. They are ruined.

She has made this happen with her carelessness, her belief that the light in the Gooley pines and the thistles in Indigo Field, her compost pile and her fertile soil, the crops that grow lush green, the goats that gave their babies and their milk, were a kind of promise that things would always stay the same, that she could keep Bobo safe in a world apart from the world, that it was even possible for a widow lady and her son to survive by milking goats and hoeing potatoes. What a fool she has been. There doesn't seem any way around it. And dear God, what will happen to Bobo? The outside world is not friendly to boys like him. Why did she ever borrow to build a dairy? Because the new health department had rules. Because Frank suggested it. Because she wanted something nice and neat and tidy in her life.

Jolene trudges upstairs, flings off her clothes, crawls into bed, pulls the covers over her head. She tucks her hands between her legs, just to warm them. Feels a gush of menstrual blood. As if it had been waiting all day for this moment to tell her: *You've lost your chance to make a child again.*

Jolene gets up, grabs a Kotex, tucks it in her panties, and crawls back into bed. It's so lonely here without Bobo in the house. She wants to leap up and get the truck and go pick him up. But let this knowledge be her payment due for a life of holding back terror, for stealing joy from birdsong: She and Bobo will be leaving here. She lets out a single cry of despair. Across the Gooley Ridge, way out in Indigo Field, a whippoorwill shouts its crazy chant of love.

34

Miss Reba wakes in the middle of the night, three-quarter moon blasting light. Sweltering hot. She throws the quilt off, turns toward the fan. She's used to it being this hot in August. But it's only early June.

There's a sound. And again. The boys?

She rises, puts on her robe. They are both fast asleep, TJ curled up in a ball in his bed, Bobo splayed all over her narrow couch. She opens the kitchen door and stands on the stoop, listening. *Rednecks on the road?* No. Just a breeze. Something cold in it, like an ice cube on her arm. There's a whispering sound from the hickory grove. Leaves shimmer in the moonlight, rise and rustle like a woman's party dress. There it is again. Someone calling from a far-off field. Like in the old days, when people hollered their calls across old fields: *danger, fire, come help.* Then a yipping sound. Dogs? Foxes after her chickens?

Reba clutches her robe around her and reaches in the closet for the shotgun. Still got a shell in her robe pocket. She creeps toward the chicken shed. But all the chickens are sleeping.

She pricks her ears. Somewhere in the distance, there's a party. People laughing. Listening to a radio. *Earl Hines and his orchestra.* Listening to a war report.

A voice speaks and does not speak: *Come.*

"Lord, Lord," Reba says. "Stand by me now." She walks through the hickory grove to the corn patch. New corn rustling the breeze, waist high already. Between the rows of Silver Queen, red Indian corn sprouts year after year, only in this corner, in a wild clump like green ribbons flaring in the breeze, like Lucy come to visit. Mama's yellow bells have dried up with the May heat, strands like yellow hair marking the place. Sheba's place.

"Why did they put her here?" Danielle child says at her elbow.

"Hush, child. I'll tell you." Reba sits on a hickory log. Motions Danielle to sit beside her.

Danielle's spirit slips her hand into Reba's.

❧

I hide behind a hickory tree, watch Papa digging by lamplight, cloth covering the lamp. When he's done, Papa cleans mud off his boots with a stick, puts the rake and shovel up in the shed. When he goes inside, I slip in behind. He doesn't see me. He doesn't see anything. He sits at the table and drinks a glass of water. Face like thunder.

Papa looks Mama in the eye, says, "Anybody ask, she ain't dead. She went to Baltimore to visit your sister." Mama nods. Papa turns his gaze to me, says, "Sister! You hear me?"

"But why, Papa? Everybody would want to come to Sheba's funeral."

Papa slams his glass down, grabs my shoulders, shakes and shakes. "Because-a-whiteman-out-there-dead-in-the-field-and-they-going-to-come-looking-for-who-to-blame.Come-to-get-you-next-'less-you-shut-your-mouth."

Mama stares at the bite mark on my cheek. Stares and stares. Seeing me, seeing nothing. Turning away.

The day after we bring Sheba home and bury her, I see trouble coming up the road, dust rising. I set my book down, hide in the damp shade behind the spirea bush, wild bees humming around my head.

Papa sees it too. Rises to greet it, his whittling still in his hand, like he forgot it was there.

"Mr. Jones," Sheriff says, "I wonder if you heard." Man is lean and tall, wide hat shades his face. Blue eyes like sky on fire. Everybody said Old Sheriff Walter Pickett was a pretty good whiteman, left colored people alone. Called them Miss and Mister and did every politeness but tip his hat.

"What's that, Mista Sheriff?" Papa says. Sets his knife down. Not polite to whittle while a whiteman talking.

"I wonder if you heard about young Billy Hooper. Got drunk and snakebit in Indigo Field, all swoll up. Dead."

Papa don't say nothing.

"Family pretty shook up. His brother Cletus says somebody cut him. There was a fight with a girl name of Black Sheba. That your girl, Mista Jones?"

"My girl Sheba gone to Baltimore two weeks ago," Papa says, in that funny high whine he uses when talking to whitemen. "She got a good govmint job, suh. Yessuh. That girl not the same one. She in trouble?"

"No," Sheriff says. "No trouble. Just a witness maybe. Only one other witness we can find. That crazy old Tussie Lucy."

Papa says, "Mm-hm," like he agrees she's crazy.

"We put her in the cell to think it out, and all she did is laugh that crazy laugh. Spooked my deputy pretty bad. He says she put red ants in his lunch bucket, some kinda Injun curse. He says she's got powers."

"Uhuh, yessuh, I heard that," Papa says, in that same high strange voice.

"Glad to hear Miss Sheba got a govmint job."

"Yessuh," Papa says. "We right proud of that one."

We right proud of that *one*. I hit at the bush with my hand, and Sheriff looks around, like he's afraid something might jump out at him.

I scooch back into the darkest shade of the spirea, where the thrasher got a nest. Bird sits there, eyeballing me. Then it takes off flying across the yard, like it seen something it didn't like.

Sheriff says goodbye, turns to walk away. Papa picks up his knife. Sheriff turns back, like he remembered something. "Maybe Miss Reba will go to Baltimore," he says. "I know she misses her sister."

The words hang in the air like a cloud of gnats you try to wave away. I close my eyes and see what he is thinking, though it makes no sense to me: *Sheriff's idea is to make me go away.*

We children watch Papa sit there for the longest time. Then he walks to where he keeps his prize cedar logs from the Gooley Ridge. Some of those logs twelve foot long, four foot around. He lays his hands on them, thinking.

There is chopping in the night. Chopping in the day. Digging a hole in the yard. Nailing boards. Sawing. Painting. Five days pass. One day Papa rigs up a winch and a chain for King Pharaoh to pull. He ties the chain to the log he's been working. He beats his King and makes him pull. The log rises, bottom slips into the hole he made, *thunk*. He packs dirt around the bottom.

It is no longer a log. It is a person.

We children stand and stare. He painted her black, with fierce blue eyes, tiny white teeth, and an open mouth with red full lips. Wings out to the side. A crown of golden spikes. One hand to the heart. One raised up, holding a silver sword.

Little Pearl runs up to her, says, "Look like Sheba!"

Papa says, "Ain't Sheba. This here the Angel of Death."

We all shrink back.

Pearl says, "When Sheba coming home, Papa?"

Papa says, "She ain't coming home. She gone to Baltimore. She don't like you children anymore."

Pearl's hands on the black wood like small brown stars. Looking up. Reaching up. Fierce blue Sheba eyes stare down.

"Don't touch it!" Papa shouts.

Pearl shrinks back, hands by her side, fingers still stretched out like stars. "She gone away?" Pearl whispers, like she don't believe her Sheba would leave her.

Papa don't say nothing, goes inside.

Pearl runs and gets her favorite cornhusk doll, two feathers and three yellow flowers, puts them at the place where Sheba's feet would be, if an angel had feet.

Danielle, baby, every morning after that, I go stare at Sheba Angel, fierce and strong. I wish to be like that, but I am not. I practice raising my arm. I use a stick for a sword. I practice being the Angel of Death. Bringing Death to all who would care to hurt my family. One day I see Papa look at my belly and he says, "Do I see what I think I see?"

"What, Papa?" I say.

Mama bows her head.

Mama says babies come from love and I am so young and foolish, I believe her. I ain't had a boy to love me. Only Cletus who hated me, pushed inside me, punched and bit, left the kiss of teeth marks on my cheek, the seed of hate behind.

"Selma," Papa says. "Get me my belt." He's going to beat me, and I don't know why.

But Sheba spirit rises up in me and says, *No, you don't. This girl named for a queen of the Bible. Ruby, Queen Esther Jones.*

I can't fight Papa so I gather up my skirt and run. Run away from Papa's hate, from Mama's sorrow, from my own ignorance. I run across cornfield and cotton field, run to the top of the Gooley Ridge, then down into the Field.

Old Lucy sees me standing on a rock in the river, comes and puts her claw hand on mine, draws me across to her island. Sets me by the fire. "Papa hate me," I say.

Lucy's eyes all beady black, a world of small hot flames in them.

"Gemstone never let me help him," she says. "But I can help you." She places her claw hand on my belly, says some words, mixes me up a cure for hate. I drink it all.

In the morning, Lucy wraps up the seed of Cletus and takes it away. Puts a poultice between my legs. My belly is sore, but I don't feel so afraid anymore. My legs feel strong. She brings me some deer hide and a knife. Says, "Sit here. Make moccasins. When you done, put them on. You got a new path to walk."

Danielle baby, I stayed with her for nigh on six years, sleeping on a pallet on her floor, learning the herbs, helping with her secret trade, midwifing. You would have loved it there. Sheba power growing in me every day. Lucy power too.

By day, I help Lucy tend her corn, red and blue kernels like jewels. I help her gather herbs and fishes. She keeps her liquor still over by Still Creek, hidden away. Call it Spill Creek now.

We go by dark of night and pull babies. Folks in Poolesville didn't have much doctoring those days. Quarryville neither.

Sometimes a woman will come to the Ridge and beat a stick on the hollow sycamore tree up there. It means she's in trouble of some kind.

Men, both Black and white, buy Lucy's hooch at Lucky's. Women, both Black and white, buy herbs by the riverside. Charms. Sometimes spells for a healthy baby. Sometimes salve for a beating. Sometimes help with making a man and his seed go away. If a love child dies in secret, Lucy says her prayer. Then she buries it the old way, in a pot in the cliff by the river. She never let me help with that. She never let me help with burying mine. But I spied on her to see where she put it, among all the rest. She saw me watching. Said, "So it will have a family."

Lucy has her pole shed covered with skins, a sage bundle and smoky fire, just like before, but now there are tiny new bundles from time to time. She shakes red root powder on the skin, covers it with bark, smokes a body ten days, like a ham in the smokehouse. Then she cuts the skin off, takes out the innards, lets them float away in the river. She scrapes bones clean, lets them smoke some more till they turn yellow with it. Then she puts it, knees up, arms crossed, skull on top, in a clean doeskin, like a baby in the womb. She slides it, bones and all, into a clay pot she made, and buries it sitting up, on the edge of Gooley Ridge, so it can look out over the river and watch the swirling patterns of this world, the travels of birds in season, the yellow butterflies.

Sometimes I think of Sheba, remember the times she called me Queen Esther, the times we ran in the Field. Sometimes I pretend she lives in Baltimore, like Papa said. Pretend she got fancy clothes, hats and gloves, nice shoes. Close my eyes, see her dance for kings and queens, and marry a prince of India.

Times when I know Papa's gone, I go visit Mama. Bring her things she needs. Mama gives me books to read, and lessons to keep up my schooling. She has another baby, a boy this time. She calls him Little Gem, for our big brother who died in the Pacific. Thomas and Pearl and Little Airy start to grow up. Poolesville starts to die out. Young men been to war, seen the world, look around, see there ain't much for them in Poolesville, so they go north to Baltimore and Washington for government jobs. Hardly a young Black man around.

Quarryville growing. Whitemen make babies, build a new school for whitechildren. At night, some of the men get together and think of ways to devil colored men. And women. There are stories about the things they do. Most of them true.

Never told you that, Danielle.

We hear everything that happens, from the women.

One day, Old Lucy teaches me about the whiteman heart. "Whiteman heart weighed down by sin," she says, "but he don't believe anybody white can be so bad. So he make up reasons sin is good. Rape a Black woman. She deserve it. Kill a Black man. He disrespectful. Kill my people. They got heathen ways. Take a slave. It in the Bible. He take all his lies and they ball up in him like snakes ball up to keep warm in a hiding place in winter. They grow and fester, lies so big they bust out and make wars so big they kill everybody, both sides. All because whiteman don't know about the circle of help. Everybody brought low from time to time. How to make it right? Help somebody else. Make a circle of help when you need help. Whiteman pretend he on top all the time. He fall out of the circle of help. It make him crazy and mean."

I think about Cletus. What could make him be that way? I can't think about it. I don't know it then, but I still have his poison inside me. I still got the hate seed in my belly. Danielle baby, all I know is my belly feels like what I saw one time: a bat with black wings folded, hanging from a peach tree in broad daylight.

One spring day I bring fat shad, a rabbit, and some herbs to Mama and the babies while Papa's out in the cornfield. "He been making more angels," Mama says. I take a peek. Sheba's still there. Now two more. One of them looks like Gem Junior, army coat on him, brass buttons.

The last one looks like me. Big eyes, wide and scared, buck teeth. He's making memorials to the dead. My papa has decided I am dead.

I go back to be with Lucy.

Sometimes when we go midwifing, I see a baby dead before it comes. I shake and quiver and fall to the ground. I stay outside. Old Lucy leaves me there. When she comes back out, she carries a bundle that does not make a sound.

One day Old Lucy looks at me with her black eyes, says, "You got the gift. The gift of sight. But you got to shut your eyes to it sometimes or your body get stuck in the spirit world and green water spirit is all you see." Old Lucy says the flower smell after is a gift from the Great Spirit, bring you back to the world of the living.

She gives me some herbs to calm the visions. Sassafras and skullcap. She shows me where to pull them in the ditch along the Gooley Ridge. I don't like to go there. Ditch right down from where I stood, frozen, while Cletus cracked Sheba in the head.

Seasons pass and I turn eighteen, still sleeping on that pallet. Lucy turns to me one day and says, "You got to go into the world now. Learn other things. You got more to do than grow up and be like me. You got to have a place in the world. You got to try to love a man."

Lord, I do not want to go.

But Lucy closes her eyes, jay feather twitching beside her cheek, *this way, that way, this way.* Then she says, "Miss Ruby Queen Esther Jones. You grown up now. You got to lead your people."

"What people?" I say. "I ain't got no people."

Well, when Tuscarora Lucy got an idea in her head, she don't budge. Lucy fixes me a bundle of herbs, sassafras root, some skins, some fish, and a jarful of money from her white liquor trade, says it is pay for all my work, and I walk across Indian Field, feet going slow, heart full of sorrow, nothing but moccasins between me and the world of men that wants to pull me down.

I go see Mama, borrow her dress-up clothes, hitch a ride to town on a mule cart, and walk around Poolesville for a day, try to get a job. I try at the library. I am still a reader of books, and this place is full of them. They give the job to a white girl. I try at the corner store, they say, *Your papa Gemstone Jones?* And it is no recommendation. Finally I ask the reverend and his family, they take me in. I care for his children, do laundry, some cooking, for pocket money, room and board. I sit in church on Sunday mornings, say the prayers and sing hymns, but I do not believe God is good. I believe Jesus must be visiting someplace else in this world.

Saturdays, I go to Poolesville Secretarial School, which is a little old colored lady been to Baltimore, worked a government job. She got a typewriter on her kitchen table and a typing book. Ribbon on the typewriter all wore out. I type on the same paper, over and over and over, looks like ghost words all across the page. She teaches me how whitepeople talk. She tells me it will help me in this world. "Think about it, missy. The world is made up of whitepeople. Our little corner is colored, but most places the whitepeople are still in charge. If you speak their language to them, you get power too. And always tell people your name is *Miss* Reba Jones. That's how whitepeople show respect." After I type, she gives me tea and tells me all about Baltimore. Big city. Jobs for young girls. Nice clothes.

I stop visiting Mama for a time. But on Sundays, I hear churchpeople talk about Papa, how he's making more angels in the yard. *More than three of them now,* they whisper. *A whole flock. And that's not all.*

They say Papa's been making signs on big sheets of plywood, placing them along the road like Burma Shave signs, but with quotes from the Bible. I edge up on them, bow my head, pretend to pray.

"He got one say, *The earth shall be laid waste.*"

"I seen one say, *God's wrath come down upon ye.*"

"Put one out last week, *Justice rain down like thunder*—that from Isaiah."

"Mmm-hmmm."

I cannot stand to stay and witness my father's grief turned to madness. I make my plan to go.

My typing teacher tells me about this boarding house in Baltimore, safe for girls like me. She tells me the PO always has jobs for clerks there. She knows somebody. She gives me a typing certificate, tells me how much it costs for the train, sends me on my way.

I get off the train and think: *I'm finally where Sheba shoulda went instead of dying.*

❧

The thread of silver dawn along the river, the smell of pine pollen and cedar trees, the loud music of blue jays, all call Miss Reba gently back to this world.

She rises, sways, and stumbles. If she doesn't go home and eat something soon she will have a sugar attack. And the boys will find her here, dead and fallen onto Sheba's grave, little green ribbons of Lucy corn sprouted all around. That's no way to do.

Reba hoists the shotgun under her arm and trudges back to the house.

She takes off her muddy shoes, leaves them on the stoop. She puts the gun in the closet behind the coats. It's Monday. TJ's got to get up and go to school. Bobo's got to go home to his mama. And she is tired, so, so tired.

Reba wakes the boys. Gets the fry pan out, cooks their eggs and bacon in her stocking feet.

"Aunt Reba!" TJ says, rubbing his eyes, dressed and ready to eat. "You cooking in your sock feet!" Reba wants to knock him silly, *Don't say aunt*, but Bobo comes up behind him, also sleepy, points at her, says, "Sock feet!" and starts to giggle so hard, and then TJ starts to giggle too, and it lifts her heart. Acting like they're four years old. Acting like girls.

Morning is no time for gloomy thoughts. It's time to feed the living.

"That's right, Auntie. Cook us up some breakfast. Biscuits too."

Lord have mercy, Danielle has followed her right here into the kitchen. Reba looks around. The boys are busy setting the table. They haven't heard a thing.

When Reba rolls out the dough, she rolls so hard and happy, flour rises into the air and fills the room.

35

Jolene wakes up Monday knowing what to do.

Joggins has been bugging her for years to do it. People pay top dollar for wood that's 400 years old, he said. "You harvest 'em right, you might could get a thousand dollars a tree."

The Gooley Ridge minus forty trees equals Bobo safe. Here at home. She doesn't want to do it. But it must be done.

Luke would hate it. He believed the Pines heard secrets, knew things. Sometimes he went and listened to the branches, which seemed to whisper without any wind. Sometimes he read poetry to them. But Luke isn't here. And, as Joggins always says, *How long before a storm will harvest them trees and ruin their value? It's a miracle they've survived this long.*

She'll miss every one. But according to the Society for Preservation, there are more than four hundred on the cliff by the river. There will be plenty left to catch the glimmer of dawn light and greet her every morning. To make a cool refuge on hot summer days. To make a roost for owls and turkeys and for warblers riding the weather south in winter. She feels like Judas, betraying the Blake family tradition, and Luke's passion, for forty pieces of silver. "I'll never cut the Gooleys," he said. But she will.

This morning, she and Bobo will be going to visit Mr. Ridley at the bank. Have a little talk. The weight on her heart shifts. After she pays the loan, the farm will be free and clear.

Morning milking done, kids and mamas fed, she picks Bobo up from Reba's. Miss Reba looks tired, but she's up and fussing over TJ, a good sign. "Boy's about to wear me out," she says, "but he'll go to school today."

Jolene brings Bobo home through the woods, over the creek, the way he likes to come. On the way, he regales her with tales of TJ.

"TJ go to church, Mama."

"That's nice." She never takes Bobo to church.

Now Bobo's singing a Jesus song. One familiar from her youth, one she never taught him. "Jesus love me this I know, 'cause the Bible tell me so. Little children with him dwell. So theh little feet don't *smell.*"

"What! That's not how it goes, Bobo!" It's funny though. She can't help laughing.

"TJ like Wambo. What would Wambo do? Bam!"

Does he mean Rambo? They must have been watching some tapes on Reba's ancient VCR. Miss Reba knows Bobo should watch Nemo. That's his favorite. A fish looking for his lost daddy.

"TJ have a girr-fend. She pitty."

Oh dear. "Did you meet her last night?"

Bobo shakes his head. "No, Mama! Duh! We at Weba's house!" He says it like, *You're so dumb, Mama.* Just like a teenager. Maybe Bobo needs to spend more time with that young man Jeff and his dog. Less time with TJ.

She also learns that TJ uses Reba's hair oil and stays up till midnight whenever he wants. Which she doubts very much. Miss Reba is strict. But Bobo is still talking. He tells her TJ is going to get a car and go to California.

"Want to go to Cah-foh-na, Mama. They have waze."

"They have what?"

"Waze, Mama! Waze! Like suhfuh on waze."

Waves. TJ wants to be a surfer boy. She wonders if Miss Reba knows about this plan.

Bobo hums some more. Who knows what other songs TJ has been teaching him.

"TJ call it his chicken neck!" Bobo points in the direction of his pants. "Chik-EN-NEK."

"Bobo," she says. "We don't talk about that." What in the world have the two of them been up to? But she's not worried. Bobo tells her all his secrets.

"Weba cook in her sock feet!" Bobo starts to giggle like crazy. He's in such a good mood. That's the boy she knows.

She doesn't tell him she's going to cut the big old trees on the Ridge. The place he thinks is heaven.

In the bank waiting room, Jolene points Bobo to the big leather chair he likes: "Sit. Do you have to pee?"

"*No,* Mama."

"I'll be right there," she says, pointing through the glass wall to Frank's office. But there's somebody already in there. One of his good old boys, chewing the fat, no doubt. "Stay here."

"I *know,* Mama," Bobo says. He's counting pennies. He wants to put them in the bank.

Jolene smooths her hair, checks the safety pin holding her skirt together, and heads down the hall to Frank's office door. But Frank's new assistant heads her off. "He's with a client," she says, the slightest smirk on her face. Is that supposed to be a smile? No.

"This was set up in advance," the assistant says. "You'll just have to wait."

"Tell him I'm about to give him forty thousand dollars. I'm about to pay my loan in full."

"Goodness!" the assistant says. "He'll be glad to hear *that*."

Frank's assistant ushers her back to the waiting room. "Let me know if you need anything," she says. She does not offer coffee.

Rand settles into the big red leather chair in the bank office and looks around. The air conditioner hums, cooling the oak paneling and book-shelves filled with leather-bound books. Frank Ridley, real estate and banking, is the kind of guy who likes wearing suits. The man's got seer-sucker on, and he's sitting in an even bigger red leather chair, his elbows resting on the desk, fingers making a church steeple. Rand had him pegged when he first met him, back when they bought the house—a big man in a small town, like a one-star general in a remote, swampy base. Banker, lawyer, real estate broker, Ridley does it all. He's the "go to" man for real estate in Stonehaven Downs. Bess said he's known for selling fast. Selling high. Rand wonders now how much they overpaid for their house.

Ridley has started talking numbers, in that half gas-station, half charm-school accent of his. "Three bedrooms, two and a half baths, and an office, in Stonehaven? We'll be able to move that in no time." Ridley smiles, but then he turns serious. "The market's turned in the last few months," he confides. "But Stonehaven properties keep their value. Everybody wants them."

Rand nods. Just what Ridley said when he and Anne bought the house for a pretty penny. You could buy three farms around here for what they paid for it.

"How about let's do a little private sale, no listing. No open house. Just a few select showings." Frank Ridley inspects his cuff, picks off a loose thread. "I can think of a few clients who may be interested."

"Okay." That sounds good. This could be easier than he expected.

"We do the credit checks. We do inspections. No muss, no fuss. And of course, it's June. You got any magnolia? People like magnolia."

Rand nods. "Yes, yes, we have magnolia."

"Mine's all burned up in this heat."

Rand nods, just to show he's agreeable. He really has no idea if theirs is blooming. Anne kept track of things like that.

"I'll come by later this week with my assistant, to check out the condition of the place. She'll let you know if we need to stage it different. Sometimes that's the ticket for a quick sale."

Anne used to watch those real estate shows on TV. They'd put potted palms around the edges and tacky vases on the mantel in wild colors. That was staging, apparently. Anne's house is already staged, but classy. Not with cheap trinkets.

Ridley rises to shake his hand, grasps and holds it, looks him in the eye. "Colonel, we're going to take care of you. Don't you worry about a thing."

And like that, it's all set. He'll call Bess's maid service. He'll sell Anne's beautiful house. The English oak dining room table, the pale blue carpet, the bird paintings, the yard with Anne's Indian stones piled high in a cairn. He'll finally get rid of the chestnut table Decker made. He wonders if he can sell the house furnished. He's got no place for these things in his new life.

As he turns down the hall to leave, he catches a glimpse of someone familiar. A youngish slender woman with a long dark braid. Sitting next to her, a big overgrown boy, kicking the coffee table. "Settle down, Bobo," she says. "It won't be long now."

It's the woman farmer with the blue-roof house. Up close she looks young, but worn. He's about to say hello, he feels he knows her so well, but that won't do. What would he say? *I've been watching you from behind a tree.* No. The woman glances through the clear glass panel into Frank Ridley's office, a look of such fierce determination in her eyes that Rand must look away. Has there ever been anything in his life that made him feel that way? Yes. Wanting Anne.

He remembers what he did to get her. A year of listening to English poets on base library recordings, trying out the words, burning off his accent. A self-imposed regiment of culture—reading Shakespeare out loud in his tiny off-base rental apartment. Memorizing lines so he could wedge them into conversation if he ever got the chance. *To be or not to be, that is the question.* He listened to Bach and Beethoven and Mozart, learned the names of the operas, studied big books of Roman sculpture, French art. Then he asked his housefrau German landlady to teach him to dance.

She led him round and round in polkas until he was dizzy. Then one day, at an officers-and-enlisted dance, he approached her, the pretty general's daughter. She grabbed his hand, laughed, placed it in proper position at her waist, and proceeded to teach him the rudiments of the jitterbug. That small hand in his. That voice, so full of laughter. Her mouth, murmuring into his ear: "I hate all these stuffed shirts. Let's get out of here."

He's standing frozen in the bank parking lot, one hand where her waist would be, one floating as if on her shoulder. He shakes it off. Remembers himself. He is no longer that boy. And she's no longer here.

He saw a Hardees on Main Street. He's got a hankering for junk food. Then the liquor store. Then the feed store for thistle seed. The painted bunting nest has hatched out. That's what they like.

Jolene is sitting in the bank waiting room, contemplating what she is about to do, when she hears Mrs. Caswell, the head teller, talking in the hallway. "…And he's been paying her late fees out of his own pocket. I think there's a law against that too."

Frank paying her late fees? That's not true.

But now the assistant returns, all smiles, and says, "Mr. Ridley is ready for you."

Frank pulls her chair out. She sits. He pushes her in, lingers for a moment, as if he's smelling her hair. He smells of bay rum aftershave, and it makes her a little nauseated.

He settles behind his enormous desk. Taps the intercom. Asks his assistant to bring coffee. "Black for me, cream for Mrs. Blake."

The assistant places a tiny china cup before her on a saucer with a little spoon. Sets the other cup in front of Frank. Jolene takes a sip to be polite. Ugh. It's not her own rich goat milk in there. It's some kind of coffee "whitener."

Frank leans back in his giant chair. "Well, here we are, Mrs. Blake," he says. "Jolene." Frank smiles at her with tenderness. As if he knows her. Knows her heart. Knows what she is going to say. She's got to get this over with. Business first. Frank leans forward, rests his elbows on the desk, puts the tips of his fingers together, rests his chin on his fingers. Stares at her with his round blue eyes. *Safety or ruin?*

Jolene sets her coffee down. Clears her throat. "Frank," she says, holding up his letter. "I'm going to pay it off. In full."

Frank looks like someone punched him. "How?"

"In a minute. I have one question. Have you been paying my late fees?"

"They were more than you could pay."

"But I *was* paying them."

"No. You were paying twenty-five dollars. The late fees went up this year."

"When did that happen?"

"With the bank merger."

"And how much was it?"

"Two hundred. Every month. I only wanted to protect you, Miss Jolene." He smiles his tenderest smile.

"And when did this new bank take over, anyway?" She can feel her spine stiffen. *How dare you try to help me behind my back?*

Frank drops his head into his hands. "If you ever read your mail—"

"Well, I've read it now."

"So you have." Frank places his hands flat on the desk. "What's your plan, then?" *And does it include me?*

Jolene explains her plan. Frank's expression changes from tenderness to confusion, to consternation. Then he lists the reasons, one by one, why her plan is not acceptable.

Miss Reba pulls into the parking lot at Quarryville Feed & Seed, pulls out her cane and pushes up the steps. She orders her chickenscratch, pays with her farmers' market dollars, counts them out one by one. Man behind the counter watches her, tapping his pencil. When she's done, he picks up the damp and raggedy bills and counts them again. She has got to tell the stock boy to put the bag on the back seat. She's so tired of feeding out of her trunk. Because instead of feeding off the porch, watching the bees rise from the crack in the sycamore tree, the sun blaze the tops of the Gooley pines, what she sees first thing every day now is a close-up view of that blessed dent and how it is only getting worse, and the bitterness rises about the whiteman who sold her a rust bucket of a car, and the whiteman who ran into it. *Jesus help me now.*

She turns toward the parking lot, and, just like Jesus must be listening, there he is, the whiteman who did it, his West Point cap on, but long pants this time. She'd know him anywhere. He's talking with the man about thistle seed, ordering a ten-pound sack. He pays thirty dollars.

What in the world would somebody go and buy thistle seed for? There's plenty of thistles in this world for free.

The trembling climbs her legs, ankles to knees. Strength of Lucy, power of Sheba rises into her belly, her throat. Her hand grips the cane, rooted to the floor, but now it wants to rise, to knock that whiteman in the head, to bring him down, all the worry he's caused.

Feed & Seed is all whitemen. Miss Reba holds it in.

She makes it to her car and sits. Stock boy has put the scratch in the trunk yet again.

When the whiteman comes out, she waits. Stockboy puts the man's seed on the back seat, on a piece of plastic. All neat and clean. Whiteman's got a nice ride. Whiteman gives the stockboy some paper money. She watches him drive away. Then she follows.

When she turns into Stonehaven Downs, the garden ladies are digging around in front of the pillars, planting new flowers, throwing out the old. They stare at her car, wave away her fumes, cough as she passes. Do they remember her from before? Hard to miss this car, the way it blows smoke.

Miss Reba slows the Cutlass to watch the whiteman pull into his drive. She knows where he lives now. Third house on the left. She keeps going for a block, then turns to pass by again. His car is parked. He's gone inside. No garden ladies here. She pulls over, sets the brake, and looks around. No number on the house. No delivery box for mail. A pile of rocks next to the front door, waist high. A jasmine vine about to bust out over the door, already smelling sickly sweet. A mail slot in the door. She's going to have to hand-deliver.

But what will the neighbors do when they see a Black woman sneaking around a whiteman's yard, going up to his front door, poking something in the slot? What will a whiteman do if she comes to his door and makes her accusation?

Miss Reba knows good and well.

She knows one whiteboy who could do it. He'll be home from school before long.

Don't be using a whiteboy to do your business.

She leaves the Cutlass running, and walks right up, bold as brass. She used to work for the post office, and she can deliver the mail just as well as anybody. She pokes the slot open. Something screams like the devil, pecks at her hand. She jerks the letter back. Flings it in the air. Runs.

36

That night, while Jolene's milking and feeding, there's a commotion in the kid pen.

"Mama, Mama, Mama!" Bobo is running back and forth in the goat barn, from pen to pen, as if he's looking for something that's missing.

"What is it, Bobo?"

"Kicks run away, Mama! Go find him!"

Oh Lord. She hasn't told him. She's got to lay it out for him. Tell him the truth.

"The baby died, Bobo. It was sick and it died."

"Wheh did it go, Mama?"

"Come with me."

She leads him out to the baby goat's grave. The stones over Ace have a grassy border now. Soon you won't be able to see them. "Here," Jolene says. "I dug a hole, Bobo. I buried it. Next to Ace."

"Ace runned away," Bobo says.

Ever since his father died, Bobo hasn't quite gotten it about death. He thinks his father lives in the Gooley pines. And now he thinks the baby goat ran away. It's her own damn fault. She buried Ace while Bobo was sleeping. She scattered Luke's ashes in the Gooley pines. She buried the baby goat while he was at Reba's. He's never seen a body go in the ground. She kept telling him about spirits.

"Oh, for goodness' sake," Jolene says. She will have to show him. "Wait here." She runs to the barn for a shovel.

She lifts the stone she placed over Ace's head. She begins to dig. When her shovel hits bone, she kneels down and digs with her hands. Bobo just stands there, arms crossed, waiting. Jolene brushes back the soil, pulls back the tattered quilt they buried him in. Under the matted fur the flesh has been eaten away by maggots and worms. It is seething with them. "Look, Bobo," she says. "Here is Ace. Over there is Folly's baby."

"Runned away," Bobo says. He looks closer. "*Not* Ace." He shakes his head, crosses his arms.

And that's that. He has decided not to listen to his mama. And she can understand. Who would want to believe your best friend was nothing but teeth and maggots?

That night after Bobo's in bed, she stays up late, freezing sugar snaps and roasting beets. They have fifty-four days before foreclosure. She has fifty-four days to say goodbye to Spill Creek Farm. She's going to by God take some of it with her. "The Gooley pines are on the land you signed as collateral," Frank said, in his just-the-facts voice. So she can't cut them to pay off her loan. "The collateral would not be worth as much that way, you see," Frank explained, sounding perfectly reasonable in his Frank-the-bank way.

"You may have other options," he'd said, "that you haven't fully considered." Was he really trying to ruin her so he could marry her? If she'd been in that room one more minute, she would have knocked his desk over.

Fifty-four days to smell the pine duff in the Gooleys. Fifty-four days to wrap her arms around the mama goats before she has to sell. Fifty-four days to say goodbye to Luke, because he's still alive to her in this place. *You have to put on a show for God sometimes, by having even rows of corn, painting the roof blue, or loving, right out in the Field.*

She plucks the lid from the steamed sugar snaps. She reaches in to sample one. Sees her hand is shaking. The snaps have gone past blanched—they're boiled to mush.

The archaeology permission letter is sitting on the kitchen counter. She picks it up. Do they pay for permission? No. A line catches her eye: *There would be a man on-site at night to protect and guard the area.*

If she gives permission, she'll at least have someone on her side. Anything to keep Frank's hands off this Field, those pines. Miss Reba would agree. *Good Lord, if you let this land fall into the bank's hands, Miss Reba will never speak to you again.*

She needs forty thousand dollars. She needs an army of people on her side. There's Reba. There's farmers' market people. The Big Tree People. She thinks of the spaced-out girl, and Justin, who writes songs to trees. She needs more. She thinks of Jeff, gets a warm feeling on her neck. It's too bad his mother is dead. She was always donating to things. She would have helped.

Jolene picks up a pen. Signs the permission letter. Writes a note: *Don't cut the fence. Don't wreck the gate. Come see me before you start.* Then she licks the envelope and sets it in the stack to mail. But panic rises in her. *You can't wait for the US mail. All you have is fifty-four days.* She picks up the phone. It must be after nine p.m.. She dials the number on the letterhead. Someone answers.

"Charles Mathers? This is Jolene Blake. You sent me a letter."

"I'm so glad to hear from you," the man says. "Call me Chuck."

When Jeff calls early Tuesday morning, Jolene is going through her week's mail, picking up each piece and shaking it, as if it might miraculously contain forty thousand dollars.

"This afternoon, right?" he says.

"Yes. Bobo can't wait. He's already made up a song about you." She flushes. It sounds like she's flirting.

"Well, I guess I need to hear that."

"Don't worry, you will."

"I just wanted to check in with you about something."

"Okay." She sits down. She can't take another surprise.

"I want to give Usen to Bobo. I just can't keep him anymore. And Bobo—well, it just seems like he belongs with Bobo."

"I don't know," she says. Goats and puppies don't mix. And what will she do when they have to leave the farm? Everything about it screams *mistake.* But it would make Bobo so very happy.

"Can I bring him by this morning?"

The farm, Bobo's happiness, the shifting pecan tree leaves, the bleats of newborns seeking their mothers. All these things so precious. All these things so close to lost. Let one good thing happen today. "Yes," she says. "Bring him. Bring him now."

Jolene looks up from her pile of papers to watch Jeff, Usen, and Bobo through the kitchen window. They're running in circles again.

Now they plop on the grass and lie back, panting. Bobo offers Jeff some gum out of his windbreaker pocket. Jeff takes the gum, tears it in half so they can share. Bobo is watching Jeff adoringly, mimicking his every move—unwrapping the gum the same slow way, wadding the paper up, putting it carefully in his pocket, chewing thoughtfully. The sun sparkles through the pecan leaves, shimmers his hair. Jeff glances up, sees her watching from the kitchen window, nods and smiles, his grin held back, then released—full-on joy. She lifts her hand in a wave, wonders if he can see her flush from that far away.

After he called, she'd caught herself looking in the mirror over the bathroom sink, smoothing her braid over one shoulder, smoothing her frown lines with a finger, licking her chapped lips, smearing on Chapstick to keep them from cracking and peeling, and finally coming to this conclusion: "He's way too young. And you are being ridiculous. You have no time for foolishness." But then she remembered waking up in the straw, her arm flung over Folly, dreaming of a kiss, and her stomach fluttered a little, like a girl trying to decide what to wear for a date. He's got an earnestness about him that makes him seem boyish, not completely grown up. But he's a man. A man who seems kind. Kindness is the sexiest quality in a man. A kind man is a man who knows how to be in this world. Luke was kind.

Today Jeff's brought a gift so much more interesting than Frank's rolls of pennies.

Bobo's face is happy now the way it was happy when Ace was alive. It's happy in the way a sunflower's face is happy, turned toward the sun.

37

Thursday morning, early, the colonel musters. Ridley is coming for inspection this afternoon. An army man knows how to clean up. How hard can it be?

He skips his run. Takes a cold shower. Puts on his work clothes. Fills his glass with RC Cola to the rim, no ice, no bourbon, and drinks it down. Then he goes looking for the vacuum cleaner. That son of his left the carpet a mess. When the hell is he ever going to grow up? *And when are you going to apologize?* Anne says. "Dammit, Anne," Rand says. "He doesn't even come here anymore."

Rand does a load of dishes. He gets a sponge and scrubs the bathrooms, the kitchen counters. He takes the pile of junk mail and magazines and dumps them in the recycle box in the pantry. He vacuums. He lines things up—pillows, glassware, liquor bottles. He tosses the sheets that still smell like Anne's perfume on the closet floor, straightens the comforter, fluffs the pillows. Anne always did that.

He tucks the bourbon behind the cans of tuna in the pantry. He bags up the socks and shirts he ruined trying to do laundry last week—he poured in bleach instead of detergent—and takes them out to the trash bin. He rolls the trash bin to the curb. By noon the house is sparkling clean. Floors vacuumed, carpet fluffed, kitchen spic and span. Anne's table shines with new lemon oil. He hopes nobody looks in the closets, now piled high with dirty sheets.

He cleans the birdcages—no way he can hide the birds, but he can make them smell better. *Happy appul,* Queen Pia says, nuzzling his hair. *Fuck.*

Christ on toast. He puts the cover back on. Queen Pia mutters and screams her displeasure. King P plucks at the cover. Molly trills a sad muffled song of protest.

Rand spritzes air freshener all over the place, then opens the windows, because the air freshener smells terrible—like a headache.

Now the room is humid and hot from letting all the AC out. *Oh bloody hell.* He shuts the windows. What else? He looks around. His mother's bird of paradise on the wall. That's nice. Leave that. And below it, Decker's table. He can't wait to never see that again. He's always wanted to toss it out with the trash. But Anne loved it. "He gave it to me," she used to say. "Not you."

"Wedding presents are supposed to be for both of us," Rand argued.

But it was a ridiculous argument, and she knew it. You can't argue that you want something when you only want to throw it out.

After the wedding on Long Island, they had a four-day leave. They could have flown to Paris, or Rome, but she wanted to meet his people, since none had come to the wedding. Rand had no intention of shocking his wife with their poverty, their backward ways. He'd spent so much time proving himself worthy of the circles she traveled in. But his new wife insisted.

"Lord, Rand, you make it sound like they're hillbillies just because they're from West Virginia. I've been to West Virginia. There are very nice people there." Rand was beginning to learn that Anne believed the world in her head, the privileged world, was all the world there was. She almost had him convinced: maybe they had changed. What she didn't know was that his brother had got strange after he finally came home— after all that time in jail. He'd got in a bar fight. Stabbed a man. His face was twisted and bitter and hard now, like he'd swallowed a black rock and it had stuck in his throat.

Rand didn't want Anne to know a person could get like that. Especially someone related to him. But she insisted.

So Rand took her home. He watched Anne greet his threadbare mother with a natural fondness. Ma had gotten small and bent over and the old house was pretty much caved in on one side. Anne kissed his brother's cheek, as if she hadn't noticed Decker was a half-mad mountain man, tending his marijuana crop with traps and snares to keep the Feds away. No doubt he was stealing the checks Rand was sending Ma.

As Ma held the framed wedding picture Anne brought, her freckled hand veiny and trembling, Rand hardened his heart. He was doing the best he could. He was sending her money every month. *You can stay and take care of her, old man,* he told himself, *or you can be with Anne.* He spent two days trying to shore up his mother's house with plywood, wrote a bigger check, gave her his remaining cash, holding back enough for the drive home.

Ma gave Anne the bird print he'd always loved, the bird of paradise in a bamboo frame. "It's from my ma," she said. "Most beautiful bird in the world." She leaned in to whisper, but Rand overheard: *"You're his beautiful bird, now. So glad he caught you."*

Before they left, Decker came down from the mountain shack he lived in now, carrying a strange load on his back. He set it down before them. "Wedding present," he said. He'd made a small rustic table out of hewn chestnut logs, the axe marks rubbed to a golden sheen and the texture of a water-smoothed rock. Anne ran her fingers across the wood grain as if she were touching watered silk.

"You made this yourself?" He nodded. "It's beautiful," she said. "Thank you." She smiled at Decker with her cornflower eyes and Decker might have smiled back, but it was hard to tell under that snarled beard.

"Chopped it from the brother tree," Decker said. "That thing finally fell." Decker wrapped the table in an old quilt and ropes, insisted on tying it to the top of Rand's rental car, threading the ties through the open windows. Rand couldn't say no. Anne loved it so much. But he was thinking, *You can't make up for what you did.*

He and Anne were halfway down the mountain when it started to rain. The ropes sagged and the quilt flapped loose on the windshield, making it impossible to see. Rand skidded to a stop, got out, and started hacking at the ropes with his knife. He planned to shove quilt, ropes, and table off the cliff. He wanted to watch it bounce off rocks and splinter, the legs break off and fly. Rand hacked away furiously, rain streaming down his face, until the rope split and the table slid halfway off the car. He felt the bitterness against his brother turning into a kind of black-hearted exulting. *I'm going to drop you off the mountain.* But part of him was broken-hearted that his brother had tried to give him something beautiful and he could not love it.

Then he looked up. Anne had gotten out and was standing there, her hair plastered against her face, her small arms pushing at the table. "What are you *doing?*" she said.

"It's got to go," he yelled. "Don't you see? He wants us to drive off the mountain. He wants us to die."

"Don't be *ridiculous,*" Anne said. "Just tie it tighter. I want that table, Rand."

Rand stood there, staring at his new young wife, and felt like an immovable object facing an irresistible force. He turned and shoved the table back on the car. Rolled the quilt under the table to brace it. Retied the whole thing with bungee cords from the trunk. Rain poured down Rand's forehead and into his eyes. *I have Anne,* he said to himself. *You get the mountain.*

But when he blinked and looked up, Anne was staring at him as if she did not know him.

Rand's gun cabinet looks a little dusty, and there's a cobweb stuck to the pistols inside. He opens the glass case and pulls out the polishing rag, the gun oil. Anne never liked it that he put the display on the wall above the dining room table. He thought it looked classy. Masculine. Historical. Guns from every war. He is not sure why he collected these. Sometimes he wonders if it wasn't because he never actually fought in a war. He pulls out the World War II-issue Colt M19. Opens the chamber. Nothing there.

The front doorbell chimes. They're early. He's still in his work clothes. But there's no time to dress properly. He wipes his hands off with a rag and runs to open the door for Frank Ridley and his young assistant.

"Colonel," Ridley says, "so this is your home. Lovely. Your arbor is blooming."

Anne's Confederate jasmine, trained on an arched trellis over the front door. He hadn't realized it was blooming. He never goes out this way.

"What's that smell?" the assistant says, looking around inside.

The smell is gun oil and solvent and bad air freshener.

The assistant scrapes her shoes on the hall rug, holds a damp white envelope, smeared with a mud footprint, by her fingertips. "This was on your porch," she says.

Rand folds it in half without looking at it, stuffs it in his pocket. Some advertising circular, no doubt. Locals have quite a racket going door to door advertising their services. Mowing. Molly Maids. Scam deals on repaving your driveway. Now the young assistant has brushed past, sniffing the air, looking around the living room/dining room. "The bird theme's got to go," she says. "And what's with all the guns?"

By the time they're done, she's advised him to toss the vase of dried hydrangeas on the dining room table, put on a new roof, repaint the interior in a coffee-latte color with white trim, take down the oil portrait of Anne in her blue gown over the mantel, have the carpet profession- ally cleaned. He's got to pull down Anne's pile of Indian rocks that the snippy girl says looks like some kind of pagan worship thing. He's got to put the powder-blue sofa in storage, it's too old fashioned, and get the guns out of here. "I'm sorry, Colonel," she says, "but about fifty percent of the people in your buying public don't like guns. You'll have to put them in storage or something. It's not like you can shoot them in your yard here anyway."

"And this den?" she says, poking her head in, getting a load of the cockatiels, who mutter and screech from under their cover. "People are allergic to birds, you'll have to move them into the garage during showings." She tells him he's got to take his boxes and papers and things, put them in the garage. "People like to see an empty closet." She hasn't even seen the bedroom, with Anne's sheets crammed in the walk-in.

There is no way he's putting on a new roof. There is no way he's putting the birds in the garage. That portrait of Anne is the classiest thing in the house. And as for guns—if people don't like them, they can lump them. Half the buying public *will* like them, if this snippy girl is right.

Back in the dining room, the assistant runs her hands across the axe-hewn surface of Decker's table as if it were an expensive silk. "This table is nice," she says. "Where did you get this?"

He got it from a wild mountain man he no longer recognizes as his brother. "It was my wife's," he says, and the words catch in his throat.

The snippy assistant calls Anne's family-heirloom carved oak table "a cliché." She turns and says, "You could take some leaves out. It's a little large for the space. Makes it seem small."

He remembers Anne asking him to help her add a leaf. He never got the chance. Someone else must have done it for the food after the funeral. Putting in leaves is a two-person job. So is taking them out. Maybe Jeff will help. Jeff, however, is not coming around much to help his old father these days. *That's your own damn fault. What did you expect?*

"Too bad you don't have a piano," the girl says. "People like pianos."

No, he doesn't have a damn piano. Talk about a cliché.

By the time Ridley and Co. leave, Rand is ready for a drink. He pours, swirls the ice in his glass, considers. If he doesn't change everything around the way they want, he can't sell the house, according to the "go to" man for real estate. If Rand can't sell the house, he could rent it, but that's way too complicated, and how could he leave all Anne's things for a stranger to touch? A clean break. That's what he needs. A fresh start.

He'll do the yard first. He inhales the sickly sweet jasmine, sneezes, pulls an Indian stone from the stack by the front door, and places it in a random spot in the garden. Then another. And another. Undoing Anne's marker. She said that spirits gather next to such cairns in Scotland. No spirits will be able to find their house now. Maybe even Anne's will be lost, untethered from this place. He leans against the side of the house for a while. Then he goes inside to do whatever's next.

Rand is down on his hands and knees, unlocking the heavy table leaves with a chisel, when he hears Pia screeching. He left the covers on the birdcages. Poor birds.

He goes to the den, pulls the cage covers, watches the cockatiels fluff up their feathers. "Poor Pia, Poor King Philip. Poor Molly too. They want me to put you in the garage." He opens Molly's door and coaxes her onto his finger. Holds her up to his face. Lets the tickling feathers brush his cheek. She chirps, shy at first. Then she leans in. What does she want? Oh. Bird kisses. Oh well. No harm in that. "Looks like I'm your new boyfriend," he whispers, and she pecks at his lips, gently, like a young girl.

He puts her back in her cage, but she pecks and fusses at the cage door. "I know," Rand says. "I know." *Motherfucker!* Queen Pia shouts. That's when he gets it: when he sells the house and goes away, he'll be leaving the birds behind.

"Oh, Molly," he says. She trembles in the back of the cage. How will she live without him? He can't leave them here. But he's got to go.

Rand pours a refill, pulls some boxes from the closet, considers the problem. When you've got an insurmountable problem, start by looking at it from every angle. Could Jeff take them? Jeff's no good at taking care of birds. And anyway, he lives in a tent. Carrie? She travels too much. Bess? No. That drunk George would knock the damn cages over. What about the garage, as temporary housing? When Rand opens the door, the blast of dank oily air makes him choke. There's no way he's putting the birds out here. It smells bad.

He goes back to the den. The birds watch his movements closely. "I don't know what to do," he says, his arms hanging helplessly at his sides. The birds do not reply.

He can't stand the thought of them with a stranger. And he's heard that showy birds like these are favorites of drug dealers. Who else would take Pia Potty Mouth?

Rand pours a double. Drinks it down. The panic in his heart subsides to a low thrum.

Stop dwelling on the negative, Anne would say. *Think about something else for a while. When you come back, you'll know what to do.*

He pops the lid on the Tropical Bird Research files, flips through the labeled folders. Which to pull for his trip? Here's one: *Wild Parrots of Rome.*

After Anne's mother died, the house on Long Island was closed down, so they took home leave in Rome. He remembers strolling through the gardens of the Villa Doria Pamphili one day and hearing what sounded like a parrot screeching in the palm tree above his head. They had been posted in the Philippines then, and knew that sound well.

"It can't be," he said. "The only birds we've ever seen in Rome are pigeons and sparrows."

"But it is," Anne insisted.

He and Anne kept craning their necks and passing the binocs back and forth, peering at the enormous pine and palm trees above their heads. Finally, as if on cue, African parrots began winging from palm to palm, in twos and threes and sevens. There must have been scores of them. "Proof!" Anne said, triumphant. She liked being right almost as much as he did.

"What do they eat, I wonder?" Rand said.

"Maybe pine nuts. You could look it up."

He did look it up. Pine nuts. Anne was right again.

It was extraordinary. Tropical birds had adapted, survived, bred, and thrived in a place where it sometimes snows in winter. They had crossed lines of habitat as if ecosystems could simply be won by force. They were tough little things. He hears there are parrot flocks now in parts of London. Dreary, rainy London. And Connecticut. He's seen the ones in San Francisco. That's when he started keeping notes for the book: *Uncommon Bird Migrations.* Anne came up with the title. He'd shown her his map tracking the directions of parrot migrations that were not part of nature's plan. Arrows from continent to continent, names in Latin, small illustrations he'd copied from the books of nineteenth-century naturalists. She got a gleam in her eye. Surprise? Admiration? "Rand," she said. "It looks like army maps of missile trajectories." And indeed it did. But how in the world did *she* know that?

Queen Pia flaps in the cage, screeches at the den window. That painted bunting again. A tough little fellow, he's survived some kind of storm, found a mate, made a nest. And now he's protecting his young. He migrated out of his home range. Maybe he'll put *him* on the map.

He has no doubt Pia could survive in the wild if she had to. She's a tough bird with attitude. If she could, King P could. Not Molly. No. He'll find someone to take her. But what would cockatiels eat in winter?

He thinks of the pines of Rome, tall bottle brushes laden with pine nuts. He thinks of the tall crowns of the Gooley pines. Their cones are prolific, no doubt stuffed with seed. *Maybe that's the way.*

His brain feels thick and sticky. He rests one palm on their cage. *No time like the present.*

He opens the cage door, says, "Bird party." The pale pink birds hop out. Molly pecks at her cage door. He leaves her chirping and frantic, *Hey, me too!* The cockatiels follow him to the living room, swooping, perching, squawking. Bird party! Pia pecks at the mail slot, rattling the brass flap. She wants *out.* He opens the front door, and a humid breeze curls into the room. The cockatiels fluff their feathers, perch on the gun case, the table, the door frame. They get a whiff of open air. They flap up and hover around his head. They zoom out into freedom.

Molly's distress call pipes behind him. She has somehow opened her cage door. She takes a warm-up lap around the room and flies out after.

38

Thursday afternoon, Jeff watches Bobo give commands to Usen: *Sit. Stay. Jump up. Dance.* "Look, Jeff! Useh dancing!"

Jolene had called, said she had to go to some kind of meeting. "No problem," he said. She's left peanut butter sandwiches for them on a plate in the kitchen. He feels like a kid after school. *Thanks, Mom.* Not the kind of thing you do for a prospective boyfriend.

She's always in such a hurry. He wants to tell her about his real job. Chuck said they'll have permission any minute now from "the Widow Blake," some old lady no doubt who doesn't care a bit about that over-grown field. Once they have permission, they'll be legit. The *Times* will be coming. He can tell anybody.

His cell rings just as they're done with the second worksheet.

"Bess called," Carrie says. "There's something wrong with Dad."

Jeff turns away from Bobo so he won't hear. "What? Is he having a heart attack?" He should have checked on him before now.

"He's out in the yard, yelling at the birds. They got loose."

"Well, crap." Has Dad lost his mind? He loves those birds.

He hadn't asked Jolene if it was okay to take Bobo for a ride. She doesn't carry a phone. But he's got to go. *Dad, you're a big pain in the ass.* "Want to ride in the truck?" he asks Bobo.

Bobo yells, "Truck!" and runs outside, heaves himself into the passenger seat. Usen hops in, sits on Bobo's lap, and hangs his head out the window. Bobo sings his Usen and Jeff song:

> Jeff and Useh
> Jeff and Useh
> Happy dog and
> Happy boy

Jeff is not sure if the happy boy is him or Bobo. Maybe it's both. "Fasten your seatbelt," he says.

"Go see Weba?" Bobo says. "Inna truck?"

"Who's Weba?" Jeff says.

"Weba have chickens," Bobo explains.

"Not this time, Bobo. Maybe later. I need to visit my dad."

Bobo thinks for a minute, then says, "You have a dad?"

Uh-oh. Maybe this is a sore subject. "Uh, yeah." He wonders what happened to Bobo's.

"Like Papa?"

"Sure. Same thing."

"Miss Ahn dead."

"Yes."

"He miss huh."

"Yeah." Gee, this kid really cuts to the bone.

"You miss huh too," Bobo says.

"Every day," Jeff says. "Every day."

"Me too," Bobo says happily. "Want some gum?"

They drive, chewing, to Stonehaven Downs.

Jeff looks around the yard. No birds. No Dad.

Jeff tells Bobo to stay in the truck with Usen for a minute. He's got to make sure Dad isn't drunk or naked before he brings Jolene's boy into the house. He slips his key in the door and walks into the kitchen. A coffee cup on the cutting board. Still warm.

He checks the living room. Dad's been moving things around. Mom's painting is leaning against the wall. He checks the den. Dad's not here. The cockatiel cage is open. And there's another cage next to it. Dad got a new bird? No, it's the lovebird cage. *But where's Molly?*

Jeff opens the door to the front yard. "Dad?" Dad's sitting in an Adirondack chair. Arms upraised. *What the fuck?* He's got sunflower seeds and macadamia nuts scattered all over the damn place, on the wide arms of the chair, in his lap, on the ground at his feet, and in a circle a couple of yards around. Empty cans and bags piled at his feet. "Dad?"

His father turns toward him. Seeds all over his shirt. "They've never been outside before," Dad says. "I don't think they know how to come back." He looks like a heartbroken ten-year-old boy. His eyes leaking tears.

Jeff looks up. King P and Queen Pia are on a pine branch, bobbing their heads up and down in greeting.

"I'll get them, Dad," Jeff says. "Don't worry. I'll get your birds." He has no clue how.

Two squirrels zip around the corner, see him, freeze. One grabs a macadamia nut, stuffs it in his cheek, then boldly grabs one more, stuffs his other cheek, hightails it away.

Jeff hears a muffled shout. "Useh!"

Usen comes tearing around the side of the house, Bobo following. Usen spies the squirrel and chases it to a tree, leaps and yips as it gets away. There is wild flapping above. *Fuck!* Pia shouts. *Oh bloody hell!*

His father rises halfway out of his chair, yells, "Go away! Go away!" waving his arms at Bobo and Usen. Usen ignores him.

"Dad, no, it's not his fault!" *Don't yell at the kid.* Dad sinks back into his chair.

"Get. That. Damn. Dog. Out. Of. Here," Dad says, pounding the arms of his chair, veins popping on his neck. Looks like he's had a few.

Bobo stands in front of Rand, bobbing from side to side like a line-man blocking a quarterback.

"Papa," he says.

Rand freezes. Jeff watches his eyes search Bobo's face, striped shirt, tie, khaki pants. "What?" Dad chokes. "What did you say?"

"You miss huh." Bobo's expression is grave.

Behind him, Usen yips at squirrels and leaps higher. The cockatiels flutter and pop their crests in high anxiety. King P begins to edge to the end of the branch. Thinks better of it and edges back.

"Miss Ahn, Miss Ahn!" Bobo says happily.

Rand sits up, stares at the boy, turns to Jeff, croaks, "Who? Who?"

"Dad!" Jeff says. "Dad, this is Bobo. He knew Mom. Mom used to help in his school. Right, Bobo?"

"Miss Ahn!" Bobo crows. "Sweet eyes. *Blue.*" He throws his head back and smiles, flings his arms out to the side. "Good hugs!"

Rand looks up at Bobo in fear. Above his head, the cockatiels flutter on their branch, flap and take wing, circle. Pink feathers land on his knees. He picks one up. Looks up. Sees them flying. "Queen P!" he croaks.

Bobo's eyes light on the circling birds. "Pink birds!" he says, his arms outstretched.

The cockatiels eye Bobo, bob their heads. From their perch high in the pine tree, the boy's body seems tethered to the ground, like a tree settled on two strong roots. The boy's face emanates joy. His arms em-anate safety. The birds flap once, rise, then flutter low, above his head.

Usen sits, completely still, fascinated.

Jeff stops breathing.

The birds alight, one on each of Bobo's outstretched arms. King Philip walks and bobs to his hand, seeking food, nibbling at his palm. "Tickles!" Bobo says happily. Queen Philippina begins grooming Bobo's hair. "Don't bite!" Bobo says. The bird bobs her head and inspects his happy face.

"They like you," Jeff says. For an instant he feels a terrible envy of this child. Dad's birds came to him just like that. He didn't even have to try.

His father sits up in his chair, a small cry escapes his lips. "Pia!"

"Give them to Dad," Jeff says. "Give Dad the birds."

Bobo turns to Rand. "Papa's birds," he says. He walks to the chair slowly, then extends one arm to Rand's outstretched hand. Queen Pia bobs and edges to Rand. Climbs onto his shoulder. Then King P follows, steps onto his other shoulder and begins grooming Rand's eyebrow.

Dad's head is surrounded by birds. "Thank you," he says to Bobo.

"Make a *wish*," Bobo says.

Dad sits in his Adirondack chair, face lit up like a baby's, eyes leaking tears of joy.

"I wish—" Dad's head drops to his chest, shakes from side to side as if he is saying, *No no no no.*

Jeff's heart hurts so badly he almost cries out. He has never seen his father emotional like this, not even when Mom died. "Hey, Dad," he says, "where's Molly?"

His dad looks at him with devastated eyes. "She flew away."

Jeff pulls into Jolene's driveway and turns to Bobo. "Listen," he says, "don't tell your mom about going to my dad's house, and the birds and everything."

"Don't tell about Papa?"

"That's right."

"See-cwet," Bobo says.

"Good."

"Come see baby goh," Bobo says. "Stay, Useh." Usen stays.

Bobo takes him into the pen with the baby goats, and it's really cute how they snuggle with him. When Usen comes bounding over the gate and into the pen, they scatter to every corner. Jeff grabs for his sparkly collar, but the pup keeps dodging him.

"Useh!" Bobo cries out, and the pup circles back and sits in front of him, his tail twitching as if he knows he shouldn't wag.

"Let me take him," Jeff says. He picks Usen up and stuffs him inside his vest. The pup barely fits anymore. He squirms and yips. "Settle down, Usen," Jeff says. "Bad dog."

Bobo stands in front of him. "Don't chase the babies," he says to Usen.

Usen whimpers.

"Useh be good?"

Usen yips. Bobo reaches for him, sets him on the other side of the fence. Usen sits. Wags his tail. Good dog.

By the time Jolene comes tearing up in her truck, they're back in the kitchen, doing worksheets.

$13 - 1 = 12$

My name is <u>BOBO</u>. My friend's name is <u>JEFF</u>.

Jolene wraps her arms around the big boy.

"Jeff like the baby gohs, Mama!"

"I'll bet he does," she says. "Usen didn't get in there, did he?"

"No, Mama."

She turns to Jeff. There's a strange expression on her face. "I told Chuck you were here, watching Bobo."

"What?" Her meeting was with *Chuck*? Why was she meeting with Chuck? Shit, he should have been there. He promised he'd be there day and night. All the time. No problem.

"He has something for you," Jolene says. She's got an armful of cords and stuff.

"What?"

"A laptop," she says, setting it down. She turns and looks him over, arms folded across her chest. "Why didn't you tell me you were working on the dig?"

Jeff thinks of all the reasons Chuck gave him, *Don't tell anybody what you're up to, they'll all be out poking around, digging holes, asking questions.* But why does she care? It's way on the other side of the Gooley Ridge.

"I guess I—"

"You didn't eat your snack," she says to Bobo. "You didn't do all your worksheets."

"We got distracted," Jeff says.

She turns away to check the sheets.

Jeff lets his eyes linger on the curve of her body barely discernible under her rough work pants. That's when he finally gets it. The Widow Blake is not an old lady. The Widow Blake is Jolene. Indigo Field, the broad expanse of abandoned rocks and brush, and the tall glimmering pines, the place where they'll find the mother lode, belongs to her. *You're such a dumbass.* He never asked her last name.

"Jolene," he says. "Mrs. Blake. I guess in all this time I didn't make the connection. I never knew it was your land."

"Well, it is." She looks pissed. "And don't you forget it."

Now Bobo is showing off tricks he's taught Usen. "Look, Mama!"

She turns away again. He wonders if she told Chuck about the dog. "You don't have to come tomorrow," she says. "I'm all set."

Crap. *You are such a fuckup.* He wants to say, *I'm sorry, you can trust me, please please please.* But people only trust you when you show you can be trusted. He knows that much.

He pulls a bag of dog food out of the truck, says his goodbyes to Usen and Bobo, and Bobo wraps his arms around him and hugs him tight. Jolene stands with her arms crossed. Jeff looks down at Usen, sitting and staying. He wants to pick him up. But Usen doesn't belong to him anymore.

When Jeff gets back to the site, Chuck isn't there, but he left a note under a potsherd on the work table. *Call me tonight, ten p.m.* When Jeff calls, Chuck doesn't seem pissed at first.

"You like the laptop?" he says.

"It's great," Jeff says. He hasn't opened it yet. In the truck, there's whole box of stuff that came with it: a solar charging station, GPS tracking and a mobile Wi-Fi hotspot unit. Plus scads of solar-rechargeable AA batteries. There's even a cookstove in there, battery operated, that says it heats water to a boil in four minutes. A little fan feeds air into the firebox at the bottom. "The stove is cool too," he says. Jeff has to ask. "Why didn't you tell me you were meeting Jolene?"

"*A,*" Chuck says, "your phone was off."

"Oh."

"*B,* I thought you were going to be here. Day and night. All the time."

"I screwed up," Jeff says. "It won't happen again."

"Good," Chuck says. "Because there's nobody left in the program this summer who doesn't already have a job. I really should fire you. Asshole."

"Yeah," Jeff says. *Damn-it-to-hell.* He's this close to getting fired. Worse, losing a friend.

"*C,* Why didn't you tell me you knew her?" Chuck says.

"I didn't know she owned the Field," Jeff said. "I met her at the farmers' market."

"You never told her what you were doing here?"

"It didn't come up." *Because I was busy staring at her lips. And green eyes. And the schoolgirl cleft in her chin.*

Chuck seems satisfied with that. "Well, she gave permission. But she was a little pissed. Let that be your punishment. No hot dates for you this weekend with hot lady farmers. And no babysitting their kids."

Hot lady farmers? Chuck is such a horn dog. Jeff wonders if he hit on her.

"And no wild little dogs. You're going to have to stand guard now, the next few days. Check the bottom of the box. I brought you six cans of beanie weenies you can heat up on your stove. Tide you over till Monday. And you like veggies, right? There's some sugar snaps in there."

"Thanks."

"She gave me a tour of her side of the highway," Chuck says. "You should have been there. Man, those pines are something. I'm not even sure they're white pines. Maybe some relict ancestor of white pines from before the ice age." Chuck's voice rises in excitement, full of wonder. "She likes the idea of a historic preserve. In fact, she's the one who brought it up. If we find what we're looking for. Could happen, you never know."

Jeff can see it, the glowing pines, the Field a preserve. Wow. And Jolene there. Happy.

"She wants to get her kid involved somehow. Can you handle that?"

"Sure thing," Jeff says. "We're good buddies." Maybe she'll forgive him.

Chuck signs off with instructions about the gate, the thistles, the fences. "And stay on site, really, all Saturday and Sunday. I know it's boring. But there's a full moon tomorrow, and full moons bring out pot hunters and crazies."

Jeff settles on a rock shaped like a sleeping deer and watches the evening light shift along the river—pink and blue to orange and blue to gold and purple to black, with Venus rising. The sun sets on the far side of the Gooley pines, gleaming through the pine branches like hot coals. The moon rises—almost full—over the river. Silver coins make a path across the dark water. Chuck didn't fire him for not being there. Chuck didn't fire him for the dog. And what else: Jolene wants them there. That's good. It's still okay with her that he's going to be around.

A whippoorwill calls. Another answers. He misses Usen.

If he can get back on Jolene's good side, he can make her dinner on his new solar stove, right out here in Indigo Field. Sugar snap peas and Beanee Weenees. What did Chuck say? *Optimism is the fallback position of archaeologists.*

39

Saturday night, the moon is high and white as a spotlight on Indigo Field. The dark pines above glimmer and shift in a light breeze. Jeff opens the gate, closes it behind him. He hears voices, laughter. Pothunters? Damn. He should have come earlier, parked the truck where people could see, be warned off. He should have brought Chuck's pellet gun to wave around. Pothunters can be armed.

Jeff turns the headlights off and nudges the truck around rocks to the open field. Fifty yards from the river, he cuts the engine and listens. Low talking. A giggle. A clink. Not the clink of a shovel. The clink of a paper bag full of beer bottles.

Jeff rolls the window down. Holds the flashlight high. Flips on the headlights and the flashlight at the same time. In the headlight glare he sees two pairs of legs, one pair in jeans, one pair bare below a fluffy pink skirt, stumbling across the tall grass. Someone pitches a bottle, glass breaks. They run.

He hears a truck start up on Quarryville Road, a boy's voice swear. So that's how they got in. They parked next to the bridge and jumped the fence. It's not much of a fence. He watches their truck barrel across the bridge. He goes to clean the glass up and finds four empties and a cold one along with shards of broken bottle. And something else: a Mason jar of clear liquid with a rusty lid, hole punched in the top. He sniffs. Moonshine. Where'd kids get that?

He twists the top off the cold one and takes a swig.

He picks up the bottle shards, drops them in the bag, scans the dirt for bottle caps. Something white and curved catches the light. A Styrofoam cup? No. Trash? No.

He steps closer. Holy shit. A human skull with a gaping eye socket stares back at him.

He hunkers down, scanning slowly with his flashlight. The nearby soil is loose and humped, like an animal dug here. Human bones laid out flat, European style. What are these doing here?

He touches the skull lightly, feels the surface, no skin, hair, or flesh remaining, some shreds that might be neck ligaments. This is no recent grave. There's a crack in the skull, dirt caked to the edges. Not a new crack. In the eye socket packed with dirt, a round flat white object glimmers, the size of his fingernail. He peers more closely. A shell bead with a hole drilled in the center. Roanoke. Like the nations of the Outer Banks made, more than 400 years ago. Could this be one of the Old Ones? Some survivor who'd lost his way, his traditions of burial? It's near the Gooley Ridge, where Chuck thought they'd find more. A shudder of dread travels up his legs to his belly. There is something very wrong here, a terrible story from the past. The dig is compromised. Animals—maybe Usen—or those kids dug this up, destroying clues that can be found only in undisturbed soil. Chuck will definitely fire him this time.

He wants to throw the beer bottle and watch it explode all over the bones and yell at the top of his lungs. *Shit, shit, shit.* Everything he touches turns to shit. *Do not screw this up, do not screw this up,* Jeff breathes, standing there. *There are moments in life,* his mother once told him, *when everything you do makes a difference.*

Don't give up, Mom would say. *Count to ten. Breathe.*

Don't be a bum, Dad would say. *Be a man.*

"Screw you, Dad." He counts to ten, blows out his breath, and knows what to do. He tips out the remaining white liquor in a circle around the bones, an offering to the spirits of this Field, *O, ha le / O, ha le!* He wonders if Geronimo's medicine song is acceptable here, especially coming from his lips. He climbs up to the Gooley pines, gathers some fallen branches, covers the bones. He goes back to his tent, gets the pellet gun, tucks it in his vest. He will sleep in his truck right here, guarding this desecrated grave all night long.

What did Chuck say? *Optimism is the fallback position for archaeologists.* This could be an incredible find. It could be the last burial of a Tuscarora descendant in this place. It could be as recent as twentieth century. Did Tuscarora live here that long? He has to find out. The drunk kids could be a stroke of luck in a way. It takes so long to find the right place to dig. This could be the right place.

He will say a prayer for the spirit of the Old One whose sleep has been disturbed. He will call Chuck Mathers in the morning. He will stay right here, guardian of the sacred dead, until Chuck tells him what to do.

Sunday morning, early, Chuck roars up to the gate in his Blazer, stretches, and empties his coffee cup onto the ground. "Let's check this baby out." Jeff leads the way to the new bones.

Chuck approaches the site with care, scanning for anything out of place. "This is where I found the kids drinking," Jeff says.

Jeff pulls back the camouflage brush, lifts the rocks holding the tarp in place, then pulls it back to reveal the bones. Chuck takes some pictures. Then he squats and pulls on latex gloves. He touches the femur, feels the tooth marks. "Coyote, maybe. A pup. Yours?"

"Maybe." Jeff is miserable.

Chuck counts the ribs. Then he turns his attention to the skull. "Twentieth century," he says. "Maybe." He runs a finger along a crack in the cranium. "Maybe not a natural death," he says.

Jeff remembers the massacre story he read. Maybe this was one of the victims. But no, that wasn't twentieth century. Chuck picks out the shell bead, holds it to the light. "The size is right, and the shape. It could be as early as 1500s." He puts it in a plastic zip bag. He slips a finger inside the mouth cavity. A molar falls from the jaw into his palm. He looks at the tooth. Turns it in his fingers, rubs. Holds it up. Slips it into a plastic zip bag. When he looks up, his face is dark red.

"Gold fillings," he says, as if that explains everything. "Cover it up. Crap. If this is a Tuscarora grave, I'll eat my socks."

Jeff knows that dental work is how you identify the dead from the latter half of the twentieth century. This is the grave of a modern man. Or woman. And it was somebody with enough money to buy gold fillings. Probably white.

"Bad timing for this," Chuck says. "The *Times* reporter was coming out tomorrow. I'll have to cancel."

"Crap," Jeff says.

"I'll have the sheriff out." Chuck stands, looks at his plastic bag: a shell bead. A gold-filled tooth. He sighs. "He'll probably shut us down. And listen. Something like this, everybody will know even before it's in the papers. You might get tourists."

"Tourists?"

"People who like to look at dead bodies just for fun."

"No problem," Jeff says. What else has he got to do?

"Damn it all to hell. The Widow Blake has got a body in her field."

40

A
t Spill Creek Farm, Usen barks like crazy when the sheriff drives up.

"More bones?" Jolene says.

"Different bones," the sheriff says.

"Sit, Useh," Bobo says.

Sheriff Walter Junior shifts the big belt of gear around his waist. "Your man Luke ever tell you about somebody buried out there in that field of yours? Would've been in the seventies, after he came back from Nam."

"No." There is a lot that Luke never told her.

"I'm shutting down the dig till forensics can come look. I'd be inclined to leave it where it lies. But it ain't up to me. You got to investigate it when you find bones."

"Bones, Mama!" Bobo says. And it's all she can do to keep him from running up into the Gooley pines, looking for the Bone Man.

They're shutting the dig down. Archaeology will not save them.

That evening, Jolene and Bobo walk to the mailbox and Usen tags along. It is a favorite ritual from when Bobo was young. She will keep these rituals alive, burn them into his memory. Luke put a turtle shell in the mailbox years ago when Bobo was little, and he keeps expecting to see it there. "Turtle in theh, Mama," he says. He opens the mailbox, lifts Usen to see.

"Is it there this time?"

"No." He is so disappointed. There is nothing like his faith in the possibility of joy. It keeps her going. Every day, though, brings new waves of sadness now. *What will become of us?*

The evening sky is alive with pink clouds and no rain. Barn swallows zoom around. Usen zooms below. "Look, Mama, Stah Wahs!" Bobo calls out. Their joke. The zooming birds look like a Star Wars battle. She's never let him see the movie. Too violent. But she's told him about the planes that fly like barn swallows.

Bobo pulls the mail out, closes the metal door, tips the flag up, crows, "Flag up, Mama!" and smiles at her. "I help, Mama."

"Yes, you helped. Such a good helper. Now flip it back down again.

That's right." She is not paying any bills today.

In the dusky pink light, she spies something odd across the pasture. A pale wooden stake with a blue flag tied to the top, rippling in the breeze. What in the world? Are they doing a new dig here? That's not part of the deal.

Two more, three, no, five, along the edge of the Gooley Ridge. She tells Bobo, "Stay here," in her Mean Mama voice, and she jogs across the pasture, reads the notation on the side of the first one: *Do Not Remove*. Then numbers and letters. Surveyor's notes. *Hell and damnation.* A survey is what people do when they are about to assess some land. Then sell it.

Sometime this afternoon, sometime while they were going about their business, freezing French filet beans, eating supper, milking and feeding goats, someone has been on her land. Someone has been walking around, pounding stakes in with a rubber mallet that makes no sound, planning the exact amount of her land to steal out from under her. She doesn't know much, but she knows it's only been a week since the bank letter said sixty days. They have no right to come here. Not till her time's up.

Jolene grips the rough pine stake in both hands and yanks it out of the earth. Then she calls Bobo, "Come on!" and he runs to help.

Together they pull out the stakes all the way up the hill halfway into the Gooley pines. Her heart pounds with rage. "No!" she shouts, "you can't have it. No!" She runs for the next stake. It's getting dark. She has to hurry to see the boundaries of what they're after.

"No, Mama," Bobo pants. "Stop."

"Help me, Bobo," she says, and as he pulls on the stake, Usen clamps on, growling, pulling and shaking like he's dragging a snake from its nest. Bobo gives one last yank, tumbles back onto the grass, a splinter in his palm. "Mama!" he cries. "Huts!"

He has gone from her helpful young man to three-year-old in two seconds flat. "Bobo," she says. "Get up. Get up now. Be a big boy, like TJ." Usen leaps on Bobo's chest. But Bobo pushes him away. A last ray of sun bounces across the pasture and lights up Bobo's round cheeks. Bobo is crying. "No, Mama!" He sits there, in his rumpled khaki pants and windbreaker, and begins to wail. It's getting dark. She can't see how far the stake line goes. She has to do something. Get help. Call Reba. Call the sheriff. Something. Jolene gathers up the stakes at her feet and strides across the pasture to the house. "Come on, Bobo. Now!"

"Maaaaamaaaaa!"

Bobo can find his way home. He's got Usen. He's a big boy. Not a baby.

She turns the porch light on, so Bobo can see his way. She picks up the phone. She dials Frank's line. Leaves a message. "I can't believe you let them on my land. Call me when you get this. Don't make me wait."

She slams the phone down. Bobo comes tumbling in the door, crying mad.

When she puts him to bed that night, he's still mad. But Usen is cuddled at his feet. He has a dog now. That's something.

When Frank calls, she's sitting in the kitchen, drinking coffee, this far from picking up the phone and calling the sheriff. *Trespass. Illegal taking.* She's heard of that. She suddenly wishes she had a damn cell phone or computer so she could look up the law.

"Mrs. Blake."

Uh-oh. He's pretending he doesn't know her.

"Your people were out here," she says. "Putting stakes all over. They gave me sixty days and you know it. You'd better call them off or I'm calling the sheriff."

"Now, now, Mrs. Blake. Miss Jolene. I'm not sure what happened. I do know they sent you a letter."

"Well, if they did send me a letter, I wouldn't have given permission."

"Miss Jolene. Have you even read your mail since Monday?"

"I read my mail when I want." She reaches out with her free hand, flips through the envelopes on the kitchen counter. There it is. A damn letter from a surveyor in town. She tears it open with her teeth. *Dear Mrs. Blake: This is to inform you of our intent to survey the land stated as collateral—*

"I can't stand this, Frank. You know Bobo can't take living in town."

"You need more help with him, that's all," he says, all conciliatory.

"I have plenty of help. I just don't have any money."

"Maybe you need a social worker evaluation. Children can get unruly at this age."

"He doesn't need—what are you talking about? Bobo has nothing to do with this."

"There are always institutions for boys like him," he says. "Places where he will be well taken care of."

"What? *What did you say?*" She can't believe it. After that song and dance about his little brother, the institution, the years of trying to find him. "How dare you."

"Miss Jolene, it's late. I can see you're upset. Your boy is your priority, I understand that. But, my dear Jolene, surely you remember there is another way. There is always another way."

Another way. Lord have mercy. She slams the phone down. She will never marry Frank Ridley. She'd rather be homeless on the streets of Quarryville, holding out a paper cup for quarters.

Jolene raises her head from the pillow. Opens the window for a breeze. There is no breeze. The whippoorwills are at it again in Indigo Field. Two of them calling back and forth. *Mating season*, Luke always said when he heard that wild frantic call. She can almost smell his breath on her shoulder.

Jolene picks up the oblong stone she keeps on her bedside table. It fits perfectly in her hand. Smooth to the touch. Luke said it was a pestle for grinding corn. It has other uses.

She dresses. Wraps a shawl around her shoulders, slips the stone into her jeans pocket, tiptoes downstairs. Pauses at Bobo's door. A soft buzz. He's snoring. A softer buzz—Usen too.

She slips out the door and walks through patches of vapor like the breath of the dead in the Gooley Ridge, then down into Indigo Field, where mist has settled above the river like a pool of molten silver. She lies down in a patch of damp grass, a place that knows the contours of her body well. A place she and Luke used to make love. A place she has visited from time to time, over the years since his passing. Her own ritual.

She holds the pestle in the moonlight, letting it catch and glint on the smooth shape of the stone. She unbuttons her jeans, slips her hand in place, and begins to rub, *pine smell of his hair, smoke smell of his shirt, her young self, opening to first love*. "Luke," she says out loud. "Oh, Luke." That face, those dark eyes, that hungry mouth. That wide, strong chest. Strong hands. Touching her. Yes. The warm place between her legs softens, rises, the strength of his arms, his kiss. But now the image shifts, the face before her changes—freckled skin, eyes earnest and blue, a sweetness in those eyes. Jeff. What is Jeff doing in her head?

She groans, and the pleasure and the sorrow of her life exhale into the night air like the song of a lovesick deer. Her hands are warm between her legs but the rest of her is cold. She sits up. Pulls the shawl close. Looks around. Rocks and grass, tall pines above, as familiar as her own body. Indigo Field. When they take this place, all the memories of Luke locked into this land will float away. All her ideas about gathering allies to help—Tree People, farmers, archaeologists—they might show up but it will be too late. The bank will have her land.

The mist rises from the river and floods the Field, swirling above her head like gauze scarves. It catches the moonlight, holds it shimmering, slips like ghosts of animals between the rocks. The Field is alive. But Luke has gone away.

Jeff steps into the thick mist spreading knee high from the river. He walks Jolene's field as far as the Gooley Ridge, ranges past the tarp covering the bones, then circles back through broomsedge and boulders toward his truck. He carries the pellet gun now—for snakes and warning shots.

There is a rustle in the tall grass. A voice calls out, "Who's there?" A woman's voice. Frightened. He hadn't thought a pothunter might be a woman.

"You're on private property," he says. "Stand and identify yourself." The script Chuck gave him. Meant to sound official.

He hears a rustle, shines the light to the sound. Nothing but foggy brightness.

"Stand up now."

Nothing but crickets and whippoorwills and mist.

"This is your last warning," he says. He fires the pellet gun into the air, it snaps like the crack of a whip.

The crickets and whippoorwills go still.

A slim dark form rises before him, arm flung up to protect her eyes from the spotlight. Shirt half-undone, as if she's been caught with a lover, but there is no one else. Eyes reflect ice-green, like a cat's. Jolene. "This is *my* land. Who the hell are *you*?" She's got a rock in her hand. Her face glints wet in the silver-blue light. She's crying.

"Jolene?" he says. "It's Jeff. Jefferson Lee. Jesus, I didn't hurt you, did I?" She doesn't know he shot up into the air, doesn't know it was just a pellet gun, harmless as gumballs. He can see it in her eyes, she's scared, defenseless, but ready to throw. To defend what is hers.

"What the blue blazes are *you* doing here?" she says.

"Jolene. Don't you remember?" he says. "I'm supposed to guard the Field at night. From intruders." He takes a step closer. "Are you okay?"

She steps back. Loses her footing, stumbles, scrambles up. "This is *my* land. It doesn't belong to you. It doesn't belong to Chuck. Get out of here, leave me alone!"

"Wait!" he yells behind her, but she is already running flat out for the Gooley pines, scrambling up the Ridge, sneakers slipping the deep pine duff.

He has to make sure she's okay. He has to explain. *Oh God, Jolene.* Jeff zips the pellet gun into his vest and runs after.

Brambles rip his jeans, a branch grazes his lip, salty blood trickles into his mouth. Is there a path? He can see her moving ahead of him in the moonlight, the bright shimmer of her shawl flickering in the dark pines. He is faster, stronger. He has long legs. He will catch up.

At the top of the Ridge is a patch of light; he stops and listens, hears her breath. She has stopped too. She must be hiding behind one of these enormous pines. He senses her watching him. "Jolene?" he whispers. The name is like the call of some sweet night bird. There is a rustling beside him. She is very close. She ducks under a branch and stands before him, panting. She reaches out, wipes the blood from his lip with her finger. He watches her, amazed. She seizes his astonished face in her hard lean hands and kisses him.

Under her loose shirt and work pants, her body is like a melon, a ripe melon, sleek and firm, and sweet and round, silver and gold. He sips her flesh, she smells of sweat and moss and ripe fruit and cloves and hay. They slide to the ground; their bodies cleave like the roots of a shaggy tree straining in a high wind. She nuzzles his ears, licks his shoulders, he clamps his fingers in the cleft of her butt and holds on. They sweat and roll and groan together. All across Indigo Field, in the curling mists along the river, in the branches of the high trees, the creatures of this place—trees and spirits too—listen to this new sound. And they are strangely pleased.

Finally the two of them lie, sweaty, moon-spangled, under the rustling pines.

She stands up, takes his hand. "Come," she says, and takes him home, up the stairs, and into her high soft bed.

ॐ

On Indigo Field, the first rays of sun throw black shadows under the rocks, polish the topsides to a gleam, and heat the tarps that cover the test holes, the four-square digs, the new bones. A few minutes and the sun is fully risen, throwing long arms of yellow light through the glimmering Gooley pines, then the edges of Jolene's pastures and garden rows, holding them in gold-rimmed darkness until the land fills with light like a green bowl. The pastures will be ready to cut again soon, and green will turn gold and dry and be pressed into square bales that capture the sun twice: in their long green blades, and in the heat of their cut flanks as they cure.

In Jolene's barn, the kids and mamas stir.

Jolene opens one eye.

She steals out of bed, checks Bobo's room. Usen whines. But Bobo's still sleeping hard. She can milk and feed the does in thirty minutes flat when Bobo's not around. She sets the percolator on the stove eye, sears sausage, leaves it in the skillet to stay warm. She runs to the milking parlor, feeds, milks, gives the kids their replacer, and steals back up the stairs to a room now filled with light. Sun's up. That golden boy in her bed. Gold hair spiky with sweat, gleaming.

Jeff wakes with the sense that he has been dreaming, and still dreams, a dream that has completely taken his body—arms, legs, chest, lungs, feet—and turned it into an element not yet listed on the periodic table. Every part of him fills with loud joy. He is radioactive, like every carbon life form, but somehow his body has gotten stuck on "on." He smells coffee. Sausage. His own sweat. A woman's musk. *Jolene.*

"Don't leave." He opens his arms and pulls her to him, smelling something new, animal and warm milk and hay.

Her body chilled and hard against his, then warming as he wraps every part of himself around her. "So beautiful," he lips into her hair.

"No," she says.

"Oh yes. Beautiful. No words for it."

"You're the beautiful one," she says. She noses his ear. Sniffs his sweaty-smelling hair.

"Are you happy?" He wants her to be happy. He feels her mouth curve next to his neck, her cheeks rise in a smile.

"Yes," she says. "Happy."

"Good," he says. "Me too." And he makes love to her again, quietly now, their breathing joining the sounds of the brilliant day, the dawn chorus shouting all across Jolene's pastures and the Gooley pines like a brilliant spell, an incantation of protection, rising up from the earth and circling them.

He stops over and over just for the pleasure of her eyes filled with light, her face and chest flushed pink, her lips holding sweetness. Her smile cracks the day open like an egg.

41

On Monday morning, when Miss Reba stops by Jolene's for whey, she finds that boy Jeff, Miss Anne's son, washing breakfast dishes.

Jeff smiles and says, "Good morning." Jolene blushes.

So that's how it is.

"I'll take Bobo outside for a while," Jeff says. Jolene nods. Miss Reba watches them go. Bobo is happy as cherry pie. That little dog following behind. Young man Jeff seems good with Bobo. That's a sign. Maybe he's got some of that Miss Anne in him. Miss Anne, who brought flowers when Danielle died. Miss Anne, the only one from Stonehaven who wrote her a letter:

> I am so sorry for your loss. Danielle was such a special young woman. I know you miss her deeply. Please know that I am thinking of you.
>
> Warm wishes, Mrs. Anne Percival Lee

Miss Reba can see how the two of them might fit together. Jolene and Jeff. It even sounds right.

She sits sipping coffee in Jolene's kitchen, something she has never done before. Miss Jolene has got something to say. Some advice to ask.

"You all settled in with this young boy Jeff," Reba says.

"I—I wouldn't say settled in," Jolene says. "This is—new." She blushes. "You think I shouldn't? You think it's bad for Bobo?"

"Miss Jolene," Reba says. "Bobo loves that boy. Jeff likes Bobo too. Maybe you ought to all be together. In the same house. At night."

"I—" Jolene stops dead. Gets a funny look on her face.

"What?"

"I didn't think you would approve. You know, without being married."

Reba considers this for a moment. "I had a man myself once," she says. "A long time ago."

Jolene half smiles. Like she doesn't believe her.

"In Baltimore," Reba says.

"What happened?" Jolene says, eyes full of wonder and surprise.

"Didn't last," Reba says, and clamps her mouth shut. *James. Sweet brown eyes, dapper clothes, that time by the shore. He was kissing and shoving on her and her spirit flew up and saw that girl being hurt. She picked up the nearest thing, a conch shell, and crashed it on his head. Trickle of blood. James wiped it off. Walked away.*

Miss Reba gathers herself. "Anyway, Jesus loves the sinner. Long as you repent." Parroting something Reverend says, like she knows anything at all about sin. About love.

"The thing is," Jolene says, "I don't feel like repenting. I feel like I'm being blessed without measure."

"Must be doing something right, then. But you know what they say?"

"What?"

"Love lasts. Blessings come and go."

Jolene puts down her coffee cup, carefully. "I know," she says. "That's just what I'm afraid of." She goes to the percolator and refills Reba's cup. Black and strong, just the way Reba likes it.

Jolene leans back against the counter, arms crossed over her chest. "You know Frank Ridley," she says.

Miss Reba nods. Here's what Miss Jolene's been holding back.

"He's got this new bank," she says. "They're going to foreclose on my loan. Take the Field. The pines. Everything. Unless."

Strength of Sheba, power of Lucy, this cannot be. The Field the precious Field.

"Unless what?"

"Unless I raise forty thousand dollars."

Great day in the morning. Jesus help me. Lucy help me. "You ain't got that kind of money."

"No."

Miss Reba feels like someone knocked her in the head with a brick. She sets down her coffee cup, hand shaking. Lucy's Field. All of Lucy's burials. Lucy's bones. Everything holy. The place they killed Sheba. The nastiness that took Lucy's land across the highway is spreading this way. She had always believed the spirit of Lucy would keep it safe.

"What will you do?" she finally says.

"I was going to give up, Miss Reba. But Jeff's going to help. Some internet thing. A lawyer. And a party. He's got all kinds of plans. I couldn't stand to tell you. I know the land belonged to your people. And the way I feel about it…well, I'm not religious really, but it's…holy ground, I think. I've been terribly afraid. For Bobo too."

"What's wrong with Bobo?"

"Frank again. He says I should send Bobo away. To an *institution*."

"Don't send him," Reba says.

"The thing is," Jolene says, "I'm afraid he'll call social services."

"He threaten you?" Miss Reba says, her forehead knotted in a scowl. Frank Ridley is like a spotted salamander, slithering around under rocks. Miss Reba feels a sound rising in her throat like a growl.

"No. It's the way he said it. Like all of a sudden he wasn't Bobo's friend anymore. He's always been so sweet to Bobo.... And there's this other thing." Miss Jolene's big green eyes like clear glass, glinting with worry. "Miss Reba, a long time ago, he asked me to marry him. I told him I'd think about it. But I think he still wants to. And I think if he knew Jeff was spending the night, and Bobo was here, I think he might call social services himself. Tell them I'm a bad mother or something. He didn't say he would do that, but I—"

The last time Jolene got this talky, she had lost Mr. Luke and did not know what to do. Miss Reba told her: *Build a garden. Increase your herd. Raise your prices. Sell to those rich Stonehaven Yankees.* What she didn't say: *Make them pay for what they did to holy land. Scraping it up. Building houses over top.* Now Miss Reba closes her eyes. *Bobo is nineteen. Social services won't mess with him. Mr. Ridley got to keep his little reputation. Can't be sending away boys like Bobo. People wouldn't like it.*

"He won't do it," Reba says.

"What?" Jolene is startled.

"He won't do it," Reba says. "Put your mind to rest. But you got to tell him no. He ain't right for you, Miss Jolene."

Jolene looks at her doubtfully. "I know. I've known it all along. I just—"

"The Lord is stronger than a rich man for all his powerful ways."

"Thank you," Jolene says. She pauses. "You don't mind taking Bobo again? Maybe Sunday?"

"Sunday is the Lord's day," Miss Reba says. "A good day for blessings."

She puts her coffee cup down and rises to go. Miss Reba wonders what Frank Ridley could be up to, after Miss Jolene like that. It's been a long time since he tried to buy her own farm and brick house across Spill Creek, buttering her up, buying more of her pound cakes than any one man could eat. What in the world would he want her brick house for? With chickens and statues all around.

Miss Reba pulls the Cutlass into the parking place in front of her porch, breeze flying up through the hole in the fender. Statues staring down. She closes her little eye. Sees the Field, rocks gone, flat as bone, shimmering. Something slithering across. She can't see if it's a snake or Mister Ridley. Then she remembers: *there is nothing he does that is not for money.*

When Sheriff Walter Pickett Jr. comes to her door that afternoon, it is no surprise to Reba. She's seen it in a vision many times. Light behind the sheriff's head, blinding white. Big sheriff hat. Trouble. Just like his grandfather sixty years ago, come to ask about that dead Hooper boy. But this is not the memory world. This is Sheriff Walter Pickett's grandson, Junior.

Reba opens the screen door. She nods in recognition. "Sheriff." He is smaller than his grandfather, but bigger around the belly. He does not tip his hat. He pulls it all the way off—hair streaked thin across a pink scalp—and holds it in front of him like an empty offering plate. "Good afternoon, Miss Reba. Got some business to discuss."

Black angels watching.

She motions him in, indicates the sofa. He sits, lays his hat on the side table.

Mama said, When trouble comes, see if manners will trick it off balance for a while.

"Something to drink, Sheriff? I got sweet tea and Mountain Dew. Let me get you some lemon pound cake. Got a few slices left over from the Market."

"Just water, if you please."

Reba heads for the kitchen. Pours the water, sets the glasses on crocheted coasters, one for her, one for him.

Sheriff Junior takes a sip. "How's TJ coming along? I hear he's been going to church."

"Fine, just fine. You know how young men are. He's got the mischief but he'll settle down. Reverend's going to baptize him at homecoming." Sheriff is taking his time getting to the point. He wants to be sociable. So she will be sociable. Making up whatever stories he might want to hear.

"You don't say. He likes church?"

"Well, he mostly likes cars. He wants to get his learner's. Got to get his grades up. How's that wife of yours?" she asks.

"Just fine, just fine."

"That's good," Miss Reba says. He looks like he wishes he'd said yes to that pound cake. She heard Marnie put him on Weight Watchers. Reba hears that spirea bush rustling outside the window. TJ's out there. Spying. She can smell his nasty Marlboro smoke. She should go roust him out by the ear. "Now, Sheriff, what's your business?"

Sheriff Junior shifts in his seat, looks like he doesn't want to say. He looks at his hat. Clears his throat. "Miss Reba. They found some bones in Indigo Field. Not the ones in the cliff. You saw that in the paper?"

"Yes, indeed." *Tiny bones, ribs and skull. Sadness tucked in a pot.*

"These are new," Sheriff Junior says. "Looks like, from first reports, it's bones from fifty years ago. Maybe more recent. You know anything about a man or woman buried in that field?"

Reba pauses. Listens to the shrubbery rustle. "Hadn't heard anything about that," she says. *Lord, Lord. Lord cover me with your wings, protect me. It is time for the reckoning. There is one I know of who is buried in that field.* Her heart begins to pound. Her leg twitches like it wants to run away.

"Who is it?" she says.

"You know I can't tell you that," Sheriff Junior says. "But we found something might be yours. Right in there with the bones."

"What something?" Reba says. She wraps her fingers around the arms of her chair, digs her nails in. Her legs begin to tremble. She wills them to be still.

"We found a bead. Looks like something from that necklace you wear all the time. Little white round flat bead right there in the eye socket, Miss Reba. Now, what would that be doing there?"

"I got my necklace right here," she says, fingering the cool shell beads strung on fishing line. "I ain't missing any beads." She moves her fingers, as if counting them. She feels a flush coming up the back of her neck. She stares at his tie. *Help me, Sheba. Help me, Lucy. Help me stare him in the eye.*

"Now, Miss Reba, I'm not saying you put a bead there. Maybe you know somebody else with the same kind of necklace. Maybe somebody stole a necklace like that from you."

"Nobody stole it. It's right here." She's had it on her neck since the day Old Lucy gave it to her. Except for that one time.

"I got to tell you," Sheriff Junior says, "we find out who this is, and the manner of death, we might be having a different conversation."

"Mmm-hmm," Miss Reba says. "If you know who it is you best come out and tell me."

"Well, Miss Reba, I hate to bring up a sad business. But you had a sister, disappeared back in 1945. Ain't that right?"

"Sister went to Baltimore," Miss Reba says. "Never saw her again." It catches in her throat. *Oh, Sheba, I wish you gone to Baltimore.*

"I see," he says. "Then it must be somebody else."

Reba feels her throat go dry. She can barely croak an answer. "Must be."

"Our people are looking into it," Sheriff says. He shifts in his seat. Pulls something out of his pocket. "Miss Reba," he says. "We found this too." He opens his palm. It is her claw-and-turtle charm, bound with red yarn. *Dear Jesus, Old Lucy, that belongs to me.* Reba wants to snatch it out of his hand. "You got any idea who this belongs to?"

"Nossir. I got no idea."

His leather belt creaks as he rises to go. He puts his hat on his head, tips it to Miss Reba. "We shall see. We shall see by and by."

Lord, the man is barely out the yard before memories come flooding. Night smell like swamp water. Hottest night in August. Man's car stuck on her road. Eyes go blank, a shimmer in the air. *What's this? Smell of cigarettes. Smell of boy.* Miss Reba opens her eyes.

Whiteboy sits down across from her. She shakes her head. *What's this whiteboy doing in my house?*

"I guess he ain't takin' either one of us to jail today," whiteboy says, all cocky.

Miss Reba brings her body and mind back to this room. This is TJ Snipes. Son of the man who killed Danielle. "You been listening at the window?"

"No, ma'am," he lies. "I saw that car in the yard. Came in to see." Eyes all innocent. Then he grins. "I guess I heard the tail end," he admits. "There's a body. Do ya think it was a murder, Aunt Reba?"

"What I think," Reba says, "is it's time for you to stroll on over to Miss Jolene's and help her for a spell, leave me be. You can tire out an old lady with your talk." She glares at him and it's enough.

"Can I drive your car?"

"You can walk on your own two feet."

He goes.

They have ways of finding out how a person dies. And where. And when. Oh Lord, it's time to pray. Reba pulls Danielle off the mantel, box heavy as a six-year-old girl now, the weight of it pulls her to the floor. Reba kneels right down on the living room rug, hands folded, but she cannot pray, her mind floods full with other things. Danielle Angel looking at her through the screen door like to break her heart. Sheba Angel looking up, like lightning might come and strike her if she tells.

"What's wrong, Auntie," Danielle says, down beside her on the floor. "Tell me."

She never has told this to a living soul, but she can't help but spill it out to the listening spirit of Danielle. For it has risen up inside her and will not be denied, like water from a spoiled well.

"But, child," she says, "you are so young. Too young to know this ugliness."

"You can tell me," Danielle says. "I'm older than you think."

Danielle, time passed, I come back from Baltimore, become old, seen many things, got me a job working in that sheriff's office, midwifing on the side. All the children have scattered to the north. Sick, dead, gone, drugs, whitemen, prison, cancer. Never coming back. Comes a time Mama and Papa die, and I come back home to live. Papa built this brick house by then. It came to me. Papa's papers say, *Burn our bones to ash*. Still afraid Old Lucy might rise up and bury him the heathen way.

I get me a TV. Watch *I Love Lucy*, *Price is Right*, whitepeople foolishness meant to make you laugh. And I watch the news. Dr. King says, *I have a dream today*, and my heart opens a crack. Then four Sunday school angels get blown up, my heart slams shut. I watch a whiteman kill President Kennedy. Then a whiteman take down Dr. King. On my little black-and-white set, I see in the eyes of the Black men on the balcony of that Memphis motel, they know what I know: we live in a cage of fear.

I watch whitepeople pass me on the road in their new cars. I watch the preacher for signs of a new world coming where Black people get a little something for all their grief. I wait and watch. But still my heart is full of bitterness.

I keep Sheba company in her cornpatch grave, listen for her voice in the hickory grove. I close my eyes and wait for a vision of how whitemen might be brought low, how the Lord might smite them for their wickedness. Put the Black people on top of His holy mountain. Indians too.

I listen for the spirit of Lucy in the Field, as she is long since dead and buried.

Sometimes, a whirlwind comes dancing across the dust, and I hear her say, *Avenge your sister.*

Danielle baby, Cletus Hooper has long since forgotten about Sheba. Sheba's just a dark piece of coal smoldering in the fiery heart of that man's sin. By now, Cletus' mind is half gone with drink and his family abandoned.

August 1975, on a night so hot and close the very air spits out a foul breath of swamp water, I get my chance. I find him with a flat tire on Field Road.

He tries to jack it up, falls down, tries again.

What's he doing on my dead-end road? you may ask. Trashing it up. Drinking his beers and his Thunderbirds, throwing his empties in my ditch, doing his business in my woods, fishing my river, killing my fish.

It's just getting dark. Tire flatter than a pancake. He's got the jack set up on the crumbly edge of the road. "You need a tow?" I say.

"Just hand me over that tire iron," Cletus says. He don't remember me.

I pick it up. Heavy metal in my hand feels hot, electric. I hand it over.

Cletus tries to make it work, but his hands are too shaky, tire iron clangs to the road. Finally he says, "Help me."

I take the tire iron from his hands and feel its fat spokes hard and heavy against my palms. I loosen the nuts, and he crouches beside me, breathing his stank liquor breath on my neck, making my fingers tremble. My hands know something I don't know. They know before I know it. They make a plan.

Finally, all five loose, I rise and wipe my hands on my skirt.

"You can do the rest," I say.

I step a small distance away, watch him struggle. He jacks the car all the way up. Tire off the pavement. He tries to get the nuts off now. Everybody knows you're supposed to take them off when the car's still stuck on the ground. He twists and pulls and the car tire wobbles and the jack wobbles too. He drops a nut and it rolls under the car.

"Pick it up, will ya?" he says.

"Oh, I can't pick that up," I say, in that high voice Papa used when whitepeople around. "Can't reach that far, I got arthritis."

"You are a ninny, aintcha?" he says. He looks me full in the face, and I don't know in the dim light if he can see the bite scar on my cheek, but he seems to shrink back for a moment. Then he lays down on one side, reaches and reaches for the nut, pokes his head into the darkness under the car, shoulder next to the jack, set into the edge of the crumbly dirt road, and I do not say a thing. I close my eyes and open my little eye and see it before it happens, *the jerk of the jack, the blown shocks creak, the weight of the car cracks a man's head like a cantaloupe.* When I open my eyes it is full dark. Thunderclouds block the sky. The jack slips. The car drops on his head.

Whiteman moans. He grunts and drags and pulls himself out from under. Whites of his eyes rolled up. Head split open over one eye. Whites of his brains showing. Whole body starts to shake and quiver.

Dear God, I pray, *What shall I do with this cracked-skull whiteman by the side of my road?*

They will blame you, Papa says.

Eye for eye, Bible says.

Then Lucy says, *Avenge her.*

Strength of Sheba rises up my legs, flows into my arms. I pick up the tire iron, with full intent to end one whiteman's misery.

A bright light shines around me. Angel of Death? No. Headlights shining up my road. A road where no one comes. Truck stops, Cletus laying there at my feet, black blood running toward my shoes. *Oh Lord,* I pray. *Let it not be the sheriff nor any whiteman turn me in for murder.*

Truck door slams. "Miss Reba?" man's voice calls out. "You all right?"

I drop the tire iron.

Luke Blake steps into the light of his own making and stands before me. Young whiteman. Home from Vietnam. Family owns the old Blake farm, trying to fix it up now. Known him since I pulled him out of his mother, back in midwife days. Mama said he used to visit Old Lucy, bring her things, while I was away in Baltimore.

Luke Blake looks down. Sees Cletus laying there. Dead as doomsday. "Who is it?" he says.

I cannot say the name.

Luke Blake kneels, says, "Hey, Mister." Headlights shine on it all. He sees the blood. The brains. The eyes rolled up white. The bad smelly teeth. He spits the name out like a curse: "Cletus Hooper."

Cletus Hooper turns his head, moans. Cletus is alive.

The foul swamp air of night opens its mouth and breathes and it begins to rain.

It rains and rains on me and Luke Blake and we stand there in the circle of his headlights, not speaking. We watch the ditch fill with water and blood. It rains and pours full buckets on our heads, Danielle, cold water down our backs, and still we do not step away. It is such a storm as only happens in deep summer, when the air so full of steam it spills and turns to water, sparks electric as it falls. Spill Creek is bad to flood when that happens.

It rains and rains and washes all signs of Cletus' blood from the road. Cletus opens one eye. Sees us watching. Makes a sound barely human. Lifts an arm as if there might be help for him. Sees there will be no help. He rolls over, claws at the road, crawls away, toward the ditch. Falls face down in the water. Man struggles, arms flail, push up, drop down. Water rises and covers him.

Still we stand there.

After a while, Luke Blake turns him over. Man's eyes stare out, teeth got mud stuck all in his gums. Not breathing anymore.

Lightning overhead. Thunder roll. Luke Blake turns to me. "We got to bury him."

A look passes between us, wet-faced in the rain.

Danielle, this is how I learnt that of all the people in the world, in Poolesville and Quarryville, in all of Ambler County, there was one other who knew all that had passed in the Field so many years ago: Luke Blake. Lucy musta told him.

There's a dead whiteman in the road. We got to bury this body in darkness. *Because they coming to get you next 'less you shut your mouth.* Luke Blake knows it. I know it. They got ways of making things up. They got ways of blaming somebody just standing there, if she is Black. Chain of evidence leads to me. Jesus be my witness, I never dropped a blow on that man. Though I wished I had.

Luke Blake's been in a war. He knows about dead bodies.

He lays Cletus out in the back of his truck bed, covers him with feed sacks. I climb up in the truck cab beside him. He drives up the hill past the Gooley Ridge, opens the gate, drives across the Field, around rocks and snares, toward the river. He gets a shovel out the back, digs a hole. The hole fills up with blue-gray water and mud. Lightning flashes show us the way. I stumble through the mud, bring rocks to cover him. Dead whiteman's hand catches my bead necklace, like to pull it off, like to drag me down into the mud with him, but I jerk away. Beads spill across the ground.

I scoop up what beads I can. Slip them in my pockets, handfuls of blue slip clay and shell mixed together in a slurry. I leave the rest.

Luke Blake fills the hole. I put the last rock in the mud over his head. Settle it there.

See, Sheba. See, Lucy. I done just what you wanted. See if you rise up now, Cletus. Lightning crashes all around us but does not harm us. A sickness rises in me. There will be a reckoning for this day. I didn't kill the man. But I let loose a wash of bile and bitterness, the poison built up inside me.

In the rage of storm we go back to where Cletus' car sits in the road. We open the doors, push it into Spill Creek. Watch it float downstream and fill with water like a great hand is pressing down. *Once Spill Creek has you, it holds you down.*

I remember what Cletus done to Sheba, cracked her head wide open with rocks. I remember what he done to that girl, in the Gooley pines up on the Ridge that night. What I kept folded inside my body for many years, the way a bat folds her wings and sleeps.

Mama sees my cheek and turns away. She has a girl to bury.

Lucy give me herbs to cure the hate. But it never took, not all the way.

Danielle, this is the truth I never told: that night in August 1975, I watched a whiteman die for the pure hard pleasure of it.

PART V

REAP THE WHIRLWIND

42

June has settled in to Ambler County like a layer of feather quilts. There is no breeze. The air is thick as syrup, moisture condenses on anything cool, making little rivers of distilled water flow down glasses of sweet iced tea, RC Cola, and bourbon. Thunderclouds rise, dissipate. There is no rain.

On the Gooley Ridge, pine needles give off the smell of hot tar and incense. Birds sit and pant on the shady lower branches in the heat of the day. In the Field, snakes burrow deep under rocks to cooler places, and in the river, the step stones that used to be a fish trap rise high out of the water, a mudline where the water used to be.

Jeff still walks the Field, on both sides of the highway, and the heat rises into his sneakers, dry grasses crunch underfoot, puffs of dust linger where he steps. Every day he drizzles water from his bottle onto the red corn kernel Chuck planted. One day, he hunkers down to see, and it has sprouted, a tiny humped thing, bent but rising.

When he tells Jolene, she nods, says, "Miss Reba has red corn." He needs to talk to Miss Reba. But everything goes out of his head when he kisses Jolene.

It's so hot Jolene's goats have stopped producing by half. Her bean blossoms wither and fall off their stems. She's so in love that she forgets to water her garden rows, then she forgets to turn off the water and the garden floods. Love ruins everything. But Jeff has set up a Go Fund Me for the Gooleys, and people are starting to donate. He's found a Stonehaven lawyer, Bess's husband, George, who thinks she's got a case. And every day the Gooley pines glimmer in the sun like a promise. She has forty-five days.

One day, watering her mama's flower bed, Miss Reba stops and looks up. Listens. A hard breeze comes flying into the dry sycamore tree. *Lucy's talking.* They may have shut down the archaeology, but whitemen still walking around looking at things. Lucy don't like it. But it's just like she said: *Whitemen coming no matter what you do.*

Lucy's breeze catches at the clothes on the line, flaps TJ's jeans, makes them rise up like a boy is inside them, climbing Jacob's ladder. She don't like TJ here either.

In Stonehaven Downs, when he gets tired of boxing things up, the colonel watches Weather Channel disaster shows and worries about his daughter, Carrie, whose beloved LA is surrounded by wildfires. The local weather pundit says the only hope of rain in Ambler County will come from the east and south: a duo of hurricanes, stalled in the Atlantic, dancing around each other in circles. But right now, the wind is coming from the wrong direction.

Friday morning, TJ takes a desk smack in the middle of the class, behind Leora, so he can watch her hair. It's the next to last week of school, and the AC doesn't work and the room smells like BO and gym socks. Everybody's still talking about Leora and Bully, how he took her to Indigo Field Saturday night after the prom, found a jar of shine next to the river, got drunk, threw up all over her dress. *That was* my *jar of shine,* he wants to say. But he knows better.

The only person in the class who ever liked him at all is Leora. And Leora's not speaking to Bully. So maybe now he has a chance. But he lost his lucky voodoo charm, red yarn and feathers, somewhere out in the Field. So maybe not.

TJ wants to reach out and stroke that hair, all crinkly and gold, hanging down her back, only inches from his hand. As long as he sits behind her and just watches her hair, he can pretend. It's been a while since he prayed. He closes his eyes tight. *Dear Jesus,* he prays silently, *please make Leora say something. Anything. JesusNameAmen.*

Teacher is looking at him now. She's been talking and talking and now she's looking at him. What did she say?

"TJ," she says. "Answer the question."

"Uh, what was the question?"

"You weren't listening," Teacher says. "What is so interesting that you can't listen in class?"

"I was looking at Leora's hair," he says. He shrugs. May as well tell the truth. Maybe Leora will like him again if he says it.

All the kids laugh, the Black boys in the back hoot, Bully Angus glowers, Leora turns around. Looks him up and down. Looks back at Teacher. "Mrs. Simons, I want to move my desk," she says. "I don't want him looking at my hair."

More laughing. More hooting.

"TJ," Teacher says. "You have got on my last nerve today. Three strikes, you're out." She sends him to the principal's office. Worst thing is, as he's leaving he can hear her say to Leora, "Honey, you can switch with Billy Angus. All right, Billy?"

Great. Just great.

He can't wait to spend the rest of his life staring at the back of Bully Angus's fat white head.

Bully Angus catches him in the hall on his way to gym class. "Tough luck today," he says, punching him in the shoulder. "See, if you were in my crew, nobody would mess with you like that. Even the teacher. We'd have you covered."

TJ looks at him. "Oh yeah? Who's *we?*"

"Wait till you see what we did," Bully says. "You won't believe it." He makes that white power sign TJ's seen the kids do at Butner. It's like saying "OK!" upside down. It's kind of ridiculous.

"Did you paint the sidewalk again?" TJ says. Bully claimed to be the one who painted swastikas on the walk in front of the school, but all the principal did was sandblast it off.

"No, man," Bully says. "This is much better than that. You'll be surprised. *They'll* be surprised."

TJ knows who "they" are without asking. Bully is always looking to torment the Black guys from church. They're always so neat and tidy with their khakis and their nice T-shirts and their clubs after school. Their moms won't let them wear jeans or baggies. Wednesdays they wear ties and white shirts, for Bible study.

"You won't have to worry about them anymore," Bully says.

"I don't *worry* about them," TJ says. "I just don't hang out with them."

"Well," Bully says, in a lowered voice, "you won't have to *hang out* with them either, anymore. If you know what I mean."

"What?" TJ says. He wishes Bully would go away. He wants to think about Leora's hair.

They enter the locker room, and in front of them the church boys are standing stock still, staring up at the cross beam over the lockers.

"Look," Bully says. He points.

There's a fat yellow rope noose hanging from the beam.

"What's *that?*" TJ says, startled. But he knows what it is. White-power guys like to draw a noose to scare the Blacks. TJ doesn't like Tyquan and Brandon and Abidsomething, but they belong to Miss Reba somehow, and he belongs to Danielle somehow, and nobody should do that to a person, that's what Danielle used to say, and right now he just hates

Bully for messing with him. Fat smelly asshole Bully who pukes on girls.

"Fuck you!" TJ whacks Bully as hard as he can with his Trapper Keeper. Bully falls into the church boys. The church boys see two white-boys falling on them like Jews fell on the Philistines, only backward, and set aside every lesson they've ever learned from their churchgoing mothers and stalwart fathers. They proceed to kick the living shit out of TJ Snipes and Bully Angus.

Miss Reba has felt it coming these last days, as the heat built from the south and the clouds built from the west, sky the color of dread. Now Sheriff's car is coming down her road, raising yellow dust behind.

He will tell her whose bones those are.

He will take her down to the county jail.

He will charge her with murder.

And TJ will have to go back to Butner.

Danielle, help me now.

Reba leans on the old hickory stick she uses for a cane. Purse on her arm, Bible in her purse, ready to put her hand on it and tell the truth. She wanted to kill Cletus Hooper. But she never cracked his head. She only let him drown. *And found pleasure in it.*

She watches the car spin gravel, the dust settle. But what's this? Her boy TJ in the back seat. *Danielle, I told you I could not take this boy. I said you would have to watch him. I knew he was trouble. Bad trouble.*

Danielle's got nothing to say.

Sheriff gets out, opens TJ's door. TJ gets out slowly. Little hooligan with his arm in a sling. Limping. Waving. That grin. Big bandage over his eye. *Lord Jesus, what have you let happen to this boy?* TJ looks a little drunk. "Hi, Auntie," he says. "I broke my arm!"

"What in the world?" Reba says. "Come inside, boy. I am not your auntie."

Sheriff sits down on the sofa while Reba inspects TJ's face. Then his arm. "What happened to your head?" she says.

"Somebody kicked me," TJ says happily. "I was in a fight."

"What you grinnin' about, boy? You not s'posed to be getting in fights." She turns to Sheriff Junior, who is waiting with his hat in his lap. Looks like he's waiting for his sweet tea and pound cake. Not this time. Not bringing TJ home like this.

"Miss Reba," Sheriff Junior says, "we're not too sure what happened.

Seems those Black boys from your church got mad at something Billy Angus did, and beat the crap out of him, excuse my language, Miss Reba. I think TJ just got in the way."

"That true, boy?" Reba asks him.

"Waaall," TJ says, "Angus wanted me in his gang, and then he put this rope in the gym, and they're your boys, Miss Reba, even though I don't like them so much, so I knocked him down and we fell on top of the Black boys, and they kicked the…stuffing out of Bully and me, Black boys call him Bully, but I hate Bully too, so I beat him up when I could get a lick in. I thought the Black boys were on my side at first but they broke my arm and called me a white devil MF, even though they go to church and everything and not supposed to use language like that. I think you oughta put a hex on them, Miss Reba, they're not Christian people—"

"All right," Reba interrupts. "Never mind. Something evil going on to get those church boys to fight. Which boys?"

"Tyquan, and Brandon, and Abid, Abid, Abidsomething."

"Abednego."

"Miss Reba?" Sheriff says, "TJ's arm ain't broken. He sprained his wrist. Should be okay in three to four days. He's suspended from school for fighting, though. One week. And something else." He nods toward the door. "Let's talk outside."

"Stay here," Reba says to TJ. "Don't move. Imma sit on what to do with you." She follows the sheriff outside to his car.

"It wasn't my fault!" TJ calls after her. But he stays put.

TJ stretches out on the long sofa. He's got more Tramadol in his pocket that he stole from the school nurse's purse. He's kind of high.

He doesn't have to go to school for a week. He might not have to go to school ever again.

Three strikes you're out.

If they try to put him in jail, he's going to run away with Miss Reba's Cutlass and drive to California. He should've killed Bully Angus. *And* the Black boys. Well, at least one of them got a black eye. *Show him for kicking me in the ribs. Asshole sissy church boy.* Tyquan. It would be Tyquan.

Miss Reba's been out there a long time.

Her Cutlass ain't gonna cut it. Crappy tires. And that side that's caving in.

Maybe he'll go live on Lucy's island.

TJ stands up. Stumbles around the room dizzy, pretending he's drunk. He's never been drunk, but now he feels like he's about to throw up. Maybe he took too many of those pills. He grabs hold of the mantel. Stares at the foil boxes there. He's always wanted to look inside.

Aunt Reba's still out there.

He picks up the gold box. Shakes it. It's heavy enough to have treasure in it. He pulls the lid off. Peers in. A plastic bag with dirt in it. Gold dust? He's heard of that. He opens the bag. Sticks his finger in. Gray dust. But there's a hard metal thing. A gold coin? He pulls it out. Looks like a dog tag. He spits on his thumb and rubs off the gritty dust like fireplace ash. Some words on it. He licks his thumb and rubs again.

Danielle Esther Johnson

And on the other side:

Maddox Funeral and Crematory Services

He drops the box. Runs to the bathroom and barfs all over the toilet seat.

Then he lies on the bathroom floor, cheek against the cool linoleum, and remembers.

It started on the bus.

The window next to him is stuck open, cold breeze on his chest. He pulls his jeans jacket tighter around him, two buttons missing in the front. Mama Danny got it for him, found it at the dump, people leave good things there. Mama Danny said she'd find more buttons and sew them on, but she hasn't found the right ones yet. They have to be silver, with the word *Lee* carved into them. He rubs the silver buttons with his thumb. They're cold too.

The bus bounces down the trailer park road to where you can see Daddy's single-wide, and the boys in the back start to chant:

> We can see from where we sit
> TJ lives in chicken shit!

And it's true. The only trailer Daddy could get was this one, wedged in next to a pile of leavings from the chicken farm next door. The pile is twice as tall as the trailer and three times as wide. They sell it to gardeners five dollars a truckload, and every time the dozer chews out one side of the pile, it lets loose a stinking fart of chicken-shit gas that burns the inside of your nose and makes your eyes water, and the whole wedge leans over a little more toward the trailer. The smell gets in your clothes. Your favorite jacket. Everything.

Bus driver honks, yells out, "TJ Snipes, get your butt up and off the bus. Got to wait for you to sit down and get up too."

Everyone is laughing at him. TJ stumbles down the aisle, two boys put their big feet out to trip him, but he knows that trick and stomps hard on both of them, *crunch, crunch*, then runs out the front before they can punch him.

Mama Danny isn't watching *Oprah*. She's in the kitchen, poking her pots and pans. "Making you some chicken pastry," she says. "And fried apple pies." He goes to get his hug. Mama D knows how to hug. She presses his whole bony ribs into her soft front and he has to wiggle to get away. "We got to fix your buttons," she says. "I got some today. They had a whole big jar at PTA Thrift, and these were right on top." She holds up two silver Lee buttons.

"Mama D, you are the *best*."

She says, "Yes, I am. Go get warm. I turned on the heat."

The heat is an electric coil on the stove that turns red. You can warm your hands over it. TJ stands there for a while. "Where's Daddy?" he says.

"In back." She jerks her head toward the other end of the trailer. "You know."

TJ's standing there, pinching hot apples out of the fry pan, popping them in his mouth, when Daddy flaps through the plastic sheet he put there, .45 in his hand, eyes gone crazy, hopped up for sure.

"Two of you sure are a sight. Talking about me. Makin' your plans. I heard what you said. Heard what you did. Danielle, don't you stand in front of that boy. Don't you stand in front. I'm gonna knock the living daylights out of him."

"What'd I do?" Daddy looks mad, but it don't take much. He makes shit up out of pure nothing, just to be mad.

"TJ didn't do nothing," Mama D says. "He's a good boy."

"Get out the way," Daddy says. He swings the gun up, points it at her, at TJ, back at her. "Or I will shoot you both, so help me God."

"You ain't shootin' nobody," Mama D says.

"Daddy!" TJ steps away from the stove, tries to get Daddy's attention.

Daddy rests the nose of the gun on his chest. TJ feels like he's going to wet his pants. Fried apples dribble out his mouth, down his jacket front. Daddy's going to shoot him? Daddy's crazy but he's never been this crazy. "No, Daddy."

"Stop it," Mama D says. She grabs the gun barrel and pushes it down.

Daddy yanks it out of her hand. "You think you going to stand between me and my boy? Between him and his punishment?" He points the gun at her chest, her neck, her cheek. Her eye. Clicks off the safety.

A boy's voice screams, "No, Daddy, no! Don't shoot, don't do it, don't do it!" and then a loud sound and Mama D falling on him, the heavy soft weight of her, and warm wet parts of her falling on him, on his face and jacket and hands, and he slides down with her, sees the back of her head is gone, blood coming out, and white stuff, presses his hands there like maybe he can stop it, go back to when the world was a mess but Mama D stood there like a wall full of love, holding it together.

Miss Reba has heard what the sheriff had to say. It wasn't any old rope. It was a noose. Class H felony charge. Hate crime. Danielle's ash box laying open on the floor. *I have nursed a viper in my breast,* she tells Danielle. Danielle does not answer.

No sign of the boy. He must be hiding up there in his room. Miss Reba calls him to come down. He comes out of the bathroom.

Reba sees he's been crying. Boy's got more to cry about. She walks across Danielle's ashes, making pale dusty tracks. She walks to the family Bible, hidden behind the other books. She flips through to a place she knows. Pulls out an old picture, black and white so faded it's brown. There's something hanging from a hollow sycamore tree, can't hardly tell it's a boy. A Black boy. Blacker places where pieces are missing.

"This what a noose is for," she says, holding it in his face so he can't look away. "My papa's Cousin Sweet. Sweetest boy in the world. Special boy like Bobo. He wanted to touch a white girl's hair and he smiled at her too hard. That was his crime."

TJ's mouth opens like a coffin. His face crumples. He falls to his knees at her feet, clutches his sticky whiteboy hands on her legs, says, "I'm sorry I'm sorry I'm sorry." She is supposed to forgive him, she knows that, but she remembers that her papa was there when they did that, just a little boy hiding in the bushes, too scared to try to stop them. *It twisted him,* Mama said. *He loved that boy.*

Whiteboy still groveling there. Clutching on her. Sticky hands. A wave of revulsion shakes her. The power of Sheba rises into her belly, the voice of Lucy says, *Make him pay.* Miss Reba is so tired of whitemen. Selling her rusty cars. Crunching her fender. Messing in the Field, desecrating the bones. Killing Cousin Sweet. Sister Sheba. Danielle.

Putting up nooses.

Reba remembers what Lucy said the day she died. *One day I shall return and the low places shall be made high, and the high places made low. You shall live to see this day.*

Lucy's been waiting long enough for her day. *Smite the whitemen and bring them low,* Reba tells her. *Bring a great wind like a wall of fire and rain. Bring the whirlwind.*

43

Monday morning Reba tells him to dress for court. Today they'll send him away for what he did. Most likely Butner Juvenile. She would bet money on that. A hate crime.

Danielle Angel looks down at her. "You going to keep him?"

"No, I ain't. And there ain't nothing an old Black lady can do about it."

"You could speak for him," Danielle says.

"No. That boy put a noose up. Sheriff said he's gonna have to pay."

The boy trudges downstairs and gets in the car without complaint. But he's got a paper sack of Nabs with him, as if he knows where he's going the food will be bad.

An hour later, Miss Reba and TJ stand sweating in their church clothes before the judge, mouths open. They hear the gavel, they look at each other and stare. Danielle must have whispered in the judge's ear. No Butner Juvenile.

TJ will stay with her—pending good behavior and completion of community service: *Clean the road, Cedar River bridge to Miss Reba's house, every week for the next six months.* And he has to write letters of apology to the church boys. Miss Reba can see the wheels turning in the boy's head: *it wasn't me.* But then he says, "They were scared of me, Miss Reba." Miss Reba nods. The whiteboy has seen an inch into the life of a Black boy and begins to understand.

Miss Reba has not forgotten calling out to Lucy for the white world to be brought low. But maybe Danielle's spirit is so strong now, she can bend the world too: one fourteen-year-old whiteboy, too small for his age, is making things right for once. And there's this: he meant to fight on the Black side.

There's a rustling beside her. A cough. "Mister Judge, Your Honor?" TJ says. "I want to testify."

What in the world? Don't he know he got a good deal? This boy is such a fool. Miss Reba grabs his arm, gives it a yank. "Hush up, TJ," she says. But he pulls away and walks right up to the judge.

"My daddy killed Danielle," he says. "I was there. I saw everything. I want to testify. They tried to get me to before, but I ran away. I don't want him to get away with murder."

"Miss Reba," the judge says, "what's this all about?"

Lord have mercy. Is there still a chance for justice for Danielle Esther Johnson? She's heard of people reopening cases with new evidence.

"Your Honor," she says, standing solid in place, and the strength that flows through her legs and into her belly is all her own. "The boy wants to testify."

The judge explains, ever so gently, that a man cannot be tried twice for the same crime. "New evidence can be brought to exonerate," he says, "but not to convict. Your father's trial is over."

TJ sits beside her in the car, crying, on the way home. "I messed up," he says. "I can't make it right. Daddy's going to find out and kill me."

Miss Reba does not answer. Nobody can make it right. But this little whiteboy too small for his age wanted to make it right. That ain't nothing.

TJ's got to go to summer school to make up English, which he has flunked. No learner's permit till you pass English. The boy doesn't like to read. When he reads Bible verses, he stumbles like he's in second grade, finger stuck on the page like he can't find his way. The five books on her mother's shelf carried her through childhood. The stories gave a window to other worlds. *Gulliver's Travels, Oliver Twist, Huckleberry Finn. Arabian Nights. The Hope of Liberty*, by George Moses Horton—Black boy sold his poems to buy his freedom.

What this whiteboy needs is reading and chores. She makes a plan.

Miss Reba sits at the kitchen table and lays down the law. "You hear what the judge said?"

"Yes, ma'am."

"Well, here's what I say. You will chop weeds, you will carry water, you will go to church, no complaining. And you will read to me. Every night. From the books on my shelf."

"Do I gotta?"

Reading is a form of suffering for him, that is clear.

"Yes."

She takes him to Tyquan's, watches while he apologizes and hands over his letter, because Tyquan's people wouldn't let this whiteboy stand on their stoop at all if she wasn't there beside him. Then she takes him to visit every other church boy until they are done.

That night, she pulls down *Gulliver's Travels*, makes him read out loud after supper. He runs his finger under the words and pulls each word out of his mouth one by one, like a fish pulled out of deep water.

"I. Felt. Something. Alive. Moving. On. My. Left. Leg. Which…"

"Advancing."

"Advancing. Gently. Forward. Over. My…"

"Breast," she says.

He makes it a few more lines until it's all Lilliputians with bows and arrows, like tiny Indians. Then he looks up, having struggled mightily to make it through, and the full meaning of what he has read comes into his head. Little men have tied down a big man. "Is this a real place?"

Wonder of wonders. The boy has a new place he wants to go besides California: Lilliput.

She remembers reading this same book and watching her father carve and set his first angel in the ground, and how he was surrounded by children, and they could not save him. She remembers watching him then, thinking that it was like he was held to the ground by tiny ropes, and tiny men with arrows, no way to get off the dark ground he had traveled to.

TJ pops the hood on her truck, stares at the engine. He's taking auto mechanics along with English. He comes back in and tells her things she's got to buy. Next day he comes home and says he knows how to fix dents now. He bought some compound with his own money. "I can fix that dent on your car, Miss Reba."

It stops her in her tracks. She doesn't want it fixed. She wants to look at it every morning and let the rage bubble up, heat her blood, keep her circulation going.

But the boy is so happy, all smiles and freckles, she gives permission. When he starts to chip away at the hole to set it up, the hole just gets bigger and bigger, and finally, while she's out watering her mama's flower bed, the whole fender falls off the frame.

"Miss Reba!" he calls out. "It fell off!"

She rises, wipes her hands on her apron, goes to see. Chunks of fender, red as earth, lie at his feet. Boy so upset. They both stare at what's underneath: a rusty frame, a spring, an axle, a wheel. There's big crack in the floorboard, right under where she sits. She feels the rage bubble up. Then she sees TJ's face. "I'm sorry, I'm sorry," he says. One whiteboy has learned to say he's sorry. Instead of "I didn't do it. It's not my fault."

Will wonders never cease.

"You didn't do anything," she says. "It was that way underneath all along."

He starts talking about new fenders and junkyards and his teacher knows a place. Face so full of hope and confidence, in all that he can do to fix it.

"You go ahead and try," she says. All that will take time. It will keep him busy. She hopes the rain will not have rusted the frame to dust by the time all that happens.

She will get arrested if she tries to drive without a fender. She's going to have to do it anyway, it's the only car she's got. But the good thing is, she can still look at the Cutlass every day and feel like she wants to run over that whiteman who did this thing to her. Old Lucy would be proud. She who kept the spirit of vengeance alive in her heart and still whispers it in Reba's ear. She who told how the Tuscarora massacred the whites at New Bern, and the telling of it made her smile. She who kept the secret of all that happened later until her dying day. Sunrise boys say they've seen dust devils rising in Indigo Field, as tall as a man, a horse, a house. The backs of Reba's arms tingle with goosebumps. *Lucy is rising.*

"What you not telling me?" Danielle says.

"Not mine to tell," Reba says.

Tell it, Lucy whispers in her ear, *when the whiteboy ain't around.*

Reba sends the boy to clean the road.

Danielle, it was 1954 when I come home from Baltimore.

Supreme Court just ruled white schools are for colored too. I read it in the paper. I am on my new path, and it seems like the rest of the world is too. But sad old Poolesville is hardly there anymore. All our fine young Black men have moved North. The ones had any sense. I find a room in Quarryville. I find a church to go to. I look for a job. I got some money saved from the post office. So I take my time. Jobs are hard to find.

I write to Mama, tell her where I am. Mama send back a letter that Papa's gotten worse. But I don't visit home. Not yet. I wait till I know Papa's going to be working in his fields. Sunny day, good for hoeing. First thing Mama tells me, Old Lucy fallen on hard times. I close my eyes, the way Lucy taught me, send my heart out to see.

She is there, but she is poorly.

Old Lucy who saved my life needs me now. I do not want to go. Indigo Field has got nothing but a world of sorrow for me. But it's got Old Lucy too.

I borrow Papa's mule cart and his old mule King. Oh yes, he still has that mule, though it's so old now it can barely stumble. Danielle baby, Ambler County still has dirt roads most places. Whitepeople throw nasty dust all over, riding around fast in cars.

I load up corncake and beans from Mama, coffee and jars of peaches. Old Lucy did love her peaches. I head out to the Field, all grown up in small pines and briars. I tie up the mule, make my way on deer trails and river rocks out to Lucy's island.

The hut is still the same. A seep of smoke from her fire pit. Lucy's got it banked. Hot coals underneath.

She's got a new pole shed with reed walls and roof, a high floor, sticks and pine needles piled for a smudge fire underneath, herb bundles close by, like she's waiting for somebody to come with a hot coal, *poof, fire.* The Old One that used to lie in the old pole shed is gone. I pull aside the skin door of Lucy's hut and poke my head in. Old Lucy laying so still, she might be dead, her dog laying beside her. Yellow Dog raises his head. Whines. Thumps his tail. He's gotten old too, baby, silver on the muzzle. I come closer. Move my hand to touch Lucy's skin, to feel the pulse of life. Claw hand rises up, grabs my wrist. Pulls me close. "You. Reba."

"Yes." Claw grip gets tighter. Breath like sassafras, dead meat, and smoke in my ear.

"When I die, you bury me the old way."

"The old way?" I say. I get a dread feeling in my belly.

"Like the babies," Old Lucy says.

I remember. What Papa calls the heathen way.

"Take ten days in the smoke," Old Lucy rasps. "You got to stay here all the time, keep fire goin'. Keep critters away."

I don't want to.

"Then you scrape the bones just like I say."

I don't want to.

"Then you put the bones in a skin, see there."

I see the skin—that old black bear she had.

"Then you put the bones in the ground, arms cross, sittin' up. Already dug the hole. Marked with snakeskin. On the cliff. Next to the sycamore."

I don't want to.

"Take the Book. Keep it close." Her claw hand points at the old box she showed me long ago, now covered in spiderwebs and dust. "The Old One in there too. Keep her close. She will protect you."

Shoulda been Sheba doing this.

Old Lucy stares at me with her black-fire glittery eyes. But she's not looking at me. She's looking at something next to me. I turn to see. When I look back, Old Lucy's looking straight at my face. Silver glitter clouding over her eyes. Old Lucy is blind.

She's been making all her plans and can't see a lick. I wonder how she did all those things. The pole shed. The fire. Then I remember Lucy did lots of things with her eyes closed. She could see without any eyes.

Lucy jerks my arm. "Sheba woulda been the one," she says. "But Sheba gone." She drops my arm.

Sheba was the brave one. I've never been brave. I'm scared of dead people. Scared of snakes. Scared of my own life, heading toward me like thunder.

I close my eyes. I try to see how it will be. All I see is me crying, scraping bones.

Lucy crooks her finger. I lean close. "Lissen here," she says. Rasp in her voice like a saw cutting old wood. "Got one last story to tell." Blind eyes glitter, blue feather twitches back and forth, *this way, that way.* "All this?" she says. "Keep it to yourself. Don't tell the whiteman."

"I promise."

"It was 1851," she says. "Thunder Moon.

"Since the Great War, the Tuscarora War, of 1715, my people been hiding in the thickets, in the quiet places, for a hundred years or more. These ones never made peace. Never stayed on any reservation. They went further west, away from the whites. Some settled on the Deep River. Some in New Hope Creek. But more whites came, till it wasn't safe anymore. So my people found a new place to live, called it Indian Field. They shelter some colored who run away, women and babies of all tribes, men wounded and weary of war. Men build huts, women plant maize and tobacco and squash and orchards of peach trees from seed they saved, traded from the Spanish, long ago. By day the children stand in the Field and beat sticks and shout to scare off flocks of colored birds that feather the sky, what my people call *estatoah*, who would pluck the fruit from the trees, eat the kernel, spoil the rest. At first, there is one small fire along the river, then two fires, then twelve. Finally, whitemen notice them.

"Johnston Blake comes talk to our leader, tells him whitemen in Quarryville planning something evil, we should run while we can. My people listen. They remember what happen west of here, a generation ago: Cherokee slaughtered, moved away from their sacred mountains. They remember what happen east of here, generations past, Tuscarora and Yemassee, Chowanoc and Meherrin, killed in the great war, land stolen, children sold for slaves. My mother raise seven boys, they all go north that summer with our men, to make a place for us in the nation of Iroquois. Women and girls and babes in arms to follow later. But then come the day.

"Child, they swoop upon us like a flood, ten men on horses with their guns. They shoot women in the Field as they tend their corn and beans. They shoot babies in the cradle, in the shade of Gooley pines. They shoot small girls, scoop up pretty ones, set them to screaming. Mama seen them coming from her place high on the cliff, where she gone to give birth. She take a basket she made tight so it can swell and hold out water. She cut the cord and lay me in it. Send me spinning down the river, around rocks and ripples, past the sawmill, past the grist mill, past red streams of blood where our girls and women lie half in the river, half on dry land.

"There is one old woman watching, the Old One, the one who can see the future, plain as day. She had told the women to leave with their men, but they denied her power to see the future. She had told the men to stay and fight, but they said whitemen could be trusted. Old One finds a place high up on the cliff, a hollow tree, and watch each death, each whiteman face, seal it to memory for the day of telling. She count the beads on her necklace and count the bodies in the Field, watch blood soak into the corn patch, tobacco patch, spill into the small stream that feeds the river. She close her eyes and smell the air and all she smell is blood. She open her eyes and call up spirits. Clouds rise and rumble, black as a crow wing, green as a curled-up leaf.

"Out of the cloud, one whirlwind poke her bony finger down, then another, then three fingers poke earth, feel their way, blind like a new-born dog, they creep across the bodies they touch, feeling the heat rise and cool from my people, girls, women, babies. Each finger become an arm, each arm make a fist and each Thunder Fist reach down and pull, pull, pull the things of whitemen into the sky: guns, horses and their saddles, the men themselves, but there is still work to do. Three whirlwinds twist and twine, pull and tug at first one mill, then the other, then the dam whitemen made, coloredmen built, stone by stone, rope and blood, turning, twisting, three black arms of thunder turn around each other, pull down stones, and the river runs free and the water swirl around the basket of reeds. That baby look up at Thunder Fist and wave both her hands and feet at this new thing as if it may be her mother. Thunder Fist look down, see this baby in the basket, only thing left moving now that is human in this place. The Old One in her sycamore see this too, say, "Take her up," and Thunder Fist reach down a bony finger, tickle the ripples around the basket, pull it up most gently, to a place in the top of a sycamore tree, a place where leaves have been stripped clean, fallen like square pages of a book down around the root, a book with many pages blank of words.

"The Old One watch Thunder Fist lift back into the sky, the rain lift away, leave flood below. The Old One see the river turn to rocks and slurry of mud. She see boulders rumble and clack against each other in the power of the river flood, now roll onto the field of corn rows, peach trees, tobacco, beans, and squash and cover them. Sky above, color of stone, like one big eye watching. One horse rise up, riderless, and run home. One girl rise up, lip cut in two, and run to the shelter of the Old One. One girl been hiding in a thicket by the river. One girl been up in the Gooley pines. She gather them up in her hollow tree. She tell them, Find dry wood from the *Gee-ree*, pine needle and sap. We making a fire.

"The Old One hear a cry. She climb the sycamore tree and find the child there, still in her basket. She see this baby of the basket all grown up, last of her kind in this fold of land. She name her Lucy, born of Whirlwind, Voice in the Sycamore Tree. She will feed her the milk of a yellow dog, raise her and teach her how to bury ones in the old way, how to live in the sacred way.

"The Old One wait for the water to slide back to the river, the earth to dry. Then she build a pole shed on this island. She dry and scrape and bury all she can, in the only part of this land that is not burdened now with rocks, the cliff along the water. When she is done, she sit on a rock and close her eyes and see with her little eye. She see the girl with the cut lip, grown and making clay pots. She see the other girls, midwiving, fishing, making corn liquor.

"Johnston Blake come and weep with the Old One, say he done the best he could, but men will be men, despite all your good intentions, and so she tell him take this land, all blood and rocks now, the Great Trees, *Tatcha na wihie Gee-ree*, for your own. Take this land, she say, and tell no one we still living. That is my bargain.

"Johnston Blake keep his bargain, and when the Old One die, I scrape her bones and bundle her in white doeskin."

Old Lucy turns her silver eyes to me. Her stank breath on my face.

"And now you will do this for me, Little Turtle."

I bow my head. I don't want to. But I will.

Old Lucy's voice rises. She says, "These are my last words: if whiteman disturb this place, these bones, my people, I will return, and there will be no rain, and I will make the low places high, and the high places low, and I will call Thunder Fist, and Thunder Fist will come like a wall of vengeance, like a wall of fire and rain, and the bones will rise and take back this place for their own. You, Reba, will live to see this day."

Wind shakes the hut, rattles the reeds and skins. I look down and see Old Lucy's mouth gone slack. Her whirlwind spirit rises up to the smoke hole. Jays *jeer jeer jeer* above the hut and whirl away. Lucy's gone.

I sit there for the longest time in the hut on the island in the middle of the river, Yellow Dog beside me, watching. Then I get up and build a fire.

I wash Old Lucy with rags dipped in warm water. Put the sweetshrub in the water and some sassafras root. Lucy liked that. Arms and legs. Breasts like dried apples on her chest. Woman parts dried and crinkle. Yellow Dog watches everything I do.

I find bear grease in an old pot. Smooth it on her skin. I soap her hair, rinse it, comb it out, make a fresh braid on one side and find a fresh jay feather for it. I tie a red thread around thirty times, one for each day of the moon. I poke around in Lucy's dangle of herbs, find a bundle of tobacco, light it, blow out the flame. Tobacco smell swirls above Old Lucy, falls down along her face and arms and legs. I lift Old Lucy's body, light as a child. Smell the Old Lucy smell. The death smell.

I carry her to the pole shed. Lay her out on the poles over the smudge fire.

Powder the skin and hair with the red root powder. Cover her with pine bark and sycamore peel.

Set the tobacco bundle on the firesticks waiting underneath. Find a coal from the fire pit, pluck it with my fingernails, pop it in there. Get a sycamore branch. Old Lucy loved that tree. Wave it to make the smoke fly, to kindle the fire.

I crouch there, making smoke, waving a branch. I know there supposed to be singing. Old Lucy didn't teach me songs for dead ones, so I sing a hymn from church. *Looked over Jordan, what did I see....* But I can't keep it going, Danielle. It's a song you can't sing alone. You got to have others to sing it with you. Like you used to do. In the church choir. Just a bitty thing.

I wish I had a drum, I wish I had a gourd rattle, I wish I was a child, running wild in Indigo Field, before I knew its name.

Ten days I stoke the smudge fire, ten nights I read the Old Book by oil lamp. It is written in English, by Johnston Blake and by different whitemen who lived before him. John White. John Lawson. John Lawson's adopted son, who was Eno Indian. And finally, Old Lucy. It tells of the Old Ones greeted the first boats full of English. It tells of the many fish in the rivers and streams. It tells of the woods buffalo, the panther, and the many nations of people who once lived here. It tells of the whitepeople settling. It tells of the pestilence they brought, the wars, the many days of hiding. It tells of the day whitemen came to this place, left the Cedar River red with blood. It tells of Lucy, who became a great beauty, and the love of Johnston Blake, Jr., and the baby that was born in Lucy's hut, and how that baby was found on the Blake doorstep in a reed basket, wrapped in skins. How the tiny girl was taken in by Johnston's wife, named Virginia Dare Blake, and raised as her own.

It tells of how this child passed as white, married a cousin, bore many children, one run off and married a Black man, Ceasar Jones, and his daughter one day gave birth to a child named Gemstone. Lucy kin to Papa. Mama musta known.

One night I turn a page and see strange markings.

Pen marks curl across the page, have to squint to see the tiny letters, they so faded. They are names. Names and more names, with lines between them like a river flowing out from one group of people to another. There is a line from Lucy to Virginia Dare Blake to her children, to their children, to Luke Blake.

Luke Blake, a whiteman, is of Lucy's blood.

And so am I.

After that, a list of names of the many who died in Indigo Field. Sheba is the last name.

There is a map showing who is buried where along the cliff, along the river, in the Field. Parts of it water-smudged, can't read it clearly.

This is how I learn the world is made of bones. We walk on them. Sleep on them. The ones before us do not need to speak. They are in the thistle and sage, sassafras and butterfly, in the river like our blood. A story can be contained inside a book. But a story is also in every place, every root and flower, every heart. Every shell bead. Every bone.

I pick up the quill pen, dip it in cinders and grease, add Old Lucy to the list of the dead. On this day Old Lucy, Born of Whirlwind, Voice in the Sycamore, left this mortal earth. She was the last of her kind.

Except for me.

And Luke Blake, who I did not yet know. And Bobo, who was not yet born.

Danielle, I can't hardly tell what I did next. I cut open Lucy's belly and take out her innards, throw them in the river for the fish. I cut off her dried-up skin from the bones. Scrape and scrape the bones with a clam shell, shreds of Lucy falling onto my arms and legs. I know I'm doing it wrong. I can't scrape her head. Blind eyes sunk into the sockets. I finally pile the scraps and loose skin of Old Lucy and burn them. I grab all the sassafras root in Lucy's hut and pile it on to make it smell like Lucy again.

The bear skin Lucy laid out is heavy and black. I fold up Lucy's bones, like hickory sticks, brown with smoking, and place them in it: Leg next to leg. Knees up. Ribs and backbone. Arms crossed over. Skull on top. Then I wrap it tight as I can with rawhide strips and honeysuckle, pack a jar of clear and Lucy's beads in a sack, plus her coals pot and her flint, put it all on King Pharaoh, press green moss to his nose, lead him to the top of the Gooley Ridge, and he don't balk at all. Like he knows death now and it don't frighten him.

The hole Lucy dug is there, next to the old sycamore, marked with a stick, and what's this? A snakeskin tied to it floating in the breeze like it's alive and hissing. I slide the bundle in so Lucy can see the river through those dead eye holes. I see a place not far away, sunken like a grave in a graveyard, marked with a stick and a jay feather. I wonder how many Old Lucy buried here over her years on earth.

I take Lucy's walking stick, tie a jay feather to it, stick it in the ground. Jay feather twirls, makes its own wind. Yellow Dog lays down on her grave, head between paws.

I rise to go. Yellow Dog stays.

I put the fire out. I take the Old One bone bundle and the Old Book and the big wooden box they come in. I hook up the mule cart and leave everything else for the deer and the scuppernong vine.

"Can't keep those bones in Papa's house," I tell King Pharaoh. I put 'em in the back of the old shed on the Blake farm. Nobody has lived there in a good long while. Somebody ought to use that house.

TJ fills two or three bags with trash, sets them by the side of the road, then hops the gate and walks the goat trail into the Field. He stays away from all the places marked with police tape. He doesn't want to know how many dead people there are out here. Aunt Reba's always talking to dead people.

TJ spies the archaeology guy across the highway, watches him checking holes, brushing things off, poking things, making coffee, sitting under his tarp reading, pouring water over his head to cool off. When the guy looks up, TJ ducks behind a bush. He doesn't want that guy to know about his secret hideout on Lucy's island. He doesn't want anybody to know about it. He's going to need it when Daddy comes to kill him.

On the island TJ clears out the fire circle, adds new rocks. He pokes the shallows with a stick, looking for clams. He pokes around for more jars of clear, finds one, tucks it in his jacket, and balances across the fish-trap rocks without falling in. He'll stash it behind the straw bales in the chicken shed.

Back at Reba's, he crouches in the shade of dry bushes and listens to the old lady muttering. He wonders if she has finally gone crazy. He thinks maybe it's his fault. He kind of ruined her car.

He looks up, sees a breeze catch in the sycamore. The leaves make a sound like people clapping. Then the breeze punches the tree in the face, and a big branch comes crashing down. Aunt Reba opens her eyes. But she doesn't seem to see him. She's talking to someone who isn't even there. He wishes there were a real person around here to talk to sometimes.

"Aunt Reba," he calls out.

The old lady blinks.

"Can Bobo come over tonight?"

"Bobo wasn't born yet," she says. "Luke was just a young boy."

It takes a while to convince her that Bobo is alive.

44

Rand is taking a break from packing, deep into his copy of *The Malaysian Archipelago*, by Alfred Russel Wallace, cockatiels grooming his head, when Frank Ridley calls and says, "I want to make an offer."

"What?" Rand says.

"I'll buy the house as is."

"My God, what for?" Rand says, unable to hide his surprise.

"Well, I've got plans to marry a little friend of mine," Ridley says. "We'll need a place near her farm." None of it makes sense, but Ridley promises full price, and he wants to close today. Is that possible? Apparently, he will not require inspection. "I saw enough when I was there. It's a fair price for what you've got."

And that's that. Rand has no clean clothes to change into, and there's no time to do laundry. A man should dress properly for the exchange of large sums of money. A man should be spruce for such an event as selling a house. But there's no time. He washes his face and hands. Brushes his hair and teeth. Gets the bourbon glasses and coffee cups off the furniture. Puts the birds in their cages, covers on. By ten a.m., Ridley and his lawyer are laying out contracts for him to sign, and fifteen minutes later, Ridley hands him a bank check for the full amount. Man must be made of money. Well, if not, he could get a loan easily enough.

"There," Ridley says. "I'll file this at the courthouse, and we'll be all set. You'll have lots of cash for that trip you're planning." Rand is still staring at the check in his hands: $225,000. What's left after paying off the mortgage. It's real now. He can go anywhere he wants, do anything he wants, and he should feel exhilarated, but a seed of panic sprouts in his belly. Anne's portrait will go into storage. Her table will be consigned to some dark corner. Her dream of dinner parties banished. No one will visit her grave. A great emptiness opens in his chest, as if it has been drained of blood. "Wait," he says.

"Seller's remorse?" Ridley says, grinning.

"No," Rand says. But he is lying. Carrie's voice rings in his ear. *Don't make any changes for two years after a spousal death.* What if she's right? But what can he possibly do with his life besides what he has planned? The decision has been made. He's leaving. He's going to hate leaving. But he's got to go. Rand holds out his hand to shake on the deal.

"All I ask," Ridley says, "is get any personal stuff out of here that you want by the end of the month. There's a storage place in Quarryville." He hands Rand a card. "Say my name, they'll give you a deal. They'll even pick it up." He pauses. "Some of this I can use." He pats Decker's table, rocks it side to side to check for sturdiness. "How about I keep this," he says. "If you don't want it, of course."

Good, Rand thinks. *I never wanted it.* But after Ridley leaves, he places his palm on the hand-rubbed surface. It's warm to the touch. *Look, the heart is still alive.*

Rand tucks the check into his briefcase, along with the house sale contract. He calls Delta for a one-way ticket to LA, San Francisco, continuing to Melbourne, Indonesia, Singapore, and Rome.

He feels goosebumps on his arms. *You're on your way*, he tells himself, and it's as though he is already rising into the air, untethered from the ground. He's got the money now to book the rest of the trip. To live the rest of his life. Without Anne. Rand calms his panic with a tall tumbler of bourbon and gets to work. He has things to do. Places to go.

He drives to Chapel Hill in his work clothes. Deposits his enormous check. Prepays a hefty amount on his credit card. Gets out a wad of cash. Drives to the post office. Pays for the money order. This time he pauses to write a note, tuck it inside: *I am coming to Malaysia. I would like to meet my son.*

Back home, he roots out the cell phone Carrie sent, pulls it out of the box, connects the charger. It will be useful on his trip. He dials her number. She'll be so pleased he's actually using it. But when Carrie picks up, she sounds strange. "Daaad," she says. "Finally. When you coming to LA? Been reading Mom's journal. Wow."

"What do you mean, wow?" Is she drunk? Not like her at all.

"Mom says a *lot* about you in there."

"What does she say?" His voice is calm. Calm. Stay calm.

"How unhappy you were. Are. I mean, in *Stonehaven*. But also overseas. She says you were unhappy pretty much all the time. She was pretty mad at you, Dad. For some things you did."

"What things?"

"Are you saying you don't know? Are you saying—"

"Dammit! You shouldn't be reading that! That's our private business!"

"I'm reading it," Carrie says. "And you don't have anything to say about it. She was my mother. And you should stay in better touch." *Click.*

What was in that journal? He can guess. But it's the last thing he'd want to see recorded in Anne's neat, slanted handwriting. Or discuss further with Carrie in LA.

He'll skip LA. He'll reroute straight to San Francisco.

Rand calls for Friday pickup. He boxes up everything remaining from the downstairs rooms and places it in the garage. He pulls the paradise bird print from its frame and tucks it in the back of a yellow pad. That will travel with him. For inspiration. There's nothing else in the den but the briefcase full of bird notes and money, Anne's portrait, and the two birds themselves, muttering quietly. He should have asked Ridley if he knew anyone who would take them. Bankers always know little old ladies. Little old ladies love birds. But he didn't ask, and he's still got no idea what he'll do with them. Molly's gone. Molly flew away. There's nothing he can do about it.

He rests his forehead on the cage wire. The cockatiels have gone very quiet. "You know something's up, don't you?" he says. Anne's portrait rests against the wall right next to them, her blue eyes just at bird level, and in this light they seem to be shadowed with a sadness deeper than her joy. "I'm leaving you," Rand says. And he remembers the time she got so mad at him that she threatened to go. *Don't think about that now,* he tells himself. *She's gone now, isn't she.*

Anne's dining room table is still half pulled apart, from when he started to take out a leaf. He's got to put it back together before they can take it away. He braces himself and shoves with all his strength, and the gap in the center shifts an inch. He follows this program for the next five minutes, and on the final push, the table jams closed and he bounces off sideways, hitting his thigh on one of the heavy oak-chair arms. He pulls his trousers down to look. A bruise is already rising, pink and hard with swelling, right on top of the old bruise. He sticks on three pain patches, but they don't seem to help. He fills a glass with bourbon. The universal anesthetic.

He finishes cleaning his guns, puts them back in the case on the wall, but now he has to decide what to do with them. Can you take a gun with you on a plane these days? Not this baker's dozen. They'll call it an arsenal and arrest him or some damn thing. He's got to store them. Or all but one. He'll keep the Bersa. It's small, fits in your pocket.

His shirt is filthy with gun oil and graphite and his pants are smeared with mud. He's been wearing the same work clothes for a week. It's time to do some laundry. He can pack the guns after that. Then all he has to do is clear out the rest of Anne's upstairs closet.

He pulls off his filthy clothes, checks his pockets. He fishes out something wadded up there. What the hell? It's that piece of junk mail the snippy assistant found on the porch. He turns to toss it in the garbage and it slips out of his fingers. When he crouches to pick it up, he yelps in pain, his thigh is so newly tender, and falls to his knees. There's a trick of light shining on the address, picking out the letters under the mud. Typed letters. *To the General.* Holy hell. That crazy old biddy again. She's hunted him down.

He picks the letter up gingerly, by the corner. It might provide evidence of her crimes against him.

What did she ever do to you? Anne's voice, mild, accusing.

His thigh throbs and he stumbles as he rises. *She did something to me, Anne. She just about ruined my leg.* The rage rises in him, he can almost see the woman's face, bleary through the windshield, Black, implacable, full of vengeful thoughts against him. He opens the letter and reads it on the kitchen island. It is the exact same letter. But this time she names a fee: ninety dollars for parts and labor. A memory tickles his ear. *Miss Reba ever catch up with you?* The boys at the Sunrise are in on the deal. They've been tracking him down together. She has tracked him to his house and she has gone too far. God only knows if she's watching him now from somewhere outside. It's too much. He will not stand for it. He may be leaving soon, but first he will take care of this business.

There is no time to do it by the book, call the sheriff, bring a witness. Who would witness for him? George or Bess? They would let this go. But it is a mistake to let things go. What he always told Anne: things must be taken care of. The crazy woman on Field Road will hear back from him today. Don't fuck with a full-bird colonel.

He puts his stained work clothes back on. Picks up the smallest gun in his collection, the Bersa, and the mud-spattered letter. He gets in the car. Sets both on the seat beside him.

This time, her big boat of a car is there. What if someone's with her? He gets out, slips the Bersa in his pocket. He limps to the porch, pulls himself up by the porch rail, senses a presence behind him. He turns. Those big, strange yard statues are bright and staring, each one like a cross between a totem pole and a child's idea of an angel. But black. And there's something different. One has been freshly painted. Red lips open in a shout, enormous blue eyes staring him down, as if it can see right through him. Arm raised with a silver sword glinting in the sun, making him wince, and making him strangely aware that he is not properly dressed for such a mission. He's wearing his filthy clothes. He could be mistaken for a workman. Not a full-bird colonel. *Not a general.* He squares his shoulders, turns, and knocks on the frame of the screen door.

There is no answer.

He knocks again.

No answer.

He peers through the screen door. "Anybody home?" he calls out. Silence.

He steps down to the yard to look around. No roosters. Chickens must be somewhere shady in the heat of the day. He stops to inspect the big black car, checks the driver's side. There is no fender on it. What the bloody hell? How can she accuse him of denting her car when the place she says was dented is gone? Old biddy. Looks like she's about to replace it without his money. Looks like the old biddy is doing just fine. The leaves on the tree above his head rustle and shake in a humid breeze. The sun shimmers on the surface of the car. He looks closer. The paint is bubbled. All over the car. Did she give it a bad paint job? He touches a bubble. It collapses, and a sifting of rust stains his finger. The damn car is falling apart. The old biddy wants him to pay for car damage for a car that's barely there. She wants to soak him.

She wants ninety dollars, Anne's voice says. *Look at what you have.*

"Ninety dollars is ninety dollars," Rand says out loud. "Plus pain and suffering." A trickle of sweat slips down the back of his neck. It's hot as hell here in the sun. He raises his head. Someone's talking back behind the shed. Rand rests his hand on the Bersa in his pocket. She could have a whole troupe of crazy people working here. He heads down the path and spies a tangled garden, fenced with chicken wire.

The garden is overrun with sweet potato vines, tomatoes, turnips, pole beans. Just like Ma's garden. Full of bounty. Someone's been watering with a bucket. That's hard work. But you've got to water when it's this hot and dry. And if you don't have a hose, a bucket will do.

Abundant crops come by the strength of the ox, Ma used to say, flex her arm muscles, and laugh. She had puny, stringy arms. But they were strong.

There's no one in the garden. The voices are coming from further on, a corn patch in a square of blazing sun. He follows the path to corn rows as tall as his head. Flat green leaves bright as new paint, flapping and rustling in the hot breeze, tassels sprouting at the top, bees and flies and hummingbirds in a cloud of yellow pollen. The corn patch is surrounded by old hickory trees, as if this place were a private refuge, a secret place. Doesn't look like sweet corn. Or field corn. The ears are short and fat. The blazing sun raises sweat on his forehead, and it trickles into his eyes, stinging. *Ye shall eat by the sweat of thy brow,* Ma used to say, hoeing corn. He wipes the sweat away with the back of his hand.

"You chopping too close to the stem." An old woman's voice. Black woman's. Clear as a bell from deep in the patch.

"No, I ain't." A young boy's voice. White boy.

Rand creeps closer, peers down corn rows until he sees them. In what must be a new planting, only knee high, two backs bent over in the sun. Two hoes, chopping. It's an old lady, bent to her work, stringy arms, big straw hat on her head. A boy, skinny and small, the back of his T-shirt streaked with sweat. Trying to keep up with the old lady, who is chopping with a vengeance. Rand slips behind a hickory tree where he won't be seen. The old lady stops. Did she hear him? No. She pulls a kerchief out of her apron pocket. Pulls off her hat. Wipes down her whole face and the back of her neck. Yes, it's her. She puts her hat back on and keeps going.

This is the old biddy who wants his money. An old lady who works by the sweat of her brow. A young boy helping. Two people who work to eat. Nobody works this hard in the summer sun unless they have to. The weight of his anger drops away and he is filled with shame. He wants to drop everything and go chop beside them. He wants to be told he is chopping too close to the stem. He wants to be told what to do.

Rand backs away from the corn patch, walks quickly to his car. He will pay the ninety dollars. He will write a check today. Put it in the mail. It is what Anne would have done all along. And she would have made a friend while doing it.

By the time he gets home, the sun is slanting sideways into the house through his newly cleaned windows, and a strange golden light glimmers off everything it touches, making it look precious and full of delight.

Maybe this was what Anne saw in the house when they first came. She fell in love with its almost-empty rooms, its possibilities. Like she did with him. He's going to miss this place. The Gooley pines glimmering with light. The Sunrise biscuits. But there is a plan. The storage men are coming tomorrow. He sets the Bersa on the dining room table. He lets the cockatiels out of their cages. "Let's get it done," he says. Then he heads upstairs to finish packing.

He bags up Anne's remaining winter coats and suits. Fine wool and cashmere. Scarves. Smell of mothballs and perfume. He'll call Second Bloom, one of her charities. She told him it takes care of pregnant girls and their babies in a big farmhouse outside of town. She gave all her old clothes to them, and sometimes, she said, it was strange to see a young girl with a baby in downtown Quarryville, wearing a Chanel jacket with jeans, knowing the jacket was hers.

He gets down on his knees, pulls out a wall of shoeboxes. The birds flutter up, perch on the open closet door, watch with interest. Rand pulls out red shoes. Blue shoes. Gold sandals. Florence leather. He loads them in a plastic trash bag, still in the boxes. He stands on his tiptoes, blindly reaches around the top shelf, comes up with a half carton of Tareytons. Really? He never knew. He never even suspected. In the back corner of the top shelf there's a white pasteboard box labeled "Private" in Anne's slanting hand. Rand opens the box. Envelopes. Scores and scores of envelopes. Airmail envelopes with a Malaysia return address, Peet's name, in the corner. The letters are addressed to Mrs. Anne Lee at PO boxes in Long Island and Quarryville. Peet wrote letters to Anne? Anne had a PO box? He has to sit down on the bed. Pia flaps to his side, pecks at the letters. He waves her away.

The envelopes are all carefully slit open with a sharp knife. He opens the one in front. No letter. Just another blue envelope, this one folded in half. Addressed to Zara. His own handwriting. Still sealed. *What the...?* Rand tears it open. Inside is a money order. Signed by him. Dated May.

How did Peet get hold of these? Something must have happened to Zara. He peers at the outer envelopes more closely. They are all stamped *no such person.* No, it is not a stamp. It is a neat, square handwritten note. Peet's writing. Anne's been piling these letters up for years. The heat rises up his chest and into his neck and face. Peet and Anne must have had a deal. And with this monthly reminder, Anne must have hated him every time she hid a thin blue envelope away in this box that smells of date sugar and curry.

Every month for fifteen years he's sent such a check. Pulled cash from private accounts he set up in Manhattan, then Chapel Hill. He would tell Anne he had errands to run or a doctor's appointment, cash a check at the bank, then take it to the post office, buy a money order made out to cash, and mail it. Back in Malaysia he'd promised to support, though he could never acknowledge. He'd lose his rank. His job. His wife's respect. But he sent money: $250 US a month, a lot of money in Malaysia.

The look on Anne's face when Zara came to the door with the baby, wanting to come in. The look of shock. Then anger. Then it was as if she flew up and looked down at him from far, far away. Weary. Disconnected. Free.

She was looking at a man who had never been battle tested. Who had joined the army during the frozen war, and who it turned out was good at the boring side of heroism: procurement, paperwork, standing firm in meetings, doing what he said he would do. Someone who had never risen in the ranks far enough, and never would. Someone who walked out into the jungle on weekend leave, away from base politics, away from sucking up to generals, dinner parties, family. A man who turned out to be faithless. A man who could never live up to what she wanted of him.

"Decide," she'd said. "One or the other." Then she walked away.

Rand clutches at his head. The birds mutter at him. He wants to go away, away.

But what did Anne always say? *Wherever you go, there you are.*

As Rand pulls the envelopes out, one by one, he finds that most of the checks are missing. A folded piece of paper falls to his hand. It is a list of things she loved: St. Dunstan's Episcopal Church, Special Needs School of Ambler, Second Bloom Home for Teen Mothers, Friends of the Library, Society for the Preservation of Old-Growth Pines, the list goes on and on. Tiny checkmarks next to each, some more than others. He always knew she volunteered. But looks like she also gave money. Lots and lots of money.

As he goes, he tosses each empty envelope to the floor, where the cockatiels glory in pecking them to pieces. The addresses on Peet's envelopes are a litany of the places they lived after Malaysia: a brief stint in Rome, then Long Island, and finally here. Each place, Anne must have had her own postal address. Each place, she slit the envelope open, cashed the check, and…finally, here's an envelope postmarked fifteen years ago, with a letter tucked inside. It's in Peet's handwriting.

My dear. I did receive your letter informing me of your new postal address. I think it best we do not write. My wife would not understand.

Once again, I have the honor of returning your husband's contribution. He was a dear friend to me. But I do not need his charity. I have my Birdland Hotel, you see. Zara is well. She works for me now. We have ecotourism. A big success! We still hope for the day that the men will come from *National Geographic*. But we are doing fine without.

And the baby does not need the money. Perhaps you need an explanation. You know there are still some among my people who do not like things that are different or strange. It makes them frightened. And they especially do not like mixed-race children. There was a man in our village who accused Zara of being a witch. He said he found birds without heads in places where she walked. He said her baby was a demon.

You may think these things do not happen in this day and age. Let me just say that we do our best to make sure you do not know. This man took the precious baby of our fine colonel and placed it in the jungle where the tiger goes. The child was never found.

My blessings on you. I will see you in heaven. I shall not write again.

With all my respect and good wishes, Peet

Rand wags his head slowly, side to side, unable to take it in. The cockatiels pause in their ripping, fix their eyes on him. He knows nothing. He understands nothing. Well, maybe just one thing. His wife loved him enough to never tell him the most terrible thing he ever heard.

But now he knows.

45

When Carrie calls Jeff Friday morning, he takes the call on Jolene's porch, where Bobo can't hear. It's always trouble when Carrie calls.

She tells him Dad is in a state, standing in the yard, yelling at the birds on the bird feeder. "Bess called," she says. "He's throwing pine cones. He said something about the wrong birds eating the thistle seed."

"*WTF*, Carrie."

"She was just going to ignore him, but he fell down. And he wouldn't let George help him up. Then he chased them back to their house. She said, and I quote, 'I think he's gone 'round the bend.'"

Jolene's gone to pick up feed. He'll have to take Bobo. Usen beats them to the truck.

When they get there Dad is nowhere to be seen. Jeff leaves Usen tied to the bumper. The safest place for Bobo, he figures, is on the kitchen stool. They're supposed to be doing math. "Count things," Jeff says. He leaves Bobo in the kitchen, counting out loud. Windows: "One, two, three, four." Cups: "One, two, three, four, five, six, seven."

"Dad?" He's not in the living room. A mug on the coffee table. Three dead stogies in the ashtray. Everything looks moved around. Piled up. In boxes. There's a big blank space above the fireplace, where Mom's portrait used to be. *What the fuck?*

"Dad?" He's not in the den. King P is perched on the top of the cage, looping his head in a crazy circle and flapping until it looks like he might fall off. There are little saucers of what looks and smells like bourbon in the cage. Dad's getting him *drunk*? Where's Pia?

Jeff walks down the hall to the bedroom. No Dad. A sound from the bathroom. Dad's sitting on the toilet lid, holding Queen Pia against his chest, cradling her like a baby. Dad looks up, his eyes dark hollow points.

"Dad," Jeff chokes. "Dad. What are you doing?"

"I fucked it up," Dad says. "I fucked the whole thing up. Army. Your mother. Everything." His voice is smeary, like a glass of watered bourbon.

"It's okay, Dad," Jeff says. He moves a little closer. His dad clutches the bird to his chest. Queen Pia struggles and peeps in protest. What is he doing to her?

"Give me the bird, Dad."

Dad opens his hands. Pia flaps up in a panic, comes to his shoulder, her claws digging in. She smells like bourbon too.

"What the hell is going on here?" Jeff says. "What are all these boxes?"

"Gone on a *trip*." Dad's voice is slurred, shaky. Dad is *wasted*.

This doesn't look like a trip. This looks like a change of address.

Dad's eyes on him again. The emptiness in them is terrifying.

"Dad. It's me, Dad. It's Jeff. Just tell me what the hell is going on."

"Shold the house."

"You're *leaving*? When the hell were you going to tell me?"

"Shoon."

"Well, where are you going?"

"Don' know. Don' know."

Pia crawls up the side of Jeff's head to the top, shivers there. She lets loose a stool. "Goddammit," Jeff mutters. Pia never does that. He wipes his hair with a piece of Kleenex.

"Take the bird," Dad says.

"Don't worry, I'm taking her. And, hey, Dad. Thanks for keeping me informed. I guess you don't really need me around, do you? You've never needed anything from me, have you? *Fuck* you, Dad. Just fuck you."

Jeff scoops Pia from his head, tucks her in his vest, heads to the kitchen. On the way, he catches Bobo standing in the dining room, counting the guns in the case. The case door is open. "Bobo!" Jeff says. "Did you touch those?"

"Too many guns!" Bobo says. "Thuh-teen!"

"Let's get you out of here, bud," he says. "The old man doesn't want company today."

Jeff grabs Bobo's shoulders, turns him around, pushes him through the kitchen. Past the open drawer. Past the twelve dessert spoons Bobo has carefully laid out, as if he's about to have an ice-cream party.

Jeff drives to the bridge, pulls off the road. One of the places he goes to think. He sets the brake. Usen licks his ear, sniffs at his vest. Bobo rocks in his seat, worried. "Papa mad?"

"He's a mess," Jeff says. "He's been drinking. Packing. I guess he's leaving." Jeff peers at Bobo. "Hey, you weren't messing with those guns, were you? In the house?"

"No! No, no, no!" Bobo shakes his head, hard, from side to side. He takes his hands out of his pockets. Opens his palms as if to say, *See?*

"Good," Jeff said. "That would be bad. Don't play with guns, okay?"

"Too many guns," Bobo says.

"Good." Jeff points his finger at Bobo. Bobo points back with his finger and shoots an imaginary gun. "What would Wambo do?" Bobo says. "Bam!" He laughs.

Jeff grimaces. "Right, *bam*. Crazy bastard." Jeff wonders if he should have left all those guns there, the kind of mood Dad's in.

Bobo stops rocking. Looks at Jeff's vest, where Pia's head is sticking out. "Pink bird!"

Usen sniffs at Pia. Pia mutters at him. "Can I have yoh bird?" Bobo says.

And it makes sense. Bobo should have the bird. He's good with birds. Pia looks so bedraggled. Like she might not make it. Just like Dad. What would Mom say? He can hear her voice as clear as if the Gooley pines are speaking: *Live your own life, dear. Let me take care of your father.*

"Her name is Pia," he says.

Bobo pulls her carefully from his vest. "Pia," he croons.

"Oh fuck," Pia mutters. Bobo pets her until she makes crooning sounds. He tucks her inside his windbreaker, her head sticking out.

"Want some gum?" Bobo offers a stick of Juicy Fruit.

Jeff takes it. Then hands it back. "You have it," he says. "Thanks anyway."

Jeff puts the truck in gear. He's got to get Bobo home. Sky's clouding over. Spatter on the windshield. Jolene's finally going to get some rain.

All Rand can do now is keep him company.

⌘

At Spill Creek Farm, the power is out in the barn. A small pine has fallen on the line. It's gotten so cloudy and dark out there, Jolene can't see what she's doing. She pokes around for the enormous electric lantern she keeps charged for just such occasions. The mama goats are making loud complaints. Their udders can't wait. She milks in the dark, head resting on Folly's flank to calm her. She never got a generator. Never had the money. Usually the power comes back on in a few hours. No need to borrow trouble.

The farm report on the radio this morning said there'd be rain bands from the hurricane. Two to three inches of rain. Thank God, because they really need it. But this rain pounds so hard, and the thunder is so loud, she's sure it means to break through the roof at any minute. The goats are safely locked in, and the barn roof is solid. *Boom.* Another lightning flash. The mama goats stamp and honk. It's getting closer.

Bobo is terrified of lightning. If she'd known a thunderstorm was coming, she never would have sent him over to Reba's, with that new pet bird tucked in his shirt. She should go pick him up. Send Jeff home. She can't keep having Jeff in her bed with Bobo here. Bobo is very curious about what they are doing. *Crack-ck-ck.* Thunder like the snap of a whip. Up on the Gooley Ridge.

Jolene glances at Jeff, crouched in the next pen. He's found the lantern, it makes a circle of light around him. He's soothing the newborn kids, feeding them with bottles. God, he is sweet. Jeff glances up at her and smiles, the lantern light glistening in his eyes, glinting on his stubbly beard. One of the kids loses the nipple, and he guides the bottle into its small mouth until the little buck sucks with energy the way he should.

Jeff is so good with Bobo. So sweet with her. Sweet and sexy and *oh my God.* She is as captured by sex as her goat mamas when they go into estrus and back up to the fence, lifting their tails, their hindquarters engorged and ready, taunting the bucks. She is just as much an animal as they are, and it frightens her a little. She has not felt like this in years. Not since that first honeymoon year with Luke. How can something this sweet last? She finishes milking and straining. She wipes the milk cans and tucks them in the fridge. It'll stay cold enough in there for a while.

Jeff takes the bottles to the sink and turns the knob. "No water!"

Jolene calls out to him. City people never get it. The well pump needs power.

Jolene lifts the lantern and shows Jeff where to put the bottles to soak. She has backup water in a stack of jugs under the sink. She pours the water over the bottles and Jeff watches her drizzle in some disinfectant. "I can do that," he says.

"We'll just leave it till the power comes back on," Jolene says. "It won't be long." The smell of him next to her makes her dizzy.

"Jesus," Jeff says, "it's raining sideways out there."

"Radio said the hurricane on the coast might send rain."

"This is not just any rain," Jeff says.

"It can't last like this. There'll be a break soon. I've got to pick up Bobo. Hold this," she says. She hands Jeff the lantern and climbs up the ladder to the hay loft. Tosses down a bale of straw, which breaks open at his feet. He hangs the lantern on a nail, scoops up the straw in his arms, and spreads it around. Then he crouches in the fresh bedding, his back against the barn wall. "I love this smell," he says.

Jolene comes down and joins him. "I love it too. Sometimes I come here and sleep with them. If I ever feel lonely, I just come and bring a pillow and hang out with the girls."

"Hen party," Jeff says.

Jolene laughs. "Yep, only goats. The does smell so good. The bucks, though, that's a different story. Bobo calls them Stinky and Poops."

"I guess I smell pretty bad too," he says. Jeff turns to her and kisses her ear, presses a hand against her breast.

She can taste his tongue, like a salty fruit, in her mouth. She can smell his hair, the salt sweat and the sweetness. Feel his hand stroking, making her rise and forget everything she knows. "We can't now," she says.

"Reba's there," he says. He slips his hand between her legs. "Don't worry so much."

Reba's there. *Did she put the milk away?* Yes. Her body arches, helpless with the heat of him. She pulls him down in the straw and wraps her legs around him. He lifts his face to look at her. There. Such an expression of sweetness, like a river pouring out of him and into her.

☙

TJ wonders where Aunt Reba has got to. She should be back by now. She always drives slow, but she drives like a turtle when it rains.

On the TV, Rambo's got that sash around his head. He's an Indian.

But he's fighting a man in a jungle. Oops! He's caught a guy. The dude hangs upside down.

TJ laughs. Bobo laughs. The bird on the lampshade flaps its wings.

Aunt Reba told him to fill empty milk jugs and pails with water while she runs her errands. As soon as the movie's over, he'll do it. The movie is keeping Bobo distracted from the thunder and lightning. Bobo is afraid of the storm. "Like a spidah," he said, when they watched it on the news. It did look like a spider, arms sticking out all around. Bobo does not like spiders.

Aunt Reba said the hurricane was coming here. The weather lady said it wasn't. He's hoping the weather lady wins that one. Bobo looked worried, so TJ said, "They never come here, they need ocean to keep their power. The land slows 'em down. They can't slow down in the water, that's why they call them Hurry-canes." His daddy told him that. It doesn't really make any sense. Daddy was drunk at the time.

Bobo is so lucky. He gets a dog and a bird and everything. There's something wrong with his brain, but everybody loves him anyway. He's a sweet kid. That's why.

More lightning. Bobo is rocking. "Uh-oh, uh-oh, uh-oh."

TJ says, "What would Rambo do?" Bobo stops, thinks, pulls an imaginary trigger. "Bam." TJ falls down. Wiggles on the floor. Lies still. "Get up, TJ!" Bobo pokes TJ with a finger. "TJ hut?" The kid pokes him again. TJ jumps up and roars like a lion. Bobo screeches. They both fall laughing to the floor. The bird goes bouncing across the ceiling.

"Here, Pia, here, Pia, dint mean to scah you." Bobo pets the bird, then puts it back on the lampshade.

The window shakes. Rain pops against the glass like BBs. Bobo's dog cries on the porch.

"Usen want to come *in*, TJ."

TJ opens the door a crack. The wind yanks the screen door open and bangs it against the house. The dog's not there. Just the black statues, wings shaking in the wind.

Bobo looks over TJ's shoulder. "Useh!"

"Probly went under the porch," TJ says. "Don't worry, little buddy. He'll be okay."

The pink bird squawks, *Fuckfuckfuck!* Geez, she shouldn't say things like that in front of Bobo.

Rambo is walking through the jungle now. His eyes bug out of his

face. His face is painted green or maybe it's just mud. It's raining in the movie too.

TJ usually gets Bobo a treat when he comes—candy or Grape Nehi or salted peanuts in the shell. Bobo loves those. This time he has something extra. He's got Cheerwine. Plus the jar of Lucy's clear he hid under his bed. Won't hurt to have a little taste before Reba comes back. Just enough to make Bobo sleep like a baby through this storm. Bobo told him about that time the goats ran away. He got stuck in the briars. Lightning tried to get him.

Now Bobo's eyes are glued to Rambo again. TJ pulls out two cans of Cheerwine. When TJ was little he used to think you could get drunk on Cheerwine, but it's just a name. There ain't no wine in it. He pops the top. Bobo glances over. "Cheeh wan!"

"Let me fix it for you," TJ says. Bobo looks back at the screen. TJ sucks off an inch of soda from the can. Pours in a couple of dribbles of the clear. Puts his thumb over the hole and swirls it around. Then hands it over. Bobo's big fingers curl around the can. He takes a gulp. "Good!" he says.

TJ laughs. He must not have put enough in. He pops the second can, sucks out a few inches, tops it off good. Doesn't bother to swirl. Chugs. The clear hits his throat. Burns like hell. TJ swallows. Chokes. Starts coughing his fool head off. Bobo looks up. TJ catches his breath. "Good!" he says. He clinks Bobo's can with his. Sits down to watch Rambo crawl through the jungle in the rain. The pink bird watches too.

Reba's windshield wipers can't keep up. Rain splashing up from Field Road, right onto her legs. Raining so hard it's already piling up in the ditches. Weather girl this morning said it was staying out to sea. But Reba knew this was coming. She closed her eyes and saw it. A swirl of rage heading this way. Lucy rising. *Oh Lord.*

She's got gas, Beanie Weenies, Sterno, canned milk, last of the C batteries, everything she needs. But she's got to get home.

Ahead of her on Field Road, there's a black sheen sliding across the dip in the road. Road's flooded. She jams on brakes. Cutlass slides across the wet asphalt and into the ditch, just to the edge of the flood. *Lord have mercy.* If it'd been dark she'd have gone right in. *Once Spill Creek has you, it holds you down.* But this isn't Spill Creek. This creek is so little it doesn't really even have a name.

The ditch is a foot deep in water and rising. She tries the ignition. Engine won't start. Wind tearing at the windows, sticks flying. Boys home all alone. No way she can get to them now. If this creek is flooded, Spill Creek is a river.

Reba sends her heart out across the creek to find them. They are safe. Something not right, though. Bobo is afraid.

"Jesus," Reba says. "Watch my boys."

She can't get to Jolene's. But somebody's always at Sunrise. They have a phone there, she can call the boys. All she's got to do is walk back up that hill to the highway.

Reba stuffs the deep pockets of her raincoat with cans—canned milk on one side, beans on the other. Pack of batteries. Sterno. Pocketknife. Wallet. The small flashlight out of the glove box. She takes the plastic grocery bag and makes a hat, handles tied under her chin. No use getting wetter than she has to. She reaches for the umbrella, nice big black one. Mama's funeral umbrella.

The wind whistles through the door frame and whips up through the missing fender, shaking this big old car, as much as it weighs. "My faith is weak," Reba says. "Lord, help thou my unbelief." She slides over to the passenger side, away from the wind. She cracks the door and ditchwater rushes in, yanking it full open. She steps into the ditch. Water swirls her calves, something catches at her coat. Old piece of plywood. Even in this driving rain she can read it: *The earth shall be laid waste.* "Lord have mercy," Reba says. One of her papa's signs. She was using them to patch the roof on the chicken shed. This one must have blown right off.

She stumbles up the ditch bank, shoving the umbrella point into the soft earth to pull herself along. She stands in the road, rain streaming down her face and glasses, can't see a thing. She closes her eyes. She knows this land like she knows the book of Isaiah. Branches crack in the woods. Field grass beaten down. The fox in her den no longer safe. It is coming.

Voice in her ear says, *Turn, open the umbrella, and face it full into the wind.* "Be thou my shield and buckler," Miss Reba says. She begins to walk.

A crash of glass in the kitchen. Rand goes to inspect. A pine branch has fallen on the bay window, knocked out three of twelve panes, and now is whacking steadily at the vinyl siding. A stream of rain is dribbling down the wall to the floor. The trees in the yard shake and bend in the

wind like inside-out umbrellas. They picked this lot for the shade. Oak
trees on the north. Pines all around. He is surrounded. Nothing to do
but wait it out, hope the roof holds, stuff the bay window with plastic
bags, tape them up with duct tape, watch the rain leak around.

Bess and George went off to the Tobacco Shed around four for a
lights-out hurricane party. That means they'll keep the generator on
long enough to serve blue slushy drinks with umbrellas and George's
chili with habañero peppers. At midnight the plan is to shut the lights
off and scream bloody murder. People here are well organized for fun.
George came back at four-thirty to pry him out of the house. Bess must
have made him come.

"Plenty to drink there," he said. "You might run out."

"No thanks."

"Suit yourself," George said.

Now Rand wonders if the Tobacco Shed will hold together. It's not
a real house. But the thing is built like a boat, all heart-pine ceilings,
tongue and groove, under the tin, more solid than any tobacco shed he's
ever seen. They had no idea this was coming. Nobody did. Even that
ever-reliable weather man at WRAL. He remembers an old hurricane
story from Texas. An island off the Gulf coast, a resort where people
came to gamble and dance, turn of the century. A ballroom glassed in
all around. People dancing, drinking, glittering with diamonds, orchestra
playing. When the storm surge came, the whole ballroom washed away.
The next morning there was no island, just a pipe sticking up from the
old artesian well, bubbling fresh water into the salt.

Rand fills his glass again, takes a long swallow.

He checks King P, quivering in his cage. Rand wishes he hadn't given
Pia away, he wishes could let King P out, tuck him inside his shirt,
hunker down, keep him warm and calm, but God knows what's going
to happen to this house. The bird could blow right out the windows.
He's safer in the cage.

Rand has lived through typhoons in Bangkok, Malaysia, and the Philippines. He never thought he'd see one here, two hundred miles inland.
But it's here, all right.

The last bourbon bottle in the house is heading alarmingly toward
empty, and he needs some light. He rummages in the dining room,
finds Anne's supply of candles in the sideboard, sets a raft of elegant
twelve-inch tapers in mauve, pink, and teal in balls of foil crushed into

the bottoms of highball glasses so they will not fall over. He finds some matches. Lights them. The room has a dinner-party glow.

He wishes Anne were here to sit out the storm with him, tipsy and quivering at every loud crash. But if she were, she might look at him, finally say what lurked in the back of her blue eyes for fifteen years: *That storm in Malaysia. Where were you?*

He picks up a framed photo from a half-filled box, peers at it in the flickering light. Anne with her sunhat, Jeff with his sunny grin, little Carrie in her dress. Jeff's expression just like Anne's. How did he never see the resemblance before? That was the year of the storm. That was the year he let his family down.

He was checking the base that afternoon, typhoon coming, when Peet told him. The village had shunned Zara. Because she was pregnant. Rand hadn't known. He'd only noticed that she disappeared for months. Peet had told him she got a job in the next town. But now Zara was alone up on the hillside, about to give birth, staying in the bird hut with Peet's enormous pink cockatoo, King Alfred, and a roomful of conures, fairy bluebirds, budgies, cockatiels. Peet's "Birdland Hotel."

Rand took the jeep and went. He stayed as the wind rose. He stayed when the roof blew off the bird hut. He stayed while Anne and the kids huddled in the tile bathroom of their base housing, fearing for their lives. He stayed when the birds rose into the sky as if sucked into the mouth of God. All except King Alfred, the cockatoo, who hid in a hole under a pile of cinderblocks, screeching almost as loud as the wind.

Somehow he got Zara and the baby half-protected in a corner out of the wind. He cut the umbilical cord with his pocketknife, eyes filled with rain and tears, ears roaring with wind and his lover's screams. She named the boy Aashka—a blessing from God.

Then came the eye of the storm. A quiet moment. A stilling of the thrashing palms. A silence. The baby was fine. Zara was okay. He thought of Anne. He left. The storm came back.

He has done so many unforgivable things.

After the storm, Peet continued to drive him on base duties, taking food and water to villages, but he never chatted about his dreams again. Rand had his heart attack. Got discharged to the states, medical disability. In the back of his mind, Rand always figured Peet's life would go on, and Zara would raise the little boy, and maybe get to go to college. The last letter in the pile was from a month ago. At least he knows Peet is still alive.

His heart thuds in his chest, a dull familiar pain. The question rises like the flame on his match: *Would anyone be inconvenienced if I died in this storm?* He lights another match. He needs more candles. The flame catches hold, flares up, singes his thumb.

The question returns, lurks in the shadowy corners of the room.

Jeff wouldn't have to put up with your crap. Carrie wouldn't have to call you up and nag. Zara doesn't need your money. The kids could split the insurance.

The only one who needs him is King P. He goes to cover the cage. King chirrups faintly.

More thuds in the yard. Another crash. Christ, his heart might give out just from the noise. "Fuckfuckfuck!" King P screeches. He's picked up a few things from potty-mouth Pia.

If it doesn't happen all on its own, you can always go out into the storm and meet it.

He is startled by the clarity of this thought. It makes perfect sense. He places his hands on the dining room table and rises, steadies. He goes to the living room window. Looks out. Decides. Sometime tonight he will invite his own death. It will be easy.

He will walk into the growing storm and let it swallow him. A fallen branch. A flying roof tile. The storm will knock him down, and if it does not, it will beat him to death. *Zara's village after the storm. Birds and houses and palm branches and people flung about like ragged toys.* So much death, it became normal, as he and his soldiers began to lift and lay out bodies in rows and zip them into bags. It had been a miracle that Zara and her boy survived that.

He has one last bit of business. He writes a check for $100—ten dollars extra for pain and suffering. He pulls a piece of paper from the yellow legal pad in his briefcase. He writes a note: *For Miss Reba Jones, 15 Field Road.* He folds the paper around the check, tucks it under one of the glasses holding a twisted red Christmas candle. No one could possibly miss it.

Strangely satisfied now, and three drinks down, he allows himself to ponder the scenario of the Tobacco Shed blowing away, spinning in the air, all the phony retired businessmen scattered into the trees. *Evil thought, take it back.*

"Randolph Jefferson Lee," he says, "you are a true bastard. You deserve whatever's coming to you." He raises his glass to it. Drinks. He will wait just a little longer.

◊

"Look, Bobo! I found a candle!" TJ says.

"Want Mama," Bobo moans.

The kid is really scared, crouched in the dark, arms around knees, head down. That crazy bird flutters around their heads. *Help! Help! Motherfucker!*

"Shut the hell up, bird," TJ says.

Bobo is making screeching sounds too now. "Help! Help! Mama!"

TJ sets the candle down on a pile of magazines. *You have to leave him alone sometimes,* Reba says. *Just let him be.* TJ doesn't like to do that. TJ pulls the afghan from the back of the sofa. Big fat pink and purple flowers crocheted so they stick out. Danielle made it. Bobo likes it. He pulls it over Bobo's shoulders. Pats his back. "It's gonna be okay, little buddy. We'll get Mama soon as the lights come back on. Soon as all this stops, I'll take you there."

The bird settles into a fold in the afghan. "Pitty bird," Bobo says, stroking her feathers.

TJ stands up and goes to peer out the window. What in *hell* happened to Aunt Reba?

For most of an hour, Miss Reba has been fighting her way up Field Road, in the shelter of the Gooley Ridge, out of the main force of the wind. She's been praying all the time, her black umbrella braced before her like a shield. Gusts tug at her, buffet her progress, billow the cloth between the umbrella's ribs. Through her glasses glazed with rain, she can see only the moving shapes of light and shadow, like spirits rising. Pockets full of cans knock her thigh bones. Her town dress sticks to her legs. Her sneakers are soaked through.

She says a prayer of shelter for God's creatures. A prayer of safety for TJ and Bobo, alone in that old house. A prayer of thanksgiving for the Gooley pines, for the beauty of the trees, for strength in their roots and trunks, for their long lives. Branches crack and fall to her right and her left. She can see the crowns of the Gooleys, *Tatcha na wihie Gee-ree,* slamming into each other, one way, then the other. *The voice of the Lord breaks the cedars of Lebanon, the voice of the Lord makes the oaks to whirl, and strips the forests bare; and in his temple all cry Glory.*

She wonders if the Gooley pines have lost heart, under the cruel pummeling of the wind, or if their hearts are steadfast and unwavering, in the love of the Lord.

Reverend says, *When we got trouble, that's when we learn to pray.* She says prayers, many prayers to banish fear.

She cannot see or hear with the roaring of the wind and the sideways rain, must take it on pure faith that the road is clear for her progress. A tree cracks and crashes across the road behind her. *Sheba, help me now. Jesus, watch over me.*

Now the top of the hill. The Field. The highway. Here the wind howls a new song, tears at her umbrella, yanks it inside out. She hangs on with both hands, her arms pulling out of their sockets. *This is Mama's umbrella. You will not take it.* The wind whirls it around and around above her head, wrenches it away, end over end, into Indigo Field.

Lightning flickers, reveals a wall of clouds and a terror of wind spreading from the east toward Stonehaven Downs. The highway curves like a black snake, electric poles point in crazy directions, sparks fly from power lines snapping like the devil's whip. All across the Field, whirlwinds, snaky narrow things, move in a jerky dance around each other, each one flickering with lightning. Reba quakes before them, falls to her knees. *Oh Lord. Spirits rising in Indigo Field. A great wind come and blow, and save my people. O Lucy, save me. O Sheba, give me strength for I am sore afraid.*

Her job is to keep walking. To find shelter. To find a phone. To call Jolene. Get help for her boys. Miss Reba pulls out six cans of weenie beanies, been dragging at her hip. Piles them in a pyramid by the side of the road. The wind picks them up, flings them behind her. "Get thee behind me, Satan," Reba says. The same wind catches her mother's umbrella, way across the Field, lifts it up in a whirlwind, and flings it back at her feet. She rises, picks up the umbrella, all ribs and black shreds, and the wind tears at her, almost knocks her down. It's getting dark. Across the highway the sky is a wall of demon shapes spewing rain and thunderbolts. She walks north. Lighthouse is out at Sunrise Gas, electric pole leaning over the top, sparking. Dark inside the grill, plate window cracked like a spiderweb. Is there no help to be found? She squints through the rain at the stone pillar entryway to where the Yankees live. Is that a flicker of light? There it is again. Somebody still got lights in Stonehaven Downs. Reba has lived all her life in Ambler County and she knows it would be best to knock on whitepeople's door while there is still enough light to see she is an old Black woman. Not a boogeyman coming to get you. *Dear Lord, let it be a woman opens the door. The whitemen all have guns.*

She clasps her broken umbrella to her heart and walks. Her raincoat opens like a wet sail and a powerful wind pushes from behind, like a great hand guiding her.

ॐ

At Spill Creek Farm, Jeff and Jolene lie in a tangle of goat mamas, sleeping, restless. They wake in the dark to a roar of wind and pounding rain.

Jeff rises from the straw, picks a stray piece out of her hair. Jittery flickers of lightning dance on the walls. "Sounds bad out there," he says.

"It's gotten worse," Jolene says. The lantern has gone dim. Does she have batteries? "Oh God, poor Bobo. I should call." Jolene braces herself against the rain and wind. Jeff raises his arm over her head and tries to shelter her as she runs. They make it to the kitchen door, push inside, and Jolene gets kitchen towels to wipe their faces. The house is dark. She checks the light switch. Power out. Phone might still work. She lifts the phone from the cradle. Lightning crackling on the line. She dials Reba. Nothing but crackling.

She feels her way to a drawer and rummages for a waxy stub, lights one with a match. She can hear the dripping all around her. She remembers something Reba said. "You a real farmer, Miss Jolene. Barn's tight, house leaks like a sieve."

Jolene hands the candle to Jeff, grabs some clean pots off the stove, and says, "The worst leaks are in the living room. See what you can do."

As they go from room to room, Jolene's uneasiness grows. There is no denying this is a freakishly bad storm. All spring, the farmers whispered about a "charmed year." Early corn, double cuts of hay, and even her goats produced way more than last year. Until the recent weeks of drought, the weather has been perfect. This storm breaks the charm. It will ruin everything. Her apple trees will cast their fruit, pumpkins and squash will drown in the downpour, the south field will wash out, pecans will drop, large branches will come down. She might lose trees.

While Jeff places pots and slams windows shut, she goes out to the porch, secures buckets and chairs, hooks the screen doors front and back so they won't bang off their hinges. Empty wren nest in that old boot. Poor wrens! She hopes they found a corner of the barn out of the rain.

Jeff's at the kitchen table, fiddling with the electric lantern. "I found some batteries," he says. "I think they'll fit." He pops them in the lantern. The lantern glows bright. "Hey," Jeff says, "do you have a radio? Something with batteries?"

"Bobo has one." Jolene feels her way to his room, rummages in his bedclothes, and finds the old transistor under his pillow. And what's this? Candy? Cracker packets? She lifts the crinkly square up next to the window for a lightning flash to illumine. *Can't be. Is.*

She confirms with her thumb, the circle of rubber, the smooth center. Bobo has been keeping a condom under his pillow. From TJ? Lord have mercy. Jeff has been using condoms—when they remember. Maybe he left a stash someplace and Bobo found it. A bolt of lightning slams into the pecan tree outside the window and drops her to her knees.

"Jolene!" She can hear Jeff calling her name, she can feel him putting arms around her, she can feel him lifting her onto the bed and covering her with Bobo's quilt. "You're okay," she hears him say. *Mouth tingling. Hands numb. Bobo's scared of lightning. Bobo is at Reba's.* Her mouth forms a word: *Bobo.*

Jeff touches her lips with his fingers. "I know," he says. "Bobo is safe with Reba. Don't worry about Bobo. My God, are you all right?"

She can still move her arms. She points to the floor where the radio dropped.

"Yeah, I see it." She hears him click it on. "Dead," he says. She still has the crinkly packet in her other hand. She lifts it up, lets her numb fingers fall open.

"What's this?" he says. "Oh. Really?"

Jolene moves her lips and this time words come out. "Bobo," she whispers. "It's Bobo's."

Jeff sets up a safe place under the stairs—sofa cushions, furniture, making a wall around them, a tarp, some apples, the electric lamp, and the candle stub in a jelly jar. He helps Jolene there, lays her down, covers her, then lies down beside her. "Try to sleep, Jo, we'll get Bobo when it's safe, I promise." Her whole body is shivering. No way to make a hot drink to warm her up. He strips her, takes off his clothes, and piles the blankets over the both of them, rubbing her back and chest and arms until the shivering stops and she starts to warm and then finally sleeps.

Jeff feels her heat against him and wraps his arms tighter around her. The candle flickers with strange darting drafts. Rain pounds like fists on the roof. He secured the tarps in the Field as best he could. But this storm will rip them off and fling them to the sky. Wind howls through the leaky doors and windows like a yard full of coyotes trying to get in.

Thank goodness Bobo is with Reba. He wonders if Dad is okay.

లు

TJ is slightly fucked up. That clear is strong. He shoves Bobo's pack over so he can lie down and use it as a pillow. There is something in there hard as a lump of iron. "Hey, what's this?" TJ pokes it with his fist.

Bobo turns away from the window. Looks at the pack. "Sec-wet," Bobo says. He pulls the drawstring, reaches in. "See?" he says.

It's a gun.

"Holy shit," TJ says. "Let me see that."

Bobo hands it over.

TJ feels the weight, points it out the window, rests one finger on the trigger. It's completely dark outside now, except for the lightning, flickering like a strobe on the cedar statues in the yard. He holds it up to the candle. "Bersa. That's a good one." His finger slips. The Bersa fires. He drops the gun.

Bobo screeches, puts his hands over his ears.

"Holy shit," TJ says.

"Like Wambo," Bobo says.

TJ looks around. What did he shoot? The bird's still alive. Bobo's still alive. *Holy crap.* What if Reba walked in just now? He feels like he's going to throw up. "Where the hell did you get this?" TJ says. "Bobo, you can't just carry around a loaded pistol."

Bobo rocks a little. "Uh-oh, uh-oh."

"Listen, little buddy, you didn't know. Let me just take the bullets out. Holy shit." Jesus, he is a little more cranked than he thought. His fingers are shaking. First, get the bullets out. Then hide it somewhere. Don't tell Reba. She'll bust him so bad. One, two, three bullets. He sets them carefully on the floor. The candle flickers. Two more to go. Bobo's eyes popping out. He looks like Rambo in the jungle. *Man, you are tripping out.* Thunder cracks next to his ear, just outside. The candle falls over and goes out.

"Mama!" Bobo yells.

"It's okay, Bobo! I'll fix it." Bobo hates the dark. TJ sets the gun down. He pulls a pack of matches out of his pocket. Snaps one, holds it up. "See?" He crawls around, looking for the candle.

Bobo rocks and whimpers. The match goes out.

TJ lights another match. Heads to the pantry. He thought he saw another candle in there on the shelf. Herb bundles hang over his head, brush against his face like spiderwebs. He feels along the cans and Mason jars with his fingers. There. A candle. One of those little tiny ones. Light it. Put it on a plate. Better see how Bobo's doing.

Bobo is crouched on the floor, looking at the open gun chamber, trying to see the bullets inside. But here's a new sound. A trickling sound. Above his head. TJ looks up.

CRACK. The room turns white. TJ's arms fly out. His head jerks back. He falls to the floor, and it's like sparks are flying off his fingers and toes. Inside his head, there are fireworks but they're all white and in slo-mo. *So this is what it's like,* TJ thinks, *getting struck by lightning.* Like being tased. Kids at school did that once. *You can't move,* they said. *You just lie there tingling.* Does it hurt? *It hurts like hell.*

He can't see Bobo. He can't see anything but what's right before his eyes: Lucy's jar spilling to the floor, the candle falling right into that puddle of clear, where there is suddenly more flickering yellow light than just one candle would make.

TJ can feel the rain. It's cold. All over his face. "Wha—th' hell?"

"TJ!" Bobo yells. That big round face shining over him, big smile flashing black and white in the storm. TJ tries to smile back. He's lying in the mud out in the yard, soaked and burned and fried by lightning, a hurry-cane coming, and his little buddy is just happy he's alive. How'd he get here? The house behind them shooting flames out of the roof. Smoke everywhere. Bobo must have got him out. "Bobo," he groans, "you are something else."

Lightning cracks over their heads. The old sycamore tree splits in half. *Holy Fuck Shit Jesus.*

Bobo yells, "Mama!" and crouches to the ground.

TJ rolls to his side and tries to get up. Falls back down. Catches his breath. Everything hurts. His head, chest, feet, arms, hair. *Dear Jesus please let me get up please let me get up. I promise I promise please.* Jesus answers: *You are in big damn trouble. This ain't no foolin' around. You gotta be a man. Your daddy couldn't hack it but you can.*

"We gotta get out of here!" he yells over the wind. "To the chicken shed!" He tries to get up, falls again. Tries to crawl. Lightning flickers all over those freaky angels. Danielle looks like she's screaming. One of them has fallen over. The one with the sword is looking straight at him, her wings shaking like they want to fly up into the sky.

"Help, Bobo!"

Bobo kneels in the mud, hooks his arms under TJ's shoulders. Stands up. Drags TJ across the yard in the pouring rain like a sack of goat feed.

In the shed, the chickens have piled up in the corner, their heads tucked under their wings. TJ knows just how they feel. He's cold, so cold. He wants to get into the pile of chickens. But he can't get up. "Bobo," he says, his teeth chattering. "Get some straw and put it on me." His voice sounds hoarse and feels like his throat is burnt a little. Like he had too much to smoke. *Maybe this is how the devil feels, after a long day in hell.*

Bobo pulls down a bale. Cuts the string with his pocketknife. *See, everybody has a pocketknife.* Bobo pulls the bale apart into flakes, stacks the flakes around TJ, then balances one on top. Now he fluffs some up. Puts it all around. Bobo knows how to make a straw house.

Now TJ's brain is singing a nursery rhyme: *Three blind mice, three blind mice. See how they run. See how they run.* Those are all the words he knows. They run over and over in his brain. Shouldn't it be three little pigs? He's in a straw house inside a wood house. This barn is made of solid oak, Reba told him once, and it's shaking like a leaf. Reba has a brick house. Had. The damn wolf is blowing them all down.

There's a loud buzzing sound, like a chainsaw, on the roof.

Bobo doesn't seem afraid anymore. Maybe the lightning jacked the scared right out of him.

It's so cold. TJ wonders if his hair has turned white. Aunt Reba said that happened to a cousin of hers. Funny to think of a Black person's hair sticking straight out, white. Would all your hair turn white or just where the lightning went in? He looks at the hairs on his arm. Too dark to see them. His arm is bleeding through a hole burned in his shirt. He touches a hole in his arm half an inch deep. It doesn't hurt. Why doesn't it hurt?

Daddy told him about this. He's in shock or hyper-something. You get it if you go hunting and get wet and you can't get warm. You have to get dry first. You have to take your clothes off. Daddy told him about a guy who killed a horse, then crawled inside the guts to keep warm. Or maybe that was in English class. Truth is, his daddy never told him any stories. TJ only pretends he did. *If you don't have a horse, you need dry clothes. You need to build a fire.* Like that story in school the teacher read to them last year. The guy finally builds a fire and the snow falls out of a tree and puts it out. Don't think about that. It's fucking getting colder.

The wind is getting louder. He can hear loud thumps in the yard. *What the Jesus happened to Reba? Damn Jesus Hell.* TJ's heart sinks, then he focuses it the way Danielle taught him. He closes his eyes, thinks about Reba, and he can feel that she is okay. She might be cold, or scared, but she is hanging tough. She is more powerful than this storm. Dang, he has burned down her house with candles and clear. She will never forgive him. He wonders if Reba is blood kin. That would mean he is Black, or she is white, or something like that. They do seem to be related in some crazy way. He is starting to doze off. Are you supposed to doze off or not? Probably not. Like that guy who fell asleep in the snow. It feels good. But you're screwed if you do.

Bobo brings more straw, fluffs it all around him. TJ's arms and legs feel like ice cubes. You're supposed to take off wet clothes, then roll up in a blanket. You have to lie next to another person. Naked. Bobo? That would be weird. You have to do things to stay alive. "Bobo?" he rasps.

Bobo crouches next to him. "Yeh?"

"Bobo, get us a blanket. Dry blanket. Or towel. Or something. Then come lie down." TJ has no idea where Bobo will get a blanket. The house has probably burned completely down by now. He could get a piece of cinder and build a fire. *You can't build a fire in a chicken shed, all the chickens would burn up. You'd be out in the rain again. But you'd have barbecue chicken!* TJ laughs to himself and shivers. He must not be all that bad off if he can make a joke. He starts to pull off his shoes, wet socks, wet jeans, but it's too hard. He has to stop and catch his breath.

"Okay, okay, okay." Bobo nods. He looks cold too. But he always has that damn blue windbreaker on, so maybe he's a little bit dry under there. *Just get under the straw with me,* TJ thinks. His lips have gone numb. *It's warm under the straw.*

Bobo peers at TJ. TJ has gone to sleep. He needs a blanket. There is a blanket in the house. There is fire in the house. Mama would be mad if he went there. But TJ is hurt. What would Rambo do? He would get the blanket.

The wind knocks him down. He stumbles. Knee hurt! Don't be a baby. He gets up. He puts his arms over his head and runs.

The front door is open. The fire has gone away. But it's dark inside.

The floor is wet. Rain is coming in. Bobo goes to Reba's bedroom. Her bed is dry. He pulls the quilt. It's big. It will keep TJ warm. How do you keep it dry when it is raining outside? He could put it in his backpack. It's in the living room. On the floor. Lightning flickers through the hole in the ceiling. *Mama!* He sees the gun. What would Rambo do? Bobo picks the gun up, puts it in his windbreaker pocket. Zips it closed. TJ likes the gun. He will give it to TJ as a present when he wakes up.

Bobo runs to the shed, pulls the straw back, sees TJ is naked. Like a little bird in his nest. Blue vein in his neck. TJ is skinny! He can see his ribs. He can see his chicken neck. His lips look blue. Bobo pokes TJ. TJ is cold. Pull the quilt on TJ, tuck it in under his chin. Get in beside him. Pull straw on top. There is a sound like broken glass. A chicken flies across the room and lands on the quilt. Another one. White chickens. He counts them. Twelve. Lucky number! It is like angels coming to watch over them. Reba likes angels, she says they are all around. So many chickens come over they are like a feather blanket. Bobo smiles. He snuggles next to TJ. It is getting warmer. It is a miracle, like Reba says, from the Bible.

47

In the darkness that is Ambler County, dams on farm ponds sag. Rain seeps into them from above, claws at them from below, swells their bellies, digs small rills that become crevices, that become ditches, and now the full collapse, washing whole herds of Black Angus and dairy cows downstream, carrying them into the forks of trees, and down into creeks and rivers. The wind howls up a notch or two, and every worm, beetle, and fly can feel the pressure drop, liquid expanding in their tissues, swelling the soft places, making them slow and stupid. Deer raise their heads from deep sleep in their dry thickets, sense the water rising, stumble with their young to crossing places, see they are trapped. The brave ones plunge into the creek, heads bobbing, eyes rolling, bodies caught in the currents, this one snagged on an underwater branch, that one making it to the thicket on the other side. A doe looks back. Her fawn bleats. She calls to it. It will not come. She steps into the water, calls again.

At Spill Creek Farm, a fox emerges from her flooded den, two kits clinging to the fur on her back. She heads for the hollow sycamore tree on the Ridge, where jays sometimes roost. On a sunny day, the jays would *jeer jeer jeer* and fly at an intruder. They do not complain now, though, when the fox curls at the bottom with her brood tucked in at her belly. They shift their wings and dig their claws in tighter to the knobs and ledges inside the trunk. They know this tree like blood kin. This tree could use a warming at the root.

Downed trees along the Cedar River now rise with the rising water, float into the main stream. Matchstick pines, old sycamores, split oak trees—they tangle and weave, make a kind of battering ram that comes careening over the old dam and into the bridge abutment. Cement pilings shake but stand firm. Tree limbs and branches build and weave until a beaver could not have done a better job: a dam. Water swirls over the banks on the north side. Then the south side. Then creeps up the cliffs at the Gooley Ridge.

At the top of the Ridge, the giant pines bend and groan. Their crowns screech and rasp against each other like the riggings of old ships. A gust catches in the head of the tallest one—a four-hundred-year-old monarch, twenty-three feet around. Too big to snap. It has lost its crown before and come back witchy and scant. It is the younger trees, the ones with fat crowns and thick branches, that catch the wind, billowing like sails, straining to turn the mast, twisting tons of bark and cambium and dense heartwood. Their anchors cannot hold; soft earth gives along the edges of surface roots. Taproots strain, stretch, break. One tree gives way. As it falls full weight, its crown tangles with sister trees and they tumble alongside. Forty trees in a sweep. The pile of trunks makes a barricade twenty feet tall. The sharp points of the crowns plunge five, ten feet into the earth. The wind shouts triumph.

The deadfall makes a wall. The wall softens the wind. The rest of the pines will stand.

Miss Reba Jones follows the faint flare of light past the grand stone columns into Stonehaven Downs. Pine needles, leaves, sticks, and acorns tear at her raincoat, bounce off her face and hair. Rain blinds her. She feels her way, palming a stone column, then a tree, then another tree, then she gets caught in shrubbery snagging and tearing at her. A pine tree falls thud just behind her. She falls to her knees. There is no longer any light. Panic rises. But there it is. The glimmer. She reaches out to push herself from the ground. Her hand finds stone. Dip in the middle. A place to grind corn. *Lucy is here.* She uses her mother's umbrella to press up from the ground. She sees it clearly now, as clearly as she can through smeary glasses: a square window of light. A step up to a porch. Her fingers find carved raised panels, her hand feels for a knob. *Lord have mercy.* Yes. It is a door. *Dear Lord,* she prays, *don't let the one who answers this door pull out a gun and shoot me.*

The colonel has lit candles in the kitchen, the living room, the bathroom. The flickering shadows in the corners look like someone watching. It's as if any minute Anne might walk in and catch him at her elegant table eating beans out of a can. He puts the can down, half finished, spoon sticking up. At least he had the grace to use a cloth napkin. *This is what it has come to, Anne, your dream of dinner parties: blazing candle stubs in whiskey glasses, an open can of beans, and a color-coordinated cloth napkin.*

One of Anne's candles is made of two ribbons of wax, one red, one white, twisted around each other. That one's dripping all over the note he wrote, and the tablecloth. He's ruined it. He ruins everything. How to make this feeling go away? It doesn't seem it ever will.

There's that knocking again. Just ignore it.

Now there's a sound like a woman's voice. A wailing sound. Rand cannot bear it. Some Xanax, Anne's old prescription, will calm him.

He picks up a candle, trudges down the hall to the bathroom, the flame flickering creepily on the walls. He gets a chill between his shoulder blades, as if someone's waiting for him in the dark shadowed place beyond the candle's light. Anne? Not Anne. Ma? He pulls the prescription bottle out of the medicine cabinet. Puts two on his tongue. He dry-swallows, slips the bottle in his pocket. Back to the dining room for a swallow of scotch. Turns out he likes scotch. The only booze left in the house, a bottle given by his father-in-law twenty years ago. Anniversary present. He found it while packing Anne's soup tureen.

What a swath of colored light, those candles, lit as if for a party! Twelve empty chairs, waiting for ghosts to fill them. Ma. Pa. Probably Decker. Anne at the head. A shadowy place next to her where there is a young boy, made of his own flesh. A boy who would be fifteen now. A boy who was torn apart before he could stand or run. *Anne, what if I could come and see you? Tell you I'm sorry? The kids will be fine. Please, Anne.* He feels a warmth in his chest, takes it for a sign. Reaches into his pocket. Empties the bottle into his mouth, letting a few spill to the floor. Doesn't matter. He washes them down with scotch. The wind is making a keening sound now, like a banshee flying through the air.

It's time to go outside. Meet his fate.

There's a smart rap at the living room window. Rand jumps up so hard the chair falls over. He squints at the black glass. Goes for a closer look, candle in hand. His own pale face flickers, reflected in the glass. Beyond that, suddenly lit by lightning, is an apparition. A hooded face. A dark cloak. A raised fist, shaking a ragged stick.

Christ on toast. If this is Death, it is time to let Him in.

Rand walks unsteadily to the door. Unbolts it. Rain blasts his face, his candle blows out. Barely visible in the giant shadow cast by his body, there's a wide Black face, with a white plastic bag puffed over the head like a football helmet, cheeks streaming water, mouth open. A shredded black umbrella, tattered in the wind. It's a woman, a Black woman, squinting at him through glasses slipping down her nose. A crazy woman, to be out in this storm.

Rand steps back. His shadow recedes. The woman's face glitters with jittering candlelight. A gust of wind blows out half the candles on the table. The woman peers at him in the dim flickering, steadies herself on the doorframe, steps inside. Closes the door, firmly, against the storm. Shakes out her umbrella. Looks around the room.

"Where is your wife?" she says.

As if she knows Anne is in here somewhere. As if she has just come for a little visit.

ॐ

Whiteman stands before her, mouth open. Miss Reba's glasses fog over. She can't see his face. She does not feature spending a storm like this alone with a whiteman. Every one of them has a gun. Every one of them has a grudge. There must be a woman in this house somewhere.

"Where is your wife?" she says again. The man stares at her, hands raised as if expecting attack.

"I thought—I thought you—she's gone," he croaks, she can barely hear him over the high whine of the wind. She watches the whiteman stumble backward, sit down hard in a chair, put his hands over his ears. Something bad wrong with this whiteman.

Candles burning on a long table. Lots of candles. Colored candles. Bottles. Bottles and glasses and the smell of hard liquor like Satan's own perfume.

She can't see. She can read a whiteman like a book, but she's got to be able to see him in the face. In the eyes. Why is he sitting there, head in his hands? Is he drunk? Afraid? Does he think she's the boogey man? *Lord, Lord.* She is wet to the bone. Can't a whiteman get a woman a towel?

"Need to dry off," Miss Reba says. "I come a long way."

Whiteman gropes on the table and holds out a pink bit of fluff. Little prissy party napkin. She's seen those at church teas for brides, but she's never seen a grown man touch one. A woman's touch is in this home. But where is the woman? Something tightens in her belly. *You testing me, Lord? You saved me through a storm to put me in a room all alone with a crazy whiteman?*

Miss Reba takes her glasses off, wipes them carefully, two, three wipes, then opens the napkin and swipes it over her face, her hair, and the back of her neck, where water still trickles down from her plastic-bag hat. The napkin is a nub of pink. She places it on the table, puts her glasses back on. Still smeary. But she can see.

Whiteman pouring another drink. Sneaking a look at her. Oh yes, just what is needed, a *drunk* crazy whiteman. Can of beans on the table.

Glass of drink making a ring. A wife would not allow all this drunkenness and mess in the middle of a storm. *There is no wife.*

She can see him better now. It is the whiteman who dented her car. Yes, the Lord is testing her. She never counted on the way in. But this must be the third house on the left. This is The General.

Sheba, help me now. Jesus Lord, stand by me. Somebody needs to take control, and it sure ain't going to be this drunk whiteman ran into my car.

Miss Reba pulls the plastic bag off her head, tucks it in her pocket, looks around for a better clue to this whiteman's state of mind. Man slumped over his drink. Not even looking. And what is this? Scattered on the table? Little pills. And there on the floor? Pill bottle and more pills flung across the carpet like colored beans between the legs of a fallen-over chair. She picks up the chair, settles it in place. She picks up the bottle. Pulls off her glasses. Reads the label, squinting. She closes her eyes. She is so tired, so very tired, of whitemen.

She opens her eyes and glares at the man, who is finally paying attention. Looking at her. Guilt all over his face. Fear. Rich whiteman made some plans to leave this world. If he leaves this world, there will be no help for her. She will be left with a dead whiteman laying on the floor. *Oh no you don't.*

A feeling flies into her arms and legs like electricity, like Sheba power. How dare this rich whiteman take pills and drink and make a mess of his life! How dare he never pay what is due. *Ninety dollars to fix my car. Best be afraid, rich whiteman. Best be afraid of the wrath of Lucy. Jesus no help to you now.* Something outside falls with a thunderous roar. The house shakes. Another giant pine has fallen in the driveway.

Whiteman turns to the sound, rises, unsteady on his feet.

"Lissen here!" she calls out to the man. She pounds her umbrella tip into the thick rug to get his attention. He turns his head and stares. "You been drinkin' and took all these pills?"

"I—I—" The man opens his mouth but nothing much comes out. He sits back down and puts his face back in his hands. "I don't feel well," he croaks.

An eerie creaking sound rises over the wind. Reba ignores it. All she feels is a storm of rage inside her, as if a charge of electricity is moving through her arms and legs, as if the Word of the Lord is speaking them into motion. *TJ caught on the other side of the creek, Bobo with him, Sheba dead, Danielle dead, Lucy dead, Gooley pines in danger, foxes in their dens running for their lives, birds and bugs and deer running for their lives, wrath of God in a wall of clouds, bones rising in the Field, trees falling all around, and this rich whiteman is playing with his life. Planning his escape. On my time. Planning to die right in front of me and leave me with a whiteman body in the only shelter I got right now. They will blame me.*

Rage rises from her belly to her heart, from her heart to her throat, and from her throat to her mouth until she must give it voice. "Oh no, you don't!" Miss Reba says. "Oh no, you don't! Lord help me, you coming with me." She strides to the whiteman, yanks him to his feet by the arm, and shoves her hand into his shoulder until he heads toward the kitchen, unresisting.

She holds his head over the sink, her wet hands deep in his short bristly hair. "Now," she says, "put a finger down that throat, or so help me, I'll be doing it myself."

Whiteman becomes docile in her hands. He tilts his head to one side, reaches into his mouth, and retches. He does it again. Then again, and the spray of pills and scotch and undigested beans covers the almond porcelain and again he vomits and again.

She lets go of his head.

Whiteman grips the counter with both hands and then lifts one. Wipes his chin with it, wipes his hand on his shirt. Stands to face his tormentor. Voice all shaky. "Who are you?" he croaks. "Who—are—you?"

"I am Miss Ruby Queen Esther Jones," she says, folding her arms over her bosom. "People call me Miss Reba. Now get me a towel, and get one for you. We going to weather this storm. Lord willing."

The colonel stands before her, stricken. So this is Miss Reba Jones. *Christ on toast, has she come to have her revenge?* It doesn't seem so. She has, after all, just tried to save his life, though she was none too gentle about it. He stares at her, finally sees a person. A person with wet, sweating skin, crooked black glasses, and a sopping raincoat. Not a batwing creature come out of the storm to torment him.

Something in the confidence of her voice is familiar, comforting. Rand meekly takes a candle and goes to the linen closet. Icy water drops on his head, slips down his neck. He looks up and gets a splat of water in his eye. *Hell.* There's a leak in the hallway ceiling. But the towels in the closet are still dry. He lifts an armload. His throat stings with acid and booze. *My God, he lost all judgment swallowing those pills. The kids would have got nothing if those insurance sharks saw pills. What was he thinking?*

He wasn't thinking.

And this Black lady came out of the storm like a banshee and caught him at it. What in the world is she doing here in Stonehaven? Miss Reba Jones lives on Field Road. Is she somebody's maid? But all the live-in maids in Stonehaven are Mexican. Is she some geezer's nurse? Now, that's entirely possible. Some geezer has croaked, or needs help, or she was heading home and got stuck in the storm. She must be pretty tough, or pretty desperate, to walk through this. With that shock of white hair, Miss Reba Jones is at least eighty years old.

He's more sober now than he's been all day. And he's a little afraid to walk back into the living room. This Reba person has manhandled him in his own house, taken control, forced him to vomit in his own kitchen sink. It's the kind of thing a nurse would do. Or an MP. Part of him bridles at the thought of what she did. Pushing him. Watching him get sick. It was so…intimate. And part of him is amazed at her guts.

Something batters the roof above his head. A new sound. He isn't as drunk as he was. He isn't as afraid. She's just an ordinary woman, a Black woman, a nurse. She did what any nurse would do in such a situation. With this conviction firmly in his head, Rand marches back into the living room with his load of towels.

Miss Reba stands dripping in the dining room, gazing about her. She has not even taken off her coat. From down the dark corridor of the back hall, King P screeches bloody murder. Miss Reba suddenly looks stricken and small in her black dress and sneakers, like some kind of waterbird, feathers smeared with oil and tar from a terrible accident. Black eyes snapping behind those glasses, defiant. "What's that?" she says.

"Don't mind that. It's just my bird. I've got him in a cage. He won't bother you."

Miss Reba looks like she doubts that very much. She shivers and clutches at her coat.

Where are his manners? "Please," he says, reaching for her raincoat. "Let me take it. You must be soaked through." He places the stack of towels on the dining room table.

She hooks her rib-sprung umbrella on a chair. Takes her coat off slowly, heavily. Hands it over. He holds it in his arms and sees finally that it's filthy, casting off leaves and twigs, and it is strangely weighted and lumpy in the pockets. He walks to the closet, gets a hanger. If he hangs it up with the rest of the coats, it will ruin whatever it's next to.

Anne's Sunday coat. His London Fog. He forgot to pack those. He doesn't want to mess them up. Rand slips the filthy raincoat onto a hanger, then places the hanger on the hook on the back of the closet door.

Miss Reba Jones has not moved from the spot.

"Please," he says. "Take a towel."

She pulls the top towel from the pile. "I need dry clothes," she says.

"I don't think I have any—" She will never fit into Anne's clothes. And anyway, they're all packed in plastic bags. What to do? He sees she is trembling. "I'll find you something. I'll be right back."

"You got a way to make hot tea?"

"No," he says. "Power's out." Isn't it obvious?

"I got Sterno in my coat pocket."

Ahh, those lumps.

"You get the Sterno," she says. "I'll get the clothes."

He watches her pick up a candle and a towel and head down the hallway to his bedroom, his closet, his bathroom, King P screeching an intruder warning. Whatever she finds packed in big plastic bags are things he does not need. He will rummage her pockets for Sterno and light one with a match. He will make some tea, just like English colonials in Singapore, with their sugar tongs and bone china. The antidote for any stressful situation. Where moments ago the whole house seemed fraught with terrors, the room now seems strangely companionable, despite the howling of the wind and the dark shadows flickering on the walls.

He hums a little as he brings out the Sterno, the cups, the teabags, and a small pot and places them on the kitchen island. What else does he need? Oh yes, a fondue stand to set the pot on. Somewhere in the pantry.

"There you are."

He turns and sees she has put on an enormous woolen bathrobe zipped up the front, something Anne ordered that came in the wrong size. Anne used to wear it anyway, dwarfed in its folds, drinking tea in the window seat and looking like a refugee wrapped in a blanket. "I like it fine this way," Anne had said.

It had once irritated him to no end that she'd been too disorganized or busy or distracted to find the label to send it back. He'd give anything now to see her sitting in that enormous robe again, freckled and big-eyed as a child.

"Ready in a minute," he says, lighting the Sterno and pouring a bottle of Aquafina into the teakettle. "Have a seat." He puts out two porcelain teacups and saucers and places some ginger snaps on a plate.

The wind has died down to a low moan. "Storm's passing," Miss Reba says. "It'll be coming back. Stronger than before."

"You think so?" Rand hears his own voice echoing oddly in the room. Her voice sounds confident. His voice sounds small.

"Phone still work?" Miss Reba says. "I got to make a call."

He pulls the cell out of his pocket. No tone. "Tower must be down," he says.

"What about that one?" She points to the wall phone.

He picks up the handset. Nope, dead.

"Cord phone might work. Old style phone. Got its own electric. You got one of those?"

Rand nods. Of course. Why didn't he think of that? Carrie had a pink princess rotary phone when she was a girl. He remembers boxing it up in the guest room. "Be right back," he says.

There is something suddenly right about Miss Reba Jones being here. Things are falling into place with an unexpected clarity. It does not occur to him that he is taking orders, a habit of motion ingrained in him since his first days in boot camp. Since being Decker's little brother.

Rand grabs a candle, takes the stairs two at a time, finds the phone in a box, tucks it under his arm, and brings it back down in triumph.

"Let's plug this baby in," he says, placing it on the counter. Hot pink princess phone, a silly toy from the seventies. Who knows, maybe it will work. He lifts the receiver. Static, more static, then a clear, low tone barely discernible under the static. "Hey!" he says. He extends the receiver to her. "There's a tone."

Miss Reba listens, then begins to dial a ten-digit number. "Speak to the sheriff?" she says. "This is Miss Reba Jones." She listens for a bit. "I know you got troubles. But lissen here. Storm's about to break for a while. You got to get the sheriff over to my house. TJ and Bobo there alone, road's flooded in."

She shakes her head, listening to the response.

"No, ma'am. You got just a little while. You got to get out there with that fancy new helicopter. That child Bobo and that child TJ there all alone. You got to do it now, gonna be a break in the storm, you tell sheriff I said he's got to go.

"Address? Just tell him Miss Reba Jones.... He knows where I live...."

No, I ain't there. I'm stuck over here in Stonehaven.... What's that? I can't hear you.... Just tell him. You hear me? Hello?"

Miss Reba holds the phone out away from her ear, shakes it a few times, puts it back to her ear, shakes her head and drops it on the cradle. "Well," she says. "It's gone."

"Your children?" Rand says. "They're stuck in the storm?" He dimly remembers a large boy named Bobo, a friend of Jeff's. Surely there can't be two Bobos around here. But the big boy was white.

"Yessir. My children." Reba nods, closes her eyes. She sees the boys. Scared, scared. She says a prayer. TJ is alive. So far. She can see his face pale and drawn surrounded by white angel feathers. *No, you don't, Jesus. That's Danielle's boy.*

She looks up at Rand. "Where your people at? You here all alone."

Rand blinks. My people? The image of the Tobacco Shed filled with people like him flashes through his mind—birds of a feather, flocked together, drinking like fishes. But she means family. My God, what about family? He hasn't even thought to worry about Jeff.

"My son Jeff is out there," he says, his voice a little shaky. "Somewhere. He's been camping out in Indigo Field."

"You say Jeff? Jeff who work in the Field?"

"Yes, that's right." Rand is surprised. "You know him?"

"Nice young man," Reba says. "Smart too. He's with my neighbor, Jolene. Bobo's mama."

"Bobo." The big boy with birds on his arms, laughing. He's never met the mother. Jolene. A mountain name, like a country song. A West Virginia name.

"Jeff has a girlfriend?" He can't believe it. Wouldn't the boy have told him? *Well, no.* Jesus, this Black woman knows his family better than he does. She knows his son.

"Oh yes, oh yes, indeed." Miss Reba squints at him.

"What?" Rand says.

"You Miss Anne's husband? Lord, Lord." Miss Reba sees it now. The General had a wife. She isn't here because she's dead. Whiteman looks like he been struck ill.

"Yes," he says. "Anne." The name twists like candle wax in his heart. A waft of her perfume, the one called "Happy," floats in the air. "You *knew* her? How?" Rand's back prickles with fear again. *Christ Almighty.* Was Miss Reba Jones some kind of spirit come to torment him after all?

"Farmers' market," she says. "She bought my flowers." *She come at the end of the day and bought all my flowers like she knew I needed the money.*

"She used to bring home buckets of flowers," he says. *Daisy and larkspur, zinnia and black-eyed Susan and sunflower with grasses and weeds mixed in.* "I never knew where she got them exactly. I thought she had a friend with a garden."

"I guess she did," Miss Reba says. "I guess she did." Miss Reba sips her tea. Pours some sugar in. "She was a friend to me. But she always paid. Sometimes she paid extra. Seemed to like doing that." That freckled face, that wispy blonde hair, those zebra-stripe glasses with crinkly blue eyes, smiling. A loving heart. Arms sweeping up those flowers and laughing with pure pleasure. *Fifty dollars for them all,* she would say, like she was driving a hard bargain, when she was really saving Reba from going home empty-handed, with a load of flowers she'd have to throw away.

"Your Jeff look just like her," Reba says.

Whiteman sits, hollow-eyed, arms hanging by his side.

"I miss her so much," he croaks. "But the truth is, the truth is I made her miserable. I hated it here so much. What in God's name have I done? What in God's name...." His shoulders shake.

Miss Reba watches the whiteman cry. No wonder he was drinking and taking pills. Man is a mess. She can feel Miss Anne in the room, watching, sad. Miss Anne who came to call on her when Danielle got killed. Brought flowers. Armfuls of them. All from her own garden, or a friend's.

Spirits rise in a storm. The bigger the storm, the more they rise.

"She seemed happy to me," Miss Reba says.

"She wasn't," Rand says. "She said—she said I was...like the Ancient Mariner. Always telling my story of woe at the bridal party."

Miss Reba has never heard that one. But she knows what's going on. "Her spirit rising," she says. "That's what you feel. We got to pray, set her to rest." She points. "In there."

She walks to the dining room table, pulls out a chair, and kneels down before it. She looks up at him, nods at the other chair. "We got to pray for your boy too. Out in the flood. I can see it. They all in bad trouble. He and Bobo and TJ and Jolene. Sheriff ain't coming. We got to pray."

Rand sinks to his knees and rests his elbows on the chair. Puts his head on his folded hands. He hasn't prayed since he was a boy, other than mouthing words in church on special occasions. Weddings. Funerals. He remembers praying with his brother, on their knees beside the bed, elbows on his mother's counterpane, which smelled like fresh balsam fir, having aired in the sun for a day. *Now I lay me down to sleep, I pray the Lord my soul to keep. If I should die before I wake, I pray the Lord my soul to take. Ayy-men.*

Another loud thud, the house shakes beneath his knees. Close. The booze that has cushioned fear has completely washed out of his brain. A prickly awareness has replaced it, a sense of danger all around. He sees it clearly now. It won't be at all surprising if he dies tonight. Or if Jeff does. This is a terrible storm, an extraordinary storm. He is suddenly very afraid. He feels Anne's slim hand on his cheek, turning his head so he must look her in the eye: *How could you let your son die in this storm?* He is down on his knees, afraid, sobs caught like something clawing his throat. *Anne, forgive me. God forgive me. Jeff out in this. With some girlfriend I don't even know. I have screwed up everything and now I'm going to die. Don't let me die without ever knowing my son.*

Across from him Miss Reba Jones is praying out loud and calling on the Lord, her eyes squeezed closed, as if she knows Him personally. She is praying for TJ, for Bobo, for Jolene, and for his son. Now she is praying for Rand. "Put your grace on this whiteman who took me in and sheltered me in the storm, put your blessing on him, O Lord." She opens one eye. "What's your name?" she hisses.

"Rand." My God, the woman knows his whole life, his whole heart, and he hasn't told her his name.

She closes her eyes again. Rand can hear her prayer like a new note of low music under the moan of the storm. "Put your blessing on this man Rand, keep him sheltered in this storm, bless him and keep him and make your face to shine upon him. Forgive him his sins. Bring the blessing of his wife Anne. Give him peace."

Peace.

The word seems to hang in the air. The quiet suddenly flooding the room seems to flow entirely from his heart. Rand wipes his eyes and lifts his head warily. The wind has stilled. Moonlight floods through the window. The eye of the storm has come.

Bobo wakes up in a house of straw. He used to make a straw playhouse with Ace. But where is Ace? Ace is in heaven. He has Usen now. Where is Usen? Usen is under the porch. "*Useh!*"

TJ is right here. Chickens on top of the straw like a big white quilt. Pink bird on his head. Poking his hair. *Get up, get up.* But TJ is sleeping.

The wind has stopped. Storm over? Bobo pushes the straw away, sits up. The moon is shining on them, and on TJ, and on the pink bird, and on the silvery feathers of chickens. He can see TJ's face in the moonlight. TJ's eyes are closed. His hair is different. He touches TJ's head. Silver hair.

Bobo pulls himself out from under the quilt. Something hard in his pocket bangs at his hip. Lucky gun. Bobo goes outside to see the moon. There's the moon! A big smile on her face. Storm over! Around it, so many stars! Millions of stars! He wants to count them. He wants to shout. It is so pretty. So quiet you can hear crickets. And running water. Soaking into the ground. Papa said after a storm the ground drinks water, you can hear it sipping.

Lots of branches in the yard. Two big trees fell. The big one where the bees live. Reba's house still there. Where is Reba? Bobo is hungry. Where is Usen? He wants Mama. Where is Mama?

Bobo goes back in the barn to tell TJ. "Stom ovah!" TJ doesn't move. "TJ, get up! Stom ovah! Come see! Stahs!"

He pokes TJ. TJ joking? "TJ!" He pokes harder. TJ doesn't move. Bobo puts the back of his hand on TJ's forehead like Mama does when he is sick. TJ's skin feels cold. When Ace went to heaven he was like this. Not moving. You could pick up his foot and drop it and it would fall. Bobo picks up TJ's arm. Drops it. Blood on his arm. A hole there. "TJ hut! Mama!" Mama is at home. Where is Reba? Reba is gone to the store.

Mama says when you are hurt, come find me. Bobo pets TJ on his silvery hair with just one finger. "Don't worry, TJ," he says. "I get Mama."

Bobo unzips his right pocket. There is always Juicy Fruit in there. He leaves one for TJ if he wakes up. He tells the chickens to cover up. They move over. They are like a big lumpy white blanket over the straw, over TJ.

Bobo walks to the old farm road, just two tracks and grass in the middle. This is the way Mama comes, the back way, shortcut through the woods, over the creek. Where is his pink bird? "Pia!" he calls. The pink bird flutters up and follows.

The moonlight shines on the farm road, a million leaves fallen and silvery green. Bobo shuffles his feet in the leaves. TJ is hurt! He shuffles faster. When he walked on this road before, it was always with Ace. He pretends Ace is walking beside him. Shuffling the leaves.

White flash in the woods. Ace! Ace knows the way. He runs to the creek crossing. Too much water. Next to the water, an animal. A mama deer. He looks closer. Is she asleep? He can see her face in the moonlight. Not asleep. Mud in her nose and mouth and eyes. Drowned.

Big trees fell across here. Water below. Mama on the other side. What would Rambo do? Rambo would walk on this log. *Don't look don't look! Don't fall in.* Bobo looks at the water. Black swirls and white foam like a mouth that wants to bite you. He shuts his eyes. Where is Ace? Ace is in heaven. Usen ran away.

Bobo crawls with his eyes closed as far as he can go. Branches stick out, block the way. He opens his eyes. The ground is below him, a long way down. *Don't fall!* He grabs a branch. Something soft and smooth moves under his fingers. A snake! He looks. Snakes in all the branches. Lots and lots of snakes. Moving around and around. Between him and the end of the log. Bobo likes the black snake that lives in the barn. This is too many snakes. Are they the bad snakes? They all look the same in the dark. *If you are hurt, come find me,* Mama says. *If you are scared.* Where is Mama? TJ is hurt! What would Rambo do? He would jump off the log and run through the woods. Bobo can see the mud below him. He does not want to go down there. But TJ is hurt. TJ needs help. Bobo closes his eyes and lets go of the log.

He falls on his side, something hard jams into his hip, *ow!* Mud in his eyes and clothes. Water just behind him. Crawl away, up and up, slipping, slipping. Nothing to hold on to. Here is something. What is it? A cow caught in a branch. The tail of a cow like a rope. Pull hard. Crawl up on the cow. Don't look at the cow's face. It might be a cow he knows. This cow is in heaven with Ace and Papa. He crawls to the top of the bank.

The trees are moving all around him. Fluttery, like a breeze. He can't see the pink bird anywhere.

❧

Rand checks the kitchen door, sees in the bright moonlight that a downed tree rests against it, the same tree whose branches now poke through the kitchen window. Fallen pines have crushed the car and made a kind of fence fifteen feet high from the back door to the road.

The kitchen is the southeast side of the house. The room floods with light from the kitchen window.

Miss Reba goes to the window. "Moon out," she says. "We ain't got long. You got any neighbors to check on?"

"No," Rand says. *They're all in the Tobacco Shed. Dear God.*

"We got to get ready," she says.

She's right, Rand thinks. After the eye comes the second half of the storm. The second half of any typhoon is always the strongest.

"Wind be coming from the north next time," she says. "You got trees on the north side?"

"Oaks," he says. "Big oaks. And pines." He opens the front door. A delicious smell flies into his nostrils. Anne's Confederate jasmine vine is stripped bare. A strong fragrance comes from the storm-tossed stuff under his feet. He bends down, picks up a handful, holds it to his nose. Shredded petals.

In the silvery light he sees that a downed oak has caught in another oak's lower branches and now hangs there, aimed at the living room. The yard is thick with shed leaves and pine needles and small branches, a mulch pile knee deep in places.

Miss Reba steps onto the stoop. Six pines have fallen in a straight line, east to west, across the front walk, like pickets in a downed fence. "Lord have mercy," she says. "All that fallen since I got here. Lord protected me all that way."

She turns to Rand. "These oaks here. Some of these gonna fall. All these windows here. You got plywood? You got nails?"

But Rand is walking into the yard, climbing over tree trunks, till he gets to the bushes where the painted bunting made its nest. The nest is still there. The silvery light catches on something ragged at his feet. The three fledglings lie strewn like rags in the yard. The larger male and female lie splayed nearby, naked as new chicks. Green, red, blue feathers everywhere. *The storm has taken the very feathers off the birds.* He picks the male up in his hand, still warm, but limp. Poor Molly is out in this. She can't have survived it. Rand feels a rustling in the air above him and looks up. The stars are like cold fire blazing. He has not seen such clear skies since the power went out in the San Francisco quake of 1989. So many stars! They are so close. They are so beautiful.

He places the painted bunting carefully back on the ground, next to his mate, and covers them all with fallen leaves. Then he rises and walks to Sir Walter Raleigh Way, past houses crushed and trees split asunder, electric lines hanging like loose skeins of yarn, lit fuses at the ends. No one else around. Should he take Reba to the Tobacco Shed? No trees there to fall and crush it. But is it even still there? He can't see it. Bess's house still stands, but with a crushed deck and the Jaguar flattened, end to end, under a pine tree trunk. George will be devastated. He loves that car.

He can hear Miss Reba following behind.

"Mister Rand," she calls out. "Best not go too far."

But he keeps walking. Where once was a Disney-village perfection, a phony English kingdom, now there is ruin. A week ago he would have rejoiced at the destruction of his neighbors' pretentious lampposts and pickety garden gates and petunia beds. Now he sees how they have kept death at bay with these things, things that could be crushed and broken on the whim of the wind.

Miss Reba stands beside him. "It's all ruint," she says.

"Yes."

"Wise man build his house on a rock," she says.

"Bunch of fools," Rand says. "Thinking we could cheat time by making things pretty."

"We best get back," Reba says. *This whiteman so crazy.*

"I'm walking to the highway," Rand says. "Maybe I can get to Jeff. But you should go back. Just go back and stay in the house. The door's unlocked."

"Jeff at Jolene's," Miss Reba says. "Trees down all over that road. Creek flooded. Can't do nothing but wait and stay alive."

"Maybe I can get across."

"You can't get across. Too late to do anything now."

Too late to repair his losses? Too late to bring back his son? When did he forget that the sandy-haired boy in that picture he loved was his son?

"It's still calm out," Rand insists. "We have time. You can come with me if you want. Check on your children."

"Mister Rand."

"It's colonel. Not mister."

"You ain't got your army with you now, Colonel. You just got me. You ain't going anywhere without me. And I'm telling you that you don't have time. You got to go home. I seen this storm coming before others seen it. I see it coming back now before you see it. You got to get inside. You'll be safe inside. Your child, my children, they safe for now. Worst is yet to come. You got to get inside."

Miss Reba plants her feet and stands before him. She has seen this whiteman sick. She has seen him cry. She has seen him guilty and afraid. And still he does not listen. Big colonel. Big whiteman thinks he knows what's up. He ain't seen nothing yet. What does she have to do, pop him over the head with a stick? She can feel the wind prickle her arms and neck. Storm is just a breath away. *Wickedness just a breath away.*

Man walks away from her, she calls out after: "You ain't helpin' your child by staying out here and getting kilt. You ain't making it better for Miss Anne. You best listen to me now, Mister *Colonel!*"

Rand steps onto the soaked grassy edge of the Commons. He can see quite a ways across the countryside from here—the Village center and the Tobacco Shed, still standing across the green, the highway to the west, Indigo Field beyond, the Gooley pines dark and glimmering above. He can hear faint voices and music and shouting from the Shed. The party must go on.

"Mister Rand?" Reba calls out. "It's comin' back. You hear me?" He doesn't move. Reba begins to be afraid. Will there be time to get back? She needs the strength of this colonel. She needs his protection to survive and to help with whatever comes next. Last thing she needs is him running across the road, being a hero, getting caught in the neck by a falling tree.

❧

Fifteen minutes ago, Jeff woke to utter silence. Then dripping. *Plop. Plop. Plop.* The roof was still leaking. But the rain had stopped. A strange light now glints through the window. Have they slept through the night? Has the storm finally passed? Jolene sighs and turns in her sleep. Jeff tucks the blankets closer around her, then rises to look outside. Moonlight shines on strange objects strewn across the yard. A roll of fence wire caught in the apple tree. A sodden pillow on the windshield of his truck. A piece of a blue tarp wrapped around the porch post, a hundred tiny plastic pots strewn under the oak tree like mutant acorns, tiny green-hulled pecans strewn like spilled beads. What could be a dead squirrel. A wedge of plywood painted black and scalloped along the edge like feathers.

Jolene stirs and raises her head. "What?" she says. "What's going on? Is it over?"

"I don't know," Jeff says. "It's quiet now. Sometimes they come back." He remembers that storm in Malaysia, it blew all night and half the morning, then went suddenly quiet. He asked his mother, "Can I go outside now? Can I?" He ran to the door. Opened it. Dad outside, a stricken look on his face. A bloody cheek. Uniform dirty and torn. Soaked. "Get inside," he said, something fierce in the way he held his mouth. "That's an order."

Dad was always giving orders. But he was right. The wind came back. *Jesus Christ.* Is Dad okay? He's probably drinking. That seems to be his solution to everything. He has neighbors, doesn't he? George and Bess. If they're still speaking to him. Christ, he should have called. But he had no idea this was coming.

"Bobo," Jolene says. "We have to get Bobo."

"We'll take my truck."

On Field Road, his headlights pick out something black and glittering where the road should be. *Jam on the brakes. Too late, too late, shit-shit-shit.* Jeff feels his bowels loosen as the truck lifts—an inch, two inches, three—off the road and starts to float downstream. The current tugs the tires left and jams them back onto pavement. He jerks the truck into reverse and guns it. But the rear wheels go into the ditch and spin.

Jolene's face is pale and her eyes luminous, clear green with pinpoint pupils. "Good God, Jeff," she says. "Holy crow."

"We're stuck," Jeff says. "Let me try." He shifts into first and rocks forward an inch or so before the tires begin to spin. He jams on brakes, puts it in park. "Stay here," he says. He swings out of the cab and grabs sticks and rocks and branches and whatever comes to hand and jams it under the wheels. "Gun it when I say go," he calls out. Jolene slips into the driver's seat and grips the gear shift. Jeff opens the passenger cab door and puts his shoulder against the frame. "One, two, three, GO." He shoves his shoulder into the frame and Jolene eases off the clutch and gives it gas and the truck pops forward a few inches, then spins out. "Give me a minute, we'll try again," Jeff calls. He grabs more branches and jams them under the wheels.

They inch the truck forward, bit by bit, until the wheels are on pavement, never noticing the wind lifting the branches around them and clouds drifting across the moon. Where did the light go? Jeff can no longer see how deep the mud is on the tires. His boots are stuck ankle deep in muck. He wipes his face with a muddy hand, leaving a streak across his forehead and cheek. Something shifts above him. Something cracks and rustles and cracks again. He looks up.

Above his head, a slender branch on a small pine tree is all that's keeping an enormous pine from crashing down on the truck cab. Something shifts again. The slender branch cracks. "Jolene!" he screams and lunges toward her, but the mud sucks at his feet and he falls to his knees. Through the cab window, he can see her narrow white face full of fear as she sees him there, then looks up.

He screams, "GET OUT OF THE TRUCK!" but the sound of a snapping tree trunk is like an explosion.

Jolene has seen this moment many times in her mind, but in her imagination it was different. A sunny day. The friendly country sound of a chain saw at work. A precarious branch high up, a little breeze lifting the branches, a small crackle, then the sound of something large and rustling, falling. A cry perhaps. Or maybe just a sudden blow to the back of the head. Jolene wandering to the woods to tell him supper's getting cold, as she has done many times, her man working into the twilight hours, his belief and hers in the magical protection of his strength and good luck, banishing misfortune. Her beautiful Luke. His face turned white and swollen, one ear trickling blood, lips twisted, showing teeth.

So when she sees Jeff's open mouth, his eyes rolled upward to a widow-maker, she sees a second chance. Her body lunges for him, flashing out the door of the truck, twisting in air like a lioness protecting a cub, flying more than jumping, to pull her man to safety, a safety granted before only in countless imaginings. The sharpened stob of a broken branch slices neatly through the rusty cab roof and into the driver's-seat upholstery, jerking to a halt in the seat springs as she tumbles onto Jeff. The stob holds back the weight of a 200-year pine, so that small side branches and delicate fans of green-scented needles brush the heads and arms of the man in the ditch and the woman now holding him, holding on, as the storm crashes down around them.

Somehow they make it back to the house, bruised and battered by flying debris. They latch the door and roll to the floor and into their closet-cave under the stairs, clutching each other and gasping for air as swirling debris pelts the windows and doors. "You're alive," Jeff sobs, kissing her face and hands, loving the smell of her, like apples and earth and pine needles. Jolene makes no answer, but kisses him fiercely in return, loving the heat of him, the lean power of his body, the very breath and sweat and fluid of him, the mud on his cheek. My God, he is alive and he is her second chance, and for a moment she forgets all about her boy. A tree falls close to the house. *Oh my God, Bobo.* He is out there somewhere across Spill Creek and there is nothing she can do but hang on.

On the Commons Rand watches the moon, the ragged clouds racing across its face, then fistulas of clouds, moving from below like the lumpy backs of demons. Slithering, surrounding, gathering. Extraordinary. Where has he seen something like this? Oh yes. Sistine Chapel. The Hell Wall.

The sky has gone dark. The wind pulls at his clothes. It's too late to find Jeff. He turns and says, "We better go."

Reba mutters, "What I been sayin' all this time?"

Rand pulls a flashlight out of his pocket, but the battery is dead. Side by side they pick their way back, past the dark ruined houses, the shadows of trees, the fallen pines, as the wind begins to lift branches and leaves. Instead of following their meandering path outward, Rand leads them in a shortcut over the deadfall. One particularly enormous pine stops Reba. Rand reaches for her hand and pulls her over. The rising wind and grumbling clouds pelt them with tiny pellets of hail like stinging bees. Rand covers his head, wants to sprint, but Reba can't run, so he slows to pull her along, sheltering her head with his arm.

Little by little, pushing, pulling, Rand and Reba make their way across the Downs to the road that leads to Rand's house. By the time they make it to the door and slam it shut, the wind has begun a new low whine. By the time Rand lights more candles, it is a roar. By the time he finds the cooling pot of tea in the kitchen and offers a swallow to Reba, it is a banshee scream.

Bobo can't see the road anymore, just feels the rut under the leaves with his feet. The moon went away. It's dark! He walks into a log. *Ow! This log is not supposed to be in the road.*

A pink bird screeches in the tree: *Motherfucker!* Make a wish. *I wish Mama was here.*

The trees are moving. A big sound, like a train coming. *Boom!* Lightning again. "Stom ovah!" Bobo cries out. He crouches down, wraps his arms around his knees. Rocks and rocks. He looks up. *CRACK.* Lightning is trying to find him. He runs and runs and runs. Another tree falls down. "*MAMA!*" Bobo cries and runs. A white dog in the woods ahead. Ace! "Here, Ace! Good boy!" He follows where Ace runs, a zigzag path through the woods.

Here is a field. Across the field is the house. *Mama!* Lightning all over the sky. What would Rambo do? Rambo would run get Mama. Bobo puts his arms over his head and runs, yelling "*Mamaaaa*," his voice drowned out by the rising yowl of wind.

Here is the porch door. The kitchen is dark. Where is Mama? There is her truck. Sleeping? Bobo pulls the screen door handle. Stuck! He pulls harder. Locked! Mama locked the door.

Mama never locks. Except in a storm, so it won't slam. *Okay, okay, okay, okay.* Go to the window. Yellow light. Yellow candle. Mama is here.

The wind makes a terrible sound. Buzzing like lots of bees. Hornets. Bobo does not like spiders, bees, or hornets. *Mama!* He is hungry. He is afraid. *TJ is hurt.* Bobo pounds his fist on the window frame. *Mamaaaaa!* The wind carries his voice away.

He goes around to the front stoop. This door is locked too. He looks in the living room window. Flickering light. He can see people! He presses his face to the glass. Mama! There is a man on Mama! Man is hurting Mama! Pushing her! Bad man! Bobo pounds on the house with his fists. Bobo yells, "*Get away, get away!*" But no one can hear him.

Rambo would shoot the bad man. Rambo would have a gun.

Bobo has a gun.

Juicy Fruit is on the right. Lucky gun is on the left. Bobo shivers and unzips his windbreaker pocket, pulls it out. He aims it at the window where the man is fighting Mama. He is crying. He shoots. *Click.* He shoots again. *Click.* And a third time. *BAM.* Hand stings! He drops the gun. He falls down. It's dark. Somebody is yelling. Mama? Bobo crouches on the stoop. Rain is pouring on his head. He puts his hands over his ears. Mama is mad. He wraps his arms around his knees and begins to rock. *Uh-oh, uh-oh, uh-oh.*

Bobo raises his head at the sound of a baby goat crying. There are five, six, seven babies standing in the yard, quivering. The babies are lost! Mama left the gate open! He found them! Now they will follow him. He stands up, forgetting the gun, forgetting TJ, forgetting Mama in trouble, and runs to the barn, babies following and crying all the while.

He does not see the pink bird rolling through the air, ass over teakettle, toward the Gooley pines.

☙

Jolene heard a clap like thunder, the crash of glass, Jeff's body jerk and roll away from her, his scream. Now her hand comes away from his buttocks wet and warm. In the lightning she sees it: red blood on her hand, on his cock, on his face where she touches him.

"Fuck!" Jeff yells. "Help!"

"What is it!" she yells. "What is it!" Something must have crashed through the window, flung shards of glass across the room. Is she cut too? She can't feel it.

She sees in a lightning flash the white of his buttocks, the black of a wound. She presses her fingers against his flesh gingerly. Not glass. A round jagged hole. Jeff rolls on the floor in pain. She presses a wad of blanket against his hip, covers his body with hers. They both hear it at the same time. A voice, almost human, calling from the porch: "*Maaaaaa.*" They look up and see a baby goat standing there, in the flicker of lightning, staring at them through a hole in the window. Then wind or God's dark hand whisks it into the air and away.

Inside the house, lightning flickers like a strobe. Rand turns and sees the oak grove outside the front windows, lined up and leaning toward the house. Now the full strength of the storm is upon them. He is afraid. This is a storm that can breach walls. This is a storm that can lift the roof off the house. This is a storm that can kill them all.

A hellish screech and buzz. What in God's name? He's heard this before. The roof is shaking, pulling upward, the screeching sound is the nails releasing their hold. The air feels electric, lifting his hair from his scalp. Deep instinct kicks in. He grabs Miss Reba around the waist, falls to the carpet, and rolls under the dining room table.

Rand can feel the shaking of the earth through her body, his belly, arms, and legs. The woman's ancient ribs swell against his arms. She is screaming bloody murder. Flailing her arms, hitting him in the face and shoulders, kicking him in the shins, hard. He grips her harder, traps her arms and legs in his, yells in her ear, "Settle down, it's all right, you're okay." He feels her ribs expand for the next lungful, and the first of the oaks smashes through the picture window, crashes onto Anne's polished table. They are surrounded by a fence of branches.

Rain and wind blast sideways into the room, skittering the candles in their glasses off the table and to the floor around them. A yellow folded paper flies up into the air and away. Fallen candles flicker and spin crazily on the carpet, like the lights of a broken amusement park ride, then go out. Whirling twigs and glass and acorns and leaves blast through their leafy fence, sting their arms and legs and faces in the dark like shrapnel. Rand tucks his face against Reba's shoulder, wraps his arms tighter around the old woman, pressing her face into the carpet away from the wind. He can feel her breathing, and a vibration in her frame, but he no longer knows if she is screaming. All he can see in the flicker and roar of lightning and wind is that they are in a bower of branches, forked limbs a kind of cage around them, like an extra set of table legs. Anne's mother's 400-year-old Tudor table holds fast, built like a boat, transported to these shores by some ancestor sea captain-privateer, who took it as booty from some rum-soaked island colony. The underside is lit by the constant lightning flash: panels six inches thick, reinforced every eight inches by crosspieces of hand-hewn oak, roses the size of small fists carved into the crosspieces and stout legs. In the sway and screech of the house, in the lash of the storm, he suddenly feels the wood's memory: a sailing vessel, tossed in a storm, the moaning of human cargo.

He can feel Miss Reba's breathing change now, a low hum coming from her belly. The wind has shifted in tone. All the acorns have been released from their branches. There is no more pummeling of his back and head with small hard pellets. But the fear remains. Metal taste in the mouth. Something else coming. Adrenaline makes you want to run but all he can do is stay still and cover his head. In the whine of the wind, he hears the old army anthem mixed with an old hymn playing crazily over and over in his ears: *Over hill, over dale, as we hit the dusty trail, and the caissons go rolling along / O God our help in ages past / our hope for years to come / our shelter from the stormy blast / and our eternal home.* He can hear her now. The woman under him is praying with all her might, the sound like a low growl and hiss, like an animal preparing to fight for its life. He can smell her sweat and soap and fear. Their bodies are so closely clamped, it is as if she is broadcasting his own mind and heart. He hears her words, and they make him sore afraid: *O Lucy, rise within me, O Sheba, my strength and buckler, O God, make them like whirling dust, and like chaff before the wind; like fire that burns down a forest, like the flame that sets mountains ablaze, drive them with thy tempest, and terrify them with thy storm, cover their faces with shame, O Lord, that they may seek your Name. Let them be disgraced and terrified forever—*

48

Jolene wakes just before dawn and lifts her head. A great quiet has settled around them, punctuated by dripping. The storm is over. She hears something else, something new. In the distance, the sound of a helicopter approaching from the direction of the highway. She turns to Jeff. She's bandaged him with sanitary pads and duct tape, forced Pedialite down his throat for loss of fluids, given him a shot of penicillin from her stash in the fridge. But he is dead weight in her arms. Barely breathing. She touches his face. "Sweetheart," she says. "My love." He turns and groans and tries to smile. That sound again. The copter's getting closer. The storm is over. Help has come.

She grabs a bloody towel from the soaked rags on the floor, runs outside and waves her arms and yells to the helicopter, now approaching from the Gooley Ridge. "Here!" she yells. "Stop!" The copter sees her, drops slowly to the ground, blowing soaked and shredded insulation into the air like wet pink feathers.

She drags the EMT inside, explains incoherently, "Loss of blood, some kind of wound, penicillin, hospital, please, please, please—" and helps him load Jeff into a gurney, load him on the copter bay. They won't let her come. The pilot reaches over to shut the bay. "Wait!" she calls out. "Wait! Promise me you will go by Reba's farm. The next house past the creek. My son is there. Please. Or send somebody." The EMT promises. She watches the helicopter rise and move back across the pasture. Sees it finally: a terrible broad swath of Gooley pines is down.

Oh, God help us, the devastation.

Oh, God help us, Bobo.

She left him out in the storm. Thank God Reba was with him. She tries that thing Reba does sometimes, closes her eyes, sends her heart's vision out across the pasture to Reba's house. Is Bobo okay? Is Reba okay? TJ?

All she can see is chickens.

❧

When Sheriff Walter Pickett Jr. finally gets his messages that morning, Reba's is the twelfth out of four hundred sixteen. Four hundred sixteen people called and got their messages through. There must be thousands more who tried. The big new cell tower in Quarryville went down around six p.m. Landline service died by eight, so many trees on the wires. He gives the EMTs directions to Reba's farm. Bobo and TJ—especially Bobo—will need help. "Abednego Underwood?" he says to the young Black man before him.

"Yessir," Abednego says.

"Don't be thinking about the TJ you know in school. This is a person to rescue. You hear me? This is your job. Take Tyquan with you."

"Yessir," Abednego says.

"Miss Reba needs you to go there, take care of those boys. Bobo too."

"Yessir."

"Okay then." Sheriff Pickett Junior turns to the next message.

Tyquan and Abednego charge their big-wheeled truck across the flooded creeks to Reba's road, chain-sawing as they go, taking sections out of fifteen pine trees blocking the Field Road and rolling the pieces into the ditches. They splash over a flooded creek, pass Jolene's house, not on the list, keep going. They come to Spill Creek. Flooded, but not too bad. This truck is about five feet up on jacked axles. Wheels big enough to cross? About to find out. They make it across. Now they pull up into Reba's yard.

Reba's brick house is black with smoke on one side, roof got a hole in it. Nobody around but those spooky Black angels in the yard. One has lost its wings and lies on the ground. One has its wings all cockeyed. Where the third one used to be, the blue-eyed one, nothing left but a hole in the ground. Musta flapped its wings and flown away.

"Miss Reba got some crazy shit in her yard," Tyquan says.

"We got to check the house," Abednego says.

Tyquan pokes his head in, looks around. "Nope. They gone."

"Let's look around," Abednego says. "Maybe they hiding."

"TJ! Bobo!" they call, walking through the yard.

They stop at the chicken shed. Open the door. Peek inside.

TJ lies still, tucked in his straw bale nest, face pale and hair strangely silver, surrounded by roosting chickens. Two of the hens have laid eggs and settled in to brood. They mutter at the approach of strangers. The rest rise on spindly legs and look around expectantly: *Reba? Food?* One young rooster tries to crow, but the hens peck him and he shuts up.

Abednego last saw TJ on the locker room floor, bruised and flattened. He's never seen a dead person before this day. He saw three this morning. A man, a woman, a child. Drowned. Mouths and noses stuffed with mud. As much as he does not care for TJ, he hopes this body ain't dead.

He nudges a hay bale with his foot, calls out, "TJ! TJ, wake up! You dead, TJ?"

"Shut up!" Tyquan says. "Don't be calling up spirits."

TJ opens one eye. Squints. Sees Abednego.

"Dude," he croaks. "I ain't dead." He lifts his head, tries to sit up. Lies back down. Swears. "I am so MF hungover."

Abednego laughs so loud Tyquan looks at him and says shut up. Abednego goes to get blankets, bandages, and some aspirin. He's happy TJ is alive. He's also happy TJ's hungover. But what's up with his hair?

Tyquan stands over TJ, watching him breathe for a moment, before he has to drag him out. Chickens fluttering all about. Boy is buck naked. *Not so tough now, are ya, dog?*

"Hey," TJ says, opening both eyes. "Where's Bobo?"

Jolene hears the chain saws working out on Field Road. Someone is finally cutting a path through the downed pines. Spill Creek goes down fast when it floods. She should be able to get to Reba's soon.

She picks her way across the yard to the barn. Roof still tight. No trees on it. Just branches all over. Gate closed. That baby goat on the porch last night. How'd it get out? She touches the wood grain on the barn door. The wind and rain have plastered loose hay against it in a brocade pattern, like ferns.

Three of the does are lined up and ready for milking. God knows where the rest are. A few kids wail in a cluster, standing on something in the straw. Nosing the straw. What is it? A patch of Carolina blue. Bobo's *windbreaker*? God help us. The windbreaker moves.

"Bobo!" Jolene runs to him, drops on her knees in the straw beside him. "Mama!" Bobo says, hugging her tight. Same old Bobo. But how in the world did he get here?

"Mama," he says, "I found the babies. They lost! I found them this time."

Jolene clasps him to her, her big boy, her grown boy, saving goats in the storm. "What a brave boy you are."

"Not a boy," Bobo says. "I the Man." He puffs up his chest and smiles.

When she releases him, she holds his big sunny face in her hands. "You all right? How in the world did you get here?" He is remembering something. Frowning. What is it?

"Bad man hut you, Mama?"

"What man? What man?"

"I shot him," Bobo says happily.

Jolene looks at him sharply. "What did you say?"

"I shot the bad man," Bobo says. He watches her face. He starts to rock. *"Okay, okay, okay, okay?"*

49

Water has power, water can flood and lift and drown and devastate. Wind, however, comes without warning, following no discernible path. There is no Army Corps that can plan the path of wind, no dam that can hold it back. No man can divert it from its play. Wind chooses its own way. Wind, like the mind of God, conquers all before it.

When the residents of Ambler County crawl from their dens—snakes from the treetops, foxes from hollow trees, and people from under twists of snapped framing, shingle roofs, and Sheetrock—it is clear that the great wind chose its track with care. This great wind was of the sort the Tuscarora call Thunder Wind, for the sound it made and the power it wrought over living things.

This great wind rode the eye of a rogue hurricane and spun out lightning and whirlwinds like warriors of a great army. These warriors flattened all they touched, and chose what they touched with care. They touched the new homes of wealthy people and left the old derelict homes of Poolesville, the farmhouses of widows, the trailer parks of the destitute, damaged but still standing. The wind brought lightning strikes so pervasive that many small fires lit rooftops, tall trees, and last year's broomsedge in Indigo Field. It brought rain so drenching that the fires did not last long. This wind skipped from high spot to high spot, so that places that had been raised up were laid low, and places that were low and humble remained intact. Meteorologists are still working on a name for such a wind.

As dawn rises across the Downs, Stonehaven raises its wounded head, scared sober. Like a convention of turtles, the people at the Tobacco Shed come slowly out of their shell. The roof on the Shed is peeled back like a sardine can. George picks the splinters out of his backside, arms, and legs and swears he'll never drink again. Bess looks around at the utter destruction and says, "Next chance I get, I'm drinking vodka straight from the bottle."

They see that the wind has played with their neighbors, picking them up and placing them down, gently, in strange places, just as the

Tuscarora positioned the Palatine settlers they slaughtered, in strange vignettes. This wind has been kinder than the Tuscarora were. Only six deaths in this place, mostly from heart attacks, and some miraculous survivals: A man on Manderly who stubbornly stayed at home in bed is found still breathing, between box spring and mattress—in the yard across the street. A Stonehaven widow wakes in the arms of her secret new love—in the ruins of someone else's house. A baby grand piano tinkles and harps, its strings played by the branches of the bark-stripped oak in which it rests. A wingback chair roosts in another.

And on Sir Walter Raleigh Way, where Colonel Randolph Jefferson Lee and one tough old Black lady held the fort under his wife Anne's mother's dining room table, two survivors raise their heads and wonder how in blue blazes they will ever crawl out of here.

The barricade of oak branches protected them from wicked projectiles—wood splinters, glass shards, roofing screws. But now they are stuck.

The able-bodied men of Stonehaven have fanned out in formation, looking for people to rescue, with their shovels and ladders. By mid-morning Bess and George have found Rand and Reba, and they've been fishing bottled water, pop-top tuna, and apples to them through the branches on six-pound test line from George's fly rod, which somehow survived his smashed garage and landed upright in a peony bush. George has offered bourbon, but Rand declines, out of deference to his companion.

George calls in the volunteer fire department, which is mostly the men who breakfast at Sunrise Grill. It takes Joggins and Joggins Junior two hours with chain saws to cut them out. They cut right through Anne's table—a rough, ragged hole just big enough to release the prisoners. They see that a smaller table, a heavy chestnut piece, took the first weight of the deadfall, cushioned the blow. Now it's in pieces.

When the captives finally emerge, first Reba, then Rand, the Stonehaven ladies take Miss Reba by the hand and dress her wounds, places where acorns flayed the skin on her arms and legs, seeping red blood. Rand's wounds are on his back and rump and head, but Miss Reba's torso is clean and clear. Bess dresses Rand's wounds and finds him a shirt and shorts from George's scattered clothing. She asks Rand what in the world brought the two of them together in the storm, but all he says is, "She came to the door. I let her in."

He doesn't say, "She saved my life." So everyone assumes he saved hers.

"How'd she get here in that storm?" Junior wonders.

"Flew up in one of them whirlwinds," Joggins says. "It's the only explanation."

King P, having spent the night rolling around in his cage on the floor of the den, now sees the cage wire is bent, an opening for escape. He squeezes his way to freedom, shouting for Pia, circumnavigating the unfamiliar branches of downed pines, fluttering to higher and higher perches. Finally he rises high, circles, finds shelter in the Gooley pines—the ones still standing—and feasts on green pine nuts, hickory nuts, and acorns, all cracked and pre-shelled in heaps around them. From time to time he rests from his feasting and flies to the top of the tallest pine left standing. Here he is surprised to find the branches cloaked in a feather cape of red and blue and yellow—a sociable band of scarlet macaws, transported in the great eye of the storm all the way from Belize. *Fuckfuckfuck!* Queen Pia cries out from the center of the brilliant flock. *Oh bloody hell!* King P says and flies up to find her, his heart light as bird bones and feathers.

Not long from now, someone will make up a story about how Indigo Field takes its name from the deep blue tail feathers that float down and rest on the rocks and mud flats here. And when storm stories are told in the coming days, tales will emerge of strange whirlwinds, siphons that caught up chickens and goats, children and dogs, and placed them down gently in safe places. Miss Phoebe will wake to find a bedraggled love-bird on her windowsill, hopping onto her finger, giving bird kisses. One of the farmers at Sunrise will tell of seeing the Angel of Death pass overhead, seven-foot wingspan, black as night. Miss Phoebe's nephew will tell of a whirlwind like a bony finger in his back field, plucked a yellow dog straight into the air. No one will believe that tale. But the Fayetteville paper will report that a yellow dog with a pink sparkly collar dropped from the sky outside town, able to perform all kinds of tricks, as if he had come straight from heaven's traveling circus.

In the land between two rivers, the roads and bridges are washed out. There are no hotels nearby to stay in. The people of Stonehaven Downs need dry clothes, and beds, and food. Some with money evacuate to Raleigh and Fayetteville via helicopter. Some fly off to live in the reluctant shelter of their children's homes across the country. At least one takes what remains of his large-cap stocks and moves to Tuscany with his secret Stonehaven-widow lover.

It will take a month or so to bring in FEMA trailers, equipment, and supplies. So those hardy souls who remain at Stonehaven make camp on the farmers' market green, using rough canvas shelters from the Quarryville Army-Navy Surplus Store, once the denizen of anarchists and Civil War reenactment militias. The Commons sprouts triangular white tents, canvas snapped taut with ropes and pegs. Stonehavenites cook Spam and canned ham on army-issue fry pans over smoky campfires made in rescued Weber grills. News crews come from WRAL and interview Stonehaven survivors. "All this smoke keeps mosquitoes away," say the stalwart sons of Stonehaven, some of whom are rather enjoying themselves. "All this smoke is ruining my hair," say their wives, who are happy to let their husbands cook.

Then the cameras set up in Poolesville, at the AME Zion Church.

"Scripture says a rich man go to heaven through the eye of a needle," Reverend Reba Queen Esther Jones says into the camera. "This is the needle." Her arm sweeps across the parish hall floor, where cots and pallets take up every inch, mostly filled with whitepeople. "We going to survive this together," she says. "Do unto others, Jesus says. So that's what we're doing."

Behind her, a retired army officer can be seen with a clipboard and a cell phone, taking orders. And behind three serious-looking young Black men, a young freckled whiteboy with spiky silver hair makes a peace sign for the camera.

Amid the debris of Ambler County, residents find small square plywood signs randomly caught in trees, rooftops, and fields, hand painted with snatches of scripture warning of the wrath of God.

The Cedar River has made a lake out of Indigo Field, and over the next three weeks, the waters of that lake will slowly ooze their way back to the shelter of the river banks, leaving a new layer of mud and logs and rocks so thick that all evidence of people and history and archaeology in the Field will lie six feet deeper than before. The skull and long thigh bones of Cletus Hooper are scattered, reburied, along with six Roanoke beads and all evidence of seven generations of Native people.

Among the bodies brought to the makeshift morgue at the sheriff's department this week is a man found in a prison uniform, drowned and cast up on the flat mud slick covering Indigo Field. A man was reported missing from the work detail near the Cedar River during the storm. This might be him.

Miss Reba gets called to bring TJ, next of kin, for positive ID.

"We ain't had time to clean him up," the man says. He pulls back the cover.

Tommy Jay Snipes, eyes popped out and staring, red smear of blood on his cheek, orange jumpsuit muddy and stained, ears and nose stuffed with blue clay. *This what I saw that day in court.* Reba cannot feel the familiar rage anymore. *Dear Jesus, I am so weary of this whiteman.*

TJ stands beside her, silent. He can't remember much good about him. Most of what was good he made up in stories. All he can think is, *Daddy, you're dead now. You can't do me or Reba any harm. Thank you, Jesus. Amen. But I wish you didn't look so bad and all messed up like that.*

"That's him," he finally says. "I guess he got out like he wanted to." He shivers a little. Daddy really did come after him. He can feel Reba standing next to him like a solid wall.

Miss Reba tells TJ to wait in the hall a moment while she speaks to the sheriff. She goes in his office and closes the door. "Miss Reba," Sheriff says. "Glad your boy's all right."

Miss Reba nods. "Come to talk about something else."

"What's that, Miss Reba?" he says. Man looks tired.

She sits down. "Take out your pen and paper. I am making a confession."

Sheriff Pickett looks at her. Doesn't say a word. Picks up his pen. Stops.

"You ready?" Miss Reba says.

"Miss Reba, listen to me. Thought you might like to know they found Cletus Hooper's old car in that mess of logs down by the bridge. Must have gone fishing at the river and got too drunk to see where he was going. Figure he drowned. Had his daughter in here yesterday. Cried like a baby. Guess it was a relief for her to know."

Once Spill Creek has you, it holds you down.

Sheriff Junior puts his hands flat on the desk. Leans in. Says, "Without a body, there is no other possible explanation."

A body. A body full of hate and bad teeth and liquor. A body whose bones are scattered and buried deep now in the Field.

"I killed him."

"Who?"

"Cletus Hooper. I could have saved him. I killed him with my hate."

"You are mistaken," he says. "Mr. Hooper died in a car accident. I'm the sheriff in this county and I get to say what the evidence provides." He rises. "You have a good day, Miss Reba."

She stands up, wanting to say more. But he turns his face away. He knows. He knows and he is walking away from knowing. He is exactly like his grandfather.

࿎

TJ has been listening at the door. *Jesus H. Christ, Miss Reba killed a man.* He looks at her with new respect. He must have done something bad wrong for her to do it. Miss Reba's not the crazy killer type.

On the way home Miss Reba pulls the car over by the side of the road, shuts it off, tells him to listen up. "Your papa dead now," she says. "Your mama gone too. But your mama's got some people on her mother's side. The Locklears—they're Lumbee. They're a hard-luck people. But I'll take you to see them, if you want. You so interested in Indians."

TJ's mouth drops open and stays there. He stares at his arm. He doesn't look Indian. But he is. He has people. He closes his eyes and he can see it: *a pow wow out in the Field. Guys in feather capes and headdresses. That step-dancing they do. The many small fires of my people.*

50

Rand stands at the door of Jeff's hospital room, the rush of air conditioning filling his nose. It smells dimly green and sweet, like death and disinfectant. Jeff is in the second bed, next to the window. He lies face down, that mop of unruly hair where his feet should be, big feet on the pillow. Bandage around his backside.

Rand hadn't even known his son was injured. Miss Reba came to him with the news. Nobody could tell him what had happened exactly. He'd been shot during the storm. It was an accident. Maybe his girlfriend shot him. *Take it back.*

Jeff hears him, turns his head. "Dad?"

"Jeff," he says. The boy looks so fragile, his eyes so wide and sweet, eyes like a sleepy child's.

"You can come in," Jeff says.

Rand steadies himself, walks to the bedside.

"Hi, Dad." The boy closes his eyes. That shaggy head. Rand wants to rest his hand on that head. Jeff sighs, opens his eyes again. "I'd sit up," he says, "but they say I can't for another day or so."

"What happened to you, son?" Rand's voice gruff.

"I got shot in the ass," he says.

"How in the hell—" Rand shuts his mouth, hears the accusing note in his voice, the old father berating his wayward son. Doesn't seem fair to kick a man who's been shot in the ass. "Shot in the ass," he says. "That's a hell of a thing."

"Don't worry," Jeff says. "I'll be fine. It was an accident. What a storm, hey?" It's just what Anne would say.

"What a storm," Rand agrees. A silence hangs in the air between them. "I'm glad you're okay, son," he says, a quaver in his voice. He clears his throat. "Now," he says, "tell me about this Jolene."

Two weeks later, Jeff is sitting up, eating real food sent from Miss Reba via Rand, with a hearty appetite. "They want me to go to rehab," Jeff says. "They have to make sure I can walk. They're going to fix up Sarge too. Good as new."

Sarge? Rand glances over at the bed beside Jeff. Young man, military cut. Legs bandaged, taken off at the knee. What was he doing here, instead of at the VA? "Where'd you serve, son?"

"Afghanistan, sir."

"Afghanistan."

"It was fantastic." The boy grins. "Looks like I missed my chance to go back."

The Taliban isn't the only reason. Rand tries not to look at where the boy's legs should be.

"Hey, don't worry," the boy says. "This place they're sending us, they have bionic legs. Not like in your day. Jeff told me all about you, sir. Pleasure to meet you, sir."

"What's wrong with *your* legs?" Rand asks Jeff, alarmed.

"Just need a little PT. Be good as new in a few weeks." Jeff slurps from something that looks suspiciously like a sippy cup. "Have a seat. Sarge has been stuck here since they couldn't transport him out for a while. He's been telling me all about Afghanistan. It sounds amazing. Were you ever there, Dad?"

"No," he says, "but Kip was. He did flyovers during the Russia war."

"Oh, man," Sarge says, "they told me about that war. Playing buzkashi with goats and hanging with the warlords. Genghis Fucking Khan used to hang out there, man. Excuse me, sir."

Rand closes his eyes. War is fun for some people. Genghis Khan, for example. This kid.

"Dad?"

He opens his eyes.

"Dad, Sarge says they had an army archaeology unit in Afghanistan. Turns out they have them all over. Chuck Mathers signed on to a unit in Vietnam. Tracking bones of MIAs. Sending them home. He says he's got a place for me."

There is a familiar sound in Jeff's voice, a tone that says, *I'm going to do this and I'm just softening you up for it, so get ready.* Rand wants to tell him how dangerous it could be. Anything could happen. Unexploded ordnance is all over the place in Vietnam.

"I think you should stay here," Rand says. "At least till you're better," he adds lamely. But by the look on his son's face, the turning away, he knows he's doing this all wrong. You don't tell a young man what to do. You watch him make his crazy zigzag flight, then help pick up the pieces when he falls.

"Vietnam," he says. "Well, what about it?"

That's all it takes for Jeff to tell him all his dreams of glory.

Jeff has other reasons for wanting to go, of course. Jolene is breaking up with him. She came with a basket of Dora's bread and aged goat cheese and a potato-onion pie—the only produce left intact these days is underground or sprouted wild in the fields. She described the gun to him. It was definitely Dad's Bersa. He's spent his whole life looking at it hanging on the wall over the dining room table at Thanksgiving dinners. Bobo must have got it from Dad's collection laid out on the table that day. Jolene thinks he got it from TJ.

The shooting, Bobo's trouble, his own ass on fire with pain, it's all his fault and she has no idea, but he is going to have to tell her. Letting Bobo into Dad's house when he was so crazy. Not even noticing he took the gun. She will hate him for putting Bobo in danger. He remembers what Dad always said: *A man does what he has to do.*

"Jolene," he starts, "it was all my fault." And as he tells her, he watches her expression turn from disbelief to anger to great sorrow. When he is done, she rises, takes her basket, and walks away.

Chuck arranges it all. Jeff is recruited to join the Archaeology Corps of the US Army for the MIA recovery project in Vietnam. He gets an army uniform, a stripe. No basic, just sidearm training. Sarge is proud. Maybe Dad will be proud. His son has finally joined his blessed army.

He shows up at Reba's doorstep in his sharp new army duds. There's a blue tarp over the corner of the roof, a place where someone's been laying brick to fill a hole. When Miss Reba opens the door, she places a hand on her heart. "Colonel?" she calls out. "Your boy Jeff is here."

Dad climbs down the ladder from the roof in an old T-shirt and ball cap, carrying a bucket of tar. Dad notices the uniform. He looks like someone hit him in the stomach.

"Already?" Rand croaks. His father sags against the brick wall, a look of dismay on his face.

"Dad," Jeff says, "the war's been over there for a while now."

Rand suddenly remembers that when he was a boy he didn't have the decency to say goodbye to his mother. He just shipped out. At least the boy told him the plan. At least he came to say goodbye. Rand stands tall, places his hands on Jeff's shoulders. "Proud of you, son," he says. Next thing he knows his son's arms are holding him close, so close he can smell the boy's hair. He takes a deep draught of his boy's smell. His only son. Then he lets him go.

"Watch over them for me?" Jeff says. "Jolene and Bobo."

Rand nods. He watches the boy walk to his truck and drive away.

It feels like someone has reached in, taken Rand's heart, and pulled it out still beating.

Rand drives Miss Reba's Cutlass into Quarryville the long way, looping around back roads to a one-lane bridge way upstream that still stands. Possum Crossing Bridge. *Why did the chicken cross the road? To prove to the possum it can be done.* He scans the side of the road. No possums.

In town, he gets chickenscratch, canned goods, kerosene, and soap. He can't find the tooth powder Miss Reba asked for, so he gets Crest. He fills the tank on the Cutlass, pours in a quart of oil. This old boat is held together with rust and duct tape, front fender gone, tires shot, no telling when the engine will give out. While he's driving, he can hear a sound like cornflakes shaking down inside the door panels. The least he can do is buy some tires.

"I got to be honest with you," the tire man says. "The axle on this thing gonna rust right through if you don't replace it soon." He points at the missing fender. "And it's against the law to drive like that." Rand crouches down and studies the exposed bones of the thing, its working parts, axle, springs, bearings, rusted floorboards. Miss Reba must have guardian angels or she would have fallen through long ago. He remembers what he overheard TJ say to Bobo: "Some jogger ran into her car. Ruined it." He finally gets it.

The man's got some cars for sale next to the tires. So today Rand buys a used car, a Volvo station wagon with 40,000 miles on it, paint tight as a tick, in teal blue, a color Anne always said went with everything.

He drives to the Quarryville bank to shut down his account there, transfer what remains to his bank in Chapel Hill. He can see Frank Ridley sitting in his office, through the glass window. He's just sitting there. Doesn't even lift a hand to wave. Rand hopes he had insurance.

Not his problem anymore. He's free as a bird, and rich too. He's got no bills to pay. He's got a pension. No car, no house. He owns very little. Clothes on his back. He's having the time of his life, getting ordered around by an old Black lady with the instincts of a brigadier general.

Today, before he left, she ordered him to go visit his wife.

"You never been to see her since the storm," she said. "You got to thank her for watching over you."

Miss Reba still believes the spirit of Anne kept them from being crushed to death. He believes it was her dining room table. Firemen said it was a combination of Decker's table and the angle of the tree fall. But who is he to argue? Miss Reba seems to know more than he'll ever know about this place and its various spiritual forces. He is alive. And he is grateful. There is no home to go back to. The only place to visit Anne is her grave.

Anne's portrait is crushed under layers of sodden Sheetrock and debris. Rand salvaged his briefcase from the house and not much else. The paradise bird painting he's tacked on the wall of the chicken shed where he's sleeping. He dragged the Adirondack chairs to Reba's for something to sit on. But she likes her porch chair. So the Adirondacks go on either side, one for him and one for TJ. Sometimes they all sit there together. When Miss Reba takes a break from ordering them around.

Miss Reba says two pink birds live with that wild new flock of scarlet macaws he's glimpsed in the Gooley pines. "Got a nasty mouth on them," she says, and he almost bursts into tears. He's amazed. It seems proof of all his theories. More tropical birds, taking over the world. A storm. A runaway. A new ecosystem. If birds can adapt like that, so can he.

Miss Reba packed him a lunch wrapped up in a piece of cloth. Fried chicken and green bean salad. A single new potato, boiled. Pound cake. A Mason jar of that strange tea she drinks. He unwraps the cloth around the chicken. Takes a bite out of a chicken leg. Miss Reba can cook.

She's got a dozen rainbow-colored afghans. She's got a house half burned, a hole in the roof, and a flock of chickens she feeds out of the trunk of the car. She's got a house dress, a church dress, some navy-blue sweatpants, an enormous black raincoat, and a busted umbrella. She's got some strange figurines in the yard, one fallen flat to the ground, gray and ashen. The one with the sword has somehow gone missing, and one still standing, cockeyed, seems to watch over things. He's caught Miss Reba talking to it. Calling it Danielle.

Miss Reba's got the AME preacher at her beck and call, plus the young boy TJ who lives upstairs and does her bidding, chopping wood, carrying water, trying to fix her truck. She's got young Black boys she feeds, who come to work for her and her neighbors from time to time.

She's like some kind of royalty here, he chuckles to himself, thinking of the Egyptian Queen hair oil he spied in the bathroom. TJ told him she was named for a great queen of the Bible. Who knew there was a whole kingdom just on the other side of the highway, past the Sunrise Gas N Grill? What did Anne always used to say? *Why don't you get out of the house and do something? Explore the world. Stop moping around.* He's finally taking her advice.

Ambler County after the storm is a different world—a ruined world requiring the sweat of his brow, pretty much all day long. A place where sleep on a lumpy straw bed is a daily reward. A place where his modest gifts of procurement and organization are useful. This world needs him. Miss Reba needs him. He's so busy he doesn't even notice his leg hurts anymore. Miss Reba poked her nose in and put poultices on it, like his ma used to do. It still twinges, but just enough to remind him how miserable he used to be. This world is such a relief from Stonehaven Downs, a place so cushioned in comfort that there was no need for effort of any kind.

At St. Dunstan's Episcopal Church, Rand settles into the cemetery bench, eats, wipes his face and hands, then contemplates Anne's stone. It got placed sometime during his week in the mountains. No one told him. Turns out she'd left instructions for a stone big enough to span two graves. Her own and that blank six feet of grass that will be his.

Anne Percival Lee
Beloved wife and mother

He lets himself dwell on Anne for a moment. A person he never understood, in all the time he lived with her. She was a person whose joy could not be twisted, or contained, or tainted by life. It had to move outward on any path it could find—one path blocked, it would take another. Joy like water flowing. And he just let it flow away.

The cemetery breathes its quiet sounds of chirping birds and light breezes. "I'm writing a new book," he says. "About those crazy macaws." He's been typing on Miss Reba's old Royal, with a carbon copy saved for each page. Now he pins a sheaf of paper into the rumpled sod with the quill end of a deep-blue tailfeather.

THE SCARLET MACAW

The scarlet macaw should have been named the rainbow bird, for as much as its bright red feathers dominate, it is the contrasting long blue tail and brilliant yellow wing coverts that combine to require our deepest admiration. With a white upper bill, a white eye and eye patch, it is a sociable bird, and the ones here in Ambler County gather by the Cedar River daily in the canopy of the remaining Gooley pines, to crack nuts, squawk, and screech the news of the day, like farmers in a gas station diner. The long blue tailfeathers are a color ranging from vivid to shadowy, depending on the light, so that one is invited to name the color according to one's mood. Indigo is the name I would choose. It was my wife's favorite color.

Rand continues his news report for Anne: "I met Miss Reba. I'm fixing her house." The rustling trees go silent above him. "Jeff's okay. That is, I think he's going to be okay. Anne, I hope to God he'll be okay." Now the branches rise and fall in the breeze above his head as if nodding in accord.

"Forgive me," he says.

A great silence. Then birdcall. A mockingbird bursts into a long, complicated song punctuated by beeps. Seems to have picked up the sounds of dump trucks backing up. Lots of those around these days, hauling away the ruin that is Ambler County.

Rand bursts out laughing. Those birds can learn anything.

If they can, then so can he.

51

S pill Creek Farm is in a state of ruin, just like everything else in Ambler County, but Jolene is strangely calm. *Let there be ruin.* Most of the mama goats and kids are safe. The barn is sound. Bobo is alive. The ruin that is the Gooley Ridge is a godsend. Fallen trees are not included in any collateral. Joggins comes by, eager to get started. He counts the rings. "Four hundred forty-two. These trees were here before white man set foot on this continent."

She nods. Ruin means more work for people around here. Ruin comes back stronger. The Gooley pines are broken. And they will rise.

One day TJ and Jeff's father bring a team out to repair her roof and clear dead branches. The colonel says, "So nice to finally meet you." She watches the two of them working, TJ so eager to please. The colonel organizing things with efficiency. Bobo comes running out from feeding the babies. "Papa!" he cries. He wraps his arms around the colonel in a blissful hug.

"Bobo," she says, mortified, "that's *Jeff's* papa."

"I know, Mama."

"It's okay," Jeff's father says. "We're old friends." The man pats Bobo awkwardly for a time, then closes his eyes, gives in.

Bobo reaches into his windbreaker pocket. "Want some gum?"

And just like that, Bobo has a new best friend.

52

Across Spill Creek and through the woods, Miss Reba sits in her chair on the new porch TJ and the colonel have built her. She's been reading the paper. Sometimes there's something new you need to know. They found new burials in the cliff. She can see it.

On the cliffs of the Gooley Ridge, the pooling water took the land in its teeth and shook and chewed until the vertical burials of seventeen more people were revealed: Five sets of tiny bones in fetal position, skulls staring, encapsulated in clay hollows like holy icons. Twelve grown women and girls wrapped in doeskin.

Dr. Charles Mathers, PhD, found them on a last reconnaissance before he left for his next assignment. "It is an extraordinary find," he says. "No one should be allowed to disturb it for centuries to come. It has to be preserved."

Local tribal organizations have been contacted. They ask to leave the bones *in situ*. That's all well and good, but nobody can figure out how to put the cliff back together again. So the bones will remain there, open to rain and wind.

All this? Old Lucy said. Keep it to yourself. Well, she's never told a living soul. The river told it. The clay pots and bones told it. She kept her promise.

Miss Reba has no need to visit these bones. She's seen them in Old Lucy's stories a hundred times: *All those girls and women. Shadowy eye sockets fllickering with the light of the river and all the life that flies and swims.* She can see the future without closing her eyes: *Sometimes, after rain, a finger bone or skull will tumble down, into the depths of the green water.*

At the bottom of the news story, something catches her eye.

It says when a hollow sycamore fell on the Ridge, roots pulled up, exposed two burials. Indian style. Both twentieth century. Old Indian woman buried with her things—shell beads, jay feather, pots, jar of clear. Young woman buried next to her—a pot broken open with Roanoke beads, a scrap of blue cloth sewn with a yellow bird.

The sheriff has had a look. He remembers a story his grandfather once told about an old Indian woman name of Tuscarora Lucy who lived here, back in the 1900s. He wonders if it's true. He wonders if it's her and another of her kind. And he says, "Who in the world buried the two of them that way? We didn't have no Indians here to do it."

Reba closes her eyes and sees: *Old Lucy musta taken Sheba's bones right out the cornfield.*

"Tell me," Danielle says.

The full weight of an eight-year-old girl, small for her age, rests in Reba's lap, warm small arms around her neck. Sweet living flesh wrapped over bones. Reba's heart aches with the pleasure of it.

You can see it, can't you? Lucy says. Yes. She can see it. The boys are off working for Jolene. Nobody will hear this but the dead.

Lucy come by dead of night, spring rain on a whirlwind breeze. Papa just planted the back corn patch. Lucy brings her digging stick, fresh deerskin bundled on her back. She finds the corner where he buried Sheba, marked by yellow bells. She says a prayer and starts to dig. Not much left but bare bones, tatters of quilt. Weevils and such who clean the earth of flesh have done their work. Old Lucy sings a song of care and healing and tenderly plucks the muddy bones: Leg bones and feet. Arm bones and hands. Ribs and pelvis and spine. Cracked skull. She puts them on the skin, folds a flap over, then another, another. Wraps it all in a blanket. Ties it with a rawhide strap.

Old Lucy scrapes soil back into the hole with a sycamore branch. She pokes holes, drops maize in rows to match the rows she dug up. When corn sprouts here it will bear red-jewel kernels. Honor Sheba's blood. Mystify Gemstone Jones.

Lucy buries Sheba sitting up, on the highest cliff of Gooley Ridge, so she can look out over the river and watch the swirling patterns of this world.

Then she waits for someone to come who can bury her right next to Sheba.

All this time, Reba sees, she's been visiting Sheba in the wrong place. But now she understands: Spirits visit freely, not bound by place, but bound by love. Sheba. Lucy. Mama. Pa. Luke Blake. They are all connected by skeins of love, like those lines in Lucy's book, no matter what hateful people do.

Danielle never let hate damage her. There are people who can do that. Miss Reba shakes her head in wonder that one little girl spirit chose to stay and listen and keep her company, when she could have flown up and away to heaven.

"Auntie," Danielle says. "I never stayed because of stories. The stories were for you."

A brisk rush of wind. Silence fills the air around her. Danielle is gone.

Miss Reba rises by dark of night. TJ's dead asleep in his room. Colonel Rand in that lean-to he built off the chicken shed, sleeping on a bed of straw. The man had no place to go. What will she do with this whiteman? Put him to work. Man is good at everything he does. She showed him how to take honey, he already knew how. Now they got five gallons from the split sycamore. She showed him where the brick needed fixing, he already knew how. Now it's mostly done.

Yesterday he brought her a tiny blue medicine bottle with a slip of paper tucked in, said he found it stuck in the hollow of a brick in the wall he's fixing. A message in a bottle. Reba fished the paper out with a stick. A page torn from the Bible. This page she always knew was gone, figured Papa tore it out and threw it away when she left his house for Indian Field. Verse is underlined, says, *A virtuous woman, who can find? For her price is above Rubies.* On the edge, Papa's handwriting: *Name her Ruby.*

Now Reba goes to the mantel, piles the boxes in a feed sack. She pulls her papa's service revolver from the hiding place in the sweet potatoes. What providence kept her boy TJ from finding it, nosy as he is, she won't tempt another day. She pushes the screen door open with her backside, hoists it all into the back seat of the Big Wheels car the colonel got her, along with a shovel. She's got business to finish.

Sliver of moon shining down. A narrow goat path to the top of the Ridge, to the cliffs. Yellow tape marking the two women's bones they found. Reba strikes at the tape with her hickory stick until it falls away. She steps in to see. A web of sycamore roots like a tent over their heads. Roots pulled up earth, like somebody dug a hole just for this moment and placed a pile of loose earth ready close by.

Sheba's pouch still there. Inside, that scrap of blue cloth. Stitches of yellow bird. Made by a young girl's hand. A young girl none too patient. Crooked stitches.

Reba kneels and tucks her foil boxes around Sheba. Pink for Mama, blue for Papa, gold for Danielle. Company for each other. Danielle will love having a big family. Papa will like being near his Sheba, even if her bones are done the heathen way. And Sheba, well, maybe she will find some comfort in all the family tucked in next to her now. Reba squats low, old bones aching, reaches out to touch the cracked skull of her sister. It seems warm to her hand. She presses her palm over the crack, says a blessing. Says goodbye. "You were a good sister, Sheba. Lucy loved you. I loved you. You done your work watching over me as best you could. Now you gotta watch over Danielle. If your spirit roam, let it remember this place, the love that held you here for a time. Jesus name, Amen."

Cloud covers the moon. The hole fills with shadow. She drops in Papa's service revolver.

Imma keep the shotgun.

Reba shovels dirt, then kneels down and uses her hands, pulls soft earth into the hole, finds rocks and piles them on top. She covers up Lucy. "You got us for family now too," she says. Reba pulls out the whiteman stakes. Balls up the yellow tape. Throws the whole mess off the cliff into the river. She watches it float away, get caught on a rock, then slide downstream.

Reba sits back on her aching knees and contemplates the Field below, shining in moonlight. Green things poking up, field cress and blackberry, scuppernong and thistle, all fine as baby hair.

She closes her eyes, smells the flowers. Instead of someone dead, she sees a day when the Field is green and broad again, when there are many cookfires, sparks rising up, whirling dancers, hollow log drums, red and blue birds flocking. Indians in the Field.

What Danielle always wanted.

53

I f you believe that the spirit, freed from the body, will fly home to visit from time to time the people it loves, then you will see, like Reba, that in the frayed ends of October morning mist among the pines Old Lucy is here, and Luke and Sheba and Danielle, even Anne.

The tiny new seedlings of *Tatcha na wihie Gee-ree* quiver with the change. There is drumming on the cliff. There are people in the Field. The spirits flock to see.

Grasses lush among the boulders, the loud cries of birds overhead, a brilliant sky. The people are having a picnic. It was Bobo's idea.

Jolene smooths white sheets over long plywood tables, feels a twinge in her belly. She hasn't told anyone. She hopes it's a girl. Reba gives her a look, up and down, and nods. Miss Reba knows a thing or two.

Jeff's father looks so happy. Smoking his cigar, gazing up at the brilliant new birds that have come to stay. Reba says he's writing a book about them. It's so funny to see her order him around. *Colonel, carry that casserole. Put it right there. Don't forget the spoon.* The man stares at the table, all the smorgasbord of food, like he's never seen a potluck before.

Now she watches Bobo tear around the Field with TJ, chasing the flock of strange bright new birds that whirl above them, and grabbing at the colored feathers they cast as they fly. Tyquan and Abednego chase the boys. Laughing and running and zigzagging under the feathered sky. It's a sight to see.

TJ grabs a blue feather. Bobo grabs a red. "Make a wish!" Bobo cries.

Jolene has no need to make a wish. Just about all her wishes have been granted.

On the long table before them is goat cheese—a new kind, aged and nutty, which requires no refrigeration—with Dora's bread. There are fried apple pies cooked on a camp stove and mashed potatoes with gravy. There are newly cured sweet potatoes baked in their jackets in the coals of a cook fire, and green beans pulled out of Mason jars. The women of the nations have brought cornbread, squash, chicken bog. Bobo waves at the Ridge and shouts, "Papa!" The other boys pass food.

Miss Reba sits, eyes closed, cocking her ear as if tuned to distant sounds. "Danielle," she says, opening her eyes, "it's time to feed the living."

Reba's preacher is here in his white collar and black suit, pulling off his jacket and setting it down, for it is a warm day. And some of Reba's church folks have come with their own casseroles and desserts. Jolene overhears one of them say, "I come to see that whiteboy I heard was struck by the hand of God. Whiter than white now, with that hair."

"He got the spirit now," another says.

"Wasn't no lightning. It was Miss Reba knocked the spirit right into him."

A fourth one says, "I come to see the Indians. You know Miss Reba's got the blood."

"My mama had the blood," the first one says. "Never told a soul till now."

After they are done, the drumbeats come faintly to Jolene's ear from the Gooley Ridge. The Big Tree People are up there, plus tribal leaders from as far as Robeson County, as close as Mebane. Who knew those people had survived all these years? Tuscarora, Lumbee, Occaneechi Band of the Saponi. There's even a young fellow from Hatteras Island. They're all singing together, a high wail, a low moan, pounding drums. Justin is here, but what the Big Tree People do is a pale imitation. These new sounds thrill her to the bone.

Three girls run up to Miss Reba, hiding something behind their backs. Eyes big with mischief. Girls from church maybe, or from the tribes on the Ridge. They pull out a crown of clover and broomstraw, bull thistle and honeysuckle vine, bright feathers tucked in every which way. They place it on Reba's head. One of them wraps her arms around Miss Reba's waist, hugs her tight. "You the Queen of the Field, my mama say."

Miss Ruby Queen Esther Jones lifts one hand to touch her crown: the spines of the thistle prick her fingers, the honeysuckle swarms with bees. *How could little children make such a thing and remain unharmed?* She can still feel the warmth where the girl's arms pressed her flesh. She wipes her glasses, strains to see where the girls have gone. But they have slipped away among the living, into the world that Danielle dreamed: colored birds flying, church people gossiping, TJ up there somewhere on the Ridge, hugging trees with Bobo, that old colonel staring at birds like he wants to be one. Tonight there will be many small fires of her people.

Two of the women come and take her by the hand. Lead her to a gathering by the river. The men have brought their drums down from the Ridge, they stand now in a circle. TJ stands among them, giving her a grin and a little wave. Bobo calls out, "Weba!" The women raise their voices in an unfamiliar song. Miss Reba finds herself right there in the thick of it: voices singing, drums pounding, water rippling and chattering among the rocks. Something lifts in her chest, batwings let go their grip, flap up and away, and life rushes in, beating like the drum of her old beating heart. She opens her mouth and lets her voice rise into brightness.

Rand leans against an enormous boulder and watches Miss Reba. She's got some kind of feather headdress on her head. There's a circle of men and boys and drums and singing. Things are going on all around him that astound him. Things he had no idea about. *You should be used to that by now, you old sonofabitch.* There is so much he doesn't understand. He feels very old and very young at the same time. Old because he can't stop tears from leaking to his cheeks. Young because he wants to run in the Field, swoop his arms, and make the colored birds fly and shout.

He never belonged in Stonehaven Downs. All that striving to be high class, to rise in the ranks, never felt right to him. He did it for Anne, he thought, but she never needed it, really. She was always telling him to venture out, see the world outside the Downs. He's finally taking her advice. And this strange Field, and the neat farm beyond that he's been spying on for comfort—well, he's an invited guest now. He belongs here as much as anyone. As much as the wildly colored birds above them do. *Fuckfuckfuck!* a cry comes from above his head. *Oh bloody hell!* He looks up. A pink flurry of wings among the macaws. King P and Queen Pia! His heart flips in his chest with an old delight. *You're an old fool,* he tells himself. But he's going to do it anyway.

He puts his cigar out on a boulder. Tucks the butt in his pocket. Miss Reba don't truck with trash. Then he lets out a whoop, wheels his arms, and runs to join the boys, the birds, this life. The birds rise and whirl, shouting curses, his brilliant companions.

A NOTE ON SOURCES

This novel contains many song references, made-up songs, Bible verses, and references to literary and historical works. For those who are interested, here are some notes.

On the epigraph page are a few lines excerpted from the poem "Where Everything Is Music," from *The Essential Rumi*, translated by Coleman Barks with John Moyne, Castle Books, HarperCollins San Francisco, 1997. I keep this book on my reading table for refreshment and morning reading.

Bobo's favorite book is *Dig A Hole in the Meadow*. This children's book is not available in stores—I made it up. But the name is also the name of a traditional song I also know as "Wake Up, Darlin' Corey." I named a dog after this song, see my essay "Drinking, Dogs, and Darlin' Corey," in *Making Notes, Music of the Carolinas*, ed. by Ann Wicker. So I have a special fondness for it.

Rand tries to sing "O Danny Boy" to his bird O'Mally, the way his wife Anne used to, but it chokes in his throat. I grew up hearing Irish tenors sing this song in a favorite bar, but it's actually written by an Englishman.

Jolene makes up a song about mulching, borrowing from "Let Us Break Bread Together On Our Knees," an African American slave-era spiritual commonly used today in many churches, especially during communion.

Jolene quotes "Pied Beauty," by Gerard Manley Hopkins (1918), a poem her husband Luke loved that makes her think of dappled flanks of goats.

When Sheba loves an unnamed blues song by the Earl Hines Orchestra, she's thinking of "Stormy Monday Blues" (Eckstein, Crowder and Hines, 1942).

Bobo sings his mother a version of "Jesus Loves Me, This I Know" that TJ has invented funny new lyrics for. The original lyrics are by Anna Bartlett Warner, 1859, and, interestingly, they were originally published as song invented for her novel *Say and Seal*.

Reba makes TJ read aloud from *Gulliver's Travels* by Jonathan Swift, published in 1726, the story of an Englishman's adventures into imaginary lands that were allegories for the social and political classes of the day. Also on that shelf is *The Hope of Liberty* (1829), by George Moses Horton, the first Black man to publish a book in the South. Horton was an enslaved man who sold his poems at a farmers market to raise money to buy his freedom.

Rand reads *The Malaysian Archipelago*, by Alfred Russel Wallace, in preparation for his return to Malaysia. Wallace was Darwin's famous rival—he wrote his article on the theory of natural selection first. One of Wallace's fascinations was finding "the paradise bird," a flock of subspecies endemic to New Guinea and Australia.

John Lawson's 1709 *A New Voyage to Carolina* is one of the most colorfully written, lovingly detailed, and historically reliable documentations of early Indigenous people of the Carolinas. An English explorer, Lawson was also a real estate developer, founding New Bern, and was a victim of the Tuscarora War. Many of the details of Old Lucy's traditional burial practices are taken from his documentation. A current scholarly edition of this book is available from UNC Press. Burial practices are also inspired by Roanoke colony governor John White's 1586 drawings.

In his moment of terror in the height of the storm, the colonel hears a crazy medly of "the caissons song," now considered the official song of the US Army (original lyrics by Edmund L. Gruber, an army general stationed in the Philippines in 1908) and "O God Our Help in Ages Past," (Isaac Watts 1708/John Wesley 1738).

Reba's Bible verses are mostly from the King James version, with the exception of Psalm 83 (O God, make them like whirling dust) which is from the English Standard version, which I chose because of the lovely "whirling dust."

I am grateful for the following sources for sparking imagination based on history and language of the Tuscarora and other tribal people: *Tuscarora Indian Language*, by Chief Elton Greene, available online from the Coastal Carolina Indian Center; *A New Voyage to Carolina*, by John Lawson (UNC Press: 1984); and *Tuscarora: Onkwehonweh, The First People*, by Marilyn Mjorado-Livingston, Scarorreh Publishing, 1997.

For more North Carolina Indigenous history, I referred to *The American Indian in North Carolina*, by Douglas L. Rights, John F. Blair, Publishers, 1991; *Native Carolinians: The Indians of North Carolina*, by Theda Perdue, Division of Archives and History, North Carolina Department of Cultural Resources, 1991; *Indian Wars in North Carolina, 1663-1763*, by E. Lawrence Lee, Reprinted by State Department of Archives and

History, Raleigh, NC, 1968; and *Transactions of the American Philosophical Society*, Vol. 54, Part 5, 1964: *Formative Cultures of the Carolina Piedmont*, Joffre Lanning Coe.

This is a work of imagination, in which facts are filtered, expanded, showcased, and sometimes invented. It is not meant to be a historical resource, though many of the stories told are firmly rooted in history. I hope readers will explore the story of the Tuscarora War, the works of Indigenous and other scholars, and the work of the Equal Justice Initiative and NAACP in your community, as well as the historical writings of John Lawson (1709) and the art of John White (1586), and the stories and celebrations of living tribal people of the South. Any errors of fact or imagination are my own, and some of the errors may be intentional. None of them are the responsibility of my sources.

ACKNOWLEDGMENTS

This book was written over a long period of years and many drafts, and it found many loyal, generous readers along the way, while I was learning to structure a complex story. At one point, the draft was more than 700 pages long.

North Carolina writer Karen Pullen read countless drafts, provided invaluable advice on edits and cuts, when my brain had stopped working. She is part of my writing group, which also read an early draft and many bits and pieces. Thanks to Frances Wood, Louise Hawes, and Donna Washington for extraordinary encouragement and advice.

Boston writer Helen Fremont of the Warren Wilson MFA Alumni Association read three full drafts, provided extraordinary encouragement and precise commentary. Other stalwart readers from that group include Peg Alford Pursell, Cass Pursell, Alison Moore, Ann Scott Knight, Dale Neal, Mimi Herman, Lee Prusick. For exceptional encouragement from this group, thanks go to Kathryn Schwille, Peg Alford Pursell, and Dale Neal.

Thanks to my Chapel Hill writer friends Walter Bennett, Jack Raper, David Lange, Marko Fong, and Tom Wolf, who sat through many scene revisions. Walter also read an entire early draft, and Tom provided essential advice and encouragement.

Heartfelt thanks to Valerie Nieman, Peggy Payne, Michele Tracy Berger, Pat Riviere-Seel, Robert Rubin, Bridgette Lacy, Nancy Peacock, Laura Vanderbeck, Dee Reid, and Sarah Anne Corbett, who read drafts and kept me going with encouragement and commentary.

Thanks to Bridgette Lacy (again) and Paul Mihas, of the North Carolina Arts Council Writing Fellows, whose fellowship and feasts make the writing life nurturing and fun.

Thanks to Lisa Dellwo, who read a full draft in two sittings and gave me my first unofficial blurb: "This fucker is ready."

Thanks to Kevin Morgan Watson, publisher of Press 53, whose passionate support for my story collection, *Accidental Birds of the Carolinas*, brought some of these characters to the published page for the first time. Thanks to Cindy Edwards, whose beach house retreat on Oak Island gave me the chance to complete a first draft, and whose good company has brightened many days.

Thanks to Weymouth Center for the Arts and Humanities, especially Katrina Denza, Andie Rose, and patriarch Sam Ragan, for providing almost 30 years of writing retreats that helped this book be born. And yes, thanks to that painted bunting print in the writers' hall, which kept inspiration going for one of my novel's bird families.

Thanks to Steven Barefoot and Sharon Moore of the Level III and Treehouse Wilmington apartment group, whose brilliant idea of a shared rental allowed me years of quiet writing weeks.

Thanks to Ucross Retreat for Writers, supported by the PEN/ Hemingway awards, where I rassled an enormous draft to the ground and visited the site of an aboriginal Crow settlement, and especially to administrators Sharon Dynak and Ruth Salvatore, artists Frank Ozereko, Ric Haynes, Suzanne Bennett, and Sharon Shapiro, and writers Christopher Beha, Lalita Tademy, and Carmiel Banasky, who provided friendly support and companionship. To the Hemingway Foundation and the PEN/Heminigway awards, which provided support for that retreat.

Thanks to Headlands Center for the Arts, located near Sausalito, CA, at the historical Fort Barry officers' quarters, and to the North Carolina Arts Council Headlands Fellowship for providing an extended residency while I mapped out scenes on rolls of paper with colored markers and drawings. Thanks also to the Nike Missile Site, part of the Golden Gate National Recreational Area, source of much of my knowledge about the history of Nike and Hercules missiles, Salt I and II, and the placement of such historic American missiles at sites around the world.

Thanks to United Arts of Raleigh and Wake County and the North Carolina Arts Council, a Division of the Department of Natural and Cultural Resources, for a writer support grant dedicated to the completion of this book.

Thanks to Doe Branch, Ink., and its founders Jim Roberts and Deborah Jakubs, who provided retreat time and space for work on this novel.

Special thanks to Geraldine DeGraffenreid, who invited me into the Black Historical Society of Chatham County, to Barbara Perry, of the Friends of the Pittsboro Memorial Library, and to author Doris Betts, who all opened my eyes to the depths and complexities of Black history all around me, and to my local NAACP chapter and the Equal Justice Initiative, who are working to lift up those depths and honor them.

Thanks also to Miss Mary Lucas, who told me one day on her front deck, "My people were never slaves. They were Indians."

Special thanks also to Louise Hobbs who, at a workshop sponsored by the Haw River Festival, taught me to make a coiled clay pot using the methods of Carolina piedmont Indigenous people. With her friend Fiddlin' Al McCanless, one afternoon of storytelling with Louise fired my imagination with talk of historical great storms and double tornadoes. Thanks also to the work of archeologist Linda Carnes-McNaughton, whose uncovering of a "baby in a pot" sparked my imagination as well.

Special thanks also to other scholars and Native Carolinians whose presence and activism opened my eyes to the living world of Indigenous people of many nations in my community. Historian Marilyn Mejorado-Livington, of the Southern Band Tuscarora; historian/activist Scott Dawson and archeologist Mark Horton, who have uncovered evidence of survival of early English settlers among Hatteras people at Croatoan (documented in Dawson's *The Lost Colony and Hatteras Island*); John "Blackfeather" Jeffries, who was the first Native person I met in the Carolinas, and whose work to illumine and support the history and present life of the Occaneechi Band of the Saponi people is extraordinary; writer MariJo Moore, who had a vision about this book; Lumbee scholar Malinda Maynard Lowry, whose *The Lumbee People: An American Struggle*, is a new classic of Native history; Larry Pait, amateur archeologist, who showed me the likely site of the Tuscarora village Catechnea on Contentea Creek; and author Scott Huler who retraced the Lawson Trail in his book *A Delicious Country*, chatting up tribal people of many nations who still live and thrive in North Carolina.

Thank you to the University of North Carolina-Chapel Hill Wilson Rounds Library and Historical Collection, especially to Robert Anthony for providing access to primary sources.

Thanks also to my many Kitchen Table Writers—too many to name, but you know who you are—whose writing and lively minds keep me inspired.

More thanks: to Sheriff Mike Robeson, whose tour of historical archives of the sheriff's office and jail were illuminating; to Annette Roberson, for providing emergency haircuts and photography; to Paul Rosenberg, who kept my computer alive and backed up; to AJ Coutu, whose ongoing support on writing retreats included delicous homemade soups and a gorgeous quilt that illuminates the world of Indigo Field; to Sarah, Kathleen and Stephen Corbett, who provided prayer and encouragement; to Jaynie Royal and Pam Van Dyk, who said YES.

And last, and always, to Sam, who keeps me in blueberries, soup, muffins, firewood, and loving support, and without whom none of these pages could have been written.

Book Club Questions

1. The author creates a mysterious grove of trees that know all the secrets. Have you ever been to a place with large trees and felt that they communicated to you? What was it like? Did you feel refreshed when you left?

2. Miss Reba keeps a list of crimes against her family in the back of her bible, but she never wanted to tell those stories to Danielle, because she wanted to protect her innocence. Did that work? Why or why not?

3. Jolene notices changes in the crop season. Were you surprised when the weather in the story became a crisis? Have you ever encountered a climate disaster in your own life?

4. Miss Reba says she believes in God and Jesus, but after her beloved niece is murdered, she doesn't like them very much. Have you ever felt like that after a great loss?

5. The colonel has lost his wife, and mixed with the grief is the complication of guilt. Do you see his working for Miss Reba as a kind of atonement? Why do you think it makes him so happy?

For a complete downloadable Readers Group Guide, see:
https://marjoriehudson.com/books/indigo-field/

For more about the lives of Jolene Blake, Bobo, Luke, Miss Reba, and the other inhabitants of Ambler County, see *Accidental Birds of the Carolinas*, available wherever books are sold.